Praise for
Debbie Macomber's bestselling novels
from Ballantine Books

Must Love Flowers

"A testament to the power of new beginnings. Wise, warm, witty, and charmingly full of hope, this story celebrates the surprising and unexpected ways that family, friendship, and love can lift us up."
—KRISTIN HANNAH,
bestselling author of *The Nightingale*

"Uplifting, warm, and hopeful. With her signature charm and wit, Debbie Macomber proves that the best relationships, like the perfect blooms, are always worth the wait. . . . This can't-miss novel is Macomber at the height of her storytelling prowess. I absolutely adored it!"
—KRISTY WOODSON HARVEY, *New York Times*
bestselling author of *The Summer of Songbirds*

"Debbie Macomber never fails to deliver an uplifting, heartwarming story. Whether you're just starting out, just starting over, or anything in between, *Must Love Flowers* should be at the top of your summer reading list!"
—BRENDA NOVAK, *New York Times*
bestselling author of *Before We Were Strangers*

The Best Is Yet to Come

"Macomber's latest is a wonderful inspirational read that has just enough romance as the characters heal their painful emotional wounds." —*Library Journal*

"This tale of redemption and kindness is a gift to Macomber's many readers and all who love tales of sweet and healing romance." —*Booklist*

It's Better This Way

"Macomber has a firm grasp on issues that will resonate with readers of domestic fiction. Well-drawn characters and plotting—coupled with strong romantic subplots and striking coincidences—will keep readers rooting for forgiveness, hope and true love to conquer all."
—KATHLEEN GERARD,
blogger at *Reading Between the Lines*

"Macomber keeps her well-shaded, believable characters at the heart of this seamlessly plotted novel as she probes the nuances of familial relationships and the agelessness of romance. This deeply emotional tale proves it's never too late for love." —*Publishers Weekly* (starred review)

A Walk Along the Beach

"Macomber scores another home run with this surprisingly heavy but uplifting contemporary romance between a café owner and a photographer. Eloquent prose . . . along with [a] charming supporting cast adds a welcome dose of light and hope. With this stirring romance, Macomber demonstrates her mastery of the genre."
—*Publishers Weekly* (starred review)

"Highly emotional . . . a hard-to-put-down page-turner, yet, throughout all the heartache, the strength and love of family shines through." —*New York Journal of Books*

Window on the Bay

"This heartwarming story sweetly balances friendship and mother-child bonding with romantic love."
—*Kirkus Reviews*

"Macomber's work is as comforting as ever." —*Booklist*

Cottage by the Sea

"Romantic, warm, and a breeze to read—one of Macomber's best." —*Kirkus Reviews*

"Macomber never disappoints. Tears and laughter abound in this story of loss and healing that will wrap you up and pull you in; readers will finish it in one sitting."
—*Library Journal* (starred review)

"Macomber's story of tragedy and triumph is emotionally engaging from the outset and ends with a satisfying conclusion. Readers will be most taken by the characters, particularly Annie, a heartwarming lead who bolsters the novel." —*Publishers Weekly*

Any Dream Will Do

"*Any Dream Will Do* is . . . so realistic, it's hard to believe it's fiction through the end. Even then, it's hard to say goodbye to these characters. This standalone novel will make you hope it becomes a Hallmark movie, or gets a sequel. It's an inspiring, hard-to-put-down tale. . . . You need to read it." —*The Free Lance–Star*

Rose Harbor

Sweet Tomorrows

"Macomber fans will leave the Rose Harbor Inn with warm memories of healing, hope, and enduring love."
—*Kirkus Reviews*

"Overflowing with the poignancy, sweetness, conflicts and romance for which Debbie Macomber is famous, *Sweet Tomorrows* captivates from beginning to end."
—*Bookreporter*

"Fans will enjoy this final installment of the Rose Harbor series as they see Jo Marie's story finally come to an end."
—*Library Journal*

Silver Linings

"Macomber's homespun storytelling style makes reading an easy venture. . . . She also tosses in some hidden twists and turns that will delight her many longtime fans."
—*Bookreporter*

"Reading Macomber's novels is like being with good friends, talking and sharing joys and sorrows."
—*New York Journal of Books*

Love Letters

"Macomber's mastery of women's fiction is evident in her latest. . . . [She] breathes life into each plotline, carefully intertwining her characters' stories to ensure that none of them overshadow the others. Yet it is her ability to capture different facets of emotion which will entrance fans and newcomers alike." —*Publishers Weekly*

"Romance and a little mystery abound in this third installment of Macomber's series set at Cedar Cove's Rose Harbor Inn. . . . Readers of Robyn Carr and Sherryl Woods will enjoy Macomber's latest, which will have them flipping pages until the end and eagerly anticipating the next installment." —*Library Journal* (starred review)

"Uplifting . . . a cliffhanger ending for Jo Marie begs for a swift resolution in the next book." —*Kirkus Reviews*

Rose Harbor in Bloom

"[Debbie Macomber] draws in threads of her earlier book in this series, *The Inn at Rose Harbor,* in what is likely to be just as comfortable a place for Macomber fans as for Jo Marie's guests at the inn." —*The Seattle Times*

"Macomber's legions of fans will embrace this cozy, heartwarming read." —*Booklist*

"Readers will find the emotionally impactful storylines and sweet, redemptive character arcs for which the author is famous. Classic Macomber, which will please fans and keep them coming back for more." —*Kirkus Reviews*

"The storybook scenery of lighthouses, cozy bed and breakfast inns dotting the coastline, and seagulls flying above takes readers on personal journeys of first love, lost love and recaptured love [presenting] love in its purest and most personal forms." —*Bookreporter*

The Inn at Rose Harbor

"Debbie Macomber's Cedar Cove romance novels have a warm, comfy feel to them. Perhaps that's why they've sold millions." —*USA Today*

"Debbie Macomber has written a charming, cathartic romance full of tasteful passion and good sense. Reading it is a lot like enjoying comfort food, as you know the book will end well and leave you feeling pleasant and content. The tone is warm and serene, and the characters are likeable yet realistic. . . . *The Inn at Rose Harbor* is a wonderful novel that will keep the reader's undivided attention."
—*Bookreporter*

"The prolific Macomber introduces a spin-off of sorts from her popular Cedar Cove series, still set in that fictional small town but centered on Jo Marie Rose, a youngish widow who buys and operates the bed and breakfast of the title. This clever premise allows Macomber to craft stories around the B&B's guests, Abby and Josh in this inaugural effort, while using Jo Marie and her ongoing recovery from the death of her husband Paul in Afghanistan as the series' anchor. . . . With her characteristic optimism, Macomber provides fresh starts for both." —*Booklist*

"Emotionally charged romance." —*Kirkus Reviews*

Blossom Street Brides

"A wonderful, love-affirming novel . . . an engaging, emotionally fulfilling story that clearly shows why [Macomber] is a peerless storyteller." —*Examiner.com*

"Rewarding . . . Macomber amply delivers her signature engrossing relationship tales, wrapping her readers in warmth as fuzzy and soft as a hand-knitted creation from everyone's favorite yarn shop." —*Bookreporter*

"Fans will happily return to the warm, welcoming sanctuary of Macomber's Blossom Street, catching up with old friends from past Blossom Street books and meeting new ones being welcomed into the fold." —*Kirkus Reviews*

"Macomber's nondenominational-inspirational women's novel, with its large cast of characters, will resonate with fans of the popular series." —*Booklist*

Starting Now

"Macomber understands the often complex nature of a woman's friendships, as well as the emotional language women use with their friends."
—*New York Journal of Books*

"There is a reason that legions of Macomber fans ask for more Blossom Street books. They fully engage her readers as her characters discover happiness, purpose, and meaning in life. . . . Macomber's feel-good novel, emphasizing interpersonal relationships and putting people above status and objects, is truly satisfying."
—*Booklist* (starred review)

"Macomber's writing and storytelling deliver what she's famous for—a smooth, satisfying tale with characters her fans will cheer for and an arc that is cozy, heartwarming and ends with the expected happily-ever-after."
—*Kirkus Reviews*

Christmas Novels

The Christmas Spirit

"Exactly what readers want from a Macomber holiday outing." —*Publishers Weekly*

"With almost all of Debbie Macomber's novels, the reader is not only given a captivating story, but also a lesson in life." —*New York Journal of Books*

Dear Santa

"[*Dear Santa*] is a quick and fun tale offering surprises and blessings and an all-around feel-good read."
—*New York Journal of Books*

Jingle All the Way

"[*Jingle All the Way*] will leave readers feeling merry and bright." —*Publishers Weekly*

"This delightful Christmas story can be enjoyed any time of the year." —*New York Journal of Books*

A Mrs. Miracle Christmas

"This sweet, inspirational story . . . had enough dramatic surprises to keep pages turning."
—*Library Journal* (starred review)

"Anyone who enjoys Christmas will appreciate this sparkling snow globe of a story." —*Publishers Weekly*

Alaskan Holiday

"Picture-perfect . . . this charmer will please Macomber fans and newcomers alike." —*Publishers Weekly*

"[A] tender romance lightly brushed with holiday magic."
—*Library Journal*

Merry and Bright

"Heartfelt, cheerful . . . Readers looking for a light and sweet holiday treat will find it here." —*Publishers Weekly*

Twelve Days of Christmas

"Another heartwarming seasonal Macomber tale, which fans will find as bright and cozy as a blazing fire on Christmas Eve." —*Kirkus Reviews*

"*Twelve Days of Christmas* is a charming, heartwarming holiday tale. With poignant characters and an enchanting plot, Macomber again burrows into the fragility of human emotions to arrive at a delightful conclusion."
—*New York Journal of Books*

Dashing Through the Snow

"This Christmas romance from Macomber is both sweet and sincere." —*Library Journal*

Mr. Miracle

"Macomber spins another sweet, warmhearted holiday tale that will be as comforting to her fans as hot chocolate on Christmas morning." —*Kirkus Reviews*

"This gentle, inspiring romance will be a sought-after read." —*Library Journal*

Starry Night

"Contemporary romance queen Macomber hits the sweet spot with this tender tale of impractical love. . . . A delicious Christmas miracle well worth waiting for."
—*Publishers Weekly* (starred review)

"[A] holiday confection . . . as much a part of the season for some readers as cookies and candy canes."
—*Kirkus Reviews*

Angels at the Table

"Rings in Christmas in tried-and-true Macomber style, with romance and a touch of heavenly magic."
—*Kirkus Reviews*

"[A] sweetly charming holiday romance."
—*Library Journal*

DEBBIE MACOMBER

What Matters Most

Shadow Chasing
and
Laughter in the Rain

BALLANTINE BOOKS
NEW YORK

2024 Ballantine Books Mass Market Edition

Published in the United States by Ballantine Books,
an imprint of Random House, a division of
Penguin Random House LLC, New York.

BALLANTINE is a registered trademark and the colophon is a
trademark of Penguin Random House LLC.

Shadow Chasing and *Laughter in the Rain* were
originally published separately in the United States by
Silhouette Romance, New York, in 1986.

ISBN 978-0-593-49618-3
Ebook ISBN 978-0-593-59952-5

Cover images: © Alan Ayers (house and hydrangea),
© Production Perig/Shutterstock (bushes at right of house),
© Peyker/Shutterstock (oars),
© Tridsanu Thopet/Shutterstock (tree next to house),
© Dorota Szymczyk/Shutterstock (rowboat)

Printed in the United States of America

randomhousebooks.com

2 4 6 8 9 7 5 3 1

Ballantine Books mass market edition: February 2024

Dear Friends,

If you were to compile a list of what matters most in your life, what would it entail? Over the years I've given a lot of thought to that and narrowed it down to three things. Mine would likely match several of your own list: God, family, and country. In the two novels you are about to read, each character recognizes what's most important in their lives, and that's love. We all need to feel cherished and accepted by another person.

These books were written early in my career as traditional romances, long before there were technological advances such as cell phones, the internet, and social media—yup, the good old days. Please keep that in mind instead of shaking your head and saying, "Good grief, why didn't she just text?" or, "This guy needs to wake up to what year it is." If he did 'wake up' I'm convinced he'd wonder if he'd arrived on another planet, but then, I digress. In other words, be kind to these poor technologically regressed heroes and heroines.

This isn't to say that I don't enjoy hearing from my readers, because I most definitely do. Your feedback has been the guiding force of my career and is always appreciated. I'm reachable on all the social platforms. You can leave me a message on my website or if you prefer, write to me at:

P.O. Box 1458, Port Orchard, WA 98366.

Warmest regards,

Debbie Macomber

Shadow Chasing

One

~

"You're kidding." Carla Walker glanced at her friend suspiciously. "What did they put in that margarita, anyway? Truth serum?"

Nancy Listten's dark eyes brightened, but her attention didn't waver from the mariachi band that played softly in the background.

"I'm serious," Nancy replied. "This happens every vacation. We now have seven glorious days in Mazatlán. What do you want to bet that we don't find a man to flirt with until day six?"

"That's because it takes awhile to scout out who's available," Carla argued, taking a sip of her drink. The granules of salt from the edge of the glass felt gritty on the inside of her bottom lip. But she enjoyed the feel and the taste.

"Exactly my point."

Nancy took off her glasses and placed them inside her purse. That action said a lot. Carla's friend had meant every word. She was dead serious.

"We spend at least two days trying to figure out who's married and who isn't."

"Your idea isn't going to help," Carla insisted. "The next two men who walk in here could be married."

"But imagine how much time it'll save if we *ask*. And"—Nancy inhaled a deep breath—"have you noticed how picky we are? We always act like our choices are going to improve if given enough time. We've simply got to realize that there're no better candidates than whoever walks through that door tonight."

"I don't know . . ." Carla hesitated, wondering if there was something wrong with her drink, too. Nancy's idea was beginning to make sense. "What if they don't speak English?" That was a stupid question, and the look Nancy gave her said as much. They each had a phrase book, and Carla had watched enough *Sesame Street* when babysitting her nieces to pick up the basics of the language. She groaned inwardly. She'd begun this vacation with such high hopes. They were in one of the most popular vacation spots in the world. Men galore. Tanned, gorgeous men. And she was going to end up introducing herself in *Sesame Street* Spanish to the next guy who walked through the door. Even worse, the idea was growing more appealing by the minute. Nancy was right. For two years they'd ruined their vacations looking for Mr. Perfect. Not only hadn't they ever found him, but as their time had grown shorter, their standards had lowered. The men they'd found marginal on day one looked like rare finds by day six. And on day seven, frustrated and discouraged, they'd flown back to Seattle, having wasted their entire vacation.

"I think we should establish some sort of criteria, don't you?"

Carla nodded. "Unencumbered."

"That goes without saying." Nancy gave her a classroom glare that Carla had seen often enough to recognize. "They should walk in here alone. And be under thirty-five." Nancy's eyes sought Carla. "Anything else?"

"I, for one, happen to be a little more particular than you."

"All right, add what you want."

"I think they should order a margarita."

"Carla! We could be here all night if we waited for that."

"We're in Mazatlán. Everyone orders margaritas," Carla countered. Well, a tourist would, and that was what she wanted. No serious stuff, just a nice holiday romance.

"Okay," Nancy agreed.

Their eyes focused on the two entrances. Waiting.

"Have you noticed how all the cocktail lounges are beginning to look like furniture showrooms?" Carla commented, just to have something to say. Her hands felt damp as she studied the entry to the nightclub.

"Shh . . . someone's coming."

A middle-aged couple walked through the door.

They both relaxed. "We'd better decide who goes first."

"You," Carla returned instantly. "It was your idea."

"All right," Nancy agreed. She straightened, nervously folding her hands on her lap.

Carla pulled up the spaghetti strap of her summer dress. Normally a redhead couldn't wear pink, but this

shade, the color of camellias, complemented the unusual color of her hair.

"Here comes a single man."

Two pairs of intense eyes followed the lumbering gait
of a dark-haired Latin American who entered the lounge
and took the closest available love seat.

"He's in a cast," Nancy observed in a high-pitched
whisper.

"Don't panic," Carla said in a reassuring tone. "He
doesn't look like the type to order a margarita."

Nancy opened her purse and put on her glasses. "Not
bad-looking."

"Yes, I suppose so," Carla agreed, although she
thought he looked too much like a movie star—smooth
and suave—to suit her. His toothy smile looked bright
enough to blind someone in broad daylight. For Nancy's
sake, she hoped the guy was into wine. "You can back
out if you want," Carla said, almost wishing Nancy
would. The whole idea was crazy.

"Not on your life."

"The guy's in a cast up to his hip. I'd say he was en-
cumbered, wouldn't you?"

"No," Nancy replied smoothly. "You're doing it
again."

"Doing what?"

"You know."

"Fine, I'll shut up. If you want to be stuck with a guy
who leaves a funny trail in the sand, that's fine with me."

"Look," Nancy whispered, "your fellow's arrived."

Quickly, Carla's attention focused on the lounge entrance at the other side of the room. She recognized him
immediately as someone from the same flight as theirs.

Not that she'd found him particularly interesting at the time. He'd sat across the aisle from Nancy and read a book during the entire trip.

"Hey, he was on the plane with us," Nancy pointed out.

"I know," Carla answered evenly, trying to disguise her disappointment. Secretly, she'd been hoping for someone compelling and forcefully masculine. She should have known better.

Both women sat in rigid silence as their eyes followed the young cocktail waitress, who delivered two margaritas: one to the looker and one to the bookworm.

"You ready?" Nancy whispered.

"What are we going to say?" Carla's hand tightened around her purse.

Nancy gave another one of those glares normally reserved for her pupils. "Good grief, Carla, we're mature women. We know what to say."

Carla shook her head. "Mature women wouldn't do something like this."

They stood together, condemned prisoners marching to the hangman's noose. "How do I look?" Nancy asked with a weak smile.

"Like you're about to throw up."

Her friend briefly closed her eyes. "That's the way I feel."

Carla hesitated.

"Come on," Nancy whispered. "We aren't backing out now."

Carla couldn't believe that calm, levelheaded, left-brained Nancy would actually agree to something like this. It was completely out of character. Carla was the impulsive one—creative, imaginative, right-brained. That was why they were such good friends: Their personalities complemented each other's perfectly. *Right-brained, left-brained,* Carla mused. That was the problem. Each of them had only half a brain.

She studied the man from the plane. He wasn't anyone she would normally have sought out. For a light romance, she wanted someone more dynamic. This guy was decidedly—she searched for the right word—undashing. He was tall, she remembered, which was lucky. At five-nine, she didn't look up to many men. And he was on the lanky side. Almost reedy. He wore horn-rimmed glasses, which gave him a serious look. His sandy hair, parted on the side, fell carelessly across his wide brow. His tan was rich, but Carla mused that he didn't look like the type to use a tanning bed or lie lazily in the sun. He probably worked outdoors—maybe he was a mailman.

He glanced at her and smiled. Carla nearly tripped on the plush carpet. His eyes were fantastic. A deep gray like overcast winter clouds with the sun beaming through. A brilliant silver shade that she had never seen. Her spirits brightened; the man's eyes, at least, were encouragingly attractive.

"Hello," she said as she stood in front of his deep cushioned chair. "I'm Carla Walker." She extended her hand. Might as well be forthright about this.

He stood, dwarfing her by a good four inches, and shook hands. "Philip Garrison."

He looked like a Philip. "We were on the same flight, weren't we?"

He pushed his glasses up the bridge of his nose with

his index finger. The action reminded her of Clark Kent. But Carla wasn't kidding herself—Philip Garrison was no Superman.

"I believe we were," he said with a smile that was surprisingly compelling. "Would you like to sit down?"

"Yes, thank you." Carla took the chair beside him. Hoping to give an impression of nonchalance, she crossed her shapely legs. "Are you from Seattle?"

"Spokane."

"On vacation?"

His smile deepened. "In a way. My parents have a condominium here that needs a few repairs."

Carla smiled absently into her drink. So he was a carpenter. The occupation suited him, she decided. He was deceptively lean and muscular. And he had a subtle, understated appeal, something she found refreshing.

"Would you like another margarita?" he asked, as he glanced at her empty glass.

"Yes. Thank you."

He raised his hand to get the waitress's attention. The lovely olive-skinned woman acknowledged his gesture and indicated that she would be there in a moment. Service here was notoriously slow, but right now Carla didn't mind. She looked around for Nancy and discovered that her friend was chatting easily and seemed to be enjoying herself. At the moment, this crazy scheme appeared to be working beautifully.

"Is this your first visit to Mazatlán?" Philip asked, and took a sip of his drink.

Carla noted the way the tip of his tongue eased the salt from the bottom of his lip. She dropped her gaze, finding his action disturbingly provocative. "Yes, my first time in Mexico, actually. To be honest, I didn't expect it to be this beautiful."

The waitress arrived, and Carla handed the girl her empty glass. She had noticed that the waitresses spoke only minimal English. Although her Spanish wasn't terrific, the urge to impress Philip with her knowledge of the language overpowered her good sense, so, proudly, without the hint of a foreign accent, Carla asked for another drink.

The waitress frowned and glanced at Philip, who was obviously trying to contain his laughter. He delivered a crisp request in Spanish to the woman, who nodded and smiled before turning away.

"What's so humorous?" Carla could feel herself blushing.

Philip composed himself quickly. "You just told the waitress that Big Bird wants a drink of water."

Carla closed her eyes and did her best to laugh, but the sound was weak and revealing. She would never watch *Sesame Street* again, she vowed, no matter how desperate she was to entertain her two nieces.

"How long will you be staying?" he asked pleasantly, deftly changing the subject.

"A week. My roommate, Nancy, and I are on a discount vacation package for teachers."

"You teach preschool?"

It was a logical assumption. "No, I'm a surgical assistant."

One thick brow arched with surprise. "You don't look much older than a student yourself."

"I'm twenty-five." *And old enough to know better*

than to make a fool of myself like this, she added silently.

Their drinks arrived, and Carla resisted the urge to gulp hers down and ease the parched feeling in her throat. Gradually she relaxed as they spoke about the flight and the weather.

After a half-hour of exchanging pleasantries, Philip asked her if she was available to join him for dinner. The invitation pleased her. Since her faux pas with the waitress, she'd imagined he'd wanted to be rid of her as quickly as he could manage to do so without appearing impolite.

"Yes, I'd like to have dinner with you." To her surprise, Carla discovered it was the truth.

He took her to a restaurant called El Marinero. The view of the harbor was excellent, as was the shrimp dinner. Philip spoke to the waiter in Spanish, then quietly translated for Carla. It was a thoughtful gesture. She would have felt excluded otherwise. Not once did he try to overwhelm her with his wit and charm. He was who he was, quiet and a little reserved, and apparently he saw no need to change because he'd been approached by her.

"I can't believe I ate that much," Carla said and groaned as they left the restaurant. The air was still sultry, but much cooler than it had been when they arrived.

"Would you like to walk along the beach? It'll be less crowded outside the hotel."

"I'd love to." Her blue eyes looked fondly into his. "But can we? I mean, it's all privately owned, isn't it?"

"Not in Mexico. The beaches are for everyone."

"How nice," Carla murmured, thinking she was beginning to like Philip more with every passing minute.

They rode back to the hotel in an open-air vehicle that resembled a golf cart—a hot-rod golf cart. The driver weaved his way in and out of lanes with complete disregard for pedestrians and traffic signals.

Philip took her by the hand and led her through the lobby, around the huge swimming pool in back of the hotel, and to the stairs that descended to the beach. The strip of white sand stretched as far as the eye could see. So did the array of hotels.

"I don't suppose you've been in the ocean yet."

"No time," Carla confessed. "The first thing Nancy and I did was take a shower." The heat that had greeted them on their arrival had been suffocating. They'd stepped from the air-conditioned plane into one-hundred-degree weather. By the time they'd arrived at the hotel room, their clothes had been damp from the humidity and clinging. "I couldn't believe that death trap of a shuttle bus actually made it all the way to the hotel."

Philip grinned in amusement. "I think the same thing every time I visit."

"Do you come often?" Carla asked as they sat in the sand and removed their sandals. Philip rolled up his tan pant legs to his knees.

"Once or twice a year."

"I think there's something I should tell you," Carla said as an ocean wave gently lapped up to her bare feet. The warm water was another surprise.

"You mean that you don't usually pick up men in bars," Philip said with a chuckle. "I already knew that."

"You did?" Carla was astonished.

"What made you do it this time?"

Carla kicked idly at the sand with her big toe. "You aren't going to like hearing this," she mumbled.

"Try me."

She took a deep breath, then exhaled slowly. "It happens every vacation. Nancy and I spend the entire time waiting to meet someone. This time, instead of wasting our vacation, we'd take the initiative ourselves. To make the decision easy, we decided we could find someone on the first day. One problem is that we're too picky, so we decided to be a bit more spontaneous. You came in alone. You're under thirty-five, and you ordered a margarita."

The pleasant sound of his laughter blended with a crashing wave that pounded the beach. "I almost asked for a beer."

"I'm glad you didn't." The words were automatic and sincere. It surprised Carla how much she meant them.

The sun became a huge red ball that slowly descended to meet a blue horizon. Carla couldn't remember ever seeing anything more spectacular. She glanced at Philip to see if he was also enjoying the beauty of their surroundings. He wasn't the chatty sort, she realized, which was fine—she could do enough talking for them both. His laugh was free and easy, and the sound of it warmed her.

"What were you reading so intently on the plane?" Carla asked, curious to know more about him.

"A book by Ann Rule. She's—"

"I know who she is," Carla interrupted. The talented

author was a policewoman turned reporter turned writer. Ann's books specialized in true-crime cases. Her novel on serial murderer Ted Bundy was a national bestseller. "My father worked with Ann before she took up writing," Carla explained. "She's from Seattle."

"I read that on the cover flap. What does your father do?"

Carla swallowed uncomfortably. "He's a cop," she murmured, not looking at Philip.

"You sound like it bothers you."

"It does," Carla replied vigorously. "Half the boys in high school wouldn't ask me out. They were afraid I'd tell my father if they tried anything, and then he'd go after them."

"Your father would arrest them for making a pass?" Philip sounded incredulous.

"Not that." She tossed him a defiant look. It was obvious that Philip, like everyone else in her life, didn't understand. "It's too hard to explain."

"Try me."

Carla felt a tightening in her stomach. Although she'd held these feelings deep inside since childhood, she had never verbalized them. She wasn't sure she was capable of expressing them now. "A good example of what I'm saying happened when I was about ten. Our family went to a friend's wedding reception. Everyone had been drinking, and an uncle had given some of the teens spiked punch. The minute Dad walked in the room the temperature dropped fifteen degrees."

"Were they afraid he was going to make a scene?"

"I don't know. But I do recall how uncomfortable everyone was."

"Including you?"

She hesitated. "Yes."

"But that's not all, is it?" he asked gently.

"No," she admitted. "It was far more than that. I can count on one hand the number of Christmases Dad spent at home. It was the same thing every holiday. And we were lucky if he was there for our birthdays. It got so that I'd dread it every time the phone rang, because I knew he was always on call. It was his job."

"I don't blame you for resenting that."

Once started, Carla discovered she couldn't stop. "He worked with the scum of the earth: pimps, muggers, murderers, wife beaters, and child abusers. Then there were the sick people, dying people, dead people, addicts, and prostitutes. Sometimes he'd come home at night and—" She stopped, realizing that everything had come out in one huge rush. When she'd caught her breath, Carla continued. "I'm sorry, I didn't mean to unload on you like this."

"You didn't," Philip said. "You've never told your father any of this, have you?"

"No. What was the use? Dad loves his work." Philip's hand cupped her shoulder. He was comforting her, and in a strange way Carla appreciated it. Never before had she voiced these thoughts, and the fierce intensity of her feelings had surprised her.

By unspoken agreement, they turned back toward the hotel. The sky had grown dark now, and the lights from the long row of hotels dimly lit the beach. Other couples were walking along the sandy shores. A few flirted with the cresting ocean waves.

"Philip." Carla stopped and turned toward him. "Thank you," she whispered.

"What for?"

Their eyes met in the moonlight, and Carla was trapped in the silvery glow of his gaze. Those beautiful, warm gray eyes held her as effectively as the arms that slipped around her waist and brought her into his embrace.

"I may never drink anything but margaritas again." His whisper was husky, but he didn't make a move to do anything more than hold her. His arms pressed her gently as he rubbed his chin across the top of her head. A mist-filled breeze off the ocean had ruined her carefully styled hair; now it fell in tight ringlets around her oval face.

Her hair was another thing that endeared her to Philip. Not once had he mentioned its color. Men invariably teased her about it, asking if her temper matched the color of her hair. The only time it did was when someone made tiresome remarks about it. Not red and not blond, the shade fell somewhere in between. Red oak, her mother claimed, like her grandmother's. Like russet potatoes, her brother suggested. The color of her hair and her fair complexion had been the bane of Carla's existence.

"Would you like to go for a swim?" Philip asked, dropping his arms and taking her hand. They continued walking toward the hotel.

"In the ocean?" She'd have to get her suit.

"No, the current's too dangerous. I meant the pool."

The hotel's swimming pool was the most luxurious Carla had ever seen. A picture of the massive pool area at the hotel had been the determining factor in their decision to book their vacation at the El Cid. Blue, watery channels stretched all around the hotel, with bridges joining one section to another.

"I'd love to go swimming," Carla replied enthusiastically. They reached the short flight of stairs that led to the hotel from the beach. "Give me ten minutes to change and I'll meet you back here."

"Ten minutes?" Philip arched one brow. Carla had noticed him do that a couple times during the evening.

"Ten minutes—easy," Carla confirmed confidently. She knew exactly which corner of her suitcase held her swimsuit. It wouldn't take her more than five minutes to change, so she figured she'd easily have five minutes to spare. But what she hadn't counted on was that Nancy had neatly stored their suitcases under the beds. Carla spent a frantic five minutes tearing their room apart, certain that they'd been robbed. Finally, she found it. She should have remembered her friend's penchant for neatness.

Fifteen minutes later, a chagrined look pinching her face, Carla met Philip at poolside.

Pointedly he glanced at his watch.

"I couldn't help it," she told him breathlessly, and offered a sketchy explanation as she placed her towel on a chaise longue. The pool was empty, which surprised Carla until she removed her wristwatch and noted that it was after midnight.

She tugged the elastic of the forest-green swimsuit over her thigh and tested the water by dipping one foot into the pool. Warm. Almost too warm.

"Are you one of those women who gets wet by degrees?" Philip asked as he took off his glasses and tossed them on his towel.

"Not me." She walked to his side, stretched out her arms, and dove in. Her slim body sliced into the water. Philip joined her almost immediately, and together they swam the width of the pool.

"Do you want to race?" he called out.

"No," Carla answered with a giggle.

"Why not?"

"Because I was on my college swim team, and I'm fast. Men can't stand to lose."

"Is that a fact?"

"It's true."

"I'm not like most men."

Carla had noticed that. But this was turning out to be a promising relationship, and she didn't want to ruin it. Floating lackadaisically on her back, she paddled rhythmically with her hands at her sides. Carla decided to ignore the challenge in his voice.

Philip joined her, floating on his back as well. "If you don't want to race, what would you like to do?"

"Kiss underwater." She laughed at the surprised look on his face as he struggled to a standing position. Philip looked different without his glasses, almost handsome. But not quite.

He stood completely still in the shoulder-deep water. "I'm not that kind of man."

He was so serious that it took Carla a moment to realize he was kidding.

"I'm not easy, you know," she said, flirting. "You have to catch me first." They were acting like adolescents, and

Carla loved it. With Philip she could be herself. There wasn't any need to put on sophisticated airs.

Laughing, she twisted and dove underwater, surfacing several feet away from him. He came after her, and Carla took off with all the energy she'd expend for an important race. Using her most powerful strokes, she surged ahead. When his hand groped for her foot, she kicked frantically and managed to escape. That he'd caught up with her so quickly was hard to believe.

She was even more amazed when his solid stroke matched hers and he gripped her waist and pulled her to the side of the pool.

"You're as slippery as an eel."

"You're good," she countered. "Who taught you to swim like that?"

"My mother." They were hidden under the shadow of a bridge that crossed a narrow section of the pool.

Carla slipped her arms around his neck. She wanted him to kiss her. She could tell he was attracted to her; she'd seen it in his eyes when they were on the beach. That look had prompted her flippant challenge about kissing underwater.

He pushed the wet strands of hair from her face. The silver light in his eyes darkened. He moved closer, but Carla assumed it was because he couldn't see her clearly without his glasses. She liked his eyes. They were so expressive. She liked the way they darkened when he was serious and how they sparkled when he was teasing. Tiny lines fanned out from the edges, and Carla recognized that this man laughed and enjoyed life. Her feelings for him were intensifying every minute they were together.

His hands rested on either side of her face, pressing her against the side of the pool. "I'm going to kiss you," he whispered. He released one hand and encircled her waist to pull her gently but firmly toward him.

Slowly, lengthening each moment, each breath, he lowered his mouth to hers. Carla felt herself relax, felt her body, her heart, opening to him. Wanting to touch him, needing to, she ran her hand along the side of his face, twisting her head so that when he found her lips their mouths slanted across each other's. The kiss was gentle and soft, gradually building in intensity until Carla melted against him.

Philip let go of the side of the pool, and they sank just below the surface. Their legs entwined, and Carla opened her mouth to him. His tongue sought hers, forcing her mouth to open farther under its exploring pressure. Carla felt as if she were drowning, but the sensation was exquisite.

They broke the surface of the water together and drew in deep, shaky breaths. Her body remained tucked in his embrace. His chest pressed against the softness of her breasts, and a crazy dizziness overcame her.

The pressure of his embrace backed her against the side of the pool, and he kissed her again. Carla gloried in the wonderful, inexplicable sensations that overwhelmed her.

Their breathing was ragged when Philip buried his face in the side of her neck.

"My word," she murmured breathlessly. "Who taught you to kiss like that?"

Philip responded with a weak laugh. "Carla." Philip

hesitated and wiped the moisture from his eyes. "I wish I could see you better."

"I'm glad you can't," she replied happily. "You might get a swelled head if you could see how much I like you."

"Carla." His voice grew strong, serious.

"What's wrong?" She placed a hand on each of his shoulders, liking the feel of her body floating against his.

"There's something you should know."

"What?" He was so serious that her heart throbbed. She didn't want anything to ruin this. If he told her he was married she wasn't sure what she'd do.

"Carla, I'm a policeman for the city of Spokane."

Two

❧

Carla woke just as the sun crested the horizon and bathed the beach in a flashy glow of color. Nancy had been asleep by the time Carla had returned last night, which was just as well. She hadn't felt much like talking.

Philip Garrison had taught her a valuable lesson. She should have trusted her instincts. From her first look at Philip, she'd felt he wasn't her type. At the time, she hadn't realized how true that was. His kisses had been . . . She couldn't find a word to describe them. *Pleasant,* she mused. *All right, very pleasant.* But that certainly wasn't enough to overcome *what* he was.

Dang. Dang. Dang. She'd liked him. In fact, she'd liked him a lot. He was sensitive, sympathetic, compassionate, kind, caring . . . Carla placed the pillow over her head to drown out her thoughts. She wouldn't allow herself to think about him again. This crazy idea of Nancy's had been ridiculous from the beginning. She'd put the episode behind her and get on with her vacation.

Throwing back the covers of her bed, she stood and

stretched. Nancy grumbled and curled into a tight ball. Typical of Nancy, who hated mornings.

"What time is it?" she demanded in a growling whisper.

"Early. The sun just came up."

"Sun!" Nancy's eyes popped open. "I forgot to set the alarm."

Carla smiled as she sat in the middle of the double bed and ran a brush through her hair to tame the wild array of red curls. "Don't worry about the time. We're on vacation, remember?"

With an uncharacteristically hurried movement, Nancy threw back the sheets. "But I promised to meet Eduardo on the beach at dawn," she cried out. "Oh good grief, how could I have been so stupid?"

For Nancy to forget anything was surprising by itself. But to have her friend show this much enthusiasm in the morning was astonishing.

"I take it you and . . . Eduardo hit it off?"

Nancy's head bobbed energetically. "What about you?"

"Not so lucky," Carla returned with a wistful sigh.

Nancy's most attractive summer dress slid over her hips as she turned her back to Carla in an unspoken request for her to help with the zipper. "What went wrong?"

"You don't have time to hear," Carla said with forced cheerfulness.

"He looked nice."

Nice was only the beginning, Carla thought. "Looks are often deceiving." That much was true. Who would have imagined that Philip Garrison would turn out to be so appealing? "If I'm not mistaken, I'd say you and Eduardo got along famously."

"He's fabulous. I can't remember a night I've enjoyed more." Nancy paused, and a dreamy look replaced the hurried frown that had marred her smooth features.

"His cast doesn't bother you?" Carla couldn't help asking.

"Good grief, no. I hardly thought about it."

That was saying something.

"He's taking me on an all-day tour of Mazatlán. You don't mind, do you?"

"Mind? Me? Of course not." Carla's mouth formed a tight smile. Now she'd be forced to spend the entire day alone. "Have a good time," she managed without a hint of sarcasm. No need to ruin Nancy's fun.

"Thanks, I will." Always practical, Nancy grabbed a hat to protect her from the sun, tucked her credit cards into a secret flap in her purse, and was out the door in a rush.

Carla flopped back on her bed and stared at the shadows on the ceiling. This vacation was rapidly turning into a disaster. Day two, and already she wished she were back in Seattle.

After an unhurried shower, Carla decided to head for the pool. With her skin color, she wasn't able to stay out in the sun long, and morning was generally the best time for her to sunbathe.

The pool area was filling up with early sun worshippers, and Carla chose a chaise longue near the deep end. That way she could dive in and cool off whenever necessary. This afternoon she'd do some shopping at the Mazatlán Arts and Crafts Center. She'd heard about the center almost immediately after her arrival. With twenty-eight shops to explore, she was certain to find souvenirs for her family. But even shopping had lost its appeal, especially since she'd be doing it alone. If she was lucky, she might meet someone at the pool—preferably someone male and handsome. She spread her towel out as a cushion for the longue and lay on her stomach, facing the pool. With her arms crossed, she pressed her cheek against her forearm. *Boring,* she admitted regretfully. Day two and she was bored to death. The turquoise tankini she wore was modest, especially when compared to the daring suit on the luscious, curvy creature across the pool from her. Carla guessed that if she had a body like that, she might be tempted to wear the same thing. She'd heard of string bikinis, but this one was hardly more than threads. The woman was attracting the attention of almost everyone at poolside. When Philip moved into her line of vision, Carla's eyes widened. He smiled, and his gray eyes twinkled. It didn't bother her that his smile wasn't directed at her. For all the attention he'd given her, be obviously hadn't noticed that she was across the pool from him.

Carla chose to ignore him, but her heart leaped just seeing him again. He wasn't muscular or strikingly masculine, but he was compelling in a way she couldn't describe. If she hadn't spent yesterday with him, she wouldn't have given him a second look today. But she'd felt the lean hardness of him against her in the water. She'd tasted the sweetness of his kiss. She'd experienced the gentle comfort of his arms. Her eyes refused to move from him, and when he looked her way, she shook herself from her musings and lowered her cheek against her arm again, pretending not to see him.

Her heart was racing, and that angered her. One look from Philip was no reason for her pulse to quicken. Although Carla refused to pay attention to him, she could feel Philip's gaze on her. She smiled as she imagined the satisfaction in his gaze, the look of admiration that would dominate those smoky-gray eyes of his. How she loved his expressive eyes! Unable to resist, she raised her head a fraction to catch a glimpse of his approval. To her dismay, Carla discovered that Philip wasn't studying her at all. His concentration was centered on the daring blond beauty at the other side of the pool.

Carla expected the woman to treat Philip like a pesky intruder. But she didn't—in fact, she seemed to encourage his attention. Grudgingly, Carla admitted there *was* a certain attractiveness to Philip, and an aura of quiet confidence that was . . . well, masculine. His sandy hair had a tendency to curl at the ends, she observed, and most men would have styled it into submission. But not Philip—professionally groomed hair wouldn't be on his list of priorities.

After several minutes of what appeared to be light conversation, Philip dived into the pool and did a number of laps. Carla couldn't help admiring the way his bronze body sliced through the water. Anyone would. A rush of pink colored her cheeks as she recalled their antics last night. Yes, Philip Garrison was indeed gifted.

When Philip came out of the pool, he maneuvered himself so that he "accidentally" dripped water on his scantily clad acquaintance. The luscious blonde sat up to hand him a towel and laughed lightly when more drops of water splashed on her bare midriff.

Forcefully, Carla directed her gaze elsewhere. For a full five minutes she refused to allow herself to turn their way. When curiosity got the better of her, she casually glanced toward Philip and the other woman, who were an unlikely match. To her dismay she found that they were laughing and enjoying a cocktail. One side of Carla's mouth curved up sarcastically. One would assume a dedicated police officer would know better than to consume alcohol at such an early hour.

Pretending that the sun was burning her tender skin, Carla made a show of standing and draping a light terry-cloth wrap over her shoulders. She tucked her towel and tanning lotion into her oversized bag and walked down the cement stairs that led to the beach.

The beach wasn't nearly as crowded as the pool area. Carla had just settled in the sandy mattress when she was approached by a vendor carrying a black case. He knelt in front of her and opened the lid to display a large number of silver earrings, bracelets, and rings. She smiled and shook her head. But the man persisted, telling her in poor English that he would sell jewelry to her at a very good price.

Politely but firmly, Carla shook her head again.

Still the man insisted, holding out a lovely silver-and-turquoise ring for her to inspect. His eyes pleaded with her, and Carla couldn't refuse. The ring was pretty.

Someone spoke in Spanish from behind her. It didn't take Carla two seconds to realize it was Philip. His words were heavy with authority, although he hadn't raised his voice. Resenting his intrusion, she tossed him an angry look.

"Do you like the ring?" He directed his comment to her.

"Well, it's more than I wanted to spend—"

She wasn't allowed to finish. Philip said something to the vendor, who nodded resignedly, took the ring back, and turned away.

"That wasn't necessary, you know," she told him stiffly.

"Perhaps not, but you could buy the same ring in the hotel gift shop for less than what he was asking." Philip spread out his towel a respectable distance from her. "Do you mind?" he asked before he sat down.

"It's a public beach," she returned coolly, recognizing it wouldn't do any good to object. "Just leave enough space between us so no one will assume we're together." She suspected that Philip would only follow her if she got up and moved. "What happened with Miss String Bikini?" Carla had hoped to resist any hint of acid in her query.

Philip chuckled. "Unfortunately, Miss is a Mrs., and hubby looked like the jealous type."

Now it was Carla's turn to laugh. She was sorry to have missed the scene of Philip meeting the irate husband. "I'll admit, though, she had quite a body."

"Passable," Philip admitted dryly as his eyes swept over the beach.

Passable! Carla's mind echoed, wondering what he considered terrific.

"Where's your roommate?" he asked breezily.

"With . . . Eduardo. They seem to have hit it off quite well."

"We did, too, as I recall. I wonder what it would take to get you to agree to have lunch with me."

"Forget it, Garrison," Carla said forcefully.

"You know what a good time we could have," he prodded softly.

"I'm not interested," Carla replied without looking at him. She felt a twinge of regret at how callous she sounded, and recalled how cold she'd been to him after he'd told her his occupation. She wouldn't have been so unfeeling, she suspected, if she hadn't previously expressed her resentment about her father being a policeman. Later, unable to sleep, she decided she was glad she'd told him. It had saved an unnecessary explanation. As it was, she'd pushed herself from his arms and swam to the opposite side of the pool. "It was a pleasure meeting you, Philip Garrison," she'd said tersely while toweling dry. "But I have one strict code regarding the men I date."

"I think I can guess what that is," he'd replied with a control that was frightening. "You realize I didn't have to tell you. We could have had a pleasant vacation together without you ever being the wiser."

"Perhaps." Carla hadn't been in any mood to reason. "But you saved us both a lot of trouble." Carla was just beginning to realize how miserable she was feeling. Disappointed in herself and disappointed in Philip. He might as well have admitted to being married; he was as off-limits as he would be if he had a wife and ten children.

"Nice-looking brunette to your left," Philip pointed out, breaking her train of thought.

"It doesn't look like she's sporting a jealous husband, either," Carla said jokingly.

Philip's laugh was good-natured. "I'll use my practiced routine on her. Care to watch me in action?"

"I'd love it," Carla answered with open delight. "At least with you out of the picture, some handsome tourist can make a play for me."

"Good luck," he called as he stood and loped lazily down the beach.

Handsome tourist. Carla almost laughed. At the rate things were going, the only men she'd be fighting off would be persistent vendors.

Carla watched with growing interest as Philip carelessly tossed his towel on the beach close to the girl and ran into the rolling surf. She'd remember to ask him later about swimming in the ocean. Last night he'd told her the tide was too dangerous, yet he was diving headlong into it without a second's hesitation.

After a few minutes in the surf, which he apparently thought suitable for a favorable impression, he stood, wiped the water from his face, and walked out of the ocean. He squinted and rubbed his eyes, giving the impression that the water was stinging. The way he groped for his towel made Carla laugh outright. Again by an apparent accident, he flicked sand on the tanning beauty. The woman sat up and brushed the offending particles from her well-oiled body. Philip fell to his knees, and although Carla couldn't hear what he was saying, she was sure it was some practiced apology. Soon the two of them were talking and laughing. Spreading out his long body, he lay beside the brown-haired beauty. His technique, tried-and-true, had worked well. Rolling his head,

Philip caught Carla's gaze and winked when she gestured with two fingers, giving the okay sign.

For the first time in recent memory, Carla wished that she were as good at acting as Philip was. For a moment she toyed with the idea of following his lead and blatantly approaching a man. Carla's devil-may-care system should work as well on the beach as it had in the cocktail lounge. But a quick survey of the area didn't turn up a single male she cared to flirt with. There wasn't anyone she particularly wanted to meet. Maybe Nancy was right, maybe she had become much too picky lately.

Ten minutes later, Carla stood, brushed the sand from her skin, and picked up her things. After lunch she'd do some shopping.

Philip gave her a brief wave, which she returned. At least one of them had been successful. At least one of them was having a good time.

The oppressive afternoon heat eventually brought Carla back into the air-conditioned cocktail lounge. Sipping a piña colada, she surveyed the growing crowd of tourists. A couple times men had asked if they could buy her a drink, but she'd declined. Men who used tanning beds, wore gold chains around their necks, and left their shirts open to their navels didn't interest Carla. Her spirits were low, and she hated to think she'd be fighting this depression the entire week. If she wasn't careful, she'd get locked in a state of self-pity.

The room was filling up rapidly, and when Philip entered, Carla pretended to be inordinately interested in her drink.

"Hi." He sauntered to her side. "Do you mind if I join you, or will I be distracting any potential margarita drinkers?"

"By all means join me," she said with a poor attempt at a smile. "I don't exactly seem to be drawing a crowd. How about you? I expected you to stroll in here with Miss September."

He cleared his throat and took the plush seat beside her. "That didn't work out."

"Was there a Mr. September?"

"No." Philip cleared his throat a second time. "Things didn't work out, that's all."

"Philip," she said and moaned impatiently, "come on, tell me what happened. You can't leave me in suspense like this." Something perverse inside her wanted to know about Philip's latest rejection. Maybe she needed to salve her pride at his expense, which was childish, Carla thought, but shared misery beats the solo kind.

He ignored her while he raised his hand to attract the waitress's attention. "What's that you're drinking?"

"Piña colada," Carla answered quickly. "Out with it, Garrison. Details, I want details."

The waitress came to take his order. Carla had lost the desire to impress him with her vast knowledge of the Spanish language. As it was, the waitress eyed her warily, as if she were afraid Carla was going *loco*.

"No margarita tonight?" His eyes mocked hers as a smile touched the corners of his mouth.

"Don't change the subject."

"I'll tell you over dinner." He raised both of his thick brows suggestively.

"Do you think bribing me is going to work?"

He smiled faintly, rather tenderly, at her. "I was hoping it would."

This was the best offer she'd had all day. And she wasn't about to refuse. "All right, as long as we understand one another."

"Of course we do," he replied formally. "You don't want to date cops, and with good reason."

"With a very good reason," she repeated emphatically.

The waitress delivered their drinks and brought a plate with two tacos, or what Carla assumed were tacos. She'd noticed that a sign outside the lounge stated that anyone buying a drink between four and five would receive a free taco. But this fried corn tortilla that had been filled with meat and rolled didn't resemble anything she'd call a taco. No lettuce, no cheese, no tomato.

One nibble confirmed that it didn't taste anything like a taco, either. "What's in this?"

Philip eyed her doubtfully. "Are you sure you want to know?"

"Of course I do."

He shrugged. "Turtle."

Carla closed her eyes and swallowed. "Turtle," she repeated. "It tastes more like week-old tuna fish to me."

"You don't have to eat it if you don't want to."

She set it back on the plate. "It's something to tell my friends about, but it's nothing I'd recommend."

"It'll grow on you," Philip commented.

"I certainly hope not," Carla said with a grimace. "Have you ever examined the skin on those things?"

Suddenly they were both laughing as if she'd said the most uproariously funny thing in the world. "Come on." His hand reached for hers. "Let's get out of here before they throw us out." He laid several bills beside their uneaten turtle tacos. They finished their drinks and together they left hand in hand, practically running out of the cocktail lounge.

Not until they were in a golf cart/taxi did Carla ask where they were headed.

"Señor Frog's," Philip shouted, the wind whipping his voice past her.

"No." She waved her hand dramatically. "Not if they serve what I think they do."

"Not to worry." Philip placed an arm around her shoulders and spoke close to her ear. "This is a famous tourist trap. The food's good, but the place is wild. You'll love it."

And just as he'd promised, Carla did love it. After almost an hour's delay, they were ushered through the restaurant doors only to be led to a cocktail lounge. The music and boisterous singing were so loud that Carla couldn't hear herself speak when she leaned over to ask Philip something. He bent closer but finally gestured that they'd have to talk afterward outside.

Two hours later, well fed and singing softly, Carla and Philip left the restaurant with their arms wrapped around each other.

"That was wild."

"I knew you'd like it," Philip said, smiling tenderly at her.

"But there's a method to your madness."

"How's that?"

"With all the noise, you weren't able to tell me about Miss September."

"All right, if you must know."

"I must," she replied firmly. "I hope you realize I baked in the hot sun while I waited to see how you did. Honestly, Philip, your approach could have been a little more original."

The look he gave told her that he was offended. "I thought my technique was one of a kind."

Carla looked at the darkening sky and rolled her eyes but refrained from comment. "I'm surprised that you didn't go up to her and ask if you'd met someplace before."

Philip shifted his weight onto the other foot. "To be honest, that occurred to me, too."

Laughing, Carla said, "You, my dear Philip, are refreshingly unimaginative."

He chuckled as he seemed to be studying the cracks in the sidewalk on which they were strolling. He didn't appear to have any clear direction.

"Now, will you spill the beans about Miss September? I'm dying to know what happened."

He was quiet for a few moments. "You prefer not to date policemen, and I have a thing about flight attendants."

Most men had a "thing" about flight attendants, too, but it wasn't to avoid them. It wasn't one of her more brilliant deductions to guess that Philip had once loved a flight attendant and been hurt. "Do you want to tell me about her? I make a great wailing wall," she murmured sympathetically.

"Not if I can avoid it." He looked at her and smiled. "Tell me about your afternoon. Any success?"

"No one," she said dejectedly, and shook her head for emphasis. "Unless you count guys in gold chains who enjoy revealing their chest hair."

"Some women like those kind of men."

"Not me."

Philip hesitated, then asked, "I wonder if I could interest you in a short-term, no-obligation, strictly regulated but guaranteed fun relationship."

Carla's mouth curved wryly. She'd had a better time with Philip tonight than she'd had the entire day she'd spent alone. Her mind was flashing a bright neon NO in bold red letters. If she had any sense whatsoever, she'd shake her head and decline without another word.

"Well?" he urged.

"I don't know," she answered truthfully. *Five days. What could possibly happen in five days?* She'd come to Mexico looking for a good time. She knew who Philip was, and, more important, *what* he was.

The silence lengthened. "I think I should make one thing clear. I have no intention of treating you like a sister."

He could have lied. But again, he'd chosen to be straight with her. She appreciated that.

"I don't want anything more than these five days. Once we leave Mazatlán, it's over."

"Agreed," he said, and a finger tenderly traced the outline of her jaw.

A tingling sensation burned across her face, and she

closed her eyes against its potency. She'd be safe. She'd walked into this with her eyes wide open. He lived in Spokane. She lived in Seattle. A light flirtation was what she'd had in mind in the first place. Knowing what he was should make it all the easier to walk away next Saturday. But it hadn't lessened the attraction she felt for him—and that appeared to be growing every minute.

"I . . . haven't agreed yet." Her self-respect demanded one last stand.

"But you will," Philip said confidently.

"How can you be so sure?" Carla returned, piqued by his attitude.

"Well, for one thing, you're looking at me with 'kiss me' eyes."

Embarrassed, Carla shot her gaze to the ground. "That's not true—" she denied hotly, and she was ready to argue further, but Philip cut her off.

"Do you agree or not?" He held out his hand for her to shake.

"I have a feeling I'm going to regret this," she said, and placed her hand in his.

Philip didn't argue. But when his arm closed around her, she didn't object. She liked the idea of being linked with this man, even if it was for only a few days.

"How about a ride on an cabriolet?" he suggested, his mouth disturbingly close to her ear.

"I don't know what you're suggesting, Philip Garrison, but that doesn't sound like something nice girls do."

His laughter filled the night. "That's a two-wheeled horse-drawn cab."

"Sounds romantic." Knowing Philip, Carla was willing to bet he'd instruct the driver to take the long way back to the hotel through scented, shady boulevards. She was in the mood for a few stolen kisses, and so was Philip, gauging by his look.

"If we can't find one, we can always jog back to the hotel," he said seriously.

"With a name like Walker, you expect me to run?"

"What's the matter with running? I thought you'd be into physical fitness."

She laughed softly. "I swim, and that's the entire repertoire of my athletic abilities."

"You mean you weren't in track? With those long legs of yours, I'd think you'd be a natural."

"So did my high school coach—until the first practice. He had to time me with a calendar. Running's out."

"Walking?" Philip suggested.

"Good grief, if we can't find a carriage, what's the matter with those golf-cart things that we've been taking lately?"

"You mean the *pulmonías*?" His gray eyes were dancing with amusement, and Carla struggled not to succumb to the invitation in their smoky depths.

"Whatever," she replied, pleased with herself now for agreeing to this crazy relationship. She honestly enjoyed this quirky man.

"If you insist," Philip said blandly, and flagged down a passing taxi when it became obvious that finding a cabriolet would take longer than they were willing to wait.

Back at the hotel, Carla mentally chastised herself for being so easily swayed by Philip's direct approach. She really ought to have played harder to get.

"There's a band playing at the—"

"I love to dance," she interrupted enthusiastically. "My feet are itching already."

Philip smoothed the hair at the side of his head. "Tell me, why was I expecting an argument?" He was regarding her with a look of amused surprise.

"I don't know." Carla laughed gaily, happiness bubbling over.

"If you're not into sports, what kinds of things do you like to do?" With his hand at her elbow, he escorted her toward the lively sounds of the mariachi band.

"Play checkers," Carla responded immediately. "I've won the King County Parks and Recreation Checker Championship three years running. It's a nice, friendly game, and I've got a terrific coach I'll tell you about sometime."

Carla felt relaxed and happy as they stood in line outside the lounge. They seemed to be waiting in a lot of lines tonight, not that she minded.

Philip studied her intently; his eyes narrowed slightly, as if he had trouble believing the fact that she was nonathletic.

"No sports, you say?"

"Just checkers." Carla's gleaming eyes didn't leave his. "Knowing that I'm a champion, Philip, would you have any trouble jumping me?" She was teasing, but the responding look in Philip's eyes was serious.

"I'd consider it," he murmured, "but I think I'd probably wait until after the game."

Three

~

Golden moonbeams softly lit a path along the beach. The gentle whisper of the ocean breeze was broken only by the sound of the waves crashing against the smooth white shore.

Philip slipped his arm around Carla's shoulders, and she brought her hand up so that they could lace their fingers together.

"Why didn't you tell me you could dance like that?" he murmured against her hair. "I've seen card sharps with slower moves."

Enjoying his surprise, Carla smiled softly to herself. "All I do is swing my hips a little."

"Yes, but I felt the least I could do was try to keep up with you. I'm dead."

"And I thought you police officers had to be in top physical condition." Not for a minute would she admit that she was as exhausted as Philip was.

"I'm in great shape," he argued, "but three hours on

the dance floor with you is above and beyond the call of duty. Next time I think I'll suggest checkers."

"You'll lose," Carla returned confidently.

"Maybe, but I have a feeling my feet won't hurt nearly as much."

Philip had been the one to suggest this stroll. But it wasn't a walk in the moonlight that interested him; Carla was convinced of that. He was seeking a few stolen kisses against the backdrop of a tropical night. And for that matter, so was she. Every time they met, Philip astonished her. One look the day on the plane and she'd instantly sized him up as dull and introspective. But he was warm, caring, and witty. There wasn't any man who could make her laugh the way Philip did.

"I enjoyed myself tonight. You're a lot of fun." She felt compelled to tell him that.

"You sound surprised." Philip moved his chin so it brushed against the crown of her head. The action was strangely comforting and erotic.

"*Surprised* is the wrong word," she said softly, struggling to express herself. "Leery, maybe. I don't want to like you too much. That would only complicate a nice, serene relationship. We're having a good time, and I don't want to ruin it."

"In other words, you don't want to fall in love with me?"

"Exactly." Carla hated the heartless way this made her sound. Already she recognized that falling for Philip wouldn't be difficult. He was many of the things she wanted in a man. And everything she didn't.

He expelled his breath in a half-angry sigh, but it was the only indication he gave that she had displeased him.

Closing her eyes, Carla felt an unexpected rush of regret settle over her. One evening together and she was already doubting that this arrangement was going to work. Spending time with Philip might not be a good idea if they were both going to end up taking it seriously. All she wanted was a good time. And he'd claimed that was all he was looking for, too. This was a holiday fling, after all, not a husband hunt.

"Don't you think you're overreacting just a little to the fact I'm a policeman?" Philip asked, his voice restrained and searching.

"Haven't we already been over this?" she answered hastily. "Besides, you have your own dating quirk. What if I'd been a flight attendant? You said yourself you prefer not to go out with them."

"But in your case I'd have made an exception."

"Why?"

"It's those lovely eyes of yours—"

"No," she interrupted brusquely, reacting with more than simple curiosity. "Why don't you date flight attendants?"

"It's a long story, and there are other things I have in mind." Clearly, he wasn't interested in relaying the details of his experience, and Carla decided she wouldn't push him. When he was ready to tell her, if he ever was, she'd be pleased to listen. She found it interesting that after only a few hours' acquaintance with Philip she had released a lifetime full of bitterness about her father and his occupation. Apparently, she hadn't generated the same kind of response in him. It troubled her a little.

"You're quiet all of a sudden." His lips found her

temple, and he kissed her there lightly. "What are you thinking?"

Tilting her head back, she smiled into those appealing smoky-gray eyes of his. "To be honest, I was mulling over the fact that you'll tell me about your hang-ups in time. But then it occurred to me that you might not."

"And that bothers you?" He studied her with amused patience.

"Yes and no." In a way that she didn't understand, Carla suddenly decided she didn't want to know. Obviously Philip had loved and presumably lost, and Carla wasn't sure she wanted the particulars.

"The curious side of you is eager to hear the gory details—"

"But my sensitive side doesn't want to have you dredge up unhappy memories," she finished for him.

"It was a long time ago."

Carla slipped an arm around his waist and laid her head against his shoulder. "And best forgotten."

They continued walking along the moonlit beach in silence. Carla felt warm and comfortable having this man at her side. The realization wasn't something she wanted to explore; for now, she was content.

"It's been six years since I broke up with Nicole," Philip said after a time.

Twisting in his embrace, Carla turned and pressed the tips of her fingers against his lips. "Don't," she whispered, afraid of how she'd react if she saw pain in his eyes. "It isn't necessary. There isn't a reason in the world for you to tell me."

His jaw tightened, and memories played across his

face. Some revealed the pleasant aspects of his relationship with Nicole, but others weren't as easily deciphered.

"I think you should know," he said, and his eyes narrowed to hard points of steel.

Carla wasn't sure which was troubling him more: the past or the sudden need to tell her about his lost love.

"Let me simplify things by saying that I loved her and asked her to marry me. But apparently she didn't care as deeply for me as I thought."

"She turned you down?" Carla murmured.

"No." His short laugh was filled with bitter sarcasm. "That's the crazy part. She accepted my ring, but she refused to move out on the guy she was living with. Naturally, neither one of us knew about the other."

Carla struggled not to laugh. "If you want my opinion, I think you made a lucky escape. This Nicole sounds a bit foolish to me."

Philip relaxed against her. His hands found the small of her back, arching her closer to him. "I don't know, there's something about me that attracts the weird ones. Just yesterday some oddball approached me in the bar with a lunatic story about me being her date for the night because I ordered a margarita."

"A real weirdo, no doubt," she said mockingly.

"That's not the half of it." His head lowered with every word, so that by the time he finished, his lips hovered over hers.

"Oh?" Breathlessly, she anticipated his kiss.

"Yes." His low voice was as caressing as his look. "The thing is, I'd been watching her from the moment I walked into the lounge, trying to come up with a way of approaching her."

Before she could react to this startling bit of news, Philip brought her into his embrace. Slowly his mouth opened over hers, taking in the softness of her trembling lips in a soul-stirring, devouring kiss. Carla stood on the tips of her toes and clung to him, devastated by the intensity of her reaction. This had happened the first time he'd kissed her. If Philip's lovemaking had been hard or urgent, maybe she could have withstood it. But he was incredibly gentle, as if she were of exquisite worth and as fragile as a rosebud, and that was irresistible.

When his tongue outlined the fullness of her mouth, Carla's willpower melted, and she couldn't pull herself away from the fiery kiss. Desire shot through her, and when she broke away, her breathing was irregular and deep.

"I . . . I think we should put a limit on these kisses," she proposed shakily.

Philip didn't look any more in control of himself than she felt. His eyes were closed as he drew in a husky breath and nodded in agreement. Only a short space separated them, but he continued to hold her, his hands running the length of her bare arms.

"Let's get you back to your hotel room."

"Yes."

But they didn't move.

Unable to resist, Carla rested her head against his muscular chest, weak with the wonder of his kiss. "I don't understand." She was surprised to hear the words, not realizing she'd spoken out loud.

"What?" Philip questioned softly.

She shrugged, flustered for a moment. "You. Me. If

you had come up to me yesterday and asked to buy me a drink, I probably would have refused."

He flashed a crooked grin. "I know. Why do you think I didn't?"

"Obviously you recognized that I was about to take the initiative," she said jokingly, to hide her discomfort.

Together they turned and headed toward the hotel, taking leisurely steps. Carla's bare toes kicked up the sand.

"What would you like to do tomorrow?" she asked, not because she was especially interested in their itinerary, but because knowing she would be seeing him in the morning would surely enhance her dreams tonight.

"Shall we get together for breakfast?"

"I'd like that."

Outside her door, Philip set a time and place for them to meet in the morning, then kissed her gently and left.

Carla walked slowly inside the room and released a long, drawn-out sigh. For such a rotten beginning, the day had turned out wonderfully well.

"Is that you, Carla?" The question came from the darkened interior of the room.

"No, it's the bogeyman," Carla teased.

"I take it you met someone?" Nancy's voice was soft and curious.

"Yup."

"Tell me about your day." The moonlight silhouetted her roommate against the wall. Nancy was sitting on the side of the mattress.

"It's the guy I met yesterday." Carla couldn't disguise the wistful note in her voice.

"What happened? When I asked this morning, the

looks you gave me said you didn't want to have anything to do with him."

"That was this morning."

Fluffing up her pillow, Nancy positioned it against the headboard, leaned against it, and put her hands behind her head. "I'm glad things worked out."

"Me, too." Carla moved into the room and began to undress.

"I can't believe how much I like Eduardo," Nancy said pensively as she stared dreamily at the ceiling. "I can't even begin to tell you what a marvelous day we had."

Carla slipped the silk nightie over her head. "The funny part was, I had no intention of seeing Philip again."

Nancy sighed unevenly and slid down so her head rested in the thick of the pillow. "He gave me a tour of Mazatlán that will hold memories to last a lifetime. And later tonight when he kissed me I could have cried, it was so incredibly beautiful."

"But then Philip was there, and I'd been so miserable all day, and he suggested we have dinner, and not for the life of me could I refuse."

"I've never felt this strongly about a man. And I've barely known Eduardo more than twenty-four hours."

Carla pulled back the bedcovers and paused, holding the pillow to her stomach. "I'm meeting Philip first thing in the morning."

"Eduardo says he can't believe that someone as beautiful as I would be interested in him. And just because he broke his leg. He keeps assuring me he really isn't a klutz. As if I'd ever think such a thing."

"I don't know if I'll be able to sleep. Every time I close my eyes I know Philip will be there. I don't know how to explain it. To look at him, you'd be unimpressed. But he's the most gentle man. Tender."

"I can't sleep. Every time I try, my heart hammers and I wonder if I'm going crazy to feel like this."

The sheets felt cool against Carla's legs as she slipped between the covers and yawned. "I guess I should get some sleep. Night, Nance."

"Night," Nancy answered with a yawn of her own.

"By the way," Carla asked absently, "how'd your day go?"

"Fantastic. How about you?"

"Wonderful."

"I'm glad. Good night."

"Night."

Philip was already seated in the hotel restaurant when Carla arrived. Her gaze met his, and she smiled. She enjoyed the way he was watching her. The sleeveless pink-and-blue crinkle-cotton sundress was her favorite, and she knew she looked good. She'd spent extra time with her makeup, and one glance from him confirmed that the effort had been well spent.

"Morning." Philip stood and pulled out her chair.

"Did you sleep well?"

He leaned forward and kissed her cheek lightly. "Like a baby. How about you?"

Setting her large-brimmed straw hat on the empty seat beside her, Carla nodded. "Great."

The waiter appeared and handed them each a menu,

but they didn't look at them. "What would you like to do today?"

"Explore," Carla replied immediately. "Would you mind if I dragged you to the arts-and-crafts center?"

Philip reached for her hand and squeezed it gently. "Not at all. And tomorrow I thought we'd take an excursion to Palmito de la Virgen."

Carla blinked. "Where?"

"An island near here. It's a bird-watcher's paradise."

The only bird Carla was interested in watching was Philip, but she didn't say as much.

"And Thursday I thought we might try our hand at deep-sea fishing."

"I'm game," she said, and giggled. "No pun intended."

"My, my, you're agreeable. Are you always like this in the mornings?"

Carla reached for the ice water, keeping her eyes lowered. "Most of the time."

"I'd like to discover that for myself."

The waiter arrived with his pen and pad, and Carla glanced up at him guiltily, realizing she hadn't even looked at the menu.

After breakfast they rode a *pulmonía* to the Mazatlán Arts and Crafts Center, and Philip insisted on buying her a lovely turquoise ring. Carla felt more comfortable purchasing her souvenirs from these people and not from the beach vendors. Here the price was set and there wasn't any haggling.

Tucking their purchases into a giant straw bag, Carla

took off her hat and waved it in front of her face. Most of the shopping areas were air-conditioned, but once they stepped outside, the heat was stifling.

"Would you like something cool to drink?" Philip asked solicitously.

Smiling up at him, Carla placed a hand over her breast. "You, my dear man, know the path to my heart."

Unexpectedly, Philip's hand tightened on the back of her neck until his grip was almost painful. He dropped his hand and took a step forward as if he'd forgotten her completely. Surprised but not alarmed, Carla reached for his arm. "What's wrong?"

"There's going to be a fight over there." He pointed to a group of youths who were having a heated exchange.

Although Carla couldn't understand what was being said, she assumed from the angry sound of their words that they would soon be coming to blows. Her gaze was drawn to Philip, and she was witness to an abrupt change in roles taking place within him. After all, she was a policeman's daughter. And Philip was an officer of the law. Once a cop, always a cop. He may be in Mazatlán, but he would never be entirely on vacation.

Philip's jaw hardened and his eyes narrowed with keen interest. Briefly he turned to her. "Stay here." The words were clipped and low, and filled with an authority that would brook no resistance.

Carla wanted to argue. Everything inside urged her to scream that this was none of his business. What right did he have to involve himself with those youths? Mexico had its own police force. She watched as Philip strode briskly across the street toward the angry young men. He asked them something in Spanish, and even from this distance Carla could hear the authority in his voice. She hadn't a clue of what he was saying, but it didn't matter. It was the law-enforcement officer in him speaking, anyway, and she didn't want to know.

Only one thing prompted her to stay. If the situation got ugly and Philip needed help, she could scream or do something to get him out of this mess. But he didn't need her assistance, and a few minutes later the group broke up. With an amused grin, Philip jogged across the street to her side.

"That was—"

"I don't care to know, thank you," she announced frostily. Opening her large bag, she took out the several small items he'd purchased during their morning's outing.

"What's this?" He looked stunned.

"Your things," she answered without looking up. "You couldn't do it, could you?"

"Do what?"

Apparently, he still didn't understand. "For once, just once, couldn't you have forgotten you're a cop? But no, Mr. Rescue had to speed to the scene of potential danger, defending truth and justice."

His face relaxed, and he reached for her. "Carla, couldn't you see—"

She sidestepped him easily. "You bet I saw," she shot back angrily. "You almost had me fooled, Philip Garrison. For a while there I actually believed we could have shared a wonderful vacation. But it's not going to work." Her voice was taut with irritation. With unnecessary roughness, she dumped the packages into his arms. "Not even for a few days could either of us manage to forget what you are. Good-bye, Philip." She spun and ran across the street, waving her hand, hoping to attract a *pulmonía* driver. At least she could be grateful that Philip didn't make an effort to follow her. But that was little comfort . . . very little.

A *pulmonía* shot past her, and Carla stamped her foot childishly. She wished she had paid closer attention to the Spanish phrase Philip had called to get the driver's attention.

Already she felt the perspiration breaking out across her face as she walked along the edge of the street. The late-morning sun could be torturous. Another driver approached, and Carla stepped off the curb and shouted something in Spanish, not sure what she'd said. With her luck, she mused wryly, it was probably something to do with Cookie Monster. But whatever it was worked, because the driver immediately pulled to the curb.

"Hotel El Cid," she mumbled, hot and miserable.

"*Sí, señorita*, the man already say."

Man? Tossing a look over her shoulder, Carla found Philip standing on the other side of the street, studying her. He'd gotten the driver for her. If she hadn't been so blasted uncomfortable, she'd have told him exactly what he could do with his driver. As it was, all Carla wanted to do was escape. The sooner, the better.

Her room was refreshingly cool when she returned. She threw herself across the bed and stared at the ceiling. Tears might have helped release some of her frustration, but she was too mad to cry.

After fifteen minutes, the hotel room gave her a bad

case of claustrophobia. From her suitcase, Carla pulled the book she'd been reading on the airplane and opened the sliding glass door to the small balcony. A thorough inspection of the pool area revealed that Philip was no-where in sight. Stuffing her book into her beach bag, Carla quickly changed into her swimsuit, slipping a cot-ton top over that, and put on the straw hat. Not for any-thing was she going to allow Philip Garrison to ruin this vacation.

Carla was fortunate to find a vacant chaise longue. The pool was busy with the early-afternoon crowd. Several vacationers were in the water, eating lunch at the coun-ter that was built up against the pool's edge. Smiling briefly, Carla recalled her first glimpse of the submerged stools and wondered what this type of meal did to the theory of not swimming after eating.

Spreading out her towel, Carla raised the back of the lounger so that she could sit up comfortably and read. Her sunglasses had a tendency to slip down the bridge of her nose, and without much thought she pushed them back up. Philip's glasses did that occasionally. Angrily, she wiped his image from her mind and viciously turned the page of her suspense novel, nearly ripping it from the book.

An older man who was lying beside her stood, stretched, and strolled lackadaisically toward the bar, seeking something cool to drink. He was barely out of sight when a familiar voice spoke in her ear.

"Is this seat taken?"

Carla's fingers gripped the page, but she didn't so

much as acknowledge his presence. Without lifting her eyes from her book, she replied, "Yes, it is."

"That's fine, I'll just sit on the edge of the pool and chat," he replied casually.

Clenching her jaw so tight her teeth hurt, Carla turned a page, having no idea of what she had just read. "I'd appreciate it very much if you didn't."

Forcefully, Philip expelled his breath. "How long are you going to be unreasonable like this? All I'm asking is that you hear me out."

"How long?" Carla repeated mockingly. "You haven't got that much time. Never, as far as I'm concerned."

"Do you mean it?" The question was issued so low, Carla had to strain to hear him.

Idly, she turned the next page. "Yes, I meant it," she replied.

"Okay." He took the towel, swung it around his neck, and strolled away.

Carla felt a deep sense of disappointment settle over her. The least he could have done was argue with her! One would assume that after yesterday she meant more to him than that. But apparently not.

Without being obvious, she glanced quickly around the pool area and discovered that Philip was nowhere in sight. Ten minutes later she did another survey. Nothing.

Tucking the book inside her beach bag, Carla settled back in her seat, joined her hands over her stomach, and closed her eyes. A splash of water against her leg was more refreshing than irritating. But the cupful of water that landed on her upper thigh was a shock.

Gasping, she opened her eyes and sat up to brush the offending wetness away.

"Did I get water on you?" came the innocent question. "Please accept my apology."

"Philip Garrison, that was a rotten thing to do!" Inside she was singing. So he hadn't left.

"So was that last, untruthful remark."

"What remark?"

"That you never wanted to talk to me again." He lay down beside her on the chaise that had been previously taken by the older sunbather. "Obviously you did, or you wouldn't have made two deliberate inspections of the pool to see if I had left."

She should have realized Philip had stayed and watched her. That was a rookie's trick. And Philip was a seasoned officer. Rather than argue, she lifted her glasses and turned toward him with a smug look. "I told you that seat was taken," she said, and repositioned herself so that the back of one hand rested against her brow. "And I don't think he'd take kindly to you lying in his place when he returns."

"Sure he would," Philip murmured confidently. "Otherwise I wasted ten very good dollars."

Struggling between outrage and delight, Carla sat up. "Do you mean to say you bribed him?" Her eyes widened as he nodded cheerfully. "What do you think you're doing, Officer Garrison? First . . . First you spy on me and . . . then . . . and then . . ." She sputtered. "You bribe the man in the chair next to me. Just how low do you plan to stoop?"

Philip yawned. "About that low."

Carla did an admirable job of swallowing her laughter.

"I suspect you aren't as annoyed as you're letting on," Philip commented.

The humor died in her eyes. "What makes you suggest that?"

"Well, you're still here, aren't you?"

Standing up, Carla pulled the thin cotton covering over her head. "Not for long," she replied, and dived into the pool.

It felt marvelous. Swimming as far and for as long as she could under the aqua-blue water helped relieve some of her pent-up frustration. Finally, she surfaced and sucked in a large breath of fresh air. In the glint of the sun, her hair was decidedly red. Carla had hoped to avoid having Philip see it wet. Like everyone else, he was sure to comment on it. Swimming at night was preferable by far.

She'd barely caught her breath when Philip surfaced beside her. Treading water at his side, she offered him a tremulous smile. "I really was angry this morning. I behaved childishly to run off like that. Thank you for seeing that I got a ride back to the hotel."

Their eyes met, and he grinned. "I know how angry you were; that's why I didn't follow you. But given time, I figured you'd forgive me." His arms found her waist and brought her close to him. Their feet kicked in unison, keeping them afloat.

"I'll forgive you on one condition," she stated firmly, and looped her arms around his neck. "You've got to promise not to do that again. Please, Philip. For me, leave your police badge in your room. We're in Mexico, and they have their own defenders of justice."

Philip went still, and she could feel him become tense.

The sparkle faded from his eyes as they darkened and became more intense. "Carla, I'll do my best, but I can't change who or what I am."

Her grip around his neck relaxed, and with a sense of defeat she lowered her eyes. "But don't you see? I can't, either," she murmured miserably, and her voice fell to a whisper.

His hold tightened as he brought his body intimately close to hers in the water. "But we can try."

"What would be the use?"

"Oh, I don't know," he said softly, and brushed aside the offending strands of wet hair from her cheek. "I can think of several things." His lips replaced his fingers, and he blazed a trail of infinitely sweet kisses along her brow and eyes, working his way to her mouth.

For an instant, Carla was caught in the rapture of his touch, but an abrupt noise behind them brought her to her senses. Breaking free, she shook her head. "I . . . I don't know, Philip. I want to think on it."

"Okay, that sounds fair."

He didn't have to be so agreeable! At least he could have argued with her. With a little sigh, Carla turned away and said, "I think I'll go to my room and lie down for a while. The sun does me in fairly easily." She started to swim away, then rapidly changed direction and joined Philip. "I almost forgot something," she murmured, as she covered his mouth with hers and kissed him thoroughly.

Obviously shaken, Philip blinked twice. "What was that for?" he asked, and cleared his throat.

"For not mentioning my frizzy hair or the color."

He cocked his head, and a puzzled frown marred his brow. "There are several other things I haven't mentioned that you may wish to thank me for."

"Later," she said with a small laugh.

"Definitely later."

Four

~

Amazingly, Carla did sleep most of the afternoon. She hadn't realized how exhausted she was. The sun, having taken its toll, had faded by the time she stirred. A glance at the clock told Carla that it was dinnertime. Although she hadn't made any arrangements to meet Philip, she knew he'd be looking for her.

Dressing quickly, she hunted for her sandals, crawling on the floor. Finally, she located them under the bed and was on her way into the bathroom to see what she could do with her hair when something stopped her. The faint sound of someone singing in Spanish drifted in past the balcony door that had been left ajar. Those deep male tones were unmistakable.

After eagerly parting the draperies, Carla opened the sliding glass door farther. The music and voice grew stronger, and the lovingly familiar voice sang loudly off-key.

"Philip!"

Standing below, playing a guitar and singing at the

top of his voice, was crazy, wonderful Philip. A band of curious onlookers had gathered around him. Now, however, they focused their attention on her.

"You're unbelievable!" she cried. "What are you doing?"

"Serenading you," he shouted, completely serious. "Do you like it?"

"I'd like it a lot better if you sang on key."

He strummed a few bars. "Can't have everything. Are you hungry?"

"Starved. I'd eat turtle tacos."

"You must be famished. Hurry down, will you? I think someone might arrest me."

Stuffing her hair under her straw hat, Carla bounded down the stairs. She paused on the bottom step, straightened her dress, and took a deep breath. Then, feeling more composed, she turned the corner and found Philip relaxing on a chaise longue.

"Hi," she said, fighting the breathlessness that weakened her voice.

He rose to his feet with an ease many would envy. "I must have sounded better than I thought."

"What makes you think that?"

A grin played at the edges of his mouth as he dug inside his pocket and pulled out a handful of loose change. "People were obviously impressed. Soon after you went inside, several started throwing coins my way."

Fighting back the bubbling laughter, Carla looped her arm around his elbow. "I hate to disappoint you, Philip, but I have the distinct feeling they were paying you *not* to sing."

The sound of his laughter tugged at her heart.

"Where are we going for dinner? I wasn't teasing about being hungry."

"Anyplace you say." Tucking her hand more securely in the crook of his arm, he escorted her through the hotel to the series of stairs that led to the busy street below.

"Anyplace I say," she repeated. "My, my, you're agreeable all of a sudden."

"With a beautiful woman on my arm, and my pockets full of change, why shouldn't I be?"

She smiled, pleased by the compliment.

"Then dinner wherever the lady chooses."

"Well, I suppose I'd better choose a restaurant where I won't have to take off my hat. I didn't wash my hair after our dip in the pool this afternoon, and now it resembles Raggedy Ann's."

"Then it's perfect for what I have in mind," he said with an enigmatic toss of his head. Sandy locks of hair fell across his brow and he brushed them aside.

"Well, are you going to tell me, or do I have to guess?" she asked with a hint of impatience. She noticed that Philip had a way of arousing her curiosity, then dropping the subject. Her father did the same thing, and Carla briefly wondered if this was a common trait among policemen. They didn't want to give out too much information —keep the world guessing seemed to be their intent. Other things about Philip reminded her of her father. He was a kind, concerned man. Like her father, he cared when the rest of the world didn't want to be bothered.

"Ever hear of La Gruta de Cerro del Crestón?" Philip asked, snapping her out of her musings.

"He was some general, right?"

"Wrong," he responded with a trace of droll tolerance. "It's a cave where, it's rumored, pirates used to store their treasure. Stolen treasure, of course. It's only accessible at low tide, but I thought we might pick up a picnic lunch and eat along the beach. Later, when the tide is low, we can explore the cave."

Carla's interest was piqued. "That sounds great."

"And of course there's always the advantage of having you to myself in a deep, dark cave."

"Honestly, Garrison, cool your hormones," she joked. One of the hot-rod golf carts Philip enjoyed so much delivered them close to the lighthouse near the heart of the city. Holding her hat, Carla climbed out from the back of the cart. Her senses were spinning, and she doubted if she'd ever get used to riding in those suicidal contraptions. The short rides weren't so bad, but anything more than three miles was like a death wish.

A drop of rain hit her hand. Carla raised her eyes to examine the darkening sky and groaned inwardly. A storm would ruin everything. Besides, if Philip saw what happened to her hair in the rain, she'd never live it down. The frizzies invariably gave her a striking resemblance to the Bride of Frankenstein.

"Philip?"

Preoccupied for the moment, Philip paid the driver and returned the folded money to his pocket. "Something wrong?"

"It's raining."

"I know!"

Twisting the strap of her purse, she swung it over her shoulder and secured the large-brimmed straw hat by holding it down over both ears. "Maybe we should go back to the hotel."

"Why?"

She swallowed nervously. "Well, we obviously can't have a picnic in the rain, and if . . . my hat should come off . . . well, my hair—"

Suddenly, the sky opened up and the earth was bombarded with heavy sheets of rain. Giving a cry of alarm, Carla ran for shelter. Mud splashed against the backs of her legs, and immediately a chill ran up her arms.

Philip caught up with her and cupped her elbow. "Let's get out of here."

"Where?" she shouted, but he didn't answer as they raced down a side street. After two long blocks, Carla stopped counting. Placing one foot in front of the other was all that she could manage in the torrent that was beating against her.

Philip led her into a building and up two flights of stairs.

Leaning against the hallway wall, Carla gasped for breath. "Where are we?"

"My parents' condo."

Vaguely, she recalled Philip mentioning that the condo was the reason he was in Mazatlán. He'd said something about repairs, but Carla didn't care where they were, as long as it was dry.

"Let's get these wet things off," Philip suggested, holding the door open for her and leading the way into the kitchen.

The condominium looked surprisingly modern, and Carla hurried inside, not wishing to leave a trail of mud across the cream-colored carpet. The washer and dryer were behind a louvered door. Philip pulled his shirt from his waist and unbuttoned it. "We'd better let these dry."

Wide-eyed, her mouth open, Carla watched him toss his drenched shirt inside. He paused and glanced expectantly at her.

"You don't honestly expect me to parade around here in my underwear, do you?"

"Well, to be honest," he said with a wry grin, "I didn't expect it, but I was hoping. Hold on and I'll get you my mom's robe."

By the time he returned, Carla had removed her sandals and found a kitchen towel to dry her feet. When she heard Philip approach, she straightened and continued to press her hat—still secure despite everything—down over her ears.

"Here." He draped the cotton robe over a chair. "I'll start a fire. Let me know when you're finished."

Shivering, Carla slipped the dress over her hips and tossed it inside the dryer. Another towel served as a turban for her hair and hid the effects of the rain.

She tied the sash of the robe and took a deep breath. Self-consciously, she stood just outside the living room. A small fire was crackling in the fireplace, and Philip was kneeling in front of it, adding one stick of wood at a time.

He seemed to sense that she was watching him. "How do you feel?" He stood and crossed the room, joining her. Placing a hand on each shoulder, he smiled into her eyes. "Mother's robe never looked so good."

"I feel like a drowned rat." The turban slipped over one eye, and Carla righted it.

His hands found the side of her neck, and his touch

sent a warm sensation through her. "Believe me when I say you don't look like one."

They continued to study each other, and Carla's heart began to pound like a locomotive racing against time. In some ways she and Philip were doing that. There were only a few days left of their vacation, and then it would be over. It had to be.

"Come in and sit down," Philip said at last, and his thumb traced her lips in a feather-light caress. "The fire should take the chill from your bones."

"I'm . . . not really cold." *Not when you're touching me,* she added silently.

"Me, neither."

Carla was convinced his thoughts were an echo of her own.

"Hungry?"

"Not really." *Not anymore.*

"Good."

Together they sat on the plush love seat that was angled to face the fireplace. Philip's arm reached for her, bringing her within the haven of his embrace.

Resting her head against the curve of his shoulder, Carla let her fingers toy with the dark hairs on his bare chest. Her body was in contact with his chest, hips, and thighs, and whenever they touched, she could feel a heat building. She struggled to control her breathing so Philip wouldn't guess the effect he had on her.

"I poured these while you were changing," Philip murmured, his voice low and slightly husky. He leaned forward and reached for the two glasses of wine sitting on the polished oak coffee table.

Straightening, Carla accepted the long-stemmed

crystal glass with a smile of appreciation and tasted the wine. It was an excellent sweet variety with a fragrant bouquet.

Removing the glass from her unresisting fingers, Philip set it aside. As he leaned back, his jaw brushed her chin, and his warm breath caressed her face. The contact stopped them both. He hadn't meant it to be sensual, Carla was sure of that, but her heart thumped wildly. Closing her eyes, she inhaled a quivering breath.

"Philip?" she whispered.

His mouth explored the side of her neck, sending rapturous shivers up and down her spine. "Yes?"

"Did you arrange for the rainstorm?" Carla couldn't believe how low and sultry her voice sounded.

"No, but I'm glad it happened."

Carla was, too, but she wouldn't admit it. She didn't need to.

Gently, Philip pressed her backward so that her head rested against the arm of the sofa; then his mouth claimed hers. His kiss was slow, leisurely, and far more intoxicating than potent wine.

Drawing in a shaky breath, Philip diverted his attention to her neck, nuzzling the scented hollow of her throat. His hands wandered over her hips, artfully arousing her so that she shifted, seeking more. She wanted to give more of herself and take more at the same time. Her restless hands explored his back, reveling in the tightness of his corded muscles. This man was deceptively strong. Her fingers found a scar, and she longed to kiss it.

Gradually, the heat that had begun to flow through her at the tenderness of his touch spread to every part of her, leaving her feverishly warm. But when Philip's hands slid across her abdomen, she tensed slightly. He murmured her name, and his mouth lingered on her lips, moving from one side of her mouth to the other in a deep exploration that left her weak and clinging. Philip turned her so that she was sitting half upright. As he did so, the towel that was covering her hair twisted and fell forward across her face. Gently, Philip lifted the offending material off her face, but her desperate hold on it prevented him from tossing it aside.

"Can we get rid of this thing?" he asked gently.

"No." She struggled to sit completely up. Both hands secured the terry-cloth towel.

"Your hair can't be that bad," he coaxed.

"It's worse. Turn around," she demanded, as she leaned forward and rewound the turban. "I . . . I don't want you to see it."

Expelling his breath, Philip leaned against the back of the sofa and closed his eyes. "Would you feel better if you showered and dried those precious locks?"

She nodded eagerly.

"Come on, I'm sure Mom's got something in the bathroom that should help."

Carla followed him down a long, narrow hallway that led to a bathroom. Investigating the vanity drawers, he managed to come up with a blow-dryer and a curling iron.

"I think my sister gave this to her for Christmas last year."

Carla's heart sank. "But I can't use this. The package isn't even open."

With a crooked grin, Philip tore off the cellophane. "If it bothers you, I'll tell her I used it."

Carla giggled delightedly. "I'd like to hear her answer to that."

Removing several fluffy towels from the hall closet, Philip handed them to her. "While you're making yourself beautiful, I'm going to make us something to eat."

Hugging the fresh towels, Carla gave him a grateful smile. "Thank you, Philip. I honestly mean that."

He shrugged and pushed his glasses up the bridge of his nose. "Are you sure you don't need someone to wash your back?" he asked in a low, seductive voice.

"I'm sure." But the look he gave her as he turned toward the kitchen was enough to inflame her senses. Never had she felt this strongly about anyone after such a short time. Maybe that was normal. They had only a week together, and already three of those precious days had been spent. All too soon the time would come when she'd say good-bye to him at the airport. And it would be good-bye.

The water felt fantastic as it sprayed against her soft skin. When she'd finished showering, she put the robe on and opened the bathroom door to allow the steam to escape.

"Your dress is dry, if you want me to bring it to you," Philip called to her from the kitchen.

"Give me a minute," she shouted. Carla's russet-red curls were blown dry and tamed with the curling iron in record time. Her face was void of makeup, and she knew she looked much paler than usual, but one kiss from Philip would correct that.

Tying the sash of the robe as she walked across the living room carpet, Carla sniffed the delicate aroma drifting from the kitchen.

"Mushrooms," she announced, and picked one out of the sizzling butter with her long fingernails and popped it into her mouth.

"Canned, I'm afraid."

"No problem, I like mushrooms any way they come." She lifted out another and fed it to Philip. His shirt was dry and tucked neatly into his waistband. Her dress, she'd noticed, was hanging off a knob from the kitchen cabinet.

Peeking inside the oven, she turned around delightedly. "I don't suppose those are T-bone steaks under the grill?"

"Yup, but they'll take time. I had to get them out of the freezer." Philip set the cooking fork beside the skillet and reached for her. His hands almost spanned her waist. "But then we have lots of time."

But not nearly enough, her heart answered.

Hours later, after they'd consumed an entire bottle of wine and eaten their fill, they washed and dried the dishes. Soft music played romantically in the background.

"Philip?" Carla tilted her head as she released the plug from the sink to drain the soapy water.

He looked at her expectantly. "Hmm?"

"There's a scar on your back. I don't think I'd noticed it before. What happened?" she asked curiously.

"It's nothing." He stooped down to place the skillet in the bottom cupboard.

"It didn't feel like it. It's long and narrow, like . . .

like . . ." She stopped cold. A painful sensation in the pit of her stomach viciously attacked her, and she leaned weakly against the counter. "Like a knife. You were stabbed, weren't you?"

Lifting up the frames of his glasses, Philip pinched the bridge of his nose. He muttered something she couldn't quite hear under his breath.

"You didn't want me to know. Well, I do now," she said, and gestured defiantly with her hand. "What happened? Did you decide to step in and break up a gang war all by yourself? You were willing to try your hand at that this morning." Her voice shook.

"No, it wasn't anything like that. I was—"

"I don't want to hear. Don't tell me." She searched frantically for her hat, moving quickly across one room and into the other.

"First you demand to know, then you claim you don't want to know. I hope you realize how unreasonable you sound," he said with a low growl.

"I . . . don't care what I sound like." Her hat was beside her purse in the other room, and she practically raced to it. "One look at you and I should have known you were bad news. But oh no, I had to follow this crazy scheme of Nancy's and make a complete fool of myself. It's not going to work, Philip. Not for another day. Not for a week. Not at all. I'm going back to the hotel."

"Carla, will you listen to me?" Philip stuffed his hands into his pants pockets, and his face hardened with a grimness she hadn't expected to see in him. "It's working, believe me, it's working."

"Maybe everything is fine for you. But I don't want to get involved. Not with you."

"You're already involved."

Defiantly, she crossed her arms in front of her. "Not anymore." Mentally and emotionally, she would have to block him out of her life before the pain became too great.

"That's twice in one day."

"Don't you see?" she cried, as if shouting helped prove her point. "All right, all right, I concede the point. I could like you very much. It probably wouldn't take a lot to fall in love with you, but I just can't. Look at me, Philip." Tossing her head back, she held out her hands, palms down, for his inspection. "I'm shaking because already I care enough for you to worry about a stabbing that happened before we even met."

"Being knifed is the only thing that's ever happened to me. I was a rookie, and stupid. . . ."

"This is supposed to reassure me?" she retorted, jamming her hat on top of her head.

He followed her to the front door and pressed against the wood to prevent her from opening it. "Carla, for heaven's sake, will you listen to reason?"

With hands clenched at her sides, she emitted a frustrated sigh. She didn't expect him to understand. "It was hopeless from the beginning."

"I'm not letting you leave until you listen to me."

Carla exhaled, her lungs aching from the effort to control her emotion. "Philip, I like you so much." Of its own volition, her hand found and explored the side of his jaw. She could feel his muscles tense as her fingertips investigated the rough feel of his day-old beard. "I won't forget you," she whispered shakily.

His hand captured hers and moved it to his mouth so that he could kiss the tender skin of her palm. As if he'd burned her, Carla jerked her fingers free.

"Come on, I'll take you back to the hotel." His quiet determination convinced her to let him escort her back. She knew him well enough to realize arguing would do little good.

Philip didn't say a word on the entire trip back. They passed a horse-drawn carriage, and Carla wanted to weep at the sight of the two young lovers who sat in the back with their arms entwined. What a perfect end to a lovely day such a ride would have been. Philip gave her a look that said he was reading her thoughts. They could have been that couple.

Bowing her head, Carla studied her clenched hands, all too aware that Philip thought she was overreacting. But she couldn't ask him to be something he wasn't, and she couldn't change, either.

His hand cupped her elbow as she climbed the short series of stairs that led to the hotel lobby. Halfway through the lobby, Carla paused and murmured, "I'll say good-bye here."

"No, you won't. I'll take you to your room."

When they reached her door, Carla's fingers nervously fumbled with her purse's latch. Her hand closed around the key card, and she drew in a deep, shuddering breath.

"I know you're angry," she said without looking up. Her gaze was centered on the room key card. "And to be honest, I don't blame you. Thank you for today and yesterday. I'll never think of Mexico without remembering you." The brittle smile she gave him as she glanced up took more of an effort than he would ever know.

Philip's mouth drew faintly upward, and Carla guessed that he wasn't in any more of a mood to smile than she was.

Her hand rested on the door handle.

"What? No farewell kiss. Surely I deserve that much."

Carla meant only to brush her lips over his. Not to tease, but to disguise the very real physical attraction she felt for him. But as she raised her mouth, his hand cupped the back of her head and she was crushed in his embrace. Where Philip had always been gentle, now he was urgent, greedily devouring her with a hunger that left her so weak she clung to him. She wanted to twist away but realized that if she struggled, Philip would release her. Instead, her arms crept around his neck. Philip groaned aloud and gathered her as close as physical boundaries would allow, his arms crushing her.

A trembling weakness attacked her, and Philip altered his method of advance. He kissed her leisurely, with a thoroughness that made her ache for more. He didn't rush, but seemed to savor each second, content to have her break the contact.

She did, but only when she thought her lungs would burst.

"Good night, Carla," he whispered against her ear, and opened the door for her.

Carla would have stumbled inside if Philip hadn't caught her. With as much dignity as possible, she broke free, entered the room unaided, and closed the door without looking back.

The cool, dark interior contained no welcome. The taste of Philip's kiss was on her mouth, and the male scent of him lingered, disturbing her further.

Pacing the floor did little to relieve the ache. Desperately, she tried watching television and was irrationally angry that every station had programs in Spanish.

After her long afternoon nap she wasn't tired. Nor was she interested in visiting the party scene that was taking place in the lounge and bars.

Her frustration mounted with every second. Standing on the balcony that overlooked the pool area, she noted again that there wasn't anyone around. A gentle breeze stirred the evening air and contained a freshness that often follows a storm. The first night she'd arrived and met Philip, they had gone for a swim. And the pool had been fantastic.

Laps would help, and with the heavy tourist crowds that filled the pool during the day, it would be impossible to do them in the morning. Besides, if she tired herself out, she might be able to sleep.

Determined now, she located a fresh suit in the bottom of her suitcase and hurriedly undressed. Tomorrow would be filled with avoiding Philip, but she didn't want to think about that now.

The water was refreshingly cool as she dived in and broke the surface twenty feet later. Her arms carried her to the far side, and the first lap was accomplished with a drive born of remorse. There wasn't anyone to blame for this but herself. She'd known almost from the beginning what Philip was. He hadn't tried to disguise it.

Her shoulders heaving as she struggled for breath ten long laps later, Carla stood in the shallow end and brushed the hair from her face.

"I didn't think you'd be able to stay away," Philip said, standing beside her. "I couldn't, either."

Five

~

Carla froze, her hands in her hair. Philip was right. When she'd come to the pool, the thought had played in the back of her mind that he would be there, too. For all her self-proclaimed righteousness, she didn't want their time together to end with an argument.

The worst part was that she'd overreacted, and like an immature child, she'd run away for the second time. It was a wonder he hadn't given up on her. "I'm sorry about tonight," she murmured in a voice that was quivery and soft. "But when I realized how you'd gotten that scar, I panicked."

Philip turned her around so that they faced each other, standing waist deep in the pool's aqua-blue water. "You don't need to explain. I know."

The moon's gentle radiance revealed a thin film of moisture glistening on his torso. Carla longed to touch him. "Turn around," she requested softly, and when he did, she slid her arms around his waist, just below the water line, and pressed her cheek against the curve of his spine. Almost shyly, she lifted her head as her fingers located the scar on his back, and she bent down and kissed it gently. The next time, Philip might not be so fortunate; such a blade could end his life. The thought was sobering, and a chill raced up Carla's arms.

"We agreed to a week," Philip reminded her as he twisted around and looped his arms over her shoulders. "This vacation is for us. Our lives, our jobs, our friends are in Washington State. But we're here. Nothing's going to spoil what we have for the remainder of the week." He said it with a determination she couldn't deny.

Nothing will ruin it, Carla's heart responded. *Everything was already ruined,* her head shouted.

They swam for an hour, making excuses to touch each other, kissing when the time seemed right. And it often seemed right.

The night had been well spent when they made arrangements to meet again in the morning. Silently, Carla climbed into the bed across from her sleeping friend. A glance at her watch told her it was after two. This time she had no trouble falling into a restful slumber.

The early-morning sounds of Nancy brushing her teeth and dressing woke Carla when the sun was barely up. Struggling to a sitting position, Carla raised her arms high above her head and yawned. "What time is it?"

"Six," Nancy whispered. "Eduardo and I are flying to Puerto Vallarta. I probably won't be back until late tonight."

Carla nodded and settled back into her bed, hugging the thick pillow.

"And before I forget, I have an invitation for you and . . . your friend."

"Philip," Carla supplied.

"Right." Nancy laughed lightly. "Who says my head isn't in the clouds? Anyway, you're both invited to dinner with Eduardo and me Saturday evening."

Carla's eyes remained closed, and she nuzzled the covers over her shoulder. "Sounds nice, I'll mention it to Philip." Her lashes fluttered open. "That's our last day here."

"It's really going by quickly, isn't it?" The sad note in Nancy's voice couldn't be disguised. "We've got only three more days."

"Three days," Carla repeated sleepily.

"But you have to admit, this has been our best vacation."

And our worst, Carla mused. Every year she hoped to have a holiday fling. But not next year. Her heart couldn't take this. Of course, not everyone would affect her the way Philip had, but she wasn't keen to have her hopes dashed every year.

"By the way, did you hear the gossip that was going around the hotel yesterday?" Nancy didn't wait for Carla's answer. "Some crazy American was standing by the pool, serenading a girl with love songs. Apparently, she's staying at the hotel."

For the third time that morning, Carla's eyes opened. A faint color began an ascent up her neck to her cheeks. "Some crazy American?"

"Right, an American. Isn't that the most incredibly romantic thing you've ever heard? Women would kill for a man like that."

"I think you're right." Carla's interest was aroused as she sat up. "Allow me to introduce you to 'some crazy American' Saturday night."

"Philip?"

"You got it." Carla blinked twice. "And it was romantic, except that everyone at the pool was staring at us."

Nancy sighed and sat on the end of Carla's mattress. "Eduardo's romantic like that." She smoothed a wrinkle from her white cotton pants as she crossed her legs. "He says the most beautiful things to me. But half the time I don't know whether to believe him or not. The lines sound so practiced, and yet he appears sincere."

"In instances like that, only time will tell," Carla said without thinking.

"But that's something we don't have. In four days I'll be flying home, and I bet I never hear from Eduardo again."

Carla searched her friend's coolly composed face, interpreting the doubts. "But I thought we were only looking for a little romance to liven up our vacation."

Nancy sighed expressively, and her eyes grew wary. "I was, but you know what? I think there's something basically wrong with me. For years now, you and I have had this dream of the perfect vacation. We've been to Southern California, Vegas, Hawaii, and now Mazatlán. Every year we plan one week when we can let down our hair and have a good time." She paused, and her shoulders sagged in a gesture of defeat. "We do it so that when we get back to Seattle and our neat, orderly lives, we'll have something to get us through another year."

"But it's never worked out that way. Our vacations are always dull."

"I know," Nancy agreed morosely. "Until this year, and all of a sudden I discover I'm not the type for a one-week fling. I'll never be the 'love 'em and leave 'em' type. I like Eduardo, and as far as I can tell, he likes me. But I could be one of any number of women he escorts during the course of a summer. He sees a fun-seeking American on vacation, and I doubt that he'd recognize the hard-working high school teacher that I really am." Nancy sighed and ran her fingers through her hair in frustration. "The funny part is that after all these years, this was exactly what I thought I wanted. And now that I've met Eduardo, I can see how wrong I've been. When I meet a man, I want a meaningful relationship that will grow. Not a one-week fling."

Carla wasn't surprised by her friend's insights. Nancy often saw things more clearly than she did, whereas she, Carla, often reacted more to her emotions. Remembering last night and the way she'd panicked at the knowledge that Philip had been stabbed produced a renewed sense of regret. With Philip, her emotions had done a lot of reacting lately.

Later, when they met for an excursion to Palmito de la Virgen, the bird-watchers' island in the bay, Carla mentioned Eduardo's invitation to dinner. Philip was agreeable, as she knew he would be.

The following morning, Philip and Carla went deep-sea fishing at the crack of dawn. Philip managed to bring in a large tuna, but all Carla caught was a bad case of seasickness.

"It wasn't the boat rocking so much," she explained later, "but the way the captain killed that poor fish, cut

him up, and passed him around for everyone to sample—
raw."

"It's a delicacy."

"Not to me."

On Saturday, their last afternoon together, while Carla
stood terrified on the beach, Philip went parasailing.
With her eyes tightly shut, his glasses clenched in her
hand, she waited until he was in the air before she
chanced a look. Even then her heart hammered in her
throat, and she struggled to beat down the fear that
threatened to overcome her. Philip had to be crazy to
allow his life to hang by a thin line. The only thing keeping him airborne was a motorboat and a cord that was
attached from the boat to the parachute.

Her fear was transmitted as an irrational form of
anger. The worst part was that Carla realized she was
reacting to her emotions again. She wanted Philip to behave like a normal, safe, and sane male. Who would have
believed that a lanky guy who wore horn-rimmed glasses
defied death every day of his life?

Carla was exactly where Philip had left her when he
returned. His glasses had made deep indentations in her
fingers, and she didn't need to be told she was deathly
pale.

Exhilarated, Philip ran to her side and took his
glasses from her hand. "It was fantastic," he said, wiping the seawater from his face with a towel and placing it
in her beach bag.

She gave him a poor imitation of a smile and lied. "It
looked like fun."

"Then why do you resemble a Halloween ghost?"

"It frightened me," she admitted, and was grateful he didn't mention that she looked as if she was going to throw up.

"Carla, I was watching you from up there. You were more than frightened. You looked like a statue with your eyes closed and your teeth clenched, standing there terrified out of your wits."

"I thought you couldn't see without your glasses," she responded, only slightly interested.

"My vision is affected only close up. I saw how terrified you were."

"I told you before, I'm a conservative person." She didn't enjoy being on the defensive.

"You're more conservative than a pin-striped suit," he growled. "There's nothing reckless in parasailing."

"And that's your opinion." Impatiently, she picked up her beach towel, stuffed it into her bag, and turned away.

"The most daring thing you've done since we arrived is eat chicken in chocolate sauce," Philip insisted, rushing up beside her.

If he wanted to fight, she wasn't going to back down. "What do you want from me, anyway?" she cried.

He slapped his hands against his sides. "I don't know. I guess I'd like for you to recognize that there's more to life than self-actualization through checkers."

Her hand flew to her hip, and she glared at him with a fierceness that stole her breath. "You know, I really tried to be the good sport. Everything you've wanted to do, including risking my life in that . . . that ocean surf." She waved her finger at the incoming tide. "Deep-sea fishing . . . everything. How can you say those things to me?"

"For heaven's sake, people come from all over the world to swim in this ocean. What makes it so dangerous for you?"

Several moments passed before she'd gained enough control of her voice to speak. "The very first day we arrived, you warned me that the current was too strong for swimming."

"It was." He pointed to a green flag beside the lifeguard station. "The flag was red."

"Oh." Carla swallowed and forged ahead, weaving her way around the sunbathing beauties that dotted the beach. "Why didn't you explain that at the time?" she demanded.

Curious stares followed her as she ran up the concrete steps that led to the hotel's outdoor restaurant. Not waiting for Philip, she pulled out a chair and sat down, purposely placing her beach bag on the empty chair beside her.

Philip joined her, taking his short-sleeve shirt out of her bag and impatiently stuffing his arms into the sleeves.

"And I suppose you're going to make a big deal out of the fact I didn't want to eat raw fish or dance on my hat," Carla cried, incensed. "I'll have you know —"

Before she could finish, the waiter came for their order. To prove a point, Carla defiantly asked for the hotel special, a hollowed-out coconut filled with a frothy alcoholic concoction. Philip looked at her in surprise, then ordered a cup of coffee.

"Carla," he said after the waiter had left, "what are you doing? You'll be under the table before you finish that drink. There must be sixteen ounces of booze in that coconut."

Gritting her teeth, Carla slowly shook her head. "Everything I do is wrong. There's no satisfying you, is there? If you find me so dull and boring, why have you insisted we spend this week together?"

"I don't find you dull." The paper straw he was fingering snapped in half.

"Then . . . then why are you so angry with me? What have I done?"

Philip ran a hand across his eyes. "Because I know what's coming. We're leaving in the morning, and when we arrive in Seattle it's good-bye, Carla. With no regrets and no looking back."

"But we agreed—"

"I know what we agreed," he growled. "But I didn't count on . . . Listen, Carla, I didn't mean for any of this to come out this way. I think I'm falling in love with you."

Carla felt the air rush out of her. "Oh Philip, you can't make a statement like that after only knowing me a week."

"Six days," he corrected grimly, and stared at her. His annoyance was barely in check, even now, when he'd admitted his feelings. "I'm not all that versed in love," he said stiffly. "Nicole was evidence of that. And if the truth be known, I thought for a long time afterward that there'd never be another woman I'd care about as much. But what I feel for you grows stronger every minute we're together. We have something special, Carla, and your cautious, conservative fears are going to ruin it."

Philip stopped talking when the waiter approached

with their drinks. Carla stared at her drink. Normally she didn't drink during the day, but Philip's accusations hurt. She took a tentative sip from the alcohol-filled coconut and winced. Philip was right; she was a fool to have ordered it.

"I can see what's going to happen," he continued. "And I don't like it."

Confusion raced through her. Philip was saying the very things she'd dreaded most—and that she most longed to hear. "Don't you attribute this attraction to the lure of the forbidden?" She sought a sane argument. "You knew from the beginning how I feel about men in law enforcement . . . and maybe in the back of your mind you thought I would change."

"No," he answered starkly. "Maybe the thought flitted through my mind at one time. But I felt that chemistry between us before you ever told me about your father."

"That soon? Philip, we'd only just met."

Her answer didn't appear to please him. "Don't you think I've told myself that a thousand times?"

The silence stretched between them, tight and unbearable. Carla shifted and pushed her drink aside. Tonight was their last night, and it seemed like they were going to spend it fighting. She was more than half in love with him herself, but she couldn't let Philip know that, especially since she had no intention of continuing to see him after they returned to Washington. What was the use? He wouldn't change, and she couldn't. There was no sense in dragging out the inevitable.

"I think I'll go up and get ready for tonight," she said, struggling to keep her voice level.

Philip didn't try to stop her as she stood, reached for her beach bag, and walked away. Tears had filled her eyes by the time she reached her room. Pressing her index finger under her eye helped to stop the brimming emotion. Somehow, with a smile on her face, she'd make it through tonight and tomorrow. When the time came, she'd thank Philip for a marvelous week and kiss him good-bye. And mean it.

A careful application of her makeup helped disguise the fact that she'd spent a good portion of the afternoon fighting back emotion. Carla thought she'd done a good job until Nancy came into the room to change, took one look at her friend, and declared: "You've been crying."

"Oh darn!" Carla raced to the bathroom mirror. "How'd you know?"

"It was either the puffy red eyes or the extra makeup. Honestly, Carla, with a complexion like yours, you can't help but tell."

"Great. Now what am I going to do?"

Nancy inspected her closet, finally deciding on a pale-blue sleeveless dress with spaghetti straps. "The same thing I'll probably end up doing. Smile and say how much you're going to miss Mexico and how this has been the best vacation of your life." She turned and laid the dress across the bed. "Now, that's what you're supposed to tell everyone else. What you say to me is the truth."

"Philip claims he's falling in love with me," she declared, and sniffled loudly. Fresh tears formed, and she grabbed a tissue and forced her head back to stare at the ceiling, hoping to discourage any new tear tracks from ruining her makeup.

"And that makes you cry. I thought you really liked Philip."

"But there's something I didn't tell you. Philip's in law enforcement. He's a cop." She didn't need to say another word.

"Good grief, Carla, how do you get yourself into these things?"

"I don't know," she lamented, pressing the tissue under her eyes. "Philip was so open and honest about it when he didn't have to be, and when he suggested that we enjoy this week I couldn't turn him down. He's wonderful. Everything about him is wonderful."

"Except that he's a policeman."

"And he's amazingly like my dad. It doesn't matter where either one of them is, the badge is always on. Even when we were shopping, Philip stopped and broke up a potential fight. Worse, Philip's been stabbed once because he was careless."

"Your dad was hurt not long ago, wasn't he?" Nancy asked from her position on the end of the bed.

"Once. He was chasing a suspect, fell, and broke his arm."

Nancy nodded. "I remember because you were so furious with him."

"And with good reason. Dad's too old to be out there running after men twenty years younger than he is."

"Take my advice and don't tell him that." Nancy's comment was punctuated with a soft laugh.

Carla decided that Nancy knew her father better than most people did. "Don't worry, Mom said it for me."

An abrupt knock on the door caused them both to

glance curiously at each other. Carla's watch told her it was forty-five minutes before they were scheduled to meet the men.

Since she was ready, Carla answered the door. "Philip!" she exclaimed. How good he looked in a suit and tie! And his eyes were the deepest gray she could remember seeing. One glance at her, and their color intensified even more.

"I thought you might be ready," he said stiffly.

"Yes . . . I am."

"Would you have a drink with me in the lounge? Nancy and Eduardo can join us there."

He sounded as if he were preparing to read Carla her rights. "Sure," she replied, and tossed a look over her shoulder to Nancy. "We'll meet you in the lounge."

Nancy arched both brows expressively. "See you there."

Philip didn't say a word until after they'd ordered their drinks. "I owe you an apology."

Carla's smile wavered only slightly as she reached for his hand. "You can't be any sorrier than I am. I wish I could change, and if there was ever a man I'd do it for, it would be you. But you've seen how I am. I just don't want our last hours together to be spent arguing."

Philip took her hand and squeezed it tightly. "I don't, either. We have tonight."

"And tomorrow," she murmured. But their flight was scheduled for the morning, and they'd be in the air a good portion of the day. Once they landed at Sea-Tac International Airport, Philip would catch a connecting flight to Spokane. They would be separated by three hundred miles that might as well have been three thousand.

"I have something for you," he announced casually, and pulled a small wrapped package from his coat pocket.

Astonished, Carla raised questioning eyes to Philip. "We must think alike. I've got something for you, too. I'd planned on giving it to you tomorrow. I didn't want you to forget me."

"There's little chance of that," he said with a wry twist of his mouth. "Go on, open it."

Eagerly, Carla tore off the ribbon and paper and was surprised to discover it was a jewelry box. Lifting the black velvet lid, she gasped in surprised pleasure. An exquisite turquoise necklace and matching earrings lay nestled in a bed of plush velvet. The ring he'd given her earlier matched the set. "Oh Philip, you shouldn't have." Fresh tears misted her eyes, and she bit her bottom lip in an effort to forestall their flow. "They're beautiful. I'll treasure them always."

"Would you like me to help you put it on?"

"Please." She moved to the edge of the chair, turned, and scooped up her hair with her forearm. Deftly, Philip placed the turquoise necklace against the hollow of her throat and fastened it in place. Carla managed the earrings on her own.

When she'd finished, she searched through her purse for a tissue to wipe away the tears that clouded her vision. She had to be crazy to walk away from the most wonderful man in the world. Crazy and stupid.

"Here comes Nancy and Eduardo," Philip announced, and stood as the introductions were being made.

The four sat together, and Carla was surprised to discover that Eduardo wasn't anything like she recalled. Her first impression had been all wrong. The Latin good looks were in evidence, but there was a natural shyness about him, a reserve that was far more appealing than his striking good looks. When he spoke English, his Spanish inflection was barely noticeable. Carla guessed that Eduardo had traveled extensively in the United States or had lived there. But more than anything else, Carla noted the way Eduardo watched Nancy. Each time his gaze swung to her friend, his dark eyes brightened and his masculine features would soften noticeably.

Conversation among the four flowed smoothly. When it came time to leave for dinner, Eduardo told them that the hotel's most expensive restaurant had a dining area designated especially for small private parties. The room resembled an intimate dining room, and had been reserved for them. A friend of his owned the hotel, Eduardo explained, and had given his permission for them to use this room. He led the way.

"It's lovely," Carla observed at first glance, impressed with the Aztec décor.

"I chose the menu myself," Eduardo explained. "I hope you will find it to your liking."

"I'm sure we will," Carla murmured. If the meal was anything like the room, this would be a dinner she'd remember all her life.

Eduardo continued by naming the dishes that they would be sampling. Carla understood little Spanish, and appreciated it when Eduardo translated for her. "The food in Mexico is a combination of indigenous Indian dishes and Spanish cuisine with some Arabic and French influences."

Carla quit counting after six courses. Replete, she settled back in her chair, her hands cupping a wineglass. "And to think none of us would be here if you two men hadn't ordered a margarita that first night." Almost instantly Carla realized that she'd said the wrong thing. Nancy's eyes widened in warning, and Carla averted her gaze to the wineglass in her hand. Nancy hadn't explained their game to Eduardo, and Carla had just stuck her foot in her mouth.

"I'm sorry?" Eduardo questioned, and a curious frown drew his thick brows together. "I don't understand."

"It's nothing," Nancy said quickly.

"Carla said something about Philip and me ordering margaritas the day we met. I'm confused."

"Really, it's nothing," Nancy insisted, a desperate edge to her voice.

An uneasy silence filled the room. "Please explain," Eduardo said stiffly. "A man doesn't like to be the only one not in on a joke."

"It wasn't a joke." Nancy avoided meeting Eduardo's probing gaze. "It's just that Carla and I never have any luck finding decent men, and we decided . . . Well, you see, we were sitting in the cocktail lounge and . . ." She tossed Carla a frantic glare. "You explain."

Carla's eyes rounded mutinously. "Nancy—I mean . . . we . . ." Good grief, she wasn't doing any better! Silently she implored Philip to take up the task.

To Carla's relief, Philip did exactly that, explaining at

length in Spanish. Three pairs of eyes studied Eduardo, and it was easy to see that he was furious. "And whose idea was this game?" His accent became thicker with every word.

"Mine," Nancy replied, accepting full responsibility. "But it wasn't like you think. I would never have—"

Pushing back his chair, Eduardo stood. "This has been an enjoyable time with my American friends, but I fear I have a business engagement and must cut our evening short."

Nancy stood up as well. "Eduardo, you can't leave now. We must . . ."

Philip leaned over to Carla.

"Let's leave these two alone to sort this out," he whispered in her ear, and they stood.

"How could I have said anything so stupid?" Carla moaned as they left the restaurant.

"You didn't know."

Philip's words did little to soothe her. "Didn't you see the look in Nancy's eyes? She'll never forgive me, and I don't blame her." Carla felt like weeping. "I've betrayed my best friend."

"Carla," Philip said, and placed an arm around her. "You can't blame yourself. Nancy should have said something to Eduardo before this."

"The bad part is that Eduardo honestly likes her, and I've ruined that." She kicked at a loose pebble. "I always did get a loose tongue when I drink too much wine."

Philip cleared his throat. "I hadn't noticed."

"And you're not helping things."

"Sorry." But his smile told her he wasn't. "You

shouldn't worry. If Eduardo cares for Nancy, he'll give her the opportunity to explain."

"But I feel rotten."

"I know you do. Come on. Let's walk off some of that fantastic dinner." His arm tightened around her waist, and she propped her head against his shoulder.

The beach was possibly even more beautiful than it had been any night that week.

"Do you remember the first time we were here?" Philip asked, his voice low, as he rubbed his chin along the top of her head.

Carla answered with a short shake of her head. "I remember thinking that you wanted to kiss me."

"I did."

"And at the time I was afraid you were the type of guy who would wait until the third date."

"Me?" He paused and pushed his glasses up the bridge of his nose. "And I was wondering what you'd do if I did make a pass."

A gentle breeze off the ocean carried Carla's soft laugh into the night. "No wonder you had a shocked look when we went swimming and I asked you to kiss me underwater."

"I thought I'd died and gone to heaven."

The laughter faded and was replaced by a sadness born of the knowledge that within a matter of hours they would be separating. "This has been a wonderful week."

"The best."

Absently, Carla fingered the turquoise necklace. "I don't ever want this to end. This is heaven being here with you. Reality is only a few hours away."

"It doesn't have to end, you know." Philip stopped walking and turned her in his arms. His smoky-gray eyes burned into hers. "I love you, Carla."

"Philip, please," she pleaded. "Don't."

"No, I'm going to say it. Believe me, I know all the arguments. One week is all we've had, and there are a thousand questions that still need to be answered. I want to get to know you, really know you. I want to meet your family and introduce you to mine."

A bubble of pain and hysteria threatened to burst inside her. "You and my dad have a lot in common."

Philip ignored the sarcasm. "You're a beautiful, warm, intelligent woman."

"Don't forget conservative."

"And conservative," he added. "Have you ever thought how beautiful our children could be?"

"Philip, don't do this to me." She had thought about it. Blending her life with Philip's had been on her mind all afternoon. But no matter how appealing the imagery, Carla couldn't see past the police uniform and badge. "I . . . I think I should go back and check on Nancy. And I still have my packing to do."

Philip pinched his mouth tightly closed when he delivered her to the hotel room. "I'll see you in the morning," she promised, not meeting his gaze.

"In the morning," he repeated, but he didn't try to kiss her. Carla couldn't decide if she was grateful or not.

A muffled sound could be heard on the other side of the door. "Good night," she murmured miserably, and slipped inside her room.

Nancy was lying across the bed, her shoulders heaving as she wept. "Oh Carla," she cried, and struggled to sit up. "Eduardo wouldn't even listen to me. He was barely polite."

Nancy and Carla looked at each other, and both burst into tears.

Six

~

The sun had barely crested the ocean, its golden strands etching their way across the morning beach, when Carla woke. Her roommate remained asleep as Carla slipped from the bed, quickly donning washed-out jeans and a warm sweatshirt. It wouldn't seem right to leave Mazatlán without one last walk along the water's edge.

Rushing down the concrete steps that led to the countless acres of white sand, Carla scanned the deserted area. Her spirits sank. This last stroll would have been perfect if Philip were here to share it with her.

Rolling up her jeans to her knees, she teased the oncoming tide with her bare feet. The water was warm and bubbly as it hit the shore. She vividly recalled the few times she'd swam in the surf with Philip. When the salt water had stung her eyes and momentarily blinded her, Philip had lifted her into his strong arms and carried her to shore.

With a wistful sigh, Carla strolled away from the water's edge, kicking up sand as she walked. Every memory of this vacation would be connected with Philip. She'd be a fool to think otherwise.

"Carla!"

Her heart swelled as she spun and waved her hand high above her head. Philip.

His shoulders were heaving by the time he ran the distance and joined her. "Morning." He reached for her and looked as if he meant to kiss her, then dropped his hands, apparently changing his mind.

"Morning. I was praying you'd be here."

"I thought I saw you by the pool."

The salty breeze carried her laughter. "I was there waiting for you to magically reappear."

"Poof. Here I am."

"Like magic," she whispered, and slipped her arm around his waist. They turned and continued strolling away from the hotel. The untouched morning beach meandered for miles in the distance.

"How's Nancy?"

Carla shrugged. "Asleep. But for how long, I don't know," she said, as a reminder to them both that she couldn't stay long. "I guess Eduardo wouldn't let her explain that picking him up in the lounge never was a game. Not really."

"His attitude is difficult to understand and seems usually indulgent toward their women."

"Are you as indulgent toward your women?" Carla inquired with rounded, innocent eyes, determined to make this a happy conversation. She'd never be able to tell him all the things in her heart.

"I must be, or you would have shared my bed before now."

Forcing her gaze toward the sea, Carla struggled to maintain control of her poise. "You sound mighty sure of yourself, Philip Garrison," she returned. If he'd said that for shock value, he'd succeeded. The evening in his parents' condo had caught her off guard. The atmosphere had been intimate, and the wine had flown too freely.

"I don't think I'm being overconfident," Philip replied. "You wanted me as much as I did you. But whether you're willing to admit it is something else."

Carla understood what he was saying and blushed.

"What were you thinking when I called you just now?" Philip asked, breaking the uneasy silence that had settled over them. "I can't remember ever seeing you look more pensive."

"About Mexico and what a wonderful time I've had," she said, and smiled up at him. "That's mostly your doing. In my mind I'll never be able to separate the two."

"Me and Mazatlán?"

She answered with a short nod.

Her response didn't seem to please him. He glanced at his watch and applied a gentle pressure to the small of her back as he turned them around and headed for the hotel. "I'll take you back before Nancy wakes."

They didn't speak as they walked toward the El Cid. Then Carla said somberly, "I was hoping you'd be here. My beach bag's up ahead. Your gift's inside." The handcrafted marlin carved from rosewood had been expensive. Carla had seen Philip admire it the day they'd gone shopping at the arts-and-crafts center and had purchased the hand-rubbed wood sculpture for him while he had been talking to some tourists.

Now her eyes shone with a happy-sad expression as Philip unwrapped the gift. He peeled back the paper and glanced at her wordlessly. Delight mingled with surprise as his eyes looked almost silver in the light of the morning sun.

"Thank you," he said simply.

"No," she replied, and swallowed against the hoarseness building in her throat. "Thank you. I'll never forget you, Philip, or this week we've shared. The reason for the marlin is so you won't forget me." She kissed him then, her hands sliding around his middle as her lips met his. It was meant to be a simple act of appreciation, but this kiss soon took on another, more intense significance. This was good-bye.

Philip's arms locked around her narrow waist, lifting her off her bare feet. Bittersweet memories merged with pure hunger. Mouths hardened against each other in a hungry, grinding demand. Their heads twisted slowly from side to side as the kiss continued and continued until Carla thought her lungs would burst. Incredibly, she couldn't give enough or take enough to satisfy the overwhelming passion consuming her resolve.

When they broke apart she was weak and panting. Her legs were incapable of holding her as she pressed her cheek to the hard wall of his chest and gloried in the thundering, erratic beat of his heart. Her shaking fingers toyed with the hair that curled along the back of his neck. But the comfort and security of his embrace was shattered when he spoke.

"Carla, I'm only going to ask you once. Can I see you once we're home?"

"Oh Philip," she moaned, caught in the trap of indecision. He was forcing her to face the very question she dreaded most. Her lips felt dry, and she moistened them. She couldn't tell him "yes," although her heart was screaming for her to do exactly that. And "no" was equally intolerable. Bright tears shimmered in her eyes as she stared up at him, silently pleading with him to understand that she couldn't say what he wanted to hear.

"Listen to me, Carla," he urged gently. "What we found in Mazatlán is rare. But two people can't know if they're in love after seven short days. We both need time to discover if what we've found is real." His hand smoothed the red curls behind her ear. "What do you say? Spokane isn't that far from Seattle, and meeting would be a simple matter of a phone call."

"Oh Philip, I'm such a coward." Her long nails made deep indentations in her palms, but she hardly noticed the pain.

"Say yes," he urged, his fingers gripping her shoulders.

Carla felt as if she were standing on the edge of the Grand Canyon, looking down. She knew the pitfalls of loving Philip, and the terror of it gripped her, making speech impossible.

Trapped as she was, she couldn't agree or disagree. "I wish you wouldn't," she murmured finally.

The gray eyes she had come to adore hardened briefly before he dropped his hands to his sides. "When you're through letting your fears and prejudices rule your life, let me know." Abruptly he turned, leaving her standing alone in the bright morning sunlight.

"Philip." Her feet kicked up sand as she raced after him. "We can talk more at the airport."

"No." He shook his head. "All along you've assumed I was booked on the same return flight as you. I won't be leaving for another two days."

"Oh." She was forced to continue running to keep up with his long strides. "Why didn't you say something?"

"Why? If you can't make up your mind now, flying back together shouldn't make any difference."

He stopped and caressed the underside of her face. "Good-bye, Carla." His eyes were infinitely sad, and he looked as if he wanted to say something more but changed his mind. Without another word, he turned and left.

Alone and hurting, she stood on the beach with the wind whipping at her from all directions.

"Phone. I think it's Cliff," Nancy announced on her way out of the kitchen.

Before Mexico, the news would have been mildly thrilling. But Carla couldn't look at Cliff Hoffman and not be reminded of Philip. Not that the two men were anything alike. Cliff was the current heartthrob of half the medical staff at Highline Medical Center. Carla had been flattered and excited when he'd started asking her out.

Unhooking her leg from the arm of the overstuffed chair, Carla set her book aside and moved into the kitchen, where the phone was mounted on the wall.

"Hello."

"Carla, it's Cliff."

"Hi." She hoped the enthusiasm in her voice didn't sound forced.

"How was Mexico?"

The question caught Carla off guard, and for one terrifying moment she couldn't breathe. "Fine."

"You don't sound enthusiastic. Don't tell me you got sick?"

"No . . . no, everything was fine." What a weak word *fine* was, Carla decided. It couldn't come close to describing the most gloriously wonderful, exciting vacation of her life. But she couldn't tell that to Cliff when she sounded on the verge of tears.

"I expected to hear from you by now. You've been back a week." She could hear an edge of disappointment in his voice but suspected it was as phony as her enthusiasm. From the beginning of their non-relationship, Cliff had let it be known that she had plenty of competition. Philip had once asked her if there was anyone special waiting for her in Seattle. At the time, mentioning Cliff hadn't even crossed her mind.

"It's been hectic around here . . . unpacking and all." No excuse could have sounded more lame.

"I was thinking we should get together soon." Cliff left the invitation open-ended.

If he expected her to jump at the opportunity to spend time in his company, he was going to be disappointed. "Sure," she agreed, without much enthusiasm.

"This weekend?"

Why not? she mused dejectedly. She wouldn't be accomplishing anything by moping around the apartment, which was exactly what she and Nancy had been doing since their return. "That sounds good."

"Let's take in a movie Saturday night, then."

"Fine." There was that word again.

Five minutes later, Carla returned to the living room and her book.

"These arrived while you were on the phone." A huge bouquet of three dozen red roses captured her attention. *Philip.* Her heart soared. That crazy, wonderful man was wooing her with expensive flowers. It was exactly like him. She'd phone him and chastise him for being so extravagant, and then she'd tell him how miserable the last week had been without him.

Nancy sniffled and wiped the tears from her cheeks. "Eduardo sent them."

"Eduardo?"

"He sent the flowers in hopes that I'll forgive him for his behavior our last night in Mazatlán."

Carla felt like crying, too, but not for the same reasons as her roommate was. "I'm really happy for you." At least one of them would be lifted from the doldrums.

"You might still hear from Philip."

"Sure," Carla said with an indifferent shrug. If anyone did anything to improve the situation between her and Philip, it would have to be her. And she couldn't, not when seeing him again would make it all the more difficult. As it was, he dominated her thoughts.

Fifteen minutes later the phone rang again. Carla's immediate reaction was to jump up and answer it, but Nancy was sitting closer to the apartment telephone and for Carla to rush to it would be a dead giveaway. Although Carla pretended she was reading, her ears were finely tuned to the telephone conversation. When Nancy gave a small, happy cry, Carla's interest piqued. Eduardo, it had to be, especially since Nancy was exclaiming how much she loved the roses. She told him how sorry she was about the mix-up and how everything had changed since Mexico.

When her friend started whispering into the receiver, Carla decided it was time to make her exit. "I think I'll go visit Gramps," she said, reaching for her bulky knit sweater and her purse.

Nancy smiled in appreciation and gave a friendly wave as Carla walked toward the door.

The sky was overcast, and Carla swung a sweater over her shoulder as she walked out the front door. Summer didn't usually arrive in the Pacific Northwest until late July.

"See you later," Nancy called with a happy lilt of her voice.

Carla's Grandpa Benoit was her mother's father. He lived in a retirement center in south Seattle, not far from Carla's apartment. Whereas Carla had always felt distant from her mother, she shared a special closeness with Gramps. Grandpa Benoit loved cards and games of any kind. From the time Carla could count, he had taught her cribbage, checkers, and chess. The three essential C's, Gramps called them. It was because of Gramps that Carla had won the checkers championship through the King County Parks and Recreation Department.

Carla pulled into the parking lot and sat in her car for several minutes. If she showed up again today, Gramps's questions would only become more probing. From the day she'd returned to Seattle, he'd guessed something had happened in Mexico. At first he hadn't pried; his questions had been general, as if her answers didn't much concern him. But Carla knew her grandfather too well to be tricked by that. Yesterday, when she'd stopped by on her way to work, they'd played a quick game of checkers, and Carla had lost on a stupid error.

"I guess that young man from Mexico must still be on your mind?" His eyes hadn't lifted from the playing board.

"What young man?"

"The one you haven't mentioned."

Carla ignored the comment. "Are you going to allow me a rematch or not?"

"Not." Still, he didn't lift his gaze to hers. "Don't see much use in playing when your mind isn't on the game."

Carla bristled. She'd lost plenty of games to Gramps over the years, and it was unfair of him to comment on this one.

"Seems you should have lots of things you'd rather be doing than playing checkers with an old man, anyways."

"Gramps!" Carla was shocked that he'd say something like that. "I love spending time with you. By now, I'd think you'd know that."

His veined hands lifted the round pieces one by one and replaced them in the tattered box. "Just seems to me a woman your age should be more interested in young men than her old Gramps."

Carla started picking up the red pieces. "His name's Philip. Does that satisfy you?"

The blue brightened on his ageless face. "He must be a special young man for you to miss him like this."

"He is special," Carla agreed.

Gramps hadn't asked anything more, and Carla hadn't voluntarily supplied additional information. But if she were to show up again today, Gramps wouldn't let her off as lightly.

Backing out of the parking space, Carla drove to a local Hallmark shop and spent an hour reading through cards. She selected two, more for the need to justify spending that much time in the store than from a desire for the cards.

That evening, as a gentle drizzle fell outside, Carla sat at the kitchen table and wrote to Philip. The letter seemed far more personal than an email. It was probably the most difficult of her life. Bunched-up sheets littered the table-top. After two hours, she read her efforts with the nagging feeling that she'd said too much—and not nearly enough.

Dear Philip,

You told me to let you know when I was ready to let go of the fears that rule my life. I don't know that I'm entirely prepared to face you in full police uniform, but I know that I can't continue the way I have these last two weeks. Nothing's the same anymore, Philip. I lost a game of checkers yesterday, and Gramps said I shouldn't play if my mind isn't on the game. The only thing on my mind is you. The moon has your image marked on its face. The wind whispers your name. I can't look at the ocean without remembering our walks along the beach.

I'm not any less of a coward than I was in Mazatlán. But I don't know what to do anymore.

I used to be happy in Seattle. Now I'm miserable.

Even checkers doesn't help.

Once, a long time ago, I read that the longest journey begins with a single step. I'm making that first attempt. Be patient with me.

> *Carla*

The letter went out in the next morning's mail. Since she didn't have Philip's address, Carla sent it to him in care of the Spokane Police Department. His return letter arrived four torturous days later.

Dear Carla,

My first reaction was to pick up the phone and call, but if I said everything that was going through my mind, I'd drive you straight to Alaska, and I'm afraid you'd never stop running.

My partner must have thought I was crazy when the watch commander handed me your letter. I've read it through a thousand times and have been walking on air ever since. Do you mean it? I never dreamed I could take the place of checkers.

Carla, I don't know what's been going through that beautiful head of yours, but with every minute that passes I'm all the more

*convinced that I'm in love with you. I didn't
want to blurt it out like this in a letter, but I'll go
crazy if I hold it inside any longer. Get used to
hearing it, love, because it feels too right to
finally be able to say it.*

*You asked me to be patient. How can I be
anything else, when that first step you're taking is
on the road that's leading you back to me?*

*Hurry and write. Your last letter is curling at
the edges from so much handling.*

*I love you.
Philip*

P.S. I can tell I'm going to like your grandfather.

If Philip claimed to have read her letter a thousand times, then Carla must have doubled his record. Her response, a twelve-page epic, went out in the next day's mail.

Monday evening the phone rang. Nancy called Carla from the kitchen. "It's for you. Cliff, I think."

Carla was tempted to have her roommate tell him she wasn't home. Their date Saturday night had been a miserable failure. The movie had been a disappointment, and their conversation afterward had been awkward. But the problem wasn't Cliff, and Carla knew as much. Nothing was wrong with Cliff that substituting Philip wouldn't cure.

"Hello."

"Who the hell is Cliff?"

"Philip," Carla cried, and the swell of emotion filled her breast. "Is it really you? Oh, Philip, I've missed you so much." Holding the phone to her shoulder with her ear, she pressed her fingertips over her eyes. "Good grief, I think I'm going to cry."

"Who's Cliff?" he repeated.

"Trust me, no one important." How could he even think anyone meant half as much to her as he did? "We went out Saturday night, and I think he was thoroughly pleased to be done with me. I'm rotten company at the moment." Her laugh was shaky. "It seems my thoughts are preoccupied of late."

"Mine, too. Jeff's ready to ask for a new partner. I haven't been worth much since I got back."

Carla stiffened, and her hand tightened over the receiver. If Philip was being careless, he could be stabbed again. Or worse.

"What's wrong? You've gone quiet all of a sudden."

"Oh Philip, please be careful. If anything happened to you because you were thinking about me, I'd never forgive myself."

"Carla, I can take care of myself." The tone of his voice told her he was on the defensive.

Carla paused, remembering that he'd already been stabbed once. "I . . . I just don't want anything to happen to you."

"That makes two of us."

"I'm so glad you called," she said, and leaned against the countertop, suddenly needing its support. "I've never felt like this. Half the time I feel like I'm living my life by rote. Every day I rush home and pray there'll be something in the mail from you."

"I do, too," he admitted, his voice low and husky. "Listen, Carla, I've got two days off next Thursday and Friday. I'd like to come over."

"Philip, I'm scheduled in surgery both days."

"Can you get off?"

Carla lifted the hair from her forehead and closed her eyes in frustration. "I doubt it. This is vacation time, and we're shorthanded as it is." Their mutual disappointment was clearly evident. "Don't be upset," Carla pleaded softly. "If it was up to me, I'd have you here in a minute. What about the weekends? Unless I'm on call, I'll be free."

"But I won't."

"Right." She sucked in an unsteady breath. For a moment she'd forgotten that he didn't work regular hours. His life had to be arranged around his job. Even love came in a poor second to his responsibility to the force.

The awkward stillness fell between them a second time.

"Now you're upset?"

"No." The denial came automatically. "I understand a lot better than you realize. I can remember how rare it was to have Dad home on a weekend. Nothing has changed to make it any easier for you."

"You're wrong." Philip's voice dropped to a husky timbre. "Everything's changed. My life is involved with this incredible person who fills every waking thought and haunts my sleep."

"Oh Philip."

"The worst part is that I get discouraged. You asked me to be patient and I promised I would be. I guess I'm looking for you to make leaps and bounds and not small steps."

Her throat tightened and she struggled not to give in to tears. "I'm trying. Really trying."

For a long moment he didn't speak, but when he did, his voice was ragged. "Please, Carla, don't cry."

"I'm not," she lied, sniffling. "I wish I could be the kind of woman you want. . . ."

"Carla—"

"Maybe it would be better if you quit wasting your time on me and found someone who can adjust to your lifestyle." Her voice shook. "Someone who doesn't know the score . . . someone who doesn't understand what being part of the police force really means. Believe me, ignorance is bliss."

"Maybe I should," Philip said sharply. "There's not much to be said about a woman who prefers to live with her head buried in the sand."

Carla placed her hands over her eyes. All this time they'd been fooling themselves to think that either of them could change.

"I think you're right," she whispered in a voice that was pitifully weak. "Good-bye, Philip."

He started to say something, but Carla didn't wait to listen. Very gently, very slowly, she replaced the receiver. She expected a flood of tears, but there were none—only a dry, aching pain that didn't ease. In some ways, Carla doubted that it ever would.

Ten minutes later the phone rang again. Carla didn't answer it, knowing it was Philip. The phone was silent for the remainder of the evening.

Carla found two messages on the kitchen counter when she returned home from work the following afternoon:

PHILIP PHONED.
CLIFF DID, TOO.

Carla returned Cliff's call. They made arrangements to go to dinner Thursday night. Carla wasn't particularly interested in continuing her non-relationship with Cliff. But not for the world would she let someone—anyone—accuse her of burying her head in the sand. That comment still hurt. Most girls should consider themselves lucky to be going out with Cliff. Obviously there was something about him she was missing. Thursday she'd make a determined effort to find out what it was.

Two days later, a letter arrived from Philip, and Carla silently cursed herself for the way her heart leaped. She managed to make it all the way into the apartment, hang up her sweater, and pour a cup of coffee before she ripped open the envelope.

Dearest Carla,

I promised myself I wouldn't rush you, and then I do exactly that. Can you find it in your heart to

*forgive me? At least give me the chance to make
it up to you.*

   Be patient with me, too, my love.

   Philip

Carla read the letter twenty times nonstop. Never had
any two people been more mismatched. Never had any
two people been more wrong for each other. But right or
wrong, Carla couldn't ignore the fact that she'd never
felt this strongly about a man. If this was what it meant
to love, she hadn't realized what a painful emotion it
could be.

Dear Officer Garrison,

*It's been brought to my attention that two
people who obviously care deeply for each
other are making themselves miserable. One
has a tendency to expect overnight changes,
and the other's got sand in her eyes from all
those years of protecting her head. I'm
writing to seek your advice on what can
be done.*

   Carla

*P.S. I'll be more patient with you if you're still
willing to stick it out with me. P.P.S. I've got a
date with Cliff Thursday night, but I promise
not to go out with him again. Maybe I should
cancel it.*

Two days later, Carla got a phone call from Western Union.

"Telegram from Mr. Philip Garrison for Miss Carla Walker."

She had never received a telegram before, and her heart leaped to her throat as she searched frantically for a pencil. "This is Carla. Will I need a piece of paper?"

"I don't think so. There are only two words: 'Break date.'"

Seven

Early Thursday evening, Carla rushed home from the hospital. "Did Philip call yet?" she asked breathlessly as she scurried inside the apartment.

Nancy looked up from her magazine, happiness lighting up her face. "Philip didn't, but Eduardo did. He's in Colorado on a business trip and wanted me to hop in the car and join him."

"You're joking."

"No," she countered, "I'm totally serious. Obviously he had no idea how far Seattle is from Denver. We did have a nice talk, though."

From the look on her roommate's face, Carla could see that the conversation with Eduardo had been satisfying. Fleetingly, she wondered where the relationship would go from here. It was obvious the two were strongly attracted to each other. For Eduardo to have swallowed his pride and contacted Nancy revealed how much he did care.

"So Philip hasn't phoned?" Disappointment settled

over Carla. Everything was going so well with Nancy that she couldn't help feeling a small twinge of envy.

"Not yet. But it's a little early, don't you think?"

Carla had already kicked off her shoes and was unbuttoning the front of her uniform. "It's not nearly early enough. I guess I can wait a few more minutes." In some ways, she'd been waiting a lifetime for Philip.

"What makes you so sure he's going to phone?" Nancy asked, following her down the hallway to the large bedroom they shared.

Carla laughed as she pulled the uniform over her head. "Easy. He'll want to know if I broke the date or not."

"And did you?"

"Of course. I'm not all that interested in Cliff, anyway."

Nancy released a sigh of relief. "I'm glad to hear that."

"Why?" Carla turned to her roommate as she slid pale blue cotton pants over her slender hips.

"Because he asked me out."

Carla was shocked. "Cliff did? Are you going?"

Nancy's eyes were evasive. "You don't mind, do you?"

Carla couldn't have been more shocked if Nancy suddenly had announced that she'd decided to date a monkey. Her roommate had practically jumped for joy because Eduardo had phoned her, yet she was going out with Cliff. It didn't make sense.

"I don't mind in the least. But . . . but why would you want to? I thought you'd really fallen hard for Eduardo."

"I have," Nancy admitted freely. "Maybe too hard. I want to know if what I feel is real or something I've blown out of proportion. We were only together for six days. And although I've been miserable without him ever since, I need to test my feelings. Eduardo's culture is different from ours, he thinks and reacts to things completely opposite of the way I do sometimes, and that frightens me."

Nancy revealing she was frightened about anything was a shock. Of the two roommates, Nancy was by far the more stouthearted. But she was the type who would be very sure before committing herself to Eduardo and once she did, it would be forever.

"But why date Cliff?" Carla wondered aloud.

"To be honest," she said a little shyly, lowering her eyes, "I've always been attracted to him, but you were seeing him and I'd never have gone out with him while you were."

"You like Cliff?"

Nancy nodded, indicating that she did. "But if it troubles you, I'll cancel the date."

"Don't," Carla said without the least hesitation. "As far as I'm concerned, Cliff is all yours."

The doorbell chimed and Nancy glanced at the front door. "That must be Cliff now. You sure you don't mind?"

"Of course not. Enjoy yourselves, I'll talk to you later."

Too excited to bother eating dinner, Carla brought in a chair and placed it beside the phone. As an afterthought, she added a pencil, some paper, and a tissue box, in case she ended up crying again. Satisfied, she moved into the living room to watch the evening newscast.

When the phone rang, she was caught off guard and glanced at her wristwatch before leaping off the sofa.

"Hello," she answered in a low, seductive voice that was sure to send Philip's heartbeat racing.

There was a lengthy pause on the other end of the line. "Carla?"

"Mom." Embarrassed, Carla stiffened and rolled her eyes toward the kitchen ceiling. "Hi . . . I was expecting someone else."

"Obviously. Is it someone I know?"

"No, his name's Philip Garrison. I met him in Mazatlán." She briefly related the story. "I thought he might be phoning tonight." *Take the hint, Mom, and make this short,* Carla pleaded silently.

"You and . . . Philip must have hit it off for you to be answering the phone like a seductress."

"I like him very much" was all Carla would admit.

"Since you're so keen on this young man, when do your father and I get to meet him?"

Clenching a fist at her side, Carla struggled to hold on to her temper. She resented her mother for asking these questions, and she wanted to get off the phone in case Philip was trying to get through to her. "I don't know. Philip lives in Spokane."

"Spokane," her mother mused aloud.

"Mom," Carla interrupted, "would you mind if we talked later? I really do need to get off the phone."

"No, that'll be fine. I just wanted to know if you could come to dinner tomorrow night."

"Sure." At this point, she would have agreed to anything. "What time?"

"Seven."

"I'll be there. Talk to you later."

"Good-bye, dear. And, Carla, it might help if you're a little more subtle with . . . what's his name again?"

"Philip."

"Right. I'll see you tomorrow. And, Carla, do try to be demure."

"Yes, Mother, I'll try."

After hanging up, Carla took several calming breaths. She had never gotten along well with her mother. Over the years, Rachel Walker had admirably portrayed the role of a docile wife, but Carla had always thought of her as weak-willed: there were too many times when she'd witnessed the anger and hurt in her mother's expressive eyes. She had wanted to shout at both her parents. Her father should have known what his career was doing to the rest of the family. Her mother should have had the courage to speak up. Carla had tried at sixteen and had been silenced immediately, so she'd moved away from home as soon as possible, eager to leave a situation that made her more miserable every year. And now . . . here she was following in her mother's footsteps. A knot tightened in the pit of her stomach. Dear heavens, what was she getting herself into with loving Philip? Again and again she'd tried to tell herself that what they shared was different—that she and Philip were different from her parents. But their chances of avoiding the same problems her parents had dealt with were slim—likely nonexistent. With stiffening resolve, Carla vowed she would never live the type of life her mother had all these years. If that meant giving up Philip, then she'd do it. There wasn't a choice.

The phone rang again a half-hour later. Carla stared

at it as if it were a mad dog, her eyes wide with fear. Chills ran up and down her spine. This was Philip phoning—the call she'd anticipated all day.

Trembling, she picked up her purse and walked out the door. A movie alone was preferable to listening to the phone ring every half-hour. If she let Philip assume that she had gone out with Cliff, then maybe, just maybe, he'd give up on her and they could put an end to this misery. Her instincts had guided her well in the past. Now, more than at any other time in her life, she had to listen to her intuition—for both their sakes. Philip deserved a woman who would love him for his dedication to law and order and his commitment to protect and serve. He needed a wife who would learn the hazards of his profession a little at a time. Carla knew too much already.

Nancy wasn't home when Carla returned to the dark, lonely apartment. And within five minutes the phone rang. She ignored it. *Coward,* she taunted silently as she moved into the bedroom. But if she was behaving like a weakling, it shouldn't be this difficult. It wasn't right that it hurt this much.

Nancy was still asleep when Carla dressed for work the following morning. She penned her roommate a note and left it propped against the sugar bowl on the kitchen table:

> *If Philip contacts you, please don't tell him I didn't go out with Cliff last night. I'll explain later. Also, don't bother with dinner. I'm going to my*

parents'. Am interested in hearing how things went with Cliff. Talk to you tonight.

Carla's first surgery was an emergency appendectomy, a teenage boy who was lucky to be alive. Carla had witnessed only a handful of deaths in the last couple years. She didn't know how the rest of the staff dealt emotionally with the loss of a patient, but each one had affected her greatly.

When she had finished assisting with the appendectomy, she found a message waiting for her. She waited to read it until she was sitting down, savoring a cup of coffee in the cafeteria. *Call Nancy,* it read. A glance at the wall clock confirmed that there wouldn't be enough time to call until after lunch. When she phoned at one-thirty, however, there wasn't any answer, so Carla assumed it couldn't have been that urgent. She'd wait to talk to Nancy at home.

Three hours later Carla headed for the hospital parking lot, rubbing the ache in the small of her back to help relieve some of the tension accumulated from a long day on her feet. Dinner with her parents would only add to that tension. And eventually she would have to talk to Philip—he'd demand as much. But she didn't want to think about that now. Not when her back hurt and her head throbbed and she was facing an uncomfortable dinner with her parents.

Carla was soaking in a tub full of scented water when Nancy knocked on the bathroom door. "Carla."

"Hmm," she answered, savoring the luxurious feel of the warm, soothing water.

"I think you should get over to your grandfather's as soon as possible."

Carla sat up, sloshing water over the edge of the bathtub. "Why? What happened?"

"I can't explain now, I'll be leaving any minute. Cliff's on his way. He's taking me to the Seattle Center for the China Exhibit."

"Is anything wrong with Gramps?" Carla called out frantically. Already standing, she reached for a thick towel to dry herself.

"No, nothing like that. It's a surprise."

"What about you and Cliff? Things must be working out if you're seeing him again." Carla could feel Nancy's hesitation on the other side of the bathroom door.

"They're working out, but not as I'd expected. I'm giving it a second chance to see if it's any better the second time."

"Oh?" Carla hoped that Nancy wasn't going to make her ask for an explanation.

"Cliff's decent, I guess."

Behind the closed door, Carla smiled smugly. That was how she felt about Cliff. He was fine, but he wasn't Philip, and now, apparently, he wasn't Eduardo, either.

"Does Eduardo know? I mean, did you tell him you were seeing another man?" Carla hated to think what would happen if he discovered Nancy was dating Cliff. Eduardo's male honor was bound to cause him to overreact.

"I . . . I told him yesterday."

"And?"

"Oh, he understands. In fact, he encouraged me to see Cliff again. I told him he should do the same thing, and you know what he said? He said he didn't need to see another woman to know how he feels about me. He mentioned something about me flying to Mexico City to meet his family, but I didn't let him know one way or the other." As if regretting she'd revealed that much, Nancy added hastily, "Listen, Carla, I promise that you'll like your surprise. I'd hurry if I were you."

The doorbell sounded and was followed by a clicking sound that told Carla she wouldn't get any more information from her friend. *A surprise!* Presumably, this was why Nancy had contacted her at the hospital.

Dressing casually in cotton pants and an antique-white blouse with an eyelet collar, Carla hardly bothered with her hair. A quick application of lip gloss and a dab of perfume and she was out the door.

Her heart was hammering by the time she arrived at the retirement center. Her shoes made clicking sounds as she hurried inside, pushing open the double glass doors with both hands. She took the elevator to Gramps's room on the third floor, thinking it would be faster than running up the stairs.

Gramps's door was closed. Carla knocked loudly twice and let herself inside. "Gramps, Nancy . . ." The words died on her lips as her startled eyes clashed with Philip's. He was sitting opposite her grandfather, playing a game of checkers.

"Philip." She stood there, stunned. "What are you doing here?"

Gramps came to his feet, using his cane to help him

stand. "Nancy brought your young man over to meet me."

"I asked her to," Philip added. "Your grandfather was someone I didn't want to miss meeting."

"Mighty fine young man you've got yourself," Gramps said, his blue eyes sparkling with approval.

"He could be saying that because he beat me in checkers," Philip explained, grinning.

Gramps's weathered face tightened to conceal a smile. "Leave an old man to his peace. Knowing my daughter, she'll have your hide if either of you is late for dinner."

"Dinner," Carla repeated with a panicked look.

"Yes, your mother was kind enough to include me in the invitation."

"My mother."

"Something's wrong with my hearing aid," Gramps complained, tapping lightly against his ear. "I'm hearing an echo."

Philip chuckled and cupped Carla's elbow. "Nice meeting you, Gramps," he said as he led the way out the door and into the hallway.

"Philip Garrison, what are you doing here?" Carla demanded. Her hands rested defiantly on her hips. Oh my, he looked good. His hair was combed to the side, and a thick lock fell carelessly across his wide brow. His appealing gray eyes were dark and intense as they met hers. To Carla he had never looked more compelling. Staying out of his arms was growing more difficult every minute.

"Are you trying to drive me crazy? Because you're

doing a mighty fine job of it. Why wouldn't you answer the phone?"

"I . . . couldn't." She wouldn't lie outright, but she had no compunction about letting him believe she'd been out with Cliff.

"And while we're at it, you can explain this." He took Carla's note to Nancy from his pocket. "'Please don't tell him I didn't go out with Cliff,'" he read with a sharp edge in his voice. "It seems to me you've got some explaining to do."

"Y-Yes . . . yes, I guess I do."

"Then let's go back to your place. At least there we can have some privacy." He flashed a look down the wide corridor.

They rode back to the apartment in silence.

"How'd you get here?" Carla asked shakily, as she pulled into her assigned parking space.

"I flew in at noon. Nancy picked me up at the airport."

"When are you going back?"

His gaze cut into hers, and one thick brow arched arrogantly. "Can't wait to be rid of me, is that it?"

"No . . . yes . . . I don't know," she replied, her voice trembling.

Her hands were unsteady as she unlocked the apartment and stepped inside. Philip had come all this way because she hadn't had the courage to talk to him last night. She'd been foolish to believe he wouldn't find out why. "Would you like a cup of coffee?" she asked, hanging her purse over the inside doorknob of the coat closet.

Gently, Philip settled a hand on each shoulder and

turned her around so that he could study her. Carla's gaze fell to the floor.

"Carla, my love." Philip's voice was low, sensuously seductive. "You know what I want."

She did know. And she wanted it, too. "Oh Philip." She groaned and slipped her arms over his shoulders, linking her fingers behind his neck. "It's so good to see you."

His mouth claimed hers in a series of long, intoxicating kisses that left her weak and trembling. Philip was becoming a narcotic she had to have; his touch was addictive.

His hands roamed over her back, pulling her soft form against his muscular frame. A warmth spread through her limbs, and she turned her head when his lips explored the smooth curve of her shoulder and the hollow of her throat.

Taking a deep breath to keep the room from spinning, Carla pushed against his chest, leaving only a narrow space between them.

"How can you refuse to speak to me, deceive me by letting me think you'd gone out with this other guy, and then kiss me like that?" Philip asked in a voice husky with emotion.

Melting against him, she explored his earlobe with her tongue as her fingertips caressed his clenched jaw. "I think I'm going crazy," she murmured at last. "I want you so much my heart's ready to pound right out of me."

"Then why?" he groaned against her ear. "Why are you running from me so hard I can barely keep up with you?"

"I'm so scared." Her low voice wavered. "I don't want to be like my mother."

"What's that got to do with anything?" He continued to nibble the side of her neck, making it impossible for her to think clearly.

"Everything," she cried desperately. "I'm not the right person for you."

"But I won't want anyone else."

"Philip, be reasonable."

"You're in my arms. I can't think straight." He bit gently at the edge of her lips. "Carla, I'm going crazy without you. I want you to marry me. I want to share my life with you, because heaven knows I can't take much more of this."

Carla's eyes shot open. "How can you talk about marriage?" she asked, struggling to break free of his hold.

"It's the normal process when two people feel as strongly about one another as we do."

"But I don't want to love you," she cried. "When my husband leaves for work in the morning, I don't want to worry about him risking his life on the streets of the city."

"Carla—"

"And when he comes home at night, I don't want him to drag his job with him. I want a husband, not a hero—"

His mouth intercepted her words, muffling them until she surrendered to his kisses, arousing her until she clung to him, seeking a deeper fulfillment. "Kissing me won't settle a thing," she murmured, breaking free with her last reserves of strength.

"I know, but it keeps you from arguing."

"When you're holding me like this," she admitted shyly, "there's not much fight in me."

"Good. All I need to do for the next seventy years is keep you at my side. Agree, and I'll whisk you to a preacher so fast it'll make your head spin."

"You're incorrigible."

"I'm in love." His hands were linked at the small of her back and slipped over her buttocks, arching her backside, lifting her up to meet his descending mouth. The kiss was shattering.

"Can we talk now?" Every minute in his arms made it more difficult to think clearly.

"Okay, explain what happened yesterday," he said, as they sat in the living room. "Why wouldn't you talk to me last night?"

"I already told you why," she said, and exhaled slowly. "I don't want to be like my mother."

"Carla." Philip captured both her hands in his and kissed her knuckles. "That doesn't make any sense. You're who you are, and I'm me. Together, we'll never be like anyone else."

Carla bowed her head, and her lashes fluttered until they closed completely. "Mom and I are a lot alike. You'll understand that when you meet her later. But she's weak and afraid and never says what she's really thinking. And, Philip, I'm trying so hard to be different."

"That still doesn't explain why you wouldn't talk to me."

Carla swallowed uncomfortably. "Mom called just before you did, and everything she said reminded me how unhappy she's been all these years."

"Ah," Philip said, and nodded thoughtfully. "And the note to Nancy?"

"I . . . I was thinking that if you assumed I was still dating Cliff, you'd give up on me."

He tucked his index finger under her chin and lifted her eyes to his. "I think there's something you'd better understand. I'm not giving up on you. Never. I love you, Carla."

"But loving someone doesn't make everything right," she argued. "We're different in so many ways."

"I don't see it like that. We complement each other. And although it seems like I'm the one who's asking you to make all the changes, I'm not. When we're married, I promise that you and our family will be my first priority. Nothing will ever mean more to me than you."

"Oh Philip." She felt herself weakening. "But it's more than that."

"I know, love." Slowly, deliberately, his eyes never leaving hers, he pulled her toward him. His mouth sought her lips, exploring their softness as if he would never get enough of the feel of her.

"Philip," she groaned, her voice ragged. "We have to leave now for my mother's."

"Your mother's," he repeated, as if he needed something to bring him back from the brink.

"You'll be meeting my dad," she said softly, teasing his neck and ear with small, biting kisses.

"Mom and Dad, I'd like to introduce Philip Garrison." Carla stood just inside her parents' living room. "Philip, my mom and dad, Joe and Rachel Walker."

Joe stepped forward and shook Philip's hand. "Nice to meet you, Philip."

Carla felt the faint stirrings of pleasure. Her father, although graying, was in top physical condition. Over the years he hadn't lost the lean, military look of his younger days. Intuitively, Carla knew that in twenty years Philip wouldn't, either.

"It's a pleasure to have you join us," Rachel added warmly. "Carla said you live in Spokane."

"Yes, I flew in this afternoon."

The four of them sat in the large living room, and Philip immediately took Carla's hand in his. The action didn't go unnoticed by either of her parents. Rachel's blue eyes sought Carla's, and she gave her daughter a small wink, indicating that she approved of this young man. Maybe Carla should have been pleased, but she wasn't. Having her family like Philip would only complicate her feelings.

"And when will you be leaving?"

Carla was as interested in his answer to her parents. "Tonight. I'd like to stay longer, but I'm on duty tomorrow morning."

"Carla said that you two met in Mazatlán."

"Yes, the first day she arrived." Philip looked at Carla, and his dark eyes flickered with barely concealed amusement.

Her eyes widened, silently warning him not to mention *how* they'd met. Then, flustered, she cleared her throat and said, "Philip helped me out with my Spanish."

"You speak Spanish?" Joe asked, but his narrowed gaze studied Carla. Her father was too observant not to recognize that there was a lot going unsaid about her meeting with Philip. Fortunately, he decided not to pursue the subject.

Rachel glanced at her gold wristwatch. "Excuse me a minute."

"Can I help, Mom?" Carla asked, and uncrossed her long legs.

"No, everything's ready, I just want to check the corn. Your father's barbecuing chicken tonight."

"You're in for a treat," Carla told Philip proudly. "I've been telling Dad for years that when he retires he should open a restaurant. He makes a barbecue sauce that's out of this world."

"It's an old family recipe that's been handed down for generations."

"He got it out of a Betty Crocker cookbook," Carla whispered, grinning. Then, before her father could open his mouth, she stood. "I'll see what I can do to give Mom a hand." Although her mother had refused her offer, there was undoubtedly something she could do to help.

Rachel was taking a large bowl of potato salad from the refrigerator when Carla came through the swinging kitchen doors. "I like your young man," she announced without preamble.

Carla couldn't hold her mother's gaze. She should have been surprised; Rachel had disapproved of most of the men Carla dated. Her excuses were usually lame ones—this boy was careless; another boy was lazy. By the time Carla moved out, she had stopped introducing her dates to her parents. Somehow, though, she'd known her mother would approve of Philip.

"He's clean-cut, polite, and he has a nice smile."

Carla bit into a sweet pickle from the relish tray. "And his eyes are the most incredible gray. Did you notice that?" Naturally, they wouldn't discuss any of the important aspects of her relationship with Philip.

"You two make a nice couple."

"Thank you," Carla answered with a hint of impatience. She opened the silverware drawer and counted out forks and spoons. "I'll set the table."

Philip was holding a beer, watching her father baste the chicken with a thick coating of pungent sauce, when Carla joined them on the sunny patio. He slipped an arm over her shoulders. His thumb made lazy, sensuous forays at the base of her neck.

Annoyed, she shrugged, and Philip dropped his hand to her waist. She didn't want him to make this kind of blanket statement to her family about their relationship. *He* was serious about her, but she had yet to deal with her feelings about him. When she stepped free of his hold, Philip firmly but gently cupped her shoulder.

"Philip," she said in an irritated whisper. "Please don't."

His eyes sparkled as he leaned toward her. "I told your father outright that I'm going to marry you."

"You didn't!" she cried in angry frustration.

Joe turned aside from the barbecue. "Hand me a spoon, would you, Carla?" he requested, and his gaze followed her as she moved to the picnic table and brought back a spoon. "Problems, Princess?"

"No." She shook her head, the red curls bouncing with the action. "I'm just sorry that Philip made it look like we're more serious than we are."

"He was rather forthright in his feelings."

Carla swallowed. "I know."

"But aren't you sure?"

"I won't marry a cop." Years of self-discipline masked any physical reaction from her father.

"I can't say I blame you for that," he said after a long moment. Some of the brightness faded from his eyes as he concentrated on his task.

"I love you, Dad, you know that. But I won't live the life Mom has."

With practiced skill, he turned the chicken over with a pair of tongs. "She's never complained."

"Oh Dad," Carla said with a rush of inner sadness. She respected and admired her father and had never thought of him as oblivious of the stress his career had placed on their family. "Are you really so blind?"

His mouth tightened, and the look he gave her was piercing. "I said she's never complained. It takes a special kind of woman to love a man like me."

Carla lifted her gaze to Philip, who was examining the meticulously kept flowerbeds, and her father's words echoed in her mind. Carla didn't know if she could ever be that special kind of woman.

Rachel appeared at the sliding glass door. "Carla, would you help me carry out the salads?"

"Sure, Mom." Carla followed her mother into the kitchen.

Rachel stuck a serving spoon in the potato salad, handed it to Carla, and turned away. "Philip mentioned that he had to be back tomorrow because he's on duty. You did say he was a doctor, didn't you?" Her voice was unnaturally high, and her hands were busily working around the sink.

"No, Mom." She'd wondered how long it would take for her mother to pick up on that. "Philip's a police officer."

A glass fell against the aluminum sink and shattered into little pieces. Rachel ignored it as she turned, her face suddenly waxen. "Oh Carla, no."

Eight

~

"Your flight will be boarding in a minute." Carla stood stiffly in the area outside of airport security. The lump in her throat was making it hard for her to talk. The crazy part was that she didn't want Philip to leave, and at the same time she couldn't bear to have him stay.

The meal with her parents had been an ordeal. As she had suspected, Philip and her father had gotten on like soul mates. They were alike in more ways than Carla had first suspected. Their personalities, ideas, and thoughts meshed as if they were father and son.

Rachel had remained subdued during most of the meal. Later, when Carla had helped clear the picnic table and load the dishwasher, a strained tension had existed between them. Her mother had asked a few polite questions about Philip, which Carla had answered in the same cordial tone.

"I don't think it would be a good idea for you to become too serious with this young man," Rachel said as they were finishing. Her casual attitude didn't fool Carla.

Fleetingly, Carla wondered what reason her mother would give. Philip wasn't the careless type, and even the most casual observer could see he wasn't lazy. She was bound to say everything but what was really on her mind.

"Why not?" Carla implored. "I thought you said you liked him."

"I do," Rachel replied quickly, in a defensive tone. "But he's too much like your father, and I'll love that man to my death." The poignant softness of Rachel's voice cracked the thin wall that stood between mother and daughter.

"And you," Rachel continued with a wry grin, "are too much like me: vulnerable, sensitive, tenderhearted. Our emotions run high, and when we love, we love with a fervor. Philip could hurt you, Princess."

Her mother so rarely called her by that affectionate term that Carla lifted her head in surprise.

"There are plenty of men in this world who will make life a thousand times easier for you than someone involved in law enforcement."

"But you married Dad," Carla argued, studying her mother intently. This was as close as they had ever come to an open conversation.

"Your father joined the force after we were married."

"I . . . I didn't know that."

"Something else you may not know is that Joe and I separated for a time before you were born."

Shocked, Carla's mouth dropped open. "You and Dad?"

Rachel busily wiped off the kitchen counter, then rinsed out the rag under the running faucet. "There are certain qualities a policeman's wife should have. I . . . I've never been the right woman—" She stopped in mid-sentence as Philip and Joe sauntered into the kitchen.

Mother and daughter had been unable to finish the conversation, but Carla had felt a closeness with her mother she had never experienced. She realized now that they had always been too much alike to appreciate each other.

"Carla?"

Philip's voice brought her back to the present, and to the reality of his leaving.

"You're looking thoughtful." His fingers caressed the gentle slope of her neck, trailing down her shoulder. "I expect a kiss good-bye, one that will hold me until I see you again."

A smile briefly touched Carla's eyes. "I don't think that kind of kissing is allowed in public places."

"I don't care." His voice was low and husky as he ran his hands up and down the length of her silken arms. "Seeing each other again has only made things worse, hasn't it?"

"No," she denied instantly. "I think it's been good for us both."

"Good and bad," he growled, and the frustration and longing in his eyes deepened. "Good, because holding you lessens the ache I feel when we're apart." His hands gripped the back of her collar, bringing her closer into his embrace. "And bad, because I don't know how much longer it'll be before I hold you again."

Their gazes met and held, and Carla felt as if she

were suffocating. His eyes, steel-gray and narrowed, slowed the torment within him, and Carla realized hers were filled with doubt. Her lips started quivering, and she pressed them tightly together.

Philip's hands tightened on Carla's blouse, and he dipped his head forward so that their foreheads touched. "I hate this."

Her arms slid around his waist, and she pressed her face to his shirt. "I do, too." Her voice was scratchy and unnaturally high as she swallowed hard, determined to be strong. "You should go," she said, and gave him a brave smile.

"Not until the last minute. Not until I have to." His voice wasn't any more controlled than her own. "Carla"—he breathed in deeply—"I want to do everything right for you. You need me to be patient and wait; then I'll do that."

"Oh . . . Ph . . . Philip. How can you love me? I'm so wrong for you."

"No one has ever been more right," he insisted, his words muffled against her hair. "I love you, and someday we'll have beautiful redheaded children."

"With warm gray eyes."

"Tall," he added.

"Naturally," she said, and offered him a shaky smile.

"Does this mean that you've reconsidered and will marry me? Because let me warn you: If it does, I'll make the arrangements tomorrow."

She couldn't answer him. Something deep and dark in her soul wouldn't allow her to speak. Instead, she blinked her eyes in an effort to hold back the emotion that threatened to overtake her.

Disappointment, regret, pain, and several other emotions Carla couldn't name played across Philip's face.

"Soon?" he asked in a whisper.

Carla forced a smile. "Maybe."

"That's good enough for now. Just make it soon, my love. Make it very soon."

Philip waited until the very last minute before going through security. Carla waited, and once he was through, he tossed an impatient glare over his shoulder and disappeared down the corridor, rushing to make his flight. His kiss had been short but ardent. As she watched him go, Carla pressed four fingers to her lips and closed her eyes.

She didn't leave the terminal until the plane was out of sight and her tears had dried. Her spirits were at an all-time low as she headed to the airport parking lot, fighting back questions that tormented her from all sides.

Philip's letter arrived in Saturday's mail.

My dearest love,

It's been only a few hours since I left you in Seattle. I couldn't sleep, and it's too late to phone. As I flew back tonight I couldn't drop the picture of you from my mind. This week is hectic, but I'll phone you Tuesday night. I'm involved with three other friends from the force in a canoe race—don't laugh. Ever hear of the Great Soap Lake Canoe Race? Well, yours truly is captain of the motley crew. We're planning to arrive at Soap Lake Friday afternoon. The race begins early Saturday morning. The others have their own cheering squad. I have only you. Tell me you'll come. I want to introduce you to my friends and their wives. And for all the trouble I've been giving Jeff Griffin, my partner, since Mexico, he claims he has a right to meet you. Let me warn you now that you shouldn't believe everything he says. Jeff likes to tease, and believe me, he's had a lot to kid me about the last few weeks. I want you to talk to Jeff's wife when you come. Sylvia is pregnant with their first child. I know you'll like her. Please tell me you'll be there.

This is torment, Carla. I can feel your kiss on my lips, and the scent of your perfume lingers, so all that I need to do is close my eyes and imagine you're with me. And, my love, don't ever doubt I want you with me. I'm praying that this feeling can hold me until Friday.

I love you.
Philip

Carla read his letter again and again, savoring each word, each line. Several times she ran her index finger back and forth over his declaration of love. Philip sounded so sure of things. Sure that they were right for each other. Sure that she could put her insecurities behind her. Sure that she would eventually marry him.

And Carla felt none of it. Every day the list of pros and cons grew longer. Philip, like her father, was an idealist. Carla wasn't convinced that being in love made everything a rose garden.

As for his invitation to have her come and root for him in the canoe race, Carla was sure that the real reason was so she could meet his friends. And she didn't need to be told that policemen usually socialized with other policemen. Her parents had few friends outside the force; the same undoubtedly held true for Philip. Friday was only a few days away, and finding someone willing to trade workdays would be difficult with half the staff scheduled for vacation time. It was a convenient excuse until she made up her mind what to do.

"Have you decided what you're going to tell him?" Nancy asked Tuesday evening, as she carted her luggage into the living room. After her last date with Cliff, Nancy had returned convinced she knew what she was feeling for Eduardo. When he'd pressed the invitation for her to meet his family, she hadn't hesitated.

"No," Carla answered dismally. "I'm afraid that I'll be dragged into his life little by little until we're married and I don't even know what happened."

"I think Philip's counting on that."

"I know." Carla nibbled on her bottom lip. Philip would be phoning later, and she still didn't know what she was going to tell him. If she told him outright that she wouldn't come, he'd accuse her of burying her head in the sand again. And he'd be right. But if she did agree, Carla realized that things would never be quite the same again. He had come to Seattle and invaded her world. He'd played checkers with Gramps and had dinner with her parents. She didn't feel safe anymore. Inch by inch, he was entwining their lives until it would be impossible for her to escape.

A happy, excited Nancy had left for Mexico by the

time Philip phoned. Carla stared at the phone for five long rings before she had the courage to answer.

"Hello." As hard as she tried, she couldn't disguise her unhappiness.

"Carla, what's wrong?" She wanted to cry at the gentle concern that coated his voice. "You aren't coming," he said, before she could answer.

"I . . . I don't know. Friday's a busy day at the hospital, and finding a replacement—"

"You don't want to come," he interrupted impatiently.

"It's not that." Carla leaned her hip against the counter and closed her eyes in defeat. "It's too soon for this sort of thing. I don't think I'm ready."

"For a canoe race!" Carla could feel his anger reverberate through her cell.

"You said you'd give me time and then you immediately start pushing at me. You're not playing fair, Philip Garrison. Don't force me into something I'm not ready to deal with yet."

"You mean to say you can't handle a social outing with my friends?"

"I don't know," she cried.

An unnatural, tension-filled silence followed. Carla struggled for some assurance to give him and found none. Maybe Philip was seeking the same. A full minute passed, and neither spoke, yet neither was willing to break off the connection.

Carla heard Philip take a deep breath. "All right, I won't push you. I said I'd be patient. When you decide if you're going to come, call me." From the tone of his voice, she knew that he was hurt and discouraged. "I'll be out most of the week—practicing with the rest of the team." Apparently, he wanted her to realize why he wouldn't be available. "If you can't reach me, I'll be waiting at the B & B Root Beer Drive-In in Soap Lake from seven to nine Friday night. It's on the main road going through town. You can't miss it. If you don't come, I'll understand."

"I'll call you before then." The lump in her throat made her voice sound tight.

"I'd appreciate that."

Again there was silence, and again it was obvious neither of them wished to end the conversation.

"I . . . I have some good news about Nancy," Carla said at last. "She's flying to Mexico City to meet Eduardo's family. From the way things have been progressing, I wouldn't be surprised if Nancy returned wearing an engagement ring."

"You could be, too," Philip told her in a tight voice, and Carla regretted having said anything. It'd been a mistake to bring up the subject of Nancy and Eduardo in light of their own circumstances.

"I know."

"But you're not ready? Right?"

"Right," Carla returned miserably.

The strained silence returned until Philip finally spoke, his voice devoid of anger. "Eduardo's a good man."

So are you, Carla mentally added.

"So you think Nancy may marry Eduardo?"

"It wouldn't surprise me," Carla said, forcing an air of cheerfulness into her voice. "Nancy's a lucky girl." The second the words were out, Carla desperately wanted to take them back. "Philip," she said contritely, and swallowed. "I didn't mean that the way it sounded."

"The problem is, I believe it's exactly what you mean. I'm not a good-looking Latin American who's going to impress your friends." His words were as cold as a blast of wind from the Arctic.

"Philip, you're everything I want in a man, except—"

"Except . . . I've heard it all before. Good-bye, Carla, if I see you Friday, that's fine. If not, that's fine, too."

The phone clicked in her ear and droned for several moments. The entire conversation had gone poorly. She'd hoped to at least start off in a lighter mood, and then explain her hesitancy about meeting him for the weekend. But she'd only succeeded in angering Philip. And he'd been furious. She knew him well enough to realize this type of cold wrath was rare. Most things rolled off him like rain on a well-waxed car. Only the important matters in his life could provoke this kind of deep anger. And Carla was important.

She still hadn't decided what to do by the time she joined her grandfather after work on Thursday for their regular game of checkers. Carla hoped he wouldn't try to influence her to go. She'd taken Gramps out to dinner Sunday afternoon, and he had done little else but talk about what a nice young man Philip was. By the end of the day, Carla had never been more pleased to take him back to the retirement home. She prayed today wouldn't be a repeat of last Sunday.

"Afternoon, Gramps," she greeted him, as she stepped into his small apartment.

Gramps had already set up the board and was sitting in his comfortable chair, waiting for her. "The more I think about that young man of yours, the more I like him."

"Philip's not my young man," she corrected, more tersely than she had intended. Carla had suspected this would happen when Philip met her family. Gramps and her dad had joined forces with Philip—it was unfair!

" 'The lady doth protest too much'—Shakespeare."

Carla laughed, her first real laugh in two days. She and Gramps played this game of quotes occasionally. " 'To be is to do'—Socrates," she tossed back lightly as she pulled out the rocking chair opposite him and sat down.

Gramps's eyes brightened and he stroked his chin, deep in contemplation. " 'To do is to be'—Sartre." He nodded curtly to Carla, and the set of his mouth said he doubted that she could match him.

" 'Do be do be do'—Sinatra," she said, and giggled. For the first time in recent memory, she'd outwitted her grandfather. Soon Gramps's deep chuckles joined her own, and his face shone with joy. "I'm going to miss you, girl."

"Miss me?" She opened the game of checkers by making the first move.

"When you and Philip marry, you'll be moving to Spokane to live with him."

Miſſed, Carla pressed her lips tightly together and removed her hand from the faded board. "Did he tell you that?"

"Nope." Gramps made his return move.

With her fingers laced together in her lap, Carla paused and looked up from the checkers. "Then what makes you think I'm going to marry him?"

"You'd be a fool not to. The boy clearly loves you, and even more obvious is the way you feel about him."

Carla returned her gaze to the checker pieces, but her mind wasn't on the game. "He's a cop, Gramps."

"So? Seems to me your daddy's been a fine officer of the law for twenty-odd years."

"And Mom's been miserable every minute of those twenty-odd years."

"Your mother's a worrier. It's in her blood," Gramps countered sharply. "She'd have fretted about your dad if he was the local dogcatcher."

"But I'm afraid of being like Mom," Carla declared vehemently. "I can't see myself pacing the floors alone at night when Philip's called on a case, or when he isn't and just goes away for a while to settle things in his head. Don't you have any idea of how much time Mom spends alone? She's by herself when she needs Dad. But he's out there"—she pointed to the world outside the apartment window—"making the city a better place to live and forgetting about his own wife and family." Her voice was high and faltering as she spewed out her doubts in one giant breath. "Gramps, I'm afraid. I'm afraid of loving the wrong man." Her fists were tightly clenched, and her nails cut painfully into her skin.

"And you think Philip is the wrong man?"

"I don't know anymore, Gramps. I'm so confused."

His gnarled hand reached across the checkers board and patted her arm. "And so in love."

Talking out her fears with Gramps had a releasing effect on her, Carla realized, as she walked around the lonely apartment hours later. Only a few days ago, Philip had been sitting on that couch, holding her as if he'd choose death rather than let her go.

Her gaze was drawn to her cell. She'd promised to call him by now and let him know if she was coming. Her heartbeat accelerated at the thought of hearing his voice. With trembling resolve, she reached for her phone and waited for the electronic bleeps to connect their lines.

Philip answered on the first ring with a disgruntled "Yes?"

"Do you always answer your phone like you want to bite off someone's head?" Just hearing his voice, unwelcome and surly as it was, had her heart pounding erratically.

A long pause followed. "Carla?"

"The one and only," she answered. Her voice throbbed with happiness. She'd pictured him lying back in an easy chair and relaxing. Now she envisioned him sitting up abruptly and rolling to his feet in disbelief. The imagery produced a deep smile of satisfaction.

"You called!" This time there was no disguising his incredulity.

"I said I would," she murmured softly.

"You've decided about the canoe race?"

"Yes."

"And?"

"First, I need to know if you're wearing your glasses."

"Good grief, Carla, what's that got to do with anything?"

"Do you have your glasses on or don't you?" she demanded arrogantly.

"Why?"

Carla was learning that he could be just as stubborn as she could. "Because what I'm about to say may steam them up, so I suggest you remove them."

Washington was known as the Evergreen State, but there was little evidence of any green in the eastern portion of the state—and none at all in the sagebrush, desertlike area in which Carla was traveling. Divided by the Cascade mountain range, Washington had a wet side and a dry side. In Seattle, summers and winters were less extreme—for example, although it was already mid-July, there had been only a handful of days above eighty-five degrees.

Carla shifted in the driver's seat of her compact car, hoping to find a more comfortable position. She'd been on the road for almost three hours and was miserably hot. Her bare thighs stuck to the seat of her car, and rivulets of perspiration trickled down the small valley between her breasts. Even Mazatlán hadn't seemed as hot.

Exiting off the interstate freeway at the town of George, Carla gassed up her car at the gas station and paused to look over the map a second time. Within an hour or so she would be meeting Philip. They'd been apart only six days, yet it felt more like six years. Carla didn't know how she was going to endure any long separations.

As he'd said he would, Philip was sitting at a picnic table in front of the B & B Drive-In. Carla savored the sight of him and did a quick self-inspection in her rearview mirror. Instantly, she was sorry she didn't freshen her makeup while at the gas station.

As she pulled into the drive-in's parking lot, she noticed that Philip had spotted her and was heading for her car. Carla's throat was dry, and she couldn't think of a thing to say.

"Hi." Philip opened the driver's-side door and gave her his hand, his face searching hers all the while, as if he couldn't quite believe she wasn't an apparition. The hand gripping hers tightened. "How was your trip?"

"Uneventful" was all Carla could manage.

Lightly, Philip brought her into his arms and brushed her cheek with his lips. Their eyes met as they parted, and still he didn't smile. "You really came," he said hoarsely.

She answered with a short nod. Philip had known without her fully explaining what her coming meant. The doubts, her determination to fight this relationship, were slowly dissolving. And coming here to meet his friends was a major step on her part.

"Jeff and Sylvia will be by in a few minutes." He led her to a picnic table. "Sit down and I'll get you something cool to drink."

"I can use that." Now that she was outside the car, the heat was even more sweltering.

Philip returned with two cold mugs of root beer. He set them on the table and sat opposite her. "I can't believe this. My heart's beating so fast I feel like an adolescent out on his first date."

"I feel the same way." She lowered her gaze to the root beer. Her fingers curled around the mug handle, and she took her first long drink. "I noticed in your note you said that you wanted me to talk to Sylvia."

Philip's hand reached for hers. "I think you two will have a lot in common."

"Does she feel the same way about Jeff's job as I do?" Carla asked tentatively.

"No." His voice was gently gruff. "But you're about the same age."

"Didn't you say she was pregnant with their first child?"

"Very." He said it with an odd little smile. "You'll be beautiful pregnant."

Carla could feel herself blushing. "Honestly, Philip," she murmured, her eyes looking troubled. "I wish you wouldn't say things like that."

"Why not? Last night after we finished talking, I was so happy that I lay in bed thinking I could run ten miles and not even feel it. But I didn't run. Instead, I lay there and closed my eyes, picturing what our lives would be like five years from now."

"And?" She was angry with herself for going along with this fantasy, but she couldn't help herself.

"You were in the kitchen cooking dinner when I walked in the back door. A little redheaded boy was playing at your feet, banging pots and pans with a wooden spoon. When you turned to me, I saw that you were pregnant. I swear, Carla, you were so beautiful I went weak. My heart stopped beating and my knees felt like putty. I don't think anything's ever affected me like that. I've never made any pretense about wanting you, and I'm not going to start now."

Carla busied herself by running her finger along the

rim of her mug, and when she lifted her gaze, their eyes met. "That's beautiful," she said, and was shocked at how low her voice was. The closeness she felt with him at that moment was beyond anything she had ever known. But she wished he wouldn't say such things to her. It only made her more miserable.

Silence fell between them, but Philip seemed content to watch her. Her hands trembled as she lifted the mug for another long drink. "Philip," she said and moaned, finding his continued scrutiny uncomfortable, "please stop looking at me like that. You're embarrassing me."

Immediately he dropped his gaze. "I didn't mean to. It seems I do everything wrong where you're concerned. I thought I'd play it cool today when you arrived. And the minute I saw you every nonchalant greeting I'd practiced died on my lips."

"Mine, too," she confessed shakily.

"I'm still having trouble believing that you came."

"We both need to thank Gramps for that."

"I think we should name our first son after him."

Carla shook her head. "He'd never forgive us for naming a boy Otis."

"We'll name him after your dad, then."

"He'd like that." Good heavens, the sun must have some effect on her mind. Here they were discussing the names of their children, and Carla wasn't even convinced she should marry Philip!

"Jeff and Sylvia are here," he announced, and his expression became sober. Carla turned and noticed a sky-blue half-ton pickup kick up gravel as it pulled into the parking lot.

A lanky fellow with a thick patch of dark hair jumped

down from the driver's seat and hurried around to help his obviously pregnant wife.

Sylvia, a petite blonde with warm blue eyes, pressed a hand to the small of her back as she ambled toward them. Carla guessed that Jeff's wife must be seven or eight months pregnant.

"Hi, you must be Carla." Jeff held out his hand, not waiting for an introduction.

"Hi. You must be Jeff."

Sylvia offered her a gracious smile. "I'm glad you could make it."

"The whole team's ecstatic she could make it. Philip hasn't been worth a damn since he got back from Mexico. I certainly hope you're going to put this poor guy out of his misery and marry him."

Carla's startled eyes clashed with Philip's. This was exactly what she'd feared would happen. She didn't want to have to answer these kinds of questions. They were bad enough coming from Philip and Gramps.

"I . . . I'm not sure what I'm going to do," she answered stiffly, her eyes challenging Philip.

Nine

～

The warm sun had disappeared beyond the horizon, and the sunbaked land cheerfully welcomed the cool breath of evening. The flickering flames of a campfire licked at the remaining pieces of dry wood.

Sylvia and Carla were the last to remain by the dying fire. The other women were busy tucking their little ones into bed, and the sound of their whispers and hushed giggles filled the still evening air. Carla and Sylvia glanced at each other and grinned. Next year Sylvia would be joining the other young mothers. And next year Carla . . . She closed her eyes and shook her head. She didn't know what she'd be doing.

Jeff, Philip, and the rest of the ten-man relay team were meeting to plan their strategy for the coming race. An air of excitement drifted through the campgrounds. The Great Soap Lake Canoe Race had dominated the conversation all afternoon. This was the first year the Spokane Police Department was competing, and their cheering squad held high expectations. For the last couple years, the eighteen-and-a-half-mile course had been won by a two-man marathon team in the amazing time of two hours and thirty minutes. Philip's teammates seemed to think that ten men in top physical condition could easily outmaneuver two. The most incredible fact, Carla thought, was that every team that had ever entered this outrageous competition had finished. "Carla?" Sylvia's voice broke into her reverie, and she looked up.

"Hmm?"

"Jeff didn't mean to put you on the spot this afternoon—about marrying Philip, I mean," Sylvia said shyly. "It's just that we all like him so much."

"I . . . like Philip, too." The toe of Carla's sandal traced lazy patterns in the dirt. "In fact, I love him."

"You didn't need to tell me that. It's obvious."

A sad smile played at the edges of Carla's mouth. She liked Sylvia. She'd discovered that she liked all of Philip's friends. They had welcomed her without hesitation and accepted her as a part of their group, going out of their way to include her in the conversation and activities. One of Philip's friends had worked in Seattle for a short time and remembered Carla's father. Perhaps that was the reason she was accepted so quickly, but Carla didn't like to think so.

"The natural thing to do when two people love one another is to get married," Sylvia suggested softly.

"Not always," Carla answered with an emotional tremor in her voice. "Oftentimes there are . . . extenuating circumstances. My father's a policeman."

"I heard." Sylvia slipped her arms into the sleeves of the thin sweater draped over her shoulders and leaned back against the folding chair. "I can understand your hesitancy. Being a policeman isn't the kind of work I would have chosen for Jeff. There are too many worries, too many potential dangers that affect both our lives. But Jeff's career is an important part of who he is. It was a package deal, and I've had to learn to accept it. Each police wife must come to grips with it sooner or later."

"Philip's got to be the most patient man in the world to put up with me."

"He loves you." Sylvia smiled. "I remember the first week after Philip returned from Mexico. Jeff complained every night." She paused and laughed softly. "A lovesick Philip took us all by surprise. We just didn't expect him to be so human. He's been as solid as a rock, and we were shocked to discover he's as vulnerable as the rest of us."

"He was in love with a flight attendant a few years ago. Did you ever meet Nicole?"

"No." Sylvia shook her head slowly. "That was before I married Jeff. But I can remember him mentioning how hard Philip took it when they split up. I think Jeff's worried the same thing is going to happen again."

Rather than offer reassurances she didn't have, Carla said, "Philip's like that. Everything is done full measure."

"Everything," Sylvia agreed.

"Nicole was a fool to let him go." Carla paused and sucked in her breath, realizing what she'd just said. She'd be a fool to allow her fears and inhibitions to ruin her life. Yet something within her, some unresolved part of herself, couldn't accept what Philip was. The other wives had come to terms, appreciating their men for what they were. Carla hadn't honored Philip's commitment to his career, just as her mother had never been able to fully respect her father's dedication to his. The thought was so profound that it caused Carla to straighten. Maybe for the first time in her life, she needed to talk with her mother.

"Would you like some help out of that chair, Mommy?" Jeff asked as he stepped behind his wife and lovingly rested his hand on her shoulder.

"Next time, I'm going to let him be the one to get pregnant," Sylvia teased, and extended her hand, accepting her husband's offer of assistance.

With their arms wrapped around each other, Jeff and Sylvia headed toward their tent.

"Night, Carla," Sylvia called back with a yawn. "I'll see you in the morning."

"Night."

"Are you tired?" Philip asked, as he took the chair Sylvia had vacated.

"Not yet." Not when she could spend a few minutes alone with Philip. Not when they could sit undisturbed in the quiet of the night and talk. There were so many things she wanted to tell him. But in the peaceful solitude by the campfire, none of them seemed important.

"It's a beautiful night," he murmured, as he leaned back and stared up at the sky. "In fact, tonight reminds me of Mexico and this incredibly lovely woman I once held in my arms."

"If I close my eyes, I can almost hear the surf against the shore," Carla responded, joining his game. "And if I try, really try, I can picture this incredibly wonderful man I met in Mexico sitting across from me."

Philip's chuckle was deep and warm. "How hard do you need to try?"

"It's not so difficult, really."

"I should hope not." Philip smiled and moved his chair so that they were sitting side by side. When he sat back down and reached for her hand, Carla glanced at him. His strong face was profiled in the moonlight, his look deep and thoughtful.

"Have you got your strategy all worked out, oh master of the canoe race?" she asked lightly. His pensive look troubled her. She didn't want anything to ruin these few minutes alone together; this wasn't the time to discuss her doubts or find the answers to nagging questions.

"Pretty much." He grimaced and quickly disguised a look of pain.

"Philip, what's wrong?" Her voice was unnaturally high with concern. "You're not feeling well, are you?" Immediately she knelt at his side and touched his brow, which was cool and revealed no sign of a fever.

"It's nothing." He tried to dispel her worry with a wide grin. "Nerves, I think. I'm always this way before a race."

Returning to her chair, Carla nodded. "I had the lead in a play when I was in the eighth grade, and I was deathly sick before the first performance. I know what you mean."

"Have you and Sylvia decided where you're going to position yourselves to cheer us on?"

Apparently, Philip didn't want to talk about his nerves: this Carla understood and could sympathize. "At the finish line. Sylvia isn't in any condition to go running from lake to lake with the rest of the team. So we've decided to plant ourselves there and wait for our dedicated heroes to bring in the trophy."

"You may have a long wait," Philip said wryly and grimaced again.

Carla decided not to comment this time, but she was concerned. "Five lakes, Philip. Are you guys honestly going to canoe across five lakes?"

"We're going to paddle like crazy across each one, then lift the boat over our heads and run like madmen to the checkpoint. From there the next two-man team will take the canoe and the whole process will start again."

"Which lakes?" Carla had heard them mentioned only fleetingly.

"Park, Blue, Alkali, Lenore, and Soap."

"I think you're all a little nuts."

"We must be," Philip agreed soberly. "But to be honest, I'd swim, hike, canoe, and run a lot farther than a few miles for an excuse to have you with me." He raised her fingers to his lips and kissed the back of her hand.

He studied her in the moonlight, and, feeling wretched, Carla lowered her eyes. "I don't know how you can love me," she murmured.

"Patience has its own rewards."

"I do love you." But a declaration of love, she knew, was only a small part of what he wanted from her.

"I know." He stood and offered her his arm. "I think we should both turn in. Tomorrow's going to be a full day." His voice was bland, almost impersonal, but his tone was at odds with the look in his eyes. Carla would have sworn he was hiding something from her, and it was a whole lot more than nerves.

Philip's kiss outside her tent was brief, as if he was

more preoccupied with the race than he was with having her near. It could be nerves, but they'd seen each other only twice since Mexico and she'd thought he'd do a whole lot more than peck her cheek when it came time to say good night. A hand on her hip, Carla tipped her head to one side and flashed him a confused glance as he turned toward the tent he was sharing with another officer. Carla didn't know what was troubling Philip, but she'd bet hard cash it had nothing to do with her or the race. But whatever it was, he wasn't going to tell her. That hurt; it seemed to prove that Philip didn't feel he could discuss his problems with her. He wanted her to share his life, but there was a part of himself he would always hold back. The same way her father had from her mother.

Carla didn't know there were this many people in all eastern Washington. The start of the race was jam-packed with participants, friends, casual observers, and cheering fans. Some of the contestants wore identifying uniforms that would distinguish themselves as being looney enough to participate in such a laughable race.

Everyone had been laughing and joking before the race, but when the gun went off, the competition began in earnest; each team was determined to win.

Jumping up and down with the others and clapping as hard as she could, Carla was caught up in the swirl of craziness that seemed to have engulfed the entire city of Soap Lake.

Three hours later, when Philip and Jeff crossed the

finish line, placing a respectable fifth, Carla and Sylvia had cheered and laughed themselves weak.

Dramatically throwing themselves down on the grass, both men lay staring at the cloudless blue sky, panting.

Jeff spoke first. "Next year," he managed breathlessly, "we'll go after the trophy."

Sitting around the picnic table at the campgrounds later that afternoon, Philip positioned himself by Carla's side and casually draped his arm over her shoulder. "Do you think we should compete again next year?"

Carla lowered her hot dog to the plate. "It'd be a shame not to. You were only twenty minutes off the best time, and with a little practice you're bound to improve. Don't you agree?"

"On one condition. That you promise to be on my cheering squad again next year." His eyes searched hers, seeming to need reassurance.

Confidently, Carla placed her hand on his. "You got it." The sun beamed off the gold band of her watch, and Carla noticed the time and groaned.

"What's the matter?"

"I've got to leave."

"Now?"

Sadly, she shook her head. "Soon. In order to have Friday afternoon free, I traded days with another girl who's on call tomorrow."

"Which means?" His eyes narrowed.

"Which means I have to be back tonight by midnight, in case there's an emergency."

Standing, Philip tossed his paper plate in the garbage

can. Carla dumped the remainder of her lunch away and followed Philip to a large oak tree, where he stood, staring at the ground.

"It was hardly worth your while to make the trip. I'm surprised you came."

"I'm glad I did. I enjoyed meeting your friends, especially Sylvia and Jeff."

He pursed his lips, and Carla studied him suspiciously. He looked as if he wanted to argue, and she couldn't understand why. Planting herself in front of him, her legs braced slightly apart, she stared at him until he met her gaze. "It's not going to work, you know."

He frowned. "What's not going to work?"

"Starting an argument. I refuse to react to your anger. I wish I could stay. If it was up to me, I would. But circumstances being what they are, I've got to leave this afternoon." She paused and drew a long breath. "Now. Will you walk me to the tent and spend the next few minutes saying good-bye to me properly, or are you going to stand here and pout?"

Philip bristled. "I never pout."

"Good." She smiled and reached for his hand. "Then let's escape for a few minutes of privacy before someone comes looking for us."

The sun was setting, whisking back the splashes of warm, golden rays, by the time Carla pulled into her apartment parking space. After emerging from the car, she stretched, raising her arms high above her head and yawning. The trip back had been leisurely and had taken the better part of three hours. Philip had promised to connect as soon as he was back in Spokane. That brooding, troubled look had returned when he'd kissed her good-bye. Carla didn't know what was bothering him, but she guessed that it had nothing to do with her. Already he was acting like her father, afraid to tell her something he knew could upset her. If she was going to consider being his wife, she didn't want him treading lightly around information she had a right to know. She'd ask him about it Monday night.

Sunday afternoon, while on call at the hospital, Carla drove to her parents' house.

"Hi, Mom," she said as she let herself in the front door. Rachel Walker was sitting on the worn sofa, knitting a sweater.

"Who's this one for?" Carla asked, as she sat across from her mother, admiring the collage of colored yarn. Rachel was constantly doing something—idle hands led to boredom, she had always said. She was a perfectionist housekeeper, and now that Carla and her brother had left home, she busied herself with craft projects.

"Julianne," her mother replied without a pause between stitches, her fingers moving with a skill that was amazing. "She'll need a warm sweater this fall for first grade. She's six now, you know."

"Yes." Both her nieces had always been special to Carla, and she'd missed them terribly since her brother and his wife had moved to Oregon.

"Where's Dad?"

Briefly, a hurt look rushed across her mother's face.

"He's playing on the men's softball team again this year." The Seattle Police Department had several teams, and Carla's father loved to participate, but her mother had never gone to watch him play, preferring to stay at home. What Joe did outside the house was his business, because it involved the police force—and Rachel had never had anything to do with the force.

"Actually, I'm glad Dad isn't here, because I'd like to talk to you alone."

"To me?" Momentarily, Rachel glanced up from her handiwork.

"I'm in love with Philip Garrison," Carla announced, and closed her eyes, preparing for the backlash that was sure to follow.

"I think I already knew that," her mother replied calmly. "In fact, your father and I were just talking about the two of you."

"And?"

"We agreed that you and Philip will do fine. What I said to you the other night isn't altogether valid. We are alike, Carla, in many ways, but in others we're completely different."

Carla marveled at the way her mother could talk so frankly with her and at the same time keep perfect pace with her knitting.

"Joe pointed out that your personality is stronger than I've given you credit for. You're not afraid to say what you feel or to speak out against injustice. Your work at the hospital proves that . . ." Rachel paused, and after taking a shuddering breath, she bit her bottom lip.

Carla moved out of the chair and kneeled at her mother's side. Rachel tossed her yarn aside and leaned forward to hug her daughter as she hadn't since Carla was a child. "I would have chosen another man for you, Princess. But I can't hold against Philip the very things that make me love your father. Be happy, baby. Be happy."

"I love you, Mom," Carla murmured. She'd never thought she'd feel this close to her mother. Philip had done that for her. He had given her the parent she had never thought she'd understand—the closeness every daughter yearns to share with her mother.

Carla laughed and said, "It's not every day your only daughter decides to get married. Could we do something together? Just you and me."

Leaning back in the cushioned sofa, Rachel reached for a tissue and blew her nose. "What do you want to do?"

"Can we go to Dad's softball game?"

For a second Rachel looked stunned. But gradually a smile formed at the edges of her mouth. "I've been waiting twenty years for an excuse to do just that."

Monday afternoon, on her way home from the hospital, Carla stopped off to visit Gramps, but she stayed just long enough for a single game of checkers and to tell him she'd made a decision about Philip.

"So you've come to your senses and decided you're going to marry him?"

"If he'll have me."

"No worry there," Gramps said with a chuckle. "The problem, as I see it, is if you're ready to be the right person for a man like Philip."

Carla didn't hesitate. "I know I am. Philip is a policeman, and I should know what that means. After all, I've been a policeman's daughter all my life."

His eyes beamed with pride as he slowly shook his head. "I see you've come to terms with that. Now I pray that you'll be as good a wife as your mother has been all these years."

"I hope I can, too," Carla added soberly.

The phone rang just as she let herself into the apartment. Carla dumped her purse on the kitchen table and grabbed the phone.

"Hello."

"Carla. Thank heaven I caught you. Where have you been? This is Jeff, Philip's partner."

Carla felt the blood rush from her face. Jeff would be phoning her only if something had happened to Philip. Her knees went weak, and she leaned heavily against the counter. "We aren't allowed to keep our cell phones with us while on duty. What is it?"

"Apparently, you didn't check your messages, either. Philip's in the hospital. I think you should get here as soon as possible. I checked with Alaska Airlines, and there's a flight leaving Seattle in two hours. If you can be on it, I'll pick you up in the patrol car and take you directly to him."

Ten

~

"What happened?" Somehow Carla managed to get the words past the bubble of hysteria that threatened to overtake her.

"We were on patrol and . . . It was my fault, I should have known what was happening. With all the medical training I've had, I can't believe I didn't know what was going on. But I got him to the hospital in record time. Listen, Carla, I can't explain everything now. Just get here. Philip asked for you when he came out of surgery. I want to tell him that you're coming."

"Yes . . . of course, I'm on my way now. And, Jeff"— her hand tightened around her phone—"thanks for letting me know."

Unable to move, Carla felt an almost tangible fear move through her body. Her senses reeled with it. Her mouth was dry, her hands were clammy, her knees felt weak. Even the rhythmic beating of her heart slowed. It seemed unfair that once she had reconciled herself to who and what Philip was, her newfound confidence should be severely tested this way. With a resolve born of love, Carla had thought she could face anything. Now she realized how wrong she was. She would never come to terms with losing Philip.

By rote, she reached for her phone and contacted her parents. "Mom," she cried, not waiting for a greeting, "Philip's been shot." Carla heard her mother's soft gasp and fought her own rising panic. "He's just out of surgery and I'm flying to be with him. Call the hospital and explain that I won't be in. And let Gramps know."

"When's your flight?"

Carla ran her hands through her hair. "In two hours. . . . There's a flight on Alaska, but I . . . I . . ."

"You pack," her mother said, taking over. "I'll call the airport for you. Your father will be there in ten minutes to drive you. Don't worry, Princess, Philip will be fine." Her mother hadn't any more information than Carla, but the gentle reassurance gave her the courage to think clearly.

Carla yanked clothes off the hanger and stuffed them into a suitcase. After adding her toothbrush, curling iron, and a comb, she slammed the lid closed. She'd be fine if only she could stop shaking. Pausing, she forced herself to take several deep, calming breaths. The shock of Jeff's call prevented tears, but she knew those would come later.

The doorbell rang, and Carla rushed across the living room to open the door.

"You ready?" Her father looked as pale as she did, Carla realized, but she knew he was far too disciplined to display his emotion openly.

She gave an abrupt nod, and he took the small suitcase out of her hand and cupped her elbow as they hurried down the flight of stairs to the apartment parking lot. During the ten-minute drive to Sea-Tac International Airport, Carla could feel her father's concerned scrutiny.

"Are you going to be okay, Princess? Do you want your mother with you?"

"No, I'm fine," she said, and with a sad smile amended, "I think I'm fine. If anything happens to Philip, I don't know that I'll ever get over it."

"Cross that bridge when you come to it," he advised. "And phone as soon as you know his condition."

"I will," she promised.

Jeff was nervously pacing the tiled airport floor when Carla spotted him just minutes after stepping off the plane. Without hesitation, she ran to him and gripped his forearm. "How's Philip?" Her eyes pleaded with him to tell her everything was fine.

"There weren't any complications. But apparently I misunderstood him. He said he *didn't* want you to know."

"Didn't want me to know?" she echoed incredulously. If that bullet didn't kill him, she would. Philip was lying on a hospital bed wanting to protect her from the unpleasant aspects of his occupation. It infuriated her, and at the same time she felt an overpowering surge of love.

"Just before I left, the doctors told me it would be several hours before he wakes."

Carla weighed Jeff's words carefully. "Take me to the hospital. I want to be there when he wakes."

A smile cracked the tight line of Jeff's mouth. "As the

lady requests. Tell him the decision was yours and I'm not responsible."

"I'll tell him," she said and winked.

"Great." He looked at his watch. "I'm afraid I can't take you to the hospital personally; I'm still on duty. But another friend of ours will get you there safely. If you like, I can take your things and drop them off at Philip's condo."

"Yes . . . that'll be fine."

Jeff introduced Bill Bower, a ruddy-faced officer Carla didn't recognize from the previous weekend. Bill nodded politely, and after saying good-bye to Jeff, the two of them headed for Bill's car.

"Can you tell me what happened?" she asked Bill when they were on the freeway. During the flight, she had prepared herself to hear the details of what exactly had gone wrong. In some ways, Carla realized that she didn't want to know. It wasn't important, as long as Philip was alive and well. There would be time for explanations later, when Philip could make them himself. But knowing that he would make light of the incident, she'd hoped to get a fuller version of the story on the way to the hospital.

"I wasn't there," Bill stated matter-of-factly, "so I don't know how it happened. But Philip was in tremendous pain, and Jeff may have saved his life by getting him to the hospital as quickly as he did."

Carla paled at the thought of Philip in agony. He'd be the type to suffer nobly. Her lips felt dry, and she moistened them.

The stoic-faced officer must have caught her involuntary action. "I wouldn't worry. Philip's healthy and strong. But he's bound to be in a foul mood, so don't pay any mind to what he says."

"No, I won't," she replied with a brave smile.

The hospital smelled faintly of antiseptic. Carla was admitted into Philip's room without question, which surprised her. Seeing him lying against the white sheets, tubes coming out of his arms, nearly undid her. She sank gratefully into the chair beside his bed.

"The doctor will be in later if you have any questions," the efficient nurse explained.

"I'll be leaving now," added Bill. "If you need anything, don't hesitate to call. Jeff will be back later tonight."

"Thanks, Bill."

"All the thanks I want is an invitation to the wedding."

"It's yours." She tried to smile, but the effort was painful.

Still wrapped in the warm comfort of sleep, Philip did little more than roll his head from one side to the other during the next two hours. Content just to be close to him, Carla did little more than hold his fingers in hers and press her cheek to the back of his hand.

"Carla?"

Forcing herself to smile, Carla raised her head and met Philip's gaze.

"Is it really you, or is this some befuddling dream?"

"If I kiss you, you'll know for sure." Gently, she moved to the head of his bed and leaned forward to press her lips to his. Philip's hand found her hair, and he wove his fingers through its rusty curls.

"Oh Philip, are you going to be all right?" she moaned, burying her face in the side of his neck.

"Stay awhile longer, and I'll prove it," he whispered against her temple.

He lifted his gaze to hers, and the intense look in those steel-gray eyes caught her breath. A muscle worked in his lean jaw as his gaze roamed possessively over her face. "I didn't want Jeff to contact you."

"I know, but I'm here now and nothing's going to make me leave." Her hand clasped his as she took the seat beside the bed.

"What did Jeff say when he phoned? He has a high sense of theatrics, you realize."

"You warned me about that once before. He said that you'd just come out of surgery and had asked for me."

"What I asked was that he not contact you. I didn't want you worrying."

"Philip Garrison, if you think you can keep something like getting shot from me"—she tried to disguise the hurt in her voice—"you've got a second think coming, because I can assure you, wild canoe racers wouldn't keep me away from you at a time like this."

"Shot?" His breath quickened as he raised his head slightly to study her. "Jeff told you I was shot? I'll kill him."

"Well, good heavens, something like a gunshot wound is a little difficult to keep from me. Just how were you planning to tell me about it? 'Carla, darling,'" she mimicked in a deep rumbling voice, "'I guess I should explain that I got scratched while on duty today. I'll be in the hospital a week or so, but it's nothing to worry about.' "

"Carla . . ." His voice was a husky growl. "If I told you I'd been shot, paranoia would overtake you so quickly that I'd never catch you, you'd be running so fast."

"It's a high opinion you've got of me, isn't it?" she asked in a shaky voice. "You're missing the point. I did learn what happened, and I'm here, because it's exactly where I want to be."

"Only because Jeff made it sound as if I were on my deathbed."

"He said you asked for me—that's all."

"And I hadn't."

Sitting became intolerable, and she stood, pacing the floor with her arms gently wrapped around her to ward off the chill in his voice.

"As it is, you've wasted a trip. There won't be any deathbed scene. I was never in any danger from a gunshot wound. I had my appendix out."

Carla pivoted sharply and her mouth dropped open. "Your appendix out?"

"If you need proof, lift the sheet and see for yourself."

She ignored the heavy sarcasm lacing his voice. "Then why did Jeff—" What kind of fool game was Philip's friend playing, anyway? Did he feel he needed to fabricate stories to convince her to come?

"That's exactly what I intend to find out."

Silence hovered over them like a heavy thundercloud.

"I don't mean to be rude, but I'm not exactly in the mood for company, Carla."

She'd thought he'd been shot and all the while it was

his appendix. To her humiliation, she sniffled and her soft breath became a hiccupping sob. Frantically, she searched for her purse, needing to get out of the room before she humiliated herself further.

"Carla. Don't go," he said and groaned in frustration. "I didn't mean that. I'm sorry."

"That's all right," she mumbled shakily, wiping the tears from her pale cheeks. A kaleidoscope of emotions whirled through her—shock, relief, hurt, anger, joy. "I understand."

"This is exactly what I didn't want. If it had been up to me, you wouldn't even have known I was in the hospital. I don't want you worrying about me."

"You didn't even want me to know you were in the hospital?" Carla closed her eyes. She didn't want to think about the life they'd have if Philip insisted on shielding her from anything unpleasant. She wondered how he'd feel if the tables were turned. By heaven, she was going to get Jeff for this. She'd arrived expecting something far worse, and he'd let her believe it!

"I may be out of line here, but didn't you ask me to marry you not long ago?" she reminded him.

Philip looked at her blankly. "What's that got to do with anything?"

"Doesn't a wife or a fiancée or even the woman in your life have a right to know certain things?"

His hand covered his weary eyes. "Do you mind very much if we discuss this at another time? Go back to Seattle, Carla. I'll call you when I'm in a better frame of mind, and we can discuss it then."

Placing four fingers at her temple, she executed a crisp military salute. "Aye, aye, Commandant."

Carla couldn't tell whether the sound Philip made was a chuckle or a snort, and she didn't stay long enough in his room to find out.

Luckily, Jeff was due to arrive at the hospital within a half-hour. Her anger mounted by the time Philip's partner arrived. The minute he appeared, she stood, prepared for battle.

"That was a rotten trick you pulled," she declared with clenched teeth.

"Trick?" Jeff looked stunned. "I didn't pull any trick."

"You told me Philip had been shot."

Jeff looked all the more taken aback. "I didn't."

"You implied as much," she returned, barely managing to keep her voice even.

"How could you have thought he'd been shot? Especially since he was feeling so crummy during the canoe race. Saturday night someone suggested it could be his appendix, and . . ." Jeff swallowed, looking chagrined. "That's right, you left early. Phil was feeling even crummier later, and I think we all should have known what was wrong. Listen, I apologize; I thought you knew. You must have been frantic. I wouldn't have frightened you, had—"

"It's all right." Carla accepted his apology with a wry grin. Obviously she had read more into his comments than he had intended. The misunderstanding hadn't been intentional.

"I'd better explain to Philip," Jeff said with a thoughtful look. "He's probably mad as hops."

"It's best to let the beast rest for now. If you want, you can explain later."

One glance at Carla was enough to convince him that Carla knew what she was talking about. The ride through Spokane seemed to take forever, and when Jeff stopped at a traffic light, Carla couldn't hold back a giggle.

"What's so funny?" Jeff glanced at her curiously.

"I don't know . . . Just my thoughts, I guess. I assumed that someone as wonderful as Philip would be a good patient. I thought he'd be the type of man to suffer silently . . . and he's terrible. Just terrible."

"Give him a day or two," Jeff advised good-humoredly. "He'll come around."

Philip's condominium was located in the heart of the city near the Spokane River. "Here are the keys to his car," Jeff said, handing them to her after unlocking the front door. They stood just inside the entryway. "Bill dropped it off on his way home tonight. Listen . . ." Jeff paused and ran his hand along the side of his short-cropped hair. "Sylvia called and said she was feeling strange. I don't know what that means, but I think I should head home. I have this irrational fear that the baby is going to come into this world without me coaching, and I'd hate to think that all those classes would go to waste. Call if you need anything, all right?"

"Sure. Go on, and give Sylvia my best."

"I will. Thanks."

Jeff was out the door, and Carla turned to interrupt Philip's orderly life even more by invading his home. Maybe he was right; maybe she should take her things and head back to Seattle. No, she wouldn't do that. Things between them had to be settled now.

The first thing that caught Carla's attention was the hand-carved marlin that she'd given Philip. He'd set it on the fireplace mantel. A photo of them together in Mexico sat on his dresser. Carla was smiling into the camera as the wind whipped up her soft russet curls. Philip's head was turned and his eyes were on her. There was so much love in his expression that Carla breathed a soft sigh as she examined the framed photo.

Her letters to him were stacked on the kitchen table. Each one had been read so many times that the edges had begun to curl. Carla took one look and recognized again that there wasn't any man on earth who would love her as much as Philip did. And, more important, there would never be anyone she could love as much.

After a reassuring phone call to her parents, she took a long shower and slept fitfully.

She waited until noon the next day before venturing outside the condominium. Driving Philip's car to the hospital proved to be eventful. Twice she got lost, but with the friendly help of a local gas station attendant, she finally located the hospital.

A nurse on Philip's floor gave her a suspicious look as she walked down the wide corridor carrying a guitar.

One loud knock against his door was all the warning she gave.

"Carla."

She suspected it was relief she heard in his voice, but she didn't pause to question him. Instead, she pulled out the chair beside his bed, sat at an angle on the cushion, and strummed one discordant chord. With that, she proceeded to serenade him in the only song she knew in Spanish.

He started to laugh, but quickly grimaced and tried to contain his amusement. "Why are you singing to me the A, B, C's?"

"It's the only Spanish song I know all the way through. However, if you'd like to hear parts of 'Mary Had a Little Lamb,' I'll be happy to comply."

Extending a hand to her, he shook his head. "The only thing I want is you."

"That's a different tune than you were singing yesterday."

"Yesterday I was an unreasonable boor." He pulled her closer to his side. "I'm glad you're here. Today I promise to be a much better patient."

"Once we're married, I suspect I'll have ways of helping you out of those irrational moods."

The room went quiet as Philip's eyes sought hers. "Once we're married."

"You did ask me, and you better not have changed your mind, because I've already given my two-week notice at the hospital."

"Carla." His gray eyes reflected an intensity she had rarely witnessed. "Do you mean it?"

"I've never been more serious in my life. But I won't have you holding out on me. If I'm going to be your wife, I expect you to trust me enough not to try to shield me from whatever comes our way. I'm stronger than I look, Philip Garrison."

"Far stronger," he agreed, as his hand slipped around

her waist. "You've already convinced me of that. I love you, Carla Walker—soon to be Carla Garrison."

Tenderness surged through her as she slipped her arms over his shoulders. "But not near soon enough," she said with a sigh of longing as her mouth eagerly sought his.

Laughter in the Rain

One

"I'm so late. I'm so late."

The words were like a chant in Abby Carpenter's mind with every frantic push of the bike pedals. She was late. A worried glance at her watch when she paused at the traffic light confirmed that Mai-Ling would already be in Diamond Lake Park, wondering where Abby was. Abby should have known better than to try on that lovely silk blouse, but she'd seen it in the store's display window and couldn't resist. Now she was paying for the impulse.

The light turned green and Abby pedaled furiously, rounding the corner to the park entrance at breakneck speed.

Panting, she stopped in front of the bike stand and secured her lock around a concrete post. Then she ran across the lush green lawn to the picnic tables, where she normally met Mai-Ling. Abby felt a rush of relief when she spotted her.

Mai-Ling had recently immigrated to Minneapolis

from Hong Kong. As a volunteer for the World Literacy Movement, Abby was helping the young woman learn to read English. Mai-Ling caught sight of her and waved eagerly. Abby, who'd been meeting her every Saturday afternoon for the past two months, was impressed by her determination to master English.

"I'm sorry I'm late," Abby apologized breathlessly.

Mai-Ling shrugged one shoulder. "No problem," she said with a smile.

That expression demonstrated how quickly her friend was adapting to the American way of speaking— and life.

Mai-Ling started to giggle.

"What's so funny?" Abby asked as she slid off her backpack and set it on the picnic table.

Mai-Ling pointed at Abby's legs.

Abby looked down and saw one red sock and one that was blue. "Oh dear." She sighed disgustedly and sat on the bench. "I was in such a rush I didn't even notice." No wonder the salesclerk had given her a funny look. Khaki shorts, mismatched socks, and a faded T-shirt from the University of Minnesota.

"I am laughing with you," Mai-Ling said in imperfect English.

Abby understood what she meant. Mai-Ling wanted to be sure Abby realized she wasn't laughing *at* her. "I know," she said as she zipped open the backpack and took out several workbooks.

Mai-Ling sat opposite Abby. "The man's here again," she murmured.

"Man?" Abby twisted around. "What man?"

Abby couldn't believe she'd been so unobservant. She

felt a slight twinge of apprehension as she looked at the stranger. There was something vaguely familiar about him, and that bothered her. Then she remembered—he was the same man she'd seen yesterday afternoon at the grocery store. Had he been following her?

The man turned and leaned against a tree not more than twenty feet away, giving her a full view of his face. His tawny hair gleamed in the sunshine that filtered through the leaves of the huge elm. Beneath dark brows were deep-set brown eyes. Even from this distance Abby could see their intense expression. His rugged face seemed to be all angles and planes. He was attractive in an earthy way that would appeal to a lot of women, and Abby was no exception.

"He was here last week," Mai-Ling said. "And the week before. He was watching you."

"Funny, I don't remember seeing him," she murmured, unable to disguise her discomfort.

"He is a nice man, I think. The animals like him. I am not worried about him."

"Then I won't worry, either," Abby said with a shrug as she handed Mai-Ling the first workbook.

In addition to being observant, Mai-Ling was a beautiful, sensitive, and highly intelligent woman. Sometimes she became frustrated with her inability to communicate, but Abby was astonished at her rapid progress. Mai-Ling had mastered the English alphabet in only a few hours and was reading level two books.

A couple of times while Mai-Ling was reading a story about a woman applying for her first job, Abby's attention drifted to the stranger. She watched in astonishment as he coaxed a squirrel down the trunk of a tree. He

pulled what appeared to be a few peanuts from his
pocket, and within seconds the squirrel was eating out
of his hand. As if aware of Abby's scrutiny, he stood up
and sauntered lazily to the nearby lakeshore. The instant
he appeared, the ducks squawked as though recognizing
an old friend. The tall man took bread crumbs from a
sack he carried and fed them. Lowering himself to a
crouch, he threw back his head and laughed.

Abby found herself smiling. Mai-Ling was right, this
man had a way with animals—and women, too, if her
pounding heart was anything to judge by.

A few times Mai-Ling faltered over a word, and Abby
paused to help her.

The hour sped by, and soon it was time for the young
woman to meet her bus. Abby walked Mai-Ling to the
busy street and waited until she'd boarded, cheerfully
waving to Abby from the back of the bus.

Pedaling her bicycle toward her apartment, Abby let
her thoughts again drift to the tall, good-looking
stranger. She had to admit she was enthralled. She wondered if he was attracted to her, too, since apparently he
came to the park every week while she was there. But
maybe she wasn't the one who attracted him; perhaps it
was Mai-Ling. No, she decided. Mai-Ling had noticed
the way the handsome stranger studied Abby. He was
interested *in her. Great,* she mused contentedly. Logan
Fletcher could do with some competition.

Abby pulled into the parking lot of her low-rise
apartment building and climbed off her bike. Automatically she reached for her backpack, which she'd placed
on the rack behind her, to get the apartment keys. Nothing. Surprised, Abby turned around to look for it. But it

wasn't there. Obviously she'd left it at the park. *Oh no!* She exhaled in frustration and turned, prepared to go and retrieve her pack.

"Looking for this?" A deep male voice startled Abby and her heart almost dropped to her knees. The bike slipped out from under her and she staggered a few steps before regaining her balance.

"Don't you know better than to sneak up on someone like that? I could have . . ." The words died on her lips as she whirled around to face the stranger. With her mouth hanging half open she stared into the deepest brown eyes she'd ever seen—the man from the park.

Her tongue-tied antics seemed to amuse him, but then it could also have been her mismatched socks. "You forgot this." He handed her the backpack. Speechless, Abby took it and hugged it to her stomach. She felt grateful . . . and awkward. She started to thank him when another thought came to mind.

"How'd . . . How'd you know where I live?" The words sounded slightly scratchy, and she cleared her throat.

He frowned. "I've frightened you, haven't I?"

"How'd you know?" She repeated the question less aggressively. He hadn't scared her. If anything, she felt a startling attraction to him, to the sheer force of his masculinity. Logan would be shocked. For that matter, so was she. But up close, this man was even more appealing than he'd been at a distance.

"I followed you," he said simply.

"Oh." A thousand confused emotions dashed through her mind. He was so good-looking that Abby couldn't manage another word.

"I didn't mean to scare you," he said, regret in his voice.

"You didn't," she hurried to assure him. "I have an overactive imagination."

Shaking his head, he thrust his hands into his pants pockets. "I'll leave before I do any more damage."

"Please don't apologize. I should be thanking you. There's a Coke machine around the corner. Would you like to—"

"I've done enough for one day." Abruptly, he turned to go.

"At least tell me your name." Abby didn't know where the request came from; it tumbled from her lips before she'd even formed the thought.

"Tate." He tossed it over his shoulder as he stalked away.

"Bye, Tate," she called as he opened his car door. When he glanced her way, she lifted her hand. "And thanks."

A smile curved his mouth. "I like your socks," he returned.

Pointedly she looked down at the mismatched pair. "I'm starting a new trend," she said with a laugh.

Standing beside her bike, Abby waited until Tate had driven away.

Later that night, Logan picked her up and they had hamburgers, then went to a movie. Logan's obligatory good-night kiss was . . . pleasant. That was the only way Abby could describe it. She had the impression that Logan kissed her because he always kissed her good night. To her dismay, she had to admit that there'd never been any driving urgency behind his kisses. They'd been dating almost a year and the mysterious Tate was capable of stirring more emotion with a three-minute conversation than Logan had all evening. Abby wasn't even sure why they continued to date. He was an accountant whose office was in a building near hers. They had many of the same friends and did plenty of things together, but their relationship was in a rut. The time had come to add a little spice to her life, and Abby knew exactly where that spice would be coming from . . .

After Logan had left, Abby settled into the overstuffed chair that had once belonged to her grandfather and picked up a new thriller she'd bought that week.

Dano, her silver-eyed cat, crawled into her lap as Abby opened the book. Absently, she stroked the length of his spine. Her hand froze in mid-stroke as she discovered the hero's name: Logan. Slightly unnerved, she dropped the book and jumped up from her chair to look for the remote. Turning on the TV, she told herself she shouldn't feel guilty because she felt attracted to another man. The first thing she saw on the screen was a commercial for Logan Furniture's once-a-year sofa sale. Abby stared at the flashing name and hit the off button. This was crazy! Logan wouldn't care if she was interested in someone else. He might even be grateful. Their relationship was based on friendship and had progressed to romance, a romance that was more about routine than passion. If Abby was attracted to another man, Logan would be the first to step aside. He was like that—warm, unselfish, accommodating.

Her troubled thoughts on Saturday evening were only

the beginning. Tate dominated every waking minute, which just went to prove how limited her social life really was. She liked Logan, but Abby longed for some excitement. He was so staid—yes, that was the word. *Staid.* Solid as a rock, and about as imaginative.

Logan came over to her apartment on Sunday afternoon, which was no surprise. He always came over on Sunday afternoons. They usually did something together, but never anything very exciting. More often than not, Abby went over to his house and made dinner. Sometimes they watched a movie. Or they played a game of backgammon, which he generally won. During the summer they'd ride their bikes; some of their most pleasant dates had been spent in Diamond Lake Park. Logan would lie on the grass and rest his head in her lap while she read whatever thriller or mystery she was currently devouring.

They'd been seeing each other so often that the last time they had dinner at her parents' Abby's father had suggested it was time they thought about getting married. Abby had been mortified. Logan had laughed and changed the subject. Later, her mother had tactfully reminded Abby that he might not be the world's most exciting man, but he was her best prospect. However, Abby couldn't see any reason to rush into marriage. At twenty-six, she had plenty of time.

"I thought we'd bike around the park," Logan said.

The day was gloriously sunny, and although Abby wished Logan had proposed something more inventive, the idea *was* appealing. She enjoyed the feel of the breeze in her hair and the sense of exhilaration that came with rapid movement.

"Hi!" Abby and Logan were greeted by Patty Martin just inside the park's boundaries. "How's it going?"

"Fine," Logan answered for them as they braked to a stop. "How about you?"

Patty had recently started to work in the same office building as Logan, which was how Abby had met her. Although Abby didn't know her well, she'd learned that Patty was living with her sister. They'd talked briefly at lunch one day, and Abby had invited her to join an office-league softball team she and Logan had played in last summer.

"I'm fine, too," Patty answered shyly, and looked away.

In some ways she reminded Abby of Mai-Ling, who hadn't said more than a few words to her the first couple of weeks they'd worked together. Only as they came to know each other did Mai-Ling blossom. Abby herself had never been shy. The world was her friend, and she felt certain Patty would soon be comfortable with her, too.

"I can't talk now. I saw you and just wanted to say hello. Have fun, you two," Patty murmured and hurried away.

Confused, Abby watched her leave. The girl looked like a frightened mouse as she scurried across the grass. The description was more than apt. Patty's drab brown hair was pulled back from her face and styled unattractively. She didn't wear makeup and was so shy it was difficult to strike up a conversation.

After biking around the lake a couple of times, they

stopped to get cold drinks. As they rested on a park bench, Logan slipped an affectionate arm around Abby's shoulders. "Have I told you that you look lovely today?"

The compliment astonished Abby; there were times she was convinced Logan didn't notice anything about her. "Thank you. I might add that you're looking very good yourself," she said with twinkling eyes, then added, "but I won't. No need for us both to get conceited."

Logan smiled absently as they walked their bikes out of the park. His expression was oddly distant; in some ways he hadn't been himself lately, but she couldn't put her finger on anything specific.

"Do you mind if we cut our afternoon short?" he asked unexpectedly.

He didn't offer an explanation, which surprised Abby. They'd spent most Sunday afternoons together for the past year. More surprising—or maybe not, considering her recent boredom with Logan—was the fact that Abby realized she didn't care. "No, that shouldn't be any problem. I've got a ton of laundry to do anyway."

Back at her apartment, Abby spent the rest of the afternoon doing her nails, feeling lazy, and ignoring her laundry. She talked to her mother on the phone and promised to stop by sometime that week. Abby had been on her own ever since college. Her job as receptionist at an orthopedic clinic had developed with time and specialized training into a position as an X-ray technician. The advancement had included a healthy pay increase—enough to start saving to buy a house. In the meantime, she relished her independence, enjoying her spacious ground-floor apartment, plus the satisfaction of her job and her volunteer work.

Several times over the next few days, Abby discovered herself thinking about Tate. Their encounter had been brief, but it had left an impression on her. He was the most exciting thing that had happened to her in months.

"What's the matter with you?" Abby admonished herself. "A handsome man gives you a little attention and you don't know how to act."

Dano mewed loudly and weaved between her bare legs, his long tail tickling her calves. It was the middle of June and the hot summer weather had arrived.

"I wasn't talking to you." She leaned over to pet the cat. "And don't tell me you're hungry. I know better."

"Meow."

"You've already had your dinner."

"Meow. Meow."

"Don't you talk to me in that tone of voice. You hear?"

"Meow."

Abby tossed him the catnip mouse he loved to hurl in the air and chase madly after. Logan had gotten it for Dano. With his nose in the air, the cat ignored his toy and sauntered into Abby's room, jumping up to sit on the windowsill, his back to her. He ignored Abby, obviously pining after whatever he could see outside. In some obscure way, Abby felt that she was doing the same thing to Logan and experienced a pang of guilt.

Since it was an older building, the apartment didn't

have air-conditioning, so Abby turned on her large fan. Then, settling in the large overstuffed chair, she draped one leg over the arm and munched on an apple as she read. She was so engrossed in her thriller that when she glanced at her watch, she gasped in surprise. Her Tuesday-evening painting class was in half an hour and Logan would arrive in less than fifteen minutes. He was always punctual, and although he seldom said anything, she could tell by the set of his mouth that he disliked it when she was behind schedule.

The "I'm late, I'm late" theme ran through her mind as she vaulted out of the chair, changed pants, and rammed her right foot into her tennis shoe without untying the lace. Whipping a brush through her long brown hair, she searched frantically for the other shoe.

"It's got to be here," she told the empty room frantically. "Dano," she cried out in frustration. "Did you take my shoe?"

She heard a faint indignant "meow" from the bedroom.

On her knees she crawled across the carpet, desperately tossing aside anything in her path—a week-old newspaper, a scarf, a CD case, the mismatched pair of socks she'd worn last Saturday, and a variety of other unimportant things.

She bolted to her feet when her apartment buzzer went off. Logan must be early.

She automatically let him into the building, threw open her door—and saw *Tate* standing in the hallway.

Abby felt the hot color seep up from her neck. He *would* come now, when she wasn't prepared and was looking her worst.

He approached her apartment. "Hello," he said, staring down at her one bare foot. "Missing something?"

"Hello again." Her voice sounded unnaturally high. She bit her lip and tried to smile. "My shoe's gone."

"Walked away, did it?"

"You might say that. It was here a few minutes ago. I was reading and . . ." She dropped to her knees and lifted the skirting around the chair. There, in all its glory, was the shoe.

"Find it?" He was still in the doorway.

"Yes." She sat on the edge of the cushion and jerked her foot into the shoe.

"It might help if you untied the laces," he said, watching her with those marvelous eyes.

"I know, but I'm in a hurry." With her heel crushing the back of the shoe, Abby hobbled over to the door. "Come on in." She closed it behind him. "I'm—"

"Abby."

"Yes. How did you know?"

"I heard your friend say it at the park. And when I got to the lobby, I asked one of your neighbors." He frowned. "You should identify your guests before you let them in, you know."

"I know. I will. But I . . . was expecting someone else and . . ." Her words drifted off.

Smiling, he offered her his hand. "Tate Harding," he said.

A tingling sensation slipped up her arm at his touch.

Tate's hand was callused and rough from work. She successfully restrained her desire to turn it over and examine the palm. His handsome face was tanned from exposure to the elements. Tate was handsome, compellingly so.

"It looks as if I came at an inconvenient time."

"Oh no," she hurried to assure him. She noticed that he'd released his grip, although she continued to hold her hand in midair. Self-consciously, she lowered it to her side. "Sit down," she said, motioning toward her favorite chair. The hot color in her face threatened to suffocate her with its intensity.

Tate sat and lazily crossed his legs, apparently unaware of the effect he had on her.

Abby was shocked by her own reaction. She'd dated a number of men. She was neither naïve nor stupid. "Would you like something to drink?" she asked as she hastily retreated to the kitchen, not waiting for his answer. Pausing, she frantically prayed that for once, just once, Logan would be late. No sooner had the thought formed than she heard the apartment buzzer again. This time she listened to her speaker.

"Abby?"

Logan. Abby hesitated, but let him in.

Tate had stood and opened the door by the time she turned around. Logan had arrived. When he stepped inside, the two men eyed each other skeptically. A slight scowl drew Logan's brows together.

"Logan, this is Tate Harding. Tate, Logan Fletcher." Abby flushed uncomfortably and darted an apologetic look at them both.

"I thought we had a class tonight." Logan spoke somewhat defensively.

"This is my fault," Tate said, his gaze resting on Abby's face and for one heart-stopping moment on her softly parted lips. "I dropped by unexpectedly."

Logan's mouth thinned with displeasure and Abby pulled her eyes from Tate's. Logan had never been the jealous type, but then he'd never had reason or opportunity to reveal that side of his nature. Still, it surprised her. Abby hadn't considered this a serious relationship. It was more of a companionable one. Logan had understood and accepted that, or so she'd thought.

"I'll come back another time," Tate suggested. "You've obviously got plans with Logan."

"We're taking classes together," Abby rushed to explain. "I'm taking painting and Logan's studying chess. We drive there together, that's all."

Tate's smile was understanding. "I won't keep you, then."

"Nice to have met you," Logan stated, sounding as if he meant exactly the opposite.

Tate turned back and nodded. "Perhaps we'll meet again."

Logan nodded briskly. "Perhaps."

The minute Tate left, Abby whirled around to face Logan. "That was so rude," she whispered fiercely. "For heaven's sake—you were acting like you owned me . . . like I was your property."

"Think about it, Abby," Logan said just as forcefully, also in a heated whisper. His dark eyes narrowed as he stalked to the other side of the room. "We've been dating exclusively for almost a year. I assumed that you would've developed some loyalty. I guess I was mistaken."

"Loyalty? Is that all our relationship means to you?" she demanded.

Logan didn't answer her. He walked to the door and held it open, indicating that if she was coming she needed to do it now. Silently, Abby followed him through the lobby and into the parking lot.

The entire way to the community center they sat without speaking. The hard set of Logan's mouth indicated the tight rein he had on his temper. Abby forced her expression to remain haughtily cold.

They parted in the hallway, Logan taking the first left while Abby continued down the hall. A couple of the women she'd become friends with greeted her, but Abby had difficulty responding. She took twice as long as normal setting up her supplies.

The class, which was on perspective, didn't go well, since Abby's attention kept returning to the scene with Logan and Tate. Logan was obviously jealous. He'd revealed more emotion in those few minutes with Tate than he had in the past twelve months. Logan tended to be serious and reserved, while she was more emotional and adventurous. They were simply mismatched. Like her socks—one red, one blue. Logan had become too comfortable in their relationship these last months, taking too much for granted. The time had come for a change, and after tonight he had to recognize that.

After class they usually met in the coffee shop beside the center. Logan was already in a booth when she arrived there.

Wordlessly, Abby slipped into the seat across from him. Folding her hands on the table, she pretended to study her nails, wondering if Logan was ever going to speak.

"Why are you so angry?" Abby finally asked. "I hardly know Tate. We only met a few days ago."

"How many times have you gone out with him?"

"None," Abby said righteously.

"But not because you turned him down." Logan shook his head grimly. "I saw the way you looked at him, Abby. It was all you could do to keep from drooling."

"That's not true," she denied vehemently—and realized he was probably right. She'd never been good at hiding her feelings. "I admit I find him attractive, but—"

"But what?" Logan taunted softly. "But you had this old boyfriend you had to get rid of first?" The hint of a smile touched his mouth. "And I'm not referring to my age." He was six years older than Abby. "I was pointing out that we've been seeing each other two or three times a week and suddenly you're not so sure how you feel about me."

Abby opened her mouth, then closed it. She couldn't argue with what he'd said.

"That's it, isn't it?"

"Logan." She said his name on a sigh. "I like you. You know that. Over the past year I've grown very . . . fond of you."

"*Fond?*" He spat the word at her. "One is *fond* of cats or dogs—not men. And particularly not me."

"That was a bad choice of words," Abby agreed.

"You're not exactly sure what you feel," Logan said, almost under his breath.

Abby's fingers knotted until she could feel the pain in her hands. Logan was right; she *didn't* know. She was attracted to Tate, but she knew nothing about him. The problem was that she liked what she saw. If her feelings for Logan were what they should be after a year, she wouldn't want Tate to ask her out so badly.

"You aren't sure, are you?" Logan said again.

She hung her head so that her face was framed by her dark hair. "I don't want to hurt you," she murmured.

"You haven't." Logan's hand reached across the table and squeezed her fingers reassuringly. "Beyond anything else, we're friends, and I don't want to do anything to upset that friendship because it's important to me."

"That's important to me, too," she said, and offered him a feeble smile. Their eyes met as the waitress came and turned over the beige cups and filled them with coffee.

"Do you want a menu?"

Abby couldn't have eaten anything and shook her head.

"Not tonight. Thanks, anyway," Logan answered for both of them.

"I don't deserve you," Abby said, after the waitress had moved to the next booth.

For the first time all night, Logan's lips curved into a genuine smile. "That's something I don't want you to forget."

For a few minutes they sipped their coffee in thoughtful silence. Holding the cup with both hands, she studied him. Logan's eyes were as brown as Tate's. Funny she hadn't remembered how brown they were. Tonight the color was intense, deeper than ever. They made quite a couple; she was so emotional—and he wasn't. Abby noticed that Logan's jaw was well defined; Tate's jaw, although different, revealed that same quality—determination. With Logan, Abby recognized there was nothing he couldn't do if he wanted to. Instinctively, she knew the same was true of Tate.

She sensed that there were definite similarities between Logan and Tate, and yet she was reacting to them in different ways.

It seemed unfair that a man she'd seen only a couple of times could affect her like this. If she fell madly in love with someone, it should be Logan.

"What are you thinking about?" His words broke into her troubled thoughts.

Abby shrugged. "Oh, this and that," she said vaguely.

"You didn't even add sugar to your coffee."

Abby grimaced. "No wonder it tastes so awful."

Chuckling, he handed her the sugar container.

Abby poured some onto her spoon and stirred it into her coffee. Logan had a nice mouth, she reflected. She couldn't remember thinking that in a long time. She had when they'd first met, but that was nearly two years ago. She watched him for a moment, trying to figure him out. Logan was so—Abby searched for the right word— sensible. Nothing ever seemed to rattle him. There wasn't an obstacle he couldn't overcome with cool reason. For once, Abby wanted him to do something crazy and nonsensical and fun.

"Logan." She spoke softly, coaxingly. "Let's drive to Des Moines tonight."

He looked at her as if she'd lost her mind. "Des Moines, Iowa?"

"Yes. Wouldn't it be fun just to take off and drive for hours—and then turn around and come home?"

"That's not fun, that's torture. Anyway, what's the point?"

Abby pressed her lips together and nodded. She shouldn't have asked. She'd known his answer even before he spoke.

The ride home was as silent as the drive to class had been. The tension wasn't nearly as great, but it was still evident.

"I have the feeling you're angry," Logan said as he parked in front of her building. "I'm sorry that spending the whole night on the road doesn't appeal to me. I've got this silly need for sleep. From what I understand, it affects older people."

"I'm not angry," Abby said firmly. She felt disappointed, but not angry.

Logan's hand caressed her cheek, curving around her neck and directing her mouth to his. Abby closed her eyes, expecting the usual featherlight kiss. Instead, Logan pulled her into his arms and kissed her soundly. Deeply. Passionately. Surprised but delighted, Abby groaned softly, liking it. Her hands slipped over his shoulders and joined at the base of his neck.

Logan had never kissed her with such intensity, such unrestrained need. His mouth moved over hers, and Abby sucked in a startled breath as pure sensation shot through her. When he released her, she sighed longingly and rested her head against his chest. Involuntarily, a picture of Tate entered her mind. This was what she'd imagined kissing *him* would be like . . .

"You were pretending I was Tate, weren't you?" Logan whispered against her hair.

Two

~

"Oh Logan, of course I wasn't," Abby answered, somewhat guiltily. She *had* thought of Tate, but she hadn't pretended Logan's kiss was Tate's.

He brushed his face along the side of her hair. Abby was certain he wanted to say something more, but he didn't, remaining silent as he climbed out of the car and walked around to her side. She smiled weakly as he offered her his hand. Logan could be such a gentleman. She was perfectly capable of getting out of a car by herself, but he always wanted to help. Abby supposed she should be grateful—but she wasn't. Those old-fashioned virtues weren't the ones that really mattered to her.

Lightly, he kissed her again outside her lobby door. Letting herself in, Abby was aware that Logan waited on the other side until he heard her turn the lock.

After changing into her pajamas, Abby went into the kitchen and made tea. She sat at the small round table and placed her feet on the edge of a chair, pulling a blanket over her knees. Did she love Logan? The answer came almost immediately. Although he'd taken offense, *fond* had aptly described her feelings. She liked Logan, but Tate had aroused far more emotion during their short acquaintance. Quickly drinking the tea, Abby turned off the light and miserably decided to go to bed. Dano joined her, purring loudly as he arranged himself at her feet.

Friday evening, she begged off when Logan invited her to a movie, saying she was tired and didn't feel well. He seemed to accept that quite readily. And, in fact, she watched a movie at home, by herself, and was in bed by ten, reading a new mystery novel, with Dano stretched out at her side.

Saturday afternoon, Abby arrived at the park a half-hour early, hoping Tate would be there and they'd have a chance to talk. She hadn't heard from him and wondered if he'd decided Logan had a prior claim to her affection. However, Tate didn't seem the type who'd be easily discouraged. She found him in the same spot he was in last week and waved happily.

"I was hoping you'd be here," she said eagerly, and sat on the grass beside him, leaning her back against the massive tree trunk.

"My thoughts exactly," Tate replied, with a warm smile that elevated Abby's heart rate.

"I'm sorry about Logan," she told him, weaving her fingers through the grass.

"No need to apologize."

"But he was so rude," Abby returned, feeling guilty

for being unkind. But she'd said no less to Logan himself.

Tate sent her a look of surprise. "He didn't behave any differently than I would have, had the circumstances been reversed."

"Logan doesn't own me," she said defiantly.

A smile bracketed the edges of his mouth. "That's one piece of news I'm glad to hear."

Their eyes met and he smiled. Abby could feel her bones melt. It was all she could do to smile back.

"Do you like Rollerblading?"

"I love it." She hadn't skated since she was a teen at the local roller rink, but if Tate suggested they stand on their heads in the middle of the road, Abby probably would have agreed.

"Would you like to meet me here tomorrow afternoon?"

"Sure," she said without hesitating. "Here?" she repeated, sitting up.

"You *have* skated?" He gave her a worried glance.

"Oh, sure." Her voice squeaked, embarrassing her. "Tomorrow? What time?"

"Three," Tate suggested. "After that, we'll go out for something to eat."

"This is sounding better all the time," Abby teased. "But be warned, I do have a healthy appetite. Logan says—" She nearly choked on the name, immediately wishing she could take it back.

"You were saying something about Logan," Tate prompted.

"Not really." She gave a light shrug, flushing involuntarily.

Mai-Ling stepped off the bus just then and walked toward them. Abby stood up. Brushing the grass from her legs, she smiled warmly at her friend.

"Why do you meet her every week?" Tate asked. The teasing light vanished from his eyes.

"I do volunteer work with the World Literacy Movement. Mai-Ling can read perfectly in Chinese, but she's an American now so I'm helping her learn to read and write English."

"Have you been a volunteer long?"

"A couple of years. Why? Would you like to help? We're always looking for volunteers."

"Me?" He looked stunned and a little shocked. "Not now. I've got more than I can handle helping at the zoo."

"The zoo?" Abby shot back excitedly. "Are you a volunteer?"

"Yes," Tate said as he stood and glanced at his watch. "I'll tell you more about it tomorrow. Right now I've got to get back to work before the boss discovers why I've taken extended lunch breaks the past four Saturdays."

"I'll look forward to tomorrow," Abby murmured, thinking she'd never known anyone as compelling as Tate.

"You met the man?" Mai-Ling asked as she came over to Abby's side and followed her gaze to the retreating male figure.

"Yes, I met him," Abby answered wistfully. "Oh Mai-Ling, I think I'm in love!"

"Love?" Mai-Ling frowned. "The American word for *love* is bad."

"Bad?" Abby repeated, not comprehending.

"Yes. In English one word means many kinds of love."

Abby turned her attention from Tate to her friend and asked, "What do you mean?"

"In America, love for a husband is the same as . . . as love for chocolate. I heard a lady on the bus say she *loves* chocolate, then say she is in love with a new man." Mai-Ling shook her head in astonishment and disbelief. "In Chinese it is much different. Better."

"No doubt you're right," Abby said with a bemused grin. "I guess it's all about context."

Mai-Ling ignored that. "You will see the man again?"

"Tomorrow," Abby said dreamily. Suddenly her eyes widened. Tomorrow was Sunday, and Logan would expect her to do something with him. Oh dear, this was becoming a problem. Not only hadn't she skated in years, but she was bound to have another uncomfortable confrontation with Logan. Her eager anticipation for tomorrow was quickly replaced by a sinking feeling in the pit of her stomach.

Abby spent another miserable night. She'd attempted to phone Logan and make up another excuse about not being able to get together, but he hadn't been home. She didn't feel it was right to leave a message, which struck her as cowardly. Consequently, her sleep was fitful and intermittent. It wasn't as if Logan called and arranged a time each week; they had a simple understanding that Sundays were *their* day. Arrangements for most other days were more flexible. But Abby couldn't remember a week when they hadn't gotten together on a Sunday. Her sudden decision would be as readable as the morning headlines. Logan would know she was meeting Tate.

Abby's first inclination was not to be there when he arrived, but that was even more cowardly. In addition, Abby knew Logan well enough to realize that her attempts to dodge him wouldn't work. Either he'd go to the park and look for her or he'd drive to her parents' house and worry them sick.

By the time he did arrive, Abby's stomach felt as if a lead balloon had settled inside.

"Beautiful afternoon, isn't it?" Logan came over to her and slipped an arm around her waist, drawing her close to his side. "Are you feeling better?" he asked in a concerned voice. So often in the past year, Abby had longed for him to hold her like this. Now, when he did, she wanted to scream with frustration.

"Yes, I'm . . . okay."

"What would you like to do?" he asked, nuzzling her neck and holding her close.

"Logan." Abby hesitated and cleared her throat, feeling guilty. "I've got other plans this afternoon." Her voice didn't even sound like her own as she squeezed her eyes shut, afraid to meet his hard gaze.

A grimness stole into his eyes as his hand tightened. "You're seeing Tate, aren't you?"

Abby caught her breath at the ferocity of his tone. "Of course not!" She couldn't look at him. For the first time in their relationship, Abby was blatantly lying to Logan. No wonder she was experiencing this terrible guilt. For one crazy minute, Abby felt like bursting into tears and running out of the apartment.

"Tell me what you're doing, then," he demanded.

Abby swallowed at the painful lump in her throat. "Last week you cut our time together short," she said. "I didn't ask where you were going. I don't feel it's too much to expect the same courtesy."

Logan's grip on her waist slackened, but he didn't release her. "What about later? Couldn't we meet for dinner? There's something I wanted to discuss."

"I can't," she said quickly. Too quickly. Telltale color warmed her face.

Logan studied her for a long moment, then dropped his arm. She should've been glad. Instead she felt chilled and suddenly bereft.

"Let me know when you're free." His words were cold as he moved toward the door.

"Logan," Abby called out to him desperately. "Don't be angry. Please."

When he paused and turned around, his eyes flickered over her. She couldn't quite read his expression, but she knew it wasn't flattering. Wordlessly, he turned again and left.

Abby wanted to crawl into a hole, curl up, and die. Logan deserved so much better than this. Any number of women would call her a fool—and they'd be right.

Dressed in white linen shorts and a red cotton shirt, Abby studied her reflection in the full-length mirror on the back of the bedroom door. Her hair hung in a long ponytail, practical for skating, she figured. Makeup did little to disguise the doubt and unhappiness in her eyes. With a jagged breath, Abby tied the sleeves of a sweater around her neck and headed out the door.

Tate was standing by the elm tree, waiting for her. He was casually dressed in jeans and a V-neck sweater that hinted at curly chest hair. Even across the park, Abby recognized the quiet authority of the man. His virile look attracted the attention of other women in the vicinity, but Tate didn't seem to notice.

He started walking toward her, his smile approving as he surveyed her long legs.

"You look like you've lost your best friend," Tate said as he slid a casual arm around her shoulder.

Abby winced; his comment might be truer than he knew.

"Problem?" he asked.

"Not really." Her voice quavered, but she managed to give him a broad smile. "I'm hoping we can rent skates. I don't have a pair."

"We can."

It didn't take long for Tate's infectious good mood to brighten Abby's spirits. Soon she was laughing at her bungling attempts to skate. A concrete pathway was very different from the smooth, polished surface of the rink. Either that or it'd been longer than she realized since her last time on skates.

Tate tucked a hand around her hip as his movements guided hers.

"You're doing great." His eyes were smiling as he relaxed his grasp.

Laughing, Abby looked away from the pathway to answer him and her skate hit a rut and she tumbled forward wildly, thrashing her arms in an effort to remain upright. She would have fallen if Tate hadn't still been holding her. His hand tightened, bringing her closer. She faltered a bit from the effect of his nearness.

"I'm a natural," she said with a grin.

"A natural klutz," he finished for her.

They skated for two hours. When Tate suggested they stop, Abby glanced at her watch and was astonished by the time.

"Hungry?" Tate asked next.

"Famished."

The place Tate took her to was one of those relatively upscale restaurants that charged a great deal for its retro diner atmosphere, but where the reputation for excellent food was well earned. Abby couldn't imagine Logan bringing her someplace like this. Knowing that made the outing all the more enticing.

When the waitress came, Abby ordered an avocado burger with a large stuffed baked potato, and strawberry shortcake for dessert.

Tate smiled. "I'll have the same," he told the waitress, who wrote down their order and stepped away from the table.

"So you do volunteer work at the zoo?" Abby was interested in learning the details he'd promised to share with her.

"I've always loved animals," he began.

"I could tell from the way you talked to the ducks and the squirrels," Abby inserted, recalling the first time she'd seen Tate.

He acknowledged her statement with a nod. "Even as a child I'd bring home injured animals—rabbits, raccoons, squirrels—and do what I could to make them well."

"Why didn't you become a veterinarian?"

Tate ignored the question. "The hardest part was setting them free once they were well. I might have been a veterinarian if things in my life had gone differently, but I'm good with cars, too."

"You're a mechanic?" Abby asked, already knowing the answer. The callused hands told her that her guess couldn't be far off.

"I work at Bessler's Auto Repair."

"Sure. I know it. That's across the street from the Albertsons' store."

"That's it."

So it *had* just been a coincidence that she'd seen Tate in the store; he worked in the immediate vicinity.

"I've been working there since I was seventeen," Tate added. "Jack Bessler is thinking about retirement these days."

"What'll happen to the shop?"

"I'm hoping to buy it," Tate said as he held his fork, nervously rotating it between two fingers.

Tate was uneasy about something. He ran his fingers up and down the fork, not lifting his gaze from his silverware.

Their meal was as delicious as Abby knew it would be. Whatever had bothered Tate was soon gone and the remainder of the evening was spent talking, getting to know each other with an eagerness that was as strong as their mutual attraction. They talked nonstop for hours, sauntering lazily along the water's edge and laughing, neither of them eager to bring their time together to a close.

When Abby finally got home it was nearly midnight.

She floated into the apartment on a cloud of happiness. Even as she readied for bed, she couldn't forget how wonderful the night had been. Tate was a man she could talk to, really talk to. He listened to her and seemed to understand her feelings. Logan listened, too, but Abby had the impression that he sometimes felt impatient with her. But perhaps that wasn't it at all. Maybe she was looking for ways to soothe her conscience. His reaction today still shocked her; as far as she was concerned, they hadn't made any commitment to each other beyond that of friendship. Sometimes Abby wondered if she really knew Logan.

The phone rang fifteen minutes after she was in the door.

Assuming it was Tate, Abby all but flew across the room to answer it, not bothering to check caller ID. "Hello," she said in a low, sultry voice.

"Abby, is that you? You don't sound right. Are you sick?"

It was Logan.

Instantly, Abby stiffened and sank into the comfort of her chair. "Logan," she said in her normal voice. "Hi. Is something wrong?" He wouldn't be phoning this late otherwise.

"Not really."

"I just got in . . . I mean . . ." She faltered as her thoughts tripped over one another. "Thought you might be in bed, so I didn't call," she finished lamely. He was obviously phoning to find out what time she got home.

Deftly Logan changed the subject to a matter of no importance, confirming Abby's suspicions. "No," he said, "I was just calling to see what time you wanted me to pick you up for class on Tuesday."

Of all the feeble excuses! "Next time I go somewhere without you, do you want me to phone in so you'll know the precise minute I get home?" she asked crisply, fighting her temper as her hand tightened around the receiver.

His soft chuckle surprised her. "I guess I wasn't very original, was I?"

"No. This isn't like you, Logan. I've never thought of you as the jealous type."

"There's a lot you don't know about me," he answered on a wry note.

"I'm beginning to realize that."

"Do you want me to pick you up for class this week, or have you . . . made other arrangements?"

"Of course I want you to pick me up! I wouldn't want it any other way." Abby meant that. She liked Logan. The problem was she liked Tate, too.

Logan hesitated and the silence stretched between them. Abby was sure he could hear her racing heart over the phone. But she hoped he couldn't read the confusion in her mind.

After work on Monday afternoon, rather than heading back to her apartment and Dano, Abby stopped off at her parents' house.

"Hi, Mom." She sauntered into the kitchen and kissed her mother on the cheek. "What's there to eat?" Opening the refrigerator door, Abby surveyed the contents with interest.

"Abby," her mother admonished, "what's wrong?"

"Wrong?" Abby feigned ignorance.

"Abby, I'm your mother. I know you. The only time you show up at the beginning of the week is if something's bothering you."

"Honestly, aren't I allowed an unexpected visit without parental analysis?"

"Did you and Logan have a fight?" her mother persisted.

Glenna Carpenter's chestnut hair was as dark as Abby's but streaked with gray, creating an unusual color a hairdresser couldn't reproduce. Glenna was a young sixty, vivacious, outgoing, and—like Abby—a doer.

"What makes you say that? Logan and I never fight." Abby chewed on a stalk of celery and closed the refrigerator. Taking the salt from the cupboard beside the stove, she sprinkled some on it.

"Salt's bad for your blood pressure." Glenna took the shaker out of Abby's hand and replaced it in the cupboard. "Are you going to tell me what's wrong?" She spoke in a warning tone that Abby knew better than to disregard.

"Honest, Mom, there's nothing."

"Abby." Sapphire-blue eyes snapped with displeasure.

Abby couldn't hold back a soft laugh. Her mother had a way of saying more with one glare than some women did with a tantrum.

Holding the celery between her teeth, Abby placed both hands on the counter and pulled herself up, sitting beside the sink.

"Abby," her mother said a second time.

"It's Logan." She gave a frustrated sigh. "He's become so possessive lately."

"Well, thank goodness. I'd have thought you'd be happy." Glenna's smiling eyes revealed her approval. "I was wondering how long it would take him."

"Mother!" Abby wanted to cry. Deep in her heart, she'd known her mother would react like this. "It's too late—I've met someone else."

Glenna froze and a shocked look came over her. "Who?"

"His name is Tate Harding."

"When?"

"A couple of weeks ago."

"How old is he?"

Abby wanted to laugh at her mother's questions. She sounded as if Abby was fifteen again and asking for permission to date. "He's twenty-seven and a hardworking, respectable citizen. I don't know how to explain it, Mom, but I was instantly attracted to him. I think I'm falling in love."

"Falling in love," Glenna echoed, reheating the day's stale coffee and pouring herself a cup. Her hand shook as she lifted the mug to her mouth a couple of minutes later.

Abby knew her mother was taking her seriously when she drank coffee, which she usually reserved for mornings. A smile tugged at Abby's mouth, but she successfully restrained it.

"I know what you must be thinking," Abby said. "You don't even have to say it because I've already chided myself a thousand times. Logan's the greatest man in the world, but Tate is—"

"The ultimate one?"

The suppressed smile came to life. "You could say that."

"Does Logan know?"

"Of all the luck, they ran into each other at my apartment last week. It would've helped if they hadn't met like that."

"I think having Logan and Tate stumble into each other was more providential than you realize," Glenna murmured with infuriating calm. "I've always liked Logan. I think he's perfect for you."

"How can you *say* that?" Abby demanded indignantly. "We aren't anything alike. We don't even enjoy the same things. Logan can be such a stuffed shirt. And you haven't even met Tate."

"No." Her mother ran the tip of one finger along the rim of her mug. "To be honest, I could never understand why Logan puts up with you. I love you, Abby, but I know your faults as well as your strengths. Apparently, Logan sees the same potential in you that I do."

"I can't believe my own mother would talk to me like this." Abby spoke to the ceiling, venting her irritation. "I come to her to pour out my heart and seek her advice and end up being judged."

Glenna laughed. "I'm not judging you," she declared. "Just giving you some sound motherly advice." An ardent light glowed from her eyes. "Logan loves you. He—"

"Mother," Abby interrupted. "How can you be so sure? If he does, which I sincerely doubt, then he's never told me."

"No, I don't imagine he has. Logan is waiting."

"Waiting?" Abby asked sarcastically. "For what? A blue moon?"

"No," Glenna said sharply, and took a long, deliberate sip of her coffee, which must have tasted foul. "He's been waiting for you to grow up. You're impulsive and quick-tempered, especially when it comes to relationships. You expect him to take the lead and yet you resent him for it."

Abby gasped; she couldn't help it. Rarely had her mother spoken this candidly to her. Abby opened her mouth to deny the accusations, then closed it again. The words hurt, especially coming from her own mother, and she lowered her gaze to hide the onrush of emotional pain. Tears gathered in her eyes.

"I'm not saying these things to hurt you," Glenna continued softly.

"I know that." Abby grimaced. "You're right. I should be more honest, but I don't want to hurt Logan."

"Then tell him what you're feeling. Stringing him along would be unkind."

"But it's hard," Abby protested, wiping her eyes. "If I told him yesterday that I was going out with Tate he would've been angry. And miserable."

"And do you suppose he wasn't? I know Logan. If you said anything to him, he'd immediately step aside until you've settled things in your own mind."

"I know," Abby breathed in frustration. "But I'm not sure I want that, either."

"You mean you want to have your cake and eat it, too," Glenna said. "As the old cliché has it . . ."

"I never have understood that saying."

"Then maybe you'd better think about it, Abby."

"In other words, you're telling me I should let Logan know how I feel about Tate."

"Yes. You can't have it both ways. You can't keep Logan hanging if you want to pursue a romance with this other man."

The seriousness of her mother's look, her words, transferred itself to Abby.

"Today," Glenna insisted. "Now, before you change your mind."

Slowly, Abby nodded. She hopped down from the counter, prepared to talk to Logan. "Thanks, Mom."

Glenna Carpenter gave Abby a motherly squeeze. "I'll be thinking about you."

"You'll like Tate."

"I'm sure I will. You always did have excellent taste."

Abby's smile was tentative.

She knew Logan was working late tonight, so she drove straight to his accounting firm, which was situated half a block from her own office. Karen, his assistant, had gone home, and Abby knocked at the outer office. Almost instantly the door opened and Logan gestured for her to come inside.

"Abby." He beamed her a warm smile. "What a nice surprise. Come in, won't you?"

Abby took the leather chair opposite his desk.

"Logan." Her fingers had knotted into a tight fist in her lap. "Can we talk?"

He looked down at his watch.

"It won't take long, I promise," she added hurriedly.

Leaning against the side of his desk, he crossed his arms. "What is it, Abby? You never look this serious about anything."

"I think you have a right to know that I was with Tate Harding yesterday." Her heart was hammering wildly as she said this.

"Abby, you're as readable as a child. I was aware from the beginning who you were with," he told her. "I only wish that you'd been honest with me."

"Oh Logan, I do apologize for that."

"Fine. It's forgotten."

How could he be so generous? So forgiving? Just when she was about to explain that she wanted to continue seeing Tate, Logan reached for her, drawing her into his embrace. As his mouth settled over hers, he drew from her a response so complete that Abby was left speechless and all the more confused. He kissed her as if he couldn't get enough of her mouth, of *her.*

"I've got a client meeting in five minutes," Logan whispered as he massaged her shoulders. "But believe me, holding you is far more appealing. Promise me you'll drop by the office again."

Then he let her go, and she sank back into the chair.

Three

~

Abby punched the pillow and determinedly shut her eyes. She shouldn't be having so much trouble falling asleep, she thought, fighting back a loud yawn. Ten minutes later, she wearily raised one eyelid and glared at the clock radio. Two-thirty! She groaned audibly. Logan was responsible for this. He should've taken the time to listen to her. Now she didn't know when she'd work up the courage to talk to him about Tate.

And speaking of Tate . . . He'd phoned after dinner and suggested going to the zoo that weekend. Abby couldn't refuse him. Now she was paying the price— remorse and self-recrimination. Worse, it was all Logan's fault that she hadn't been able to explain the situation to him. She didn't mean to do anything behind his back. She liked both men, but the attraction she felt toward Tate was far more intense than the easy camaraderie she shared with Logan.

Bunching the pillow, Abby forced her eyes to close.

She'd gone to Logan to tell him she wanted to date other men. She'd tried, really tried. What else could she do?

When the alarm went off at six, Abby wanted to scream. Sleep had eluded her the entire night. The few hours she'd managed to catch wouldn't be enough to see her through the day. Her eyes burned as she tossed aside the covers and sat on the edge of the bed.

More from habit than anything, Abby brushed her teeth and dressed. Coffee didn't help. And the tall glass of orange juice tasted like tomato, but she didn't open her eyes to investigate.

Half an hour later, she let herself into the clinic. The phone was already ringing.

"Morning." Cheryl Hansen, the receptionist, smiled at Abby before answering the call.

Abby returned the friendly gesture with a weak smile of her own.

"You look like the morning after a wild-and-crazy night," Cheryl said as Abby hung her jacket in the room off the reception area.

"It was wild and crazy, all right," Abby said after an exaggerated yawn. "But not the way you think."

"Another late night with Logan?"

Abby's eyes widened. "No!"

"Tate, then?"

"No. Unfortunately."

"I'm telling you, Ab, keeping track of your love life is getting more difficult all the time."

"I haven't got a love life," she murmured, unable to stop yawning. Covering her mouth, Abby moved to the end of the long hallway.

The day didn't get any better. By noon, she recognized that she couldn't possibly attend tonight's class with Logan. For one thing, she was too tired to concentrate on painting theory and technique. For another, as soon as he saw her troubled expression, he'd know immediately that she was deceiving him and seeing Tate again. And something she didn't need today was another confrontation with Logan. She didn't want to hurt him. But more than that—she didn't want to lie to him.

On her way back from lunch, Abby decided to call his office. Her guilt grew heavier at the pleasure in his voice.

"Abby! What's up?"

"Hi, Logan." She groaned inwardly. "I hope you don't mind me phoning you like this."

"Not at all."

"I'm not feeling well." She paused, her hand tightening around the receiver. "I was thinking that maybe it'd be best if I skipped class tonight."

"What's wrong?" His genuine concern was nearly her undoing. "You weren't well on Friday, either."

Did he really believe her excuse on Friday evening, which had been nothing but a way of avoiding him?

"You must be coming down with something," he said.

"I think so." *Like a terminal case of cowardice,* her mind shot back.

"Have you seen a doctor?"

"It isn't necessary. Not yet. But I thought I'd stay home again tonight and go to bed early," Abby mumbled, feeling more wretched every second.

"Do you need me to do anything for you?" His voice was laced with gentleness.

"No," she assured him quickly. "I'm fine. Really. I just thought I'd nip this thing in the bud and take it easy."

"Okay. But promise me that if you need anything, you'll call."

"Oh sure."

Abby felt even worse after making that phone call. By the time she returned to her apartment late that afternoon, her excuse for not attending her class had become real. Her head was throbbing unmercifully, her throat felt dry and scratchy, and her stomach was queasy.

With her fingertips pressing her temple, Abby located the aspirin in the bathroom cabinet and downed two tablets. Afterward she lay on the sofa, the phone beside her, head propped up with a soft pillow, and closed her eyes. She didn't open them when the phone rang, and she scrabbled around for it blindly.

"Hello." Her reluctant voice was barely above a whisper.

"Abby, is that you?"

She breathed easier. It was her mother.

"Hi, Mom."

"What's wrong?"

"I've got a miserable headache."

"What's bothering you?"

"What makes you think anything's bothering me?" Her mother displayed none of the sympathy Logan had.

"Abby, I know you. When you get a headache it's because something's troubling you."

Breathing deeply, Abby glanced at the ceiling with wide-open eyes, unable to respond.

Her mother resumed the interrogation. "Did you talk to Logan yesterday?"

"Only for a little while. He was on his way to a meeting."

"Did you tell him you want to continue seeing Tate?"

"I didn't get the chance," Abby said, more aggressively than she'd intended. "Mom, I tried, but he didn't have time to listen. Then Tate phoned me and asked me out this weekend and . . . I said yes."

"Does Logan know?"

"Not yet," she mumbled.

"And you've got a whopper of a headache?"

"Yes." The word trembled on her lips.

"Abby." Her mother's voice took on the tone Abby knew all too well. "You've *got* to talk to Logan."

"I will."

"Your headache won't go away until you do."

"I know."

Dano strolled into the room and leaped onto the sofa, settling in Abby's lap. Grateful to have one friend left in the world, Abby stroked her cat.

It took her at least twenty minutes to work up enough fortitude to call Logan's home number. His phone rang six times, and Abby sighed, not leaving a message. She assumed he'd gone to class on his own, that he was on his way, so she didn't bother trying his cell. She'd talk to him tomorrow.

She closed her eyes again, wondering how—if—she could balance her intense attraction to Tate with her feelings of friendship for Logan. Friendship that sometimes hinted at more. His ardent kiss yesterday had taken her by surprise. But she *had* to tell him about Tate . . .

The apartment buzzer woke Abby an hour later. She

sat up and rubbed the stiff muscles of her neck. Dano remained on her lap and meowed angrily when she stood, forcing the cat to leap to the floor.

"Yes?" she said into the speaker.

"It's Logan."

Abby buzzed him in. Her hand was shaking visibly as she unlocked the door. "Hi," she said in a high-pitched voice.

Logan stepped inside. "How are you feeling?"

"I don't know." She yawned, stretching her arms. "Better, I guess." Her attention was drawn to a white sack Logan was holding. "What's that?"

A crooked smile slanted his mouth. "Chicken soup. I picked some up at the deli." He handed her the bag. "I want to make sure you're well enough for the game tomorrow night."

Abby's head shot up. "Game? What game?"

"I wondered if you'd forgotten. We signed up a couple of weeks ago for the softball team. Remember?"

This was the second summer they were playing in the office league. With her recent worries, softball had completely slipped Abby's mind. "Oh, *that* game." Abby wanted to groan. She'd *never* be able to avoid Logan. Too many activities linked them together—closeness of their workspaces, classes, and now softball.

She took the soup into the kitchen, removing the large plastic cup from the sack. The aroma of chicken and noodles wafted through the small room. Logan followed her in and slipped his arms around her waist from behind. His chin rested on her head as he spoke. "I woke you up, didn't I?"

She nodded, resisting the urge to turn and slip her

arms around his waist and bury her face in his chest. "But it's probably a good thing you did. I've gotten a crick in my neck sleeping on the couch with Dano on my lap."

Logan's breath stirred the hair at the top of her head. The secure feeling of his arms holding her close was enough to bring tears to her eyes.

"Logan." She breathed his name in a husky murmur. "Why are you so good to me?"

He turned her to face him. "I would've thought you'd have figured it out by now," he said as he slowly lowered his mouth to hers.

A sweetness flooded Abby at the tender possession of his mouth. She wanted to cry and beg him *not* to love her. Not yet. Not until she was sure of her feelings. But the gentle caress of his lips prevented the words from ever forming. Her hands moved up his shirt and over his shoulders, reveling in his strength.

His hands, at the small of her back, arched her closer as he inhaled deeply. "I've got to go or I'll be late for class. Will you be all right?"

Speaking was impossible, and it was almost more than Abby could do to simply nod.

He straightened, relaxing his grip. "Take care of yourself," he said as his eyes smiled lovingly into hers.

Again, it was all Abby could do to nod.

"I'll pick you up tomorrow at six-thirty, if you're up to it. We can grab a bite to eat after the game."

"Okay," she managed shakily, and walked him to the door. "Thanks for the soup."

Logan smiled. "I've got to take care of the team's first

base player, don't I?" His mouth brushed hers and he was gone.

Leaning against the door, Abby looked around her grimly. If she felt guilty before, she felt wretched now.

Shoving the baseball cap down on her long brown hair, which she'd tied back in a loose ponytail, Abby couldn't stifle a sense of excitement. She did enjoy softball. And Logan was right—she was the best first base player the team was likely to find. Not to mention her hitting ability.

Logan wasn't as good a player but enjoyed himself as much as she did. He just didn't have the same competitive edge. More than once he'd been responsible for an error. But no one seemed to mind, and Abby didn't let it bother her.

As usual, he was punctual when he came to pick her up. "Hi. I can see you're feeling better."

"Much better."

The game was scheduled to be played in Diamond Lake Park, and Abby was half afraid Tate would stumble across them. She wasn't sure how often he went into the park and—She reined in her worries. There was no reason to assume he'd show up or that he'd even recognize her.

Most of the team had arrived by the time Abby and Logan sauntered onto the field. The co-ed Softball League was recreational. Of all their team members, Abby was the one who took the game most seriously. The team positions alternated between men and women. Since Abby played first base, a man was at second. Logan was in the outfield.

The team they were playing was from a local church, and Abby remembered her team beating them last summer.

Dick Snyder was their office team's coach and strategist. "Hope that arm's as good as last year," Dick said to Abby, who beamed at him. It was gratifying to be appreciated.

After a few warm-up exercises and practice pitches, their team left the field. Logan was up to bat first. Abby cringed at the stiff way he held himself. He wasn't a natural athlete, despite his biking prowess.

"Logan," she shouted encouragingly, "bend your knees."

He did as she suggested and swung at the next pitch. The ground ball skidded past the shortstop and Logan was safe on first.

Abby breathed easier and sent him a triumphant smile.

Patty Martin was up to bat next. Abby took one look at the shy, awkward young woman and knew she'd be an immediate out. Patty was new to the team this year, and Abby hoped she'd stick with it.

"Come on, Patty," she called out, hoping to instill some confidence, "you can do it!"

Patty held the bat clumsily and bit her lip as she glared straight ahead at the pitcher. She swung at the first three balls and missed each one.

Dick pulled Patty aside and gave her a pep talk before she took her place on the bench.

Abby hurried over to Patty and patted her knee. "I'm

glad you decided to play with us." She meant that honestly. She suspected Patty could do with some friends.

"But I'm terrible." Patty stared at her clenched hands and Abby noticed how white her knuckles were.

"You'll improve," Abby said, with more certainty than she felt. "Everyone has to learn, and believe me, every one of us strikes out. Don't worry about it."

By the time Abby was up to bat, there were two outs and Logan was still at first. Her stand-up double and a home run by the hitter following her made the score 3–0.

It remained the same until the bottom of the eighth. Logan was playing the outfield when a high fly ball went over his head. He scrambled to retrieve it.

Frantically jumping up and down at first base, Abby screamed, "Throw the ball to second! Second." She watched in horror as Logan turned and faced third base. "Second!" she yelled angrily.

The woman on third base missed the catch, and the batter went on to make it home, giving his team their first run.

Abby threw her glove down and, with her hands placed defiantly on her hips, stormed into the outfield and up to Logan. "I told you to throw the ball to second."

He gave her a mildly sheepish look. "Sorry, Abby. All your hysterics confused me."

Groaning, Abby returned to her position.

They won the game 3–1 and afterward gathered at the local restaurant for pizza and pitchers of beer.

"You're really good," Patty said, sitting beside Abby.

"Thanks," she said, smiling into her beer. "I was on

the high school team for three years, so I had lots of practice."

"I don't know if I'll ever learn."

"Sure you will," Logan insisted. "Besides, we need you. Didn't you notice we'd be one woman short if it wasn't for you?"

Abby hadn't noticed that, but was pleased Logan had brought it up. This quality of making people feel important had drawn Abby to him on their first date.

"I'm awful, but I really like playing. And it gives me a chance to know all of you better," Patty added shyly.

"We like having you," Abby confirmed. "And you *will* improve." Patty seemed to want the reassurance that she was needed and appreciated, and Abby didn't mind echoing Logan's words.

They ate their pizza and joked while making plans for the game the following Wednesday evening.

Dick Snyder and his wife gave Patty a ride home. Patty hesitated in the parking lot. "Bye, Abby. Bye, Logan," she said timidly. "I'll see you soon."

Abby smiled secretly to herself. Patty was attracted to Logan. She'd praised his skill several times that evening. Abby didn't blame her. Logan was wonderful. True, he wasn't going to be joining the Minnesota Twins anytime soon—or ever. But he'd made it to base every time he was up at bat.

Logan dropped Abby off at her apartment but didn't accept her invitation to come in for a glass of iced tea. To be honest, Abby was grateful. She didn't know how much longer she could hide from Logan that she was continuing to see Tate. And she refused to lie if he asked her. She planned to tell him soon . . . as soon as an appropriate opportunity presented itself.

The remainder of the week went smoothly. She didn't talk to Logan, which made things easier. Abby realized that Sunday afternoon with him would be difficult after spending Saturday with Tate, but she decided to worry about it then.

She woke Saturday morning with a sense of expectation. Tate was taking the afternoon off and meeting her in the park after she'd finished tutoring Mai-Ling. From there they were driving out to Apple Valley and the Minnesota Zoo, where he did volunteer work.

She wore a pale pink linen summer dress and had woven her long brown hair into a French braid. A glance in the mirror revealed that she looked her best.

Mai-Ling met her and smiled knowingly. "You and Tate are seeing each other today?"

"We're going to the zoo."

"The animal place, right?"

"Right."

Abby's attention drifted while Mai-Ling did her lesson. The woman's ability was increasing with each meeting. Judging by the homework Mai-Ling brought for Abby to examine, the young woman wouldn't be needing her much longer.

They'd finished their lesson and were laughing when Abby looked up and saw Tate strolling across the lawn toward her.

Again she was struck by the sight of this ruggedly appealing male. He was dressed in jeans, a tight-fitting T-shirt, and cowboy boots.

His rich brown eyes seemed to burn into hers. "Hello,

Abby." He greeted Mai-Ling, but his eyes left Abby's for only a second.

"I'll catch my bus," said Mai-Ling, excusing herself, but Abby barely noticed.

"You're looking gorgeous today," Tate commented, taking her hand in his.

A tingling sensation shot up her arm at his touch. Her nerves felt taut just from standing beside him. Abby couldn't help wondering what kissing Tate would be like. Probably the closest thing to heaven this side of earth.

"You seem deep in thought."

Abby smiled up at him. "Sorry. I guess I was."

They chatted easily as Tate drove toward Apple Valley. Abby learned that he'd been a volunteer for three years, working at the zoo as many as two days a week.

"What animals do you care for?"

Tate answered her without taking his eyes off the road. "Most recently I've been working with a llama for the Family Farm, but I also do a lot of work with birds. In fact, I've been asked to assist in the bird show."

"Will you?" Abby remembered seeing Tate that first day with the ducks . . .

"Yes."

"What other kinds of things do you do?"

Tate's returning smile was quick. "Nothing that glamorous. I help at feeding time and I clean the cages. Sometimes I groom and exercise the animals."

"What are you doing with the llama?"

"Mostly I've been working to familiarize him with people. We'd like Larry to join his brother in giving children rides."

Tate parked the car and came around to her side to open the passenger door. He kept her hand tucked in his as he led the way to the entrance.

"You love it here, don't you?" Abby asked as they cleared the gates.

"I do. The zoo gives us a rare opportunity to discover nature and our relationship to other living things. We have a responsibility to protect animals, as well as their habitats. Zoos, good zoos like this, are part of that." A glint of laughter flashed in his eyes as he turned toward her. "I didn't know I could be so profound."

Someone called out to Tate, and Abby watched him respond with a brief wave.

"Where would you like to start?"

The zoo was divided into five regions, and Abby chose Tropics Trail, an indoor oasis of plants and animals from Asia.

As they walked, Tate explained what they were seeing, regaling her with fascinating bits of information. She'd been to the zoo before, but she'd never had such a knowledgeable guide.

Three hours later, it was closing time.

"Promise you'll bring me again," Abby begged, her eyes held by Tate's with mesmerizing ease.

"I promise," he whispered as he led her toward his car.

The way he said it made her feel weak in the knees, made her forget everything and everyone else. She lapsed into a dreamy silence on the drive home.

Tate drove back to Minneapolis and they stopped at a Mexican restaurant near Diamond Lake Park. Abby had passed it on several occasions but had never eaten there.

A young waitress smiled at them and led them to a table.

Tate spoke to the woman in Spanish. She nodded and turned around.

"What did you ask?" Abby whispered.

"I wanted to know if we could eat outside. You don't mind, do you? The evening is lovely."

"No, that sounds great." But she did mind. Because it immediately occurred to her that Logan might drive past and see her eating there with Tate. Abby managed to squelch her worries as she sat down at a table on the patio and opened her menu. She studied its contents, but her appetite had unexpectedly disappeared.

"You've got that thoughtful look again," Tate remarked. "Is everything okay, Abby?"

"Oh sure," she said.

Abby decided what she'd order and took the opportunity to watch Tate as he reviewed the menu. His brow was creased, his eyes narrowed in concentration. When he happened to glance up and found her looking at him, he set the menu aside.

An awkwardness followed. It continued until the waitress finally stopped at their table. Abby ordered cheese enchiladas and a margarita; Tate echoed her choice but asked for a Corona beer. "I had a good time today," Abby said, in an attempt to breach the silence after the waitress left.

"I did, too." Tate sounded stiff, as if he suddenly felt uneasy.

"Is something wrong?" Abby asked after another silence.

It could have been Abby's imagination, but she sensed that Tate was struggling within himself.

"Tate?" she prompted.

He leaned forward and pinched the bridge of his nose before exhaling loudly. "No . . . nothing."

Long after he'd dropped her off at the apartment, Abby couldn't shake the sensation that something was troubling him. Twice he'd seemed about to speak, but both times he'd stopped himself.

Abby's thoughts were heavy as she drifted into sleep. Tomorrow she'd be spending the afternoon with Logan. She had to tell him she'd decided to see Tate; delaying it any longer was a grave disservice to them both—to Logan *and* to Tate.

Sunday afternoon, Logan sat on the sofa beside Abby and reached for her hand. She had to force herself not to snatch it away. So often in the past Abby had wanted Logan to be more demonstrative. And now that he was, it caused such turmoil inside her that she wanted to cry.

"You're looking pale, Abby. Are you sure you're feeling all right?" he asked her, his voice concerned.

"Logan, I've got to talk to you," she blurted out miserably. "I need to—"

"What you need is to get out of this stuffy apartment." He stood up, bringing her with him. Slipping an arm around her waist, Logan directed her out of the apartment and to his car.

Abby didn't have time to protest as he opened the

door. She climbed inside and he leaned across to fasten her seat belt.

"Where are we going?" she asked, confused and unhappy as he backed out of the parking area.

"For a drive."

"I don't want to go for a drive."

Logan glanced away from the road long enough to narrow his eyes slightly at her. "Abby, what is it? You look like you're about to cry."

"I am." She swallowed convulsively and bit her bottom lip. "I want to go back to the apartment."

Logan pulled over and cut the engine. "Abby, what's wrong?" he asked solicitously.

Abby got out and leaned against the side of the car. The blood was pounding wildly in her ears. She hugged her waist with both arms.

"Abby?" he prompted softly as he joined her.

"I tried to tell you on Monday evening," she said. "I even went to your office, but you had some stupid meeting."

He didn't argue with her. "Is this about Tate?"

"Yes!" she shouted. "I went to the zoo with him yesterday. All week I've felt guilty because I know you don't want me to see anyone except you."

Abby chanced a look at him. He displayed no emotion, his eyes dark and unreadable. "Do you want to continue seeing him?" he asked carefully.

"I like Tate. I've liked him from the time we met," Abby admitted in a low whisper. "I don't know him all that well, but—"

"You want to get to know him better?" His eyes seemed to draw her toward him like a magnet.

"Yes," she whispered, gazing up at him.

"Then you should," he said evenly.

"Oh Logan," she breathed. "I was hoping you'd understand."

"I do, Abby." He placed his hands deep inside his pants pockets, but then opened the passenger door.

"Where are we going?"

He looked mildly surprised. "I'm taking you home."

The smile that touched the corners of his mouth didn't reach his eyes. "Abby, if you're seeing Tate, you won't be seeing me."

Four

~

Shocked, Abby stared at him, and her voice trembled slightly. "What do you mean?"

"Isn't it obvious?" Logan turned toward her. His eyes had darkened and grown more intense. There was an almost imperceptible movement along his jaw. "Remind me. How long have we been dating?" he asked, but his voice revealed nothing.

"You know how long we've been dating. About a year now. What's that got to do with anything?"

Logan frowned. "If you don't know how you feel about me in that length of time, then I can't see continuing a relationship."

Abby clenched her fist, feeling impotent anger well up within her. "You're trying to blackmail me, aren't you?"

"Blackmail you?" Logan snapped. He paused and breathed in deeply. "No, Abby, that isn't my intention."

"But you're saying that if I go out with Tate, then I can't see you," she returned with a short, bitter laugh.

"You're not being fair. I like you both. You're wonderful, Logan, but . . . but so is Tate."

"Then decide. Which one of us do you want?"

Logan made it sound so simple. "I can't." She inhaled a shaky breath and raked a weary hand through her hair. "It's not that easy."

"Do you want Tate and me to slug it out? Is that it? Winner takes the spoils?"

"No!" she cried, shocked and angry.

"You've got the wrong man if you think I'll do that."

Tears spilled from Abby's eyes. "That's not what I want, and you know it."

"Then what *do* you want?" The low question was harsh.

"Time. I . . . I need to sort through my feelings. When did it become a crime to feel uncertain? I barely know Tate—"

"Time," Logan interrupted, but the anger in his tone didn't seem directed at her. "That's exactly what I'm giving you. Take as long as you need. When you've decided what you feel, let me know."

"But you won't see me?"

"Seeing you will be unavoidable. Our offices are half a block apart—and we have the softball team."

"Classes?"

"No. There's no need for us to go together or to meet each other there."

Tilting her chin downward, Abby swiped at her tears, trying to quell the rush of hurt. Logan could remove her from his life so effortlessly. His apparent indifference pierced her heart.

Without a word, he drove her back to the apartment building and parked, but didn't shut off the engine.

"Before you go," Abby said, her voice quavering, "would you hold me? Just once?"

Logan's hand tightened on the steering wheel until his knuckles were strained and white. "Do you want a comparison? Is that it?" he asked in a cold, stiff voice.

"No, that wasn't what I wanted." She reached for the door handle. "I'm sorry I asked."

Logan didn't move. They drew each breath in unison. Unflinching, their eyes held each other's until Logan, his jaw clenched, hard and proud, became a watery blur and Abby lowered her gaze.

"Call me, Abby. But only when you're sure." The words were meant as a dismissal, and the minute she was out of his car, he drove away.

Abby's knees felt so weak, she sat down as soon as she got inside her apartment. She was stunned. She'd expected Logan to be angry, but she'd never expected this—that he'd refuse to see her again. She'd only tried to be fair. Hurting Logan—or Tate, for that matter— was the last thing she wanted. But how could she possibly know what she felt toward Tate? Everything was still so new. As she'd told Logan, they barely knew each other. They hadn't so much as kissed. But she and Logan were supposed to be friends . . .

She moped around the apartment for a couple of hours, then thought she'd pay her parents a visit. Her mother would be as shocked at Logan's reaction as she'd been. Abby needed reassurance that she'd done the right thing, especially since nothing had worked out as she'd hoped.

The short drive to her parents' house was accomplished in a matter of minutes. But there was no response to her knock; her parents appeared to be out. Belatedly, Abby recalled her mother saying that they were going camping that weekend.

Abby slumped on the front steps, feeling enervated and depressed. Eventually she returned to her car, without any clear idea of where she should go or what she should do.

Never had a Sunday been so dull. Abby drove around for a time, picked up a hamburger at a drive-in, and washed her car. Without Logan, the day seemed empty.

Lying in bed that night, Dano at her feet, Abby closed her eyes. If she'd missed Logan, he must have felt that same sense of loss. This could work both ways. Logan would soon discover how much of a gap she'd left in *his* life.

The phone rang Monday evening and Abby glanced at it anxiously. It had to be Logan, she thought hopefully. Who else would be calling? She didn't recognize the number, so maybe he had a new cell, she told herself.

"Hello," she said cheerfully. If it *was* Logan, she didn't want him to get the impression that she was pining away for him.

"Abby, it's Tate."

Tate. An unreasonable sense of disappointment filled her. What was the matter with her? This whole mess had come about because she wanted to be with Tate.

"How about a movie Friday evening?"

"I'd like that." She exhaled softly.

"You don't sound like yourself. Is something wrong?"

"No," she denied quickly. "What movie would you like to see?"

They spoke for a few more minutes and Abby managed to steer the conversation away from herself. For those few minutes, Tate helped her forget how miserable she was, but the feelings of loss and frustration returned the moment she hung up.

Tuesday evening, Abby waited outside the community center, hoping to see Logan before class. She planned to give him a regal stare that would show how content she was without him. Naturally, if he gave any hint of his own unhappiness, she might succumb and speak to him. But he'd arrived either before her or after she'd gone into the building, because Abby didn't catch a glimpse of him anywhere. Maybe he'd even skipped class, but she doubted that. Logan loved chess.

The painting class remained a blur in her mind as she hurried out the door to the café across the street. She'd met Logan there after every class so far. He'd come; Abby was convinced of it. She pictured how their eyes would meet and intuitively they'd know that being apart like this was wrong for them. Logan would walk to her table, slip in beside her, and take her hand. Everything would be there in his eyes for her to read.

The waitress gave Abby a surprised glance and asked if she was sitting alone tonight as she handed her the menu. Dejectedly, Abby acknowledged that she was alone . . . at least for now.

When Logan entered the café, Abby straightened, her

heart racing. He looked as good as he always did. What she didn't see was any outward sign of unhappiness . . . or relief at her presence. But, she reminded herself, Logan wasn't one to display his emotions openly. Their eyes met and he gave her an abrupt nod before sliding into a booth on the opposite side of the room.

So much for daydreams, Abby mused. Well, fine, he could sit there all night, but she refused to budge. Logan would have to come to her. Determinedly, she studied the menu, pretending indifference. When she couldn't stand it any longer, she glanced at him from the corner of her eye. He now shared his booth with two other guys and was chatting easily with his friends. Abby's heart sank.

"I'm telling you, Mother," Abby said the next afternoon in her mother's kitchen. "He's blown this whole thing out of proportion."

"What makes you say that?" Glenna Carpenter closed the oven door and set the meatloaf on top of the stove.

"Logan isn't even talking to me."

"It doesn't seem like there's been much opportunity. But I wouldn't worry. He will tonight at the game."

"What makes you so sure of that?" Abby hopped down from her position on the countertop.

Glenna straightened and wiped her hands on her ever-present terry-cloth apron. "Things have a way of working out for the best, Abby," she continued nonchalantly.

"Mom, you've been telling me that all my life and I've yet to see it happen."

Glenna chuckled, slowly shaking her head. "It happens every day of our lives. Just look around." Deftly, she turned the meatloaf onto a platter. "By the way, didn't you say your game's at six o'clock?"

Abby nodded and glanced at her watch, surprised that the time had passed so quickly. "Gotta rush. Bye, Mom." She gave her mother a peck on the cheek. "Wish me well."

"With Logan or the game?" Teasing blue eyes so like her own twinkled merrily.

"Both!" Abby laughed and was out the door.

Glenna followed her to the porch, and Abby felt her mother's sober gaze as she hurried down the front steps and to her car.

Almost everyone was on the field warming up when Abby got there. Immediately her gaze sought out Logan. He was in the outfield, pitching to another of the male players. Abby tried to suppress the emotion that charged through her. Who would've believed she'd feel so lost and unhappy without Logan? If he saw that Abby had arrived, he gave no indication.

"Hi, Abby," Patty called, waving from the bench.

Abby smiled absently. "Hi."

"Wait until you see me bat." Patty beamed happily, pretending to swing at an imaginary pitch. Then, placing her hand over her eyes as the fantasy ball flew into left field, she added, "I think I'll be up for an award by the end of the season."

"Good." Abby was preoccupied as she stared out at Logan. He looked so attractive. So vital. Couldn't he have the decency to develop some lines at his eyes or a few gray hairs? He *had* to be suffering. She was, although it wasn't what she'd wanted or expected.

"Logan took me to see the Twins play on Monday night and he gave me a few pointers afterward," Patty continued.

Abby couldn't believe what she was hearing. *A few pointers? I'll just bet he did!* Logan and Patty?

The shock must have shown in her eyes because Patty added hurriedly, "You don't mind, do you? When Logan phoned, I asked him about the two of you and he said you'd both decided to start seeing other people."

"No, I don't mind," Abby returned flippantly, remembering her impression last week—that Patty had a crush on him. "Why should I?"

"I . . . I just wanted to be sure."

If Patty thought she'd get an award for softball, Abby was sure someone should nominate *her* for an Oscar. By the end of the game her face hurt from her permanent smile. She laughed, cheered, joked, and tried to suggest that she hadn't a care in the world. At bat she was dynamite. Her pain was readily transferred to her swing and she didn't hit anything less than a double and got two home runs.

Once, when Logan had patted her affectionately on the back to congratulate her, Abby had shot him an angry glare. It'd taken him only one day. *One day* to ask Patty out. That hurt.

"Abby?" Logan's dark brows rose questioningly. "What's wrong?"

"Wrong?" Although she gave him a blank look, she realized her face must have divulged her feelings. "What could possibly be wrong? By the way, Tate said hello. He wanted to be here tonight, but something came up." Abby knew her lie was childish, but she couldn't help her reaction.

She didn't speak to him again.

Gathering the equipment, Abby tried not to remember the way Patty had positioned herself next to Logan on the bench and how she made excuses to be near him at every opportunity.

"You're coming for pizza, aren't you?" Dick asked Abby for the second time.

Abby wanted to go. The get-togethers after the game were often more fun than the game itself. But she couldn't bear the curious stares that were sure to follow when Logan sat next to Patty and started flirting with her.

"Not tonight," Abby responded, opening her eyes wide to give Dick a look of false candor. "I've got other plans." Abby noticed the way Logan's mouth curved in a mirthless smile. He'd heard that and come to his own conclusions. *Good!*

Abby regretted her hasty refusal later. The apartment was hot and muggy. Even Dano, her temperamental cat, didn't want to spend time with her.

After a cool shower, Abby fixed a meal of scrambled eggs, toast, and a chocolate bar. She wasn't the least bit hungry, but eating was at least a distraction.

She couldn't concentrate on her newest suspense novel, so she sat on the sofa and turned on the TV. A rerun of an old sitcom helped block out the image of Patty in Logan's arms. Abby didn't doubt that Logan had kissed Patty. The bright, happy look in her eyes had said as much.

Uncrossing her legs, Abby released a bitter sigh. She shouldn't care if Logan kissed a hundred women. But she did. It bothered her immensely—regardless of her own hopes and fantasies about Tate. She recognized how irrational she was being, and her confusion only increased.

With the television blaring to drown out the echo of Patty telling her about the fun she'd had with Logan, Abby reached for the chocolate bar and peeled off the wrapper. The sweet flavor wouldn't ease the discomfort in her stomach, because Abby knew it wasn't chocolate she wanted, it was Logan. Feeling wretched again, she set the candy bar aside and leaned her head back, closing her eyes.

By Friday evening, Abby was convinced all the contradictory feelings she had about Logan could be summed up in one sentence: The grass is always greener on the other side of the fence. It was another of those clichés her mother seemed so fond of and spouted on a regular basis. She was surprised Glenna hadn't dragged this one into their conversations about Logan and Tate. The idea of getting involved with Tate had been appealing when she was seeing Logan steadily. It stood to reason that the reverse was also true—that Logan would miss her and lose interest in Patty. At least that was what Abby told herself repeatedly as she dressed for her date.

With her long brown hair a frame around her oval face, she put on more makeup than usual. With a secret little smile she applied an extra dab of perfume. Tate wouldn't know what hit him! The summer dress was one of her best—a pale blue sheath that could be dressed up or down, so she was as comfortable wearing it to a movie as she would be to a formal dinner.

When Tate arrived, he had on a pair of cords and a cotton shirt, open at the neck, sleeves rolled up. It was an undeniably sexy look.

"You're stunning," he said appreciatively, kissing her lightly on the cheek.

"Thank you." Abby couldn't restrain her disappointment. He'd looked at her the way one would a sister and his kiss wasn't that of a lover—or someone who intended to be a lover.

Still, they joked easily as they waited in line for the latest blockbuster action movie and Abby was struck by their camaraderie. It didn't take her long to realize that their relationship wasn't hot and fiery, sparked by mutual attraction. It was . . . friendly. Warm. Almost lacking in imagination. Ironically, that had been exactly her complaint about Logan . . .

Tate bought a huge bucket of popcorn, which they shared in the darkened theater. But Abby noted that he appeared restless, often shifting his position, crossing and uncrossing his legs. Once, when he assumed she wasn't watching, he laid his head against the back of the seat and closed his eyes. Was Tate in pain? she wondered.

Abby's attention drifted from the movie. "Tate," she whispered. "Are you okay?"

He immediately opened his eyes. "Of course. Why?"

Rather than refer to his restlessness, she simply shook her head and pretended an interest in the screen.

When they'd finished the popcorn, Tate reached for her hand. But Abby noted that it felt tense. If she didn't know better, she'd swear he was nervous. But Abby couldn't imagine what possible reason Tate would have to be nervous around her.

The evening was hot and close when they emerged from the theater.

"Are you hungry?" Tate asked, taking her hand, and again, Abby was struck by how unnaturally tense he seemed.

"For something cold and sinful," she answered with a teasing smile.

"Beer?"

"No," Abby said with a laugh. "Ice cream."

Tate laughed, too, and hand in hand they strolled toward the downtown area, where Tate assured her he knew of an old-fashioned ice-cream place. The Swanson Parlor was decorated in pink—pink walls, pink chairs, pink linen tablecloths, and pink-dressed waitresses.

Abby decided quickly on a banana split and mentioned it to Tate.

"That does sound good. I'll have one, too."

Abby shut her menu and set it aside. This was the third time they'd gone for something to eat, and each time Tate had ordered the same thing she did. He didn't seem insecure. But maybe she was being oversensitive. Besides, it didn't make any difference.

Their rapport made conversation comfortable and lighthearted. They talked about the movie and other films they'd both seen. Abby discussed some of her favorite mystery novels and Tate described animal behavior he'd witnessed. But several times Abby noted that his laughter was forced. His gaze would become intent and his sudden seriousness would throw the conversation off stride.

"I love Minneapolis," Abby said as they left the ice-cream parlor. "It's such a livable city."

"I agree," Tate commented. "Do you want to go for a walk?"

"Yes, let's." Abby tucked her hand in the crook of his elbow.

Tate looked at her and smiled, but again Abby noted the sober look in his eyes. "I was born in California," he began.

"What's it like there?" Abby had been to New York, but she'd never visited the West Coast.

"I don't remember much. My family moved to New Mexico when I was six."

"Hot, I'll bet," Abby said.

"It's funny, the kinds of things you remember. I don't recall what the weather was like. But I have a very clear memory of my first-grade teacher in Albuquerque, Ms. Grimes. She was pretty and really tall." Tate chuckled. "But I suppose all teachers are tall to a six-year-old. We moved again in the middle of that year."

"You seem to have moved around quite a bit," Abby said, wondering why Tate had started talking about himself so freely. Although they had talked about a number of different subjects, she knew little about his personal life.

"We moved five times in as many years," Tate continued. "We had no choice, really. My dad couldn't hold down a job, and every time he lost one we'd pack up and move, seeking another start, another escape." Tate's face hardened. "We came to Minneapolis when I was in the eighth grade."

"Did your father finally find his niche in life?" Abby sensed that Tate was revealing something he rarely shared with anyone. She felt honored, but surprised. Their relationship was promising in some ways and disappointing in others, but the fact that he trusted her with his pain, his difficult past, meant a lot. She wondered why he'd chosen her as a confidante.

"No, Dad died before he ever found what he was looking for." There was no disguising the anguish in his voice. "My feelings for my father are as confused now as they were then." He turned toward Abby, his expression solemn. "I hated him and I loved him."

"Did your life change after he was gone?" Abby's question was practically a whisper, respecting the deep emotion in Tate's eyes.

"Yes and no. A couple of years later, I dropped out of school and got a job as a mechanic. My dad taught me a lot, enough to persuade Jack Bessler to hire me."

"And you've been there ever since?"

His mouth quirked at one corner. "Ever since."

"You didn't graduate from high school, then, did you?"

"No."

That sadness was back in his voice. "And you resent that?" Abby asked softly.

"I may have for a time, but I never fit in a regular classroom. I guess in some ways I'm a lot like my dad. Restless and insecure. But I'm much more content working at the garage than I ever was in a classroom."

"You've worked there for years now," Abby said, contradicting his assessment of himself. "How can you say you're restless?"

He didn't acknowledge her question. "There's a chance I could buy the business. Jack's ready to retire and wants out from under the worry."

"That's what you really want, isn't it, Tate?"

"The business is more than I ever thought I'd have."

"But something's stopping you?" Abby could sense this more from his tension than from what he said.

"Yes." The stark emotion in his voice startled her.

"Are you worried about not having graduated from high school? Because, Tate, you can now. There's a program at the community center where I take painting classes. You can get what they call a GED—General Education Diploma, I think is what it means. Anyway, all you need to do is talk to a counselor and—"

"That's not it." Tate interrupted her harshly and ran a hand across his brow.

"Then what is it?" Abby asked, her smile determined.

Tate hesitated until the air between them was electric, like a storm ready to explode in the muggy heat.

"Where are you going with this discussion? What can I do to help? I don't understand." One minute Tate was exposing a painful part of his past, and the next he was growling at her. What was it with men? Something had been bothering him all evening. First he'd been restless and uneasy, then brooding and thoughtful, now angry. Nothing made sense.

And it wasn't going to. Abruptly, he asked her if she was ready to leave.

He hardly said a word to her when he dropped her off at her apartment.

For a moment, Abby was convinced he'd never ask her out again.

"What about Sunday?" he finally said. "We can bring a picnic."

"Okay." But after this evening, Abby wasn't sure. He didn't sound as if he really wanted her company. "How about three o'clock?"

"Fine." His response was clipped.

Again he gave her a modest kiss, more a light brushing of their mouths than anything passionate or intense. Not a real kiss, in her opinion.

She leaned against the closed door of her apartment, not understanding why Tate was bothering to take her out. It seemed apparent that his interest in her wasn't romantic—although she didn't know what it actually was, didn't know what he wanted or needed from her. And for that matter, the bone-melting effect she'd experienced at their first meeting had long since gone. Tate was a handsome man, but he wasn't what she'd expected.

Maybe the grass wasn't so green after all.

After a restless Sunday morning, Abby decided that she'd go for a walk in the park. Logan often did before he came over to her place, and she hoped to run into him. She'd make a point of letting him know that their meeting was pure coincidence. They'd talk. Somehow she'd inform him—casually, of course—that things weren't working out as she'd planned. In fact, yesterday, during her lesson with Mai-Ling, Tate didn't come to the park, and she'd secretly been relieved. Despite today's picnic, she suspected that their romance was over before it could really start. And now she had doubts about its potential, anyway. *Hmm*. Maybe she'd hint to Logan that she missed his company. That should be enough to break the ice without either of them losing their pride. And that was what this came down to—pride.

The park was crowded by the time Abby arrived. Entering the grounds, she scanned the lawns for him and released a grateful sigh to find that he was sitting on a park bench, reading. By himself. To her relief, Patty wasn't with him.

Deciding on her strategy, Abby stuck her hands in her pockets and strolled down the paved lane, hoping to look as if she'd merely come for a walk in the park. Their meeting would be by accident.

Abby stood about ten feet away, off to one side, watching Logan. She was surprised at the emotion she felt just studying him. He looked peaceful, but then he always did. He was composed, confident, in control. Equal to any situation. They'd been dating for almost a year and Abby hadn't realized that so much of her life was interwoven with Logan's. She'd taken him for granted until he was gone, and the emptiness he'd left behind had shocked her. She'd been stupid and insensitive. And heaven knew how difficult it was for her to admit she'd been wrong.

For several minutes Abby did nothing but watch him. A calm settled over her as she focused on Logan's shoulders. They weren't as broad or muscular as Tate's, but somehow it didn't matter. Not now, not when she was hurting, missing Logan and his friendship. Without giving it much thought, she'd been looking forward to Sunday all week and now she knew precisely why: Sundays had always been special because they were spent with Logan. It was Logan she wanted, Logan she needed, and Abby desperately hoped she wasn't too late.

Abby continued to gaze at him. After a while her determination to talk to him grew stronger. Never mind her ego—Logan had a right to know her feelings. He'd been patient with her far longer than she deserved. Her stomach felt queasy, her mouth dry. Just when she'd gathered enough courage to approach him, Logan clasped his book and stood up. Turning around, he looked in her direction, but didn't hesitate for a second. He glanced at his watch and walked idly down the concrete pathway toward her until he was within calling distance. Abby's breath froze as he looked her way, blinked, and looked in the opposite direction. She couldn't believe he'd purposely avoid her, and she doubted he would've been able to see her standing off to the side.

The moment she was ready to step forward, Logan stopped to chat with two older men playing checkers. From her position, Abby saw them motion for him to sit down, which he did. He was soon deep in conversation with them. The three were obviously good friends, although she'd never met the other men before.

Abby loitered as long as she could. Half an hour passed and still Logan stayed.

Defeated, Abby realized she'd have to hurry or be late for her picnic with Tate. Silently she slipped from her viewing position and started across the grounds. When she glanced over her shoulder, she saw that Logan was alone on a bench again and watching a pair of young lovers kissing on the grass. Even from this distance, she saw a look of such intense pain cross his face, she had to force herself not to run to his side. He dropped his head in his hands and hunched forward as if a heavy burden was weighing on him.

Abby's throat clogged with tears until it was painful to breathe. They filled her eyes. Logan loved her and had loved her from the beginning, but she'd carelessly thrown his love aside. It had taken only a few days' separation to know with certainty that she loved him, too.

Tears rolled down her face, but Abby quickly brushed them away. Logan wouldn't want to know she'd seen him. She'd stripped him of so much, it wouldn't be right to take his self-confidence, as well. Today she'd tell Tate she wouldn't be seeing him again. If that was all Logan wanted, it would be a small price to pay. She'd run back to his arms and never leave him again.

By the time she got to her building, Tate was at the front door. They greeted each other and Tate told her about a special place he wanted to show her near Apple Valley.

She ran into her apartment to get a few things, then joined him in the car.

Both seemed preoccupied during the drive. Abby helped him unload the picnic basket, her thoughts racing at breakneck speed. She folded the tablecloth she'd brought over a picnic table while Tate spread out a blanket under a shady tree. They hardly spoke.

"Abby—"

"Tate—"

They both began together.

"You first," Abby murmured, and sat down, drawing

up her legs and circling them with both arms, then resting her chin on her bent knees.

Tate remained standing, hands in his pockets as he paced. Again, something was obviously troubling him.

"Tate, what is it?"

"I didn't know it would be so hard to tell you," he said wryly, and shook his head. "I meant to explain weeks ago."

What was he talking about?

His gaze settled on her, then flickered to the ground. "I tried to tell you Friday night after the movie, but I couldn't get the words out." He ran a weary hand over his face and fell to his knees at her side.

Abby reached for his hand and held it.

"Abby." He released a ragged breath. "*I can't read.* I'll pay you any amount if you'll teach me."

Five

~⁀

In one brilliant flash everything about Tate fell into place. He hadn't been captivated by her charm and natural beauty. He'd overheard her teaching Mai-Ling how to read and known she could help him. That was the reason he'd sought her out and cultivated a friendship. She could help him.

Small things became clear in her mind. No wonder Tate ordered the same thing she did in a restaurant. Naturally their date on Friday night had been awkward. He'd been trying to tell her then. How could she have been so blind?

Even now he studied her intently, awaiting her response. His eyes glittered with pride, insecurity, and fear. She recognized all those emotions and understood them now.

"Of course I'll teach you," she said reassuringly.

"I'll pay you anything you ask."

"Tate." Her grip on his hand tightened. "I wouldn't take anything. We're friends."

"But I can afford to pay you." He took a wad of bills from his pocket and breathed in slowly, glancing at the money in his hand.

Again Abby realized how difficult admitting his inability to read had been. "Put that away," Abby said calmly. "You won't be needing it."

Tate stuffed the bills back in his pocket. "You don't know how relieved I am to have finally told you," he muttered hoarsely.

"I don't think I could have been more obtuse," she said, still shocked at her own stupidity. "I'm amazed you've gotten along as well as you have. I was completely fooled."

"I've become adept at this. I've done it from the time I was in grade school."

"What happened?" Abby asked softly, although she could guess.

A sadness stole into his eyes. "I suppose it's because of all those times I was pulled out of school so we could move," he said unemotionally. "We left New Mexico in the middle of first grade and I never finished the year. Because I was tall for my age, my mother put me in second grade the following September. The teacher wanted to hold me back but we moved again. And again and again." A bitterness infected his voice. "By the time I was in junior high and we'd moved to Minneapolis, I had devised all kinds of ways to disguise the fact that I couldn't read. I was the class clown, the troublemaker, the boy who'd do anything to get out of going to school."

"Oh Tate." Her heart swelled with compassion.

Sitting beside her, Tate rubbed his hand across his

face and smiled grimly. "But the hardest part was getting up the courage to tell you."

"You've never told anyone else, have you?"

"No. It was like admitting I have some horrible disease."

"You don't. We can fix this," she said. She was trying to reassure him and felt pathetically inadequate.

"Will you promise me that you'll keep this to yourself? For now?"

She nodded. "I promise." She understood how humiliated he felt, why he wanted his inability to read to remain a secret, and felt she had to agree.

"When can we start? There's so much I want to learn. So much I want to read. Books and magazines and computer programs . . ." He sounded eager, his gaze level and questioning.

"Is tomorrow too soon?" Abby asked.

"I'd say it's about twenty years too late."

Tate brought Abby back to her apartment two hours later. Tomorrow she'd call the World Literacy Movement and have them email the forms for her to complete regarding Tate. He looked jubilant, excited. Telling her about his inability to read had probably been one of the most difficult things he'd ever done in his life. She understood how formidable his confession had felt to him because now she had to humble herself and call Logan. And that, although major to her, was a small thing in comparison.

Abby wasn't unhappy at Tate's confession. True, her dignity was stung for a moment. But overall she was relieved. Tate was the kind of man who'd always attract women's attention. For a brief time she'd been caught up in his masculine appeal. And if it hadn't been for Tate, it would have taken her a lot longer to recognize how fortunate she was to have Logan.

Phoning him and admitting that she was wrong had been unthinkable a week ago. Had it been only a week? In some ways it felt like a year.

Abby glanced at the ceiling and prayed that Logan would answer her call. There was so much stored in her heart that she wanted to tell him. Her hand trembled as she lifted the receiver and tried to form positive thoughts. *Everything's going to work out. I know it will.* She repeated that mantra over and over as she dialed.

She was so nervous her fingers shook and her stomach churned until she was convinced she was going to be sick. Inhaling, Abby held her breath as his phone rang the first time. Her lungs refused to function. Abby closed her eyes tightly during the second ring.

"Hello?"

Abby took a deep breath.

"Logan, this is Abby."

"Abby?" He sounded shocked.

"Can we talk? I mean, I can call back if this is inconvenient."

"I'm on my way out the door. Would you like me to come over?"

"Yes." She was surprised at how composed she sounded. "That would be great." She replaced the phone and tilted her head toward the ceiling. "Thank you," she murmured gratefully.

Looking down, Abby realized how casually she was

dressed. When Logan saw her again, she wanted to bowl him over.

Racing into her room, she ripped the dress she'd worn Friday night off the hanger, then decided it wouldn't do. She tossed it across her bed. She tried on one outfit and then another. Never had she been more unsure about what she wanted to wear. Finally she chose a pair of tailored black pants and a white blouse with an eyelet collar. Simple, elegant, classic.

Abby was frantically brushing her hair when the buzzer rang. *Logan.* She gripped the edge of the sink and took in a deep breath. Then she set the brush down, practiced her smile, and walked into the living room.

"Hello, Abby," Logan said a moment later as he stepped into the apartment.

Her first impulse was to throw her arms around him and weep. A tightness gripped her throat. Whatever poise she'd managed to gather was shaken and gone with one look from him.

"Hello, Logan. Would you like to sit down?" She gestured toward the chair. Her gaze was fixed on his shoulders as he walked across the room and took a seat.

"And before you ask," he interjected sternly, "no, I don't want anything to drink. Sit down, Abby."

She complied, grateful because she didn't know how much longer her knees would support her.

"You wanted to talk?" The lines at the sides of his mouth deepened, but he wasn't smiling.

"Yes." She laced her hands together tightly. "I was wrong," she murmured. Now that the words were out, Abby experienced none of the calm she'd expected. "I'm—I'm sorry."

"It wasn't a question of my being right or your being wrong," Logan said. "I'm not looking for an apology."

Abby's lips trembled and she bit into the bottom corner. "I know that. But I felt I owed you one."

"No." He stood, and with one hand in his pocket paced the width of the carpet. "That's not what I wanted to hear. I told you to call me when you were sure it was me you wanted and not Tate." His eyes rested on her, his expression hooded.

Abby stood, unable to meet his gaze. "I *am* sure," she breathed. "I know it's you I want."

His mouth quirked in what could have been a smile, but he didn't acknowledge her confession.

"You have every right to be angry with me." She couldn't look at him, afraid of what she'd see. If he were to reject her now, Abby didn't think she could stand it. "I've missed you so much," she mumbled. Her cheeks flamed with color, and she couldn't believe how difficult this was. She felt tears in her eyes as she bowed her head.

"Abby." Logan's arms came around her shoulders, bringing her within the comforting circle of his arms. He lifted her chin and lovingly studied her face. "You're sure?"

The growing lump in her throat made speech impossible. She nodded, letting all the love in her eyes say the words.

"Oh Abby . . ." He claimed her lips with a hungry kiss that revealed the depth of his feelings.

Slipping her arms around his neck, Abby felt him shudder with a longing he'd suppressed all these months. He buried his face in the dark waves of her hair and held her so tightly it was difficult to breathe.

"I've been so wrong about so many things," she confessed, rubbing her hands up and down his spine, reveling in the muscular feel of him.

Lowering himself to the sofa, Logan pulled Abby onto his lap. His warm breath was like a gentle caress as she wound her arms around his neck and kissed him, wanting to make up to him for all the pain she'd caused them both. The wild tempo of her pulse made clear thought impossible.

Finally, Logan dragged his mouth from hers. "You're sure?" he asked, as if he couldn't quite believe it.

Abby pressed her forehead against his shoulder and nodded. "Very sure. I was such a fool."

His arm held her securely in place. "Tell me more. I'm enjoying this."

Unable to resist, Abby kissed the side of his mouth. "I thought you would."

"So you missed me?"

"I was miserable."

"Good!"

"Logan," she cried softly. "It wouldn't do you any harm to tell me how lonely *you* were."

"I wasn't," he said jokingly.

Involuntarily, Abby stiffened and swallowed back the hurt. "I know. Patty mentioned that you'd taken her to the Twins game."

Logan smiled wryly. "We went with several other people."

"It bothers me that you could see someone else so soon."

"Honey." His hold tightened around her waist, bringing her closer. "It wasn't like what you're thinking."

"But . . . you said you weren't lonely."

"How could I have been? I saw you Tuesday and then at the game on Wednesday."

"I know, but—"

"Are we going to argue?"

"A thousand kisses might convince me," she teased, and rested her head on his shoulder.

"I haven't got the willpower to continue kissing you without thinking of other things," he murmured in her ear as his hand stroked her hair. "I love you, Abby. I've loved you from the first time I asked you out." His breathing seemed less controlled than it had been a moment before.

"Oh Logan." Fresh tears sprang to her eyes. She started to tell him how much she cared for him, but he went on, cutting off her words.

"As soon as I saw Tate I knew there was no way I could compete with him. He's everything I'll never be. Tall. Movie-star looks." He shook his head. "I don't blame you for being attracted to him."

Abby straightened so she could look at this man she loved. Her hands framed his face. "You're a million things Tate could never be."

"I know this has been hard on you."

"But I was so stupid," Abby inserted.

He kissed her lightly, his lips lingering over hers. "I can't help feeling grateful that you won't be seeing him again."

Abby lowered her eyes. She *would* be seeing Tate, but not in the way Logan meant.

A stillness filled the room. "Abby?"

She gave him a feeble smile.

"You aren't seeing Tate, are you?"

She couldn't reveal Tate's problem to anyone. She'd promised. And not for the world would she embarrass him, especially when admitting he couldn't read had been so difficult. No matter how much she wanted to tell Logan, she couldn't.

"I'd like to explain," Abby replied, her voice trembling.

Logan stiffened and lightly pushed her from his lap. "I don't want explanations. All I want is the truth. Will you or will you not be seeing Tate?"

"Not romantically," she answered, as tactfully and truthfully as possible.

Logan's eyes hardened. "What other explanation could there be?"

"I can't tell you that," she said forcefully, and stood up.

"Of course you can." A muscle worked in his jaw. "We're right back where we started, aren't we, Abby?"

"No." She felt like screaming at him for being so unreasonable. Surely he recognized how hard it had been for her to call him and admit she was wrong?

"Will you stop seeing Tate, then?" he challenged.

"I can't." Her voice cracked in a desperate appeal for him to understand. "We live in the same neighborhood . . ." she said, stalling for time as her mind raced for an excuse. "I'll probably run into him . . . I mean, it'd be only natural, since he's so close and all."

"Abby." Logan groaned impatiently. "That's not what I mean and you know it. Will you or will you not be *seeing* Tate?"

She hesitated. Knowing what her promise was doing

to her relationship with Logan, Tate would want him to know. But she couldn't say anything without clearing it with him first.

"Abby?"

"I'll be seeing him, but please understand that it's not the way you assume."

For an instant, Abby saw pain in Logan's eyes. The pain she witnessed was the same torment she was experiencing herself.

They stood with only a few feet separating them, and yet Abby felt they'd never been farther apart. Whole worlds seemed to loom between them. Logan's ego was at stake, his honor, and he didn't want her to continue seeing Tate, no matter what the reason.

"You won't stop seeing him," Logan challenged furiously.

"I can't," Abby cried, just as angry.

"Then there's nothing left to say."

"Yes," Abby said, "there is, but you're in no mood to hear it. Just remember that things aren't always as they appear."

"Good-bye, Abby," he responded. "And next time don't bother calling me unless—"

Abby stalked across the room and threw open the door. "Next time I won't," she said with a cutting edge.

Reaction set in the minute the door slammed behind him. Abby was so angry that pacing the floor did little to relieve it. How could Logan say he loved her in one breath and turn around and storm out the next? Yet he'd done exactly that.

Once the anger dissipated, Abby began to tremble and she felt the tears burning for release. Pride demanded that she forestall them. She wouldn't allow Logan to reduce her to that level. She shook her head and kept her chin raised. *I won't cry, I won't cry,* she repeated over and over as one tear after another slid down her cheeks.

"Who did you say was responsible for the literacy movement?" Tate asked, leafing respectfully through the first book.

"Dr. Frank Laubach. He was a missionary in the Philippines in the 1920s. At that time some of the island people didn't have a written language. He invented one and later developed a method of teaching adults to read."

"Sounds like he accomplished a lot."

Abby nodded. "By the time he died in 1970, his work had spread to one hundred five countries and three hundred thirteen languages."

Tate continued leafing through the pages of the primary workbook. Abby wanted to start him at the most fundamental skill level, knowing his progress would be rapid. At this point, Tate would need all the encouragement he could get, and the speed with which he completed the lower-level books was sure to help.

Abby hadn't underestimated Tate's enthusiasm. By the end of the first lesson he had relearned the alphabet and was reading simple phrases. He proudly took the book home with him.

"Can we meet again tomorrow?" he asked, standing near her apartment door.

"I've got my class tomorrow evening," Abby explained, "but if you like, we could meet for a half-hour before—or after, if you prefer."

"Before, I think."

The following afternoon, Tate showed up an hour early, just after she got home from work, and seemed disappointed that Abby would be occupied with softball on Wednesday evening.

"We could get together afterward if you want," she told him.

Affectionately, Tate kissed her on the cheek. "I want."

Again she noted that his fondness for her was more like that of a brother—or a pupil for his teacher. She was grateful for that, at least. And he was wonderful to her. He brought over takeout meals and gave her small gifts as a way of showing his appreciation. The gifts weren't necessary, but they salvaged Tate's dignity, and that was something she was learning more about every day—male pride.

Abby was dressing for the game Wednesday evening when the phone rang. No longer did she expect or even hope it would be Logan. He'd made his position completely clear. Fortunately, caller ID told her it was her parents' number.

"Hello, Mom."

"Abby, I've been worried about you."

"I'm fine!" She forced some enthusiasm into her voice.

"Oh dear, it's worse than I thought."

"What's worse?"

"Logan and you."

"There is no more Logan and me," she returned.

A strained silence followed. "But I thought—"

"Listen, Mom," Abby cut in, unwilling to listen to her mother's postmortem. "I've got a game tonight. Can I call you later?"

"Why don't you come over for dinner?"

"Not tonight." Abby hated to turn down her mother's invitation, but she'd already agreed to see Tate for his next lesson.

"It's your birthday Friday," Glenna reminded her.

"I'll come for dinner then," Abby said with a feeble smile. Her birthday was only two days away and she wasn't in any mood to celebrate. "But only if you promise to make my favorite dish."

"Barbecued chicken!" her mother announced. "You bet."

"And, Mom," Abby continued, "you were right about Logan."

"What was I right about?" Her mother's voice rose slightly.

"He does love me, and I love him."

Abby thought she heard a small, happy sound.

"What made you realize that?" her mother asked.

"A lot of things," Abby said noncommittally. "But I also realized that loving someone doesn't make everything perfect. I wish it did."

"I have the feeling there's something important you're not telling me, Abby," Glenna said, on a note of puzzled sadness. "But I know you will in your own good time."

Abby couldn't disagree with her mother's observation. "I'll be at your place around six on Friday," she murmured. "And thanks, Mom."

"What are mothers for?" Glenna teased.

The disconnected phone line droned in Abby's ear

before she hung up, suddenly surprised to see that it was time to head over to the park. For the first time that she could remember, she didn't feel psyched up for the game. She wasn't ready to see Logan, which would be more painful than reassuring. And if he paid Patty special attention, Abby didn't know how she'd handle that. But Logan wouldn't do anything to hurt her. At least she knew him well enough to be sure of that.

The first thing Abby noticed as she walked onto the diamond was that Patty Martin had cut and styled her hair. The transformation from straight mousy-brown hair to short, bouncy curls was astonishing. The young woman positively glowed.

"What do you think?" Patty asked in a hurried voice. "Your hair is always so pretty and . . ." She let the rest of what she was going to say fade.

Abby held herself motionless. Patty had made herself attractive for Logan. She desperately wanted Logan's interest, and for all Abby knew, she was getting it. "I think you look great," Abby commented, unable to deny the truth or to be unkind.

"I was scared out of my wits," Patty admitted shyly. "It's been a long time since I was at the hairdresser's."

"Hey, Patty, they're waiting for you on the field," the team's coach hollered. "Abby, you, too."

"Okay, Dick," Patty called back happily, her eyes shining. "I've gotta go. We'll talk later, okay?"

"Fine." Softening her stiff mitt against her hand with unnecessary force, Abby ran to her position at first base.

Logan was practicing in the outfield.

"Abby," he called, and when she turned, she found his gaze level and unwavering. "Catch."

Nothing appeared to affect him. They'd suffered through the worst four days of their relationship and he looked at her as coolly and unemotionally as he would a . . . a dish of potato salad. She didn't respond other than to catch the softball and pitch it to second base.

The warm-up period lasted for about ten minutes. Abby couldn't recall a time she'd felt less like playing, and it showed.

"What's the matter, Ab?" Dick asked her at the bottom of the fifth, after she'd struck out for the third time. "You're not yourself tonight."

"I'm sorry," she said with a frustrated sigh. Her eyes didn't meet his. "This isn't one of my better nights."

"She's got other things on her mind." Logan spoke from behind her, signaling that he was sitting in the bleachers one row above. "Her boyfriend just showed up, so she'll do better."

Abby whirled around to face Logan. "What do you mean by that?"

Logan nodded in the direction of the parking lot. Abby's gaze followed his movement and she wanted to groan aloud. Tate was walking toward the stands.

"Tate isn't my boyfriend." Abby's voice was taut with impatience.

"Oh, is that terminology passé?" Logan returned.

Stunned at the bitterness in him, Abby found no words to respond. They were both hurting, and in their pain they were lashing out at each other.

Logan slid from the bleachers for his turn at bat.

Abby focused her attention on him, deciding she didn't want to make a fuss over Tate's unexpected arrival.

Logan swung wildly at the first pitch, hitting the ball with the tip of his bat. Abby could hear the wood crack as the ball went flying over the fence for a home run. Logan looked as shocked as Abby. He tossed the bat aside and ran around the bases to the shouts and cheers of his teammates. Abby couldn't remember Logan ever getting more than a single.

"Hi." Tate slid into the row of seats behind her. "You don't mind if I come and watch, do you?" he asked as he leaned forward with lazy grace.

"Not at all," Abby said blandly. It didn't make any difference now. She stared at her laced fingers, attempting to fight off the depression that seemed to have settled over her. She was so caught up in her own sorrows that she didn't see the accident. Only the startled cries of those around her alerted her to the fact that something had happened.

"What's wrong?" Abby asked frantically as the bench cleared. Everyone was running toward Patty, who was clutching her arm and doubled over in pain.

Logan's voice could be heard above the confusion. "Stand back. Give her room." Gently, he aided Patty into a sitting position.

Even to Abby's untrained eye it was obvious that Patty's arm was broken. Logan tore off his shirt and tied it around her upper body to create a sling and support the injured arm.

The words *hospital* and *doctor* were flying around, but everyone seemed stunned and no one moved. Again it was Logan who helped Patty to her feet and led her to his car. His calm, decisive actions imparted confidence to both teams. Only minutes before, Abby had been angry because he displayed so little emotion.

"What happened?" Abby asked Dick as they walked off the field.

"I'm not sure." Dick looked shaken himself. "Patty was trying to steal a base and collided with the second baseman. When she fell, she put out her arm to catch herself and it twisted under her."

"Will she be all right?"

"Logan seemed to think so. He's taking her to the emergency room. He said he'd let us know her condition as soon as possible."

The captain of the opposing team crossed the diamond to talk to Dick and it was decided that they'd play out the remainder of the game.

But without Logan the team was short one male player.

"Do you think your friend would mind filling in?" Dick asked somewhat sheepishly, glancing at Tate.

"I can ask."

"No problem," Tate said, smiling as he picked up Logan's discarded mitt and ran onto the field.

Although they'd decided to finish the game, almost everyone was preoccupied with the accident. Abby's team ended up winning, thanks to Tate, but by only a slight margin.

The group as a whole proceeded to the pizza parlor to wait for word about Patty.

Tate sat across the long wooden table from Abby, chatting easily with her teammates. Only a few slices of the two large pizzas had been eaten. Their conversation was a low hum as they recounted their versions of the accident and what could have been done to prevent it.

Abby was grateful for Logan's clear thinking and quick actions. He wasn't the kind of skilled softball player who'd stand out, but he gave himself in a way that was essential to every member of the team. Only a few days earlier she'd found Logan lacking. Compared to the muscular Tate, he'd seemed a poor second. Now she noted that his strengths were inner ones. Again she was reminded that if given the chance, she would love this man for the rest of her life.

Abby didn't see Logan enter the restaurant, but the immediate clamor caused her to turn. She stood with the others.

"Patty's fine," he assured everyone. "Her arm's broken, but I don't think that's news to anyone."

"When will she be back?"

"We want to send flowers or something."

"When do you think she'll feel up to company?"

Everyone spoke at once. Calmly, Logan answered each question, and when he'd finished, the mood around the table was considerably lighter.

A tingling awareness at the back of her neck told Abby that Logan was near. With a sweeping action he swung his foot over the long bench and joined her.

He focused on Tate, sitting across from Abby. "I wish I could say it's good to see you again," he said with stark unfriendliness.

"Logan, please!" Abby hissed.

The two men eyed each other like bears who'd violated each other's territory. Tate had no romantic interest in her, Abby was convinced of that, but Logan was openly challenging him and Tate wouldn't walk away from such blatant provocation.

Unaware of the dangerous undercurrents swirling around the table, Dick Snyder sauntered over and slapped Logan on the back.

"We owe a debt of thanks to Tate here," he informed Logan cheerfully. "He stepped in for you when you were gone. He batted in the winning run."

Logan and Tate didn't so much as blink. "Tate's been doing a lot of that for me lately, isn't that right, Abby?"

Wrenching her gaze from him, Abby stood and, with as much dignity and self-confidence as she could muster, walked out of the restaurant and went home alone.

The phone was ringing when she walked into the apartment. Abby let it ring. She didn't want to talk to anyone. She didn't even want to know who'd called.

"Abby, would you take the bread out of the oven?" her mother asked, walking out to the patio.

"Okay." Abby turned off the broiler and pulled out the cookie sheet, on which slices of French bread oozed with melted butter and chopped garlic. Her enthusiasm for this birthday celebration was nil.

The doorbell caught her by surprise. "Are you expecting anyone?" she asked her mother, who'd returned to the kitchen.

"Not that I know of. I'll get it."

Abby was placing the bread slices in a warming basket when she heard her mother's surprised voice.

Turning, Abby looked straight at Logan.

Six

A shocked expression crossed Logan's face. "Abby." He took a step inside the room and paused.

"Hello, Logan." A tense silence ensued as Abby primly folded her hands.

"I'll check the chicken," Glenna Carpenter murmured discreetly as she hurried past them.

"What brings you to this neck of the woods?" Abby forced a lightness into her voice. He looked tired, as if he hadn't been sleeping well. For that matter, neither had Abby, but she doubted either would admit as much.

Logan handed her a wrapped package. "I wanted your mother to give you this. But since you're here—happy birthday."

A small smile parted her trembling lips as Abby accepted the brightly wrapped gift. He had come to her parents' home to deliver this, but he hadn't expected her to be there.

"Thank you." She continued to hold it.

"I, uh, didn't expect to see you." He stated the obvious, as though he couldn't think of anything else to say.

"Where else would I be on my birthday?"

Logan shrugged. "With Tate."

Abby released a sigh of indignation. "I thought I'd explained that I'm not involved with Tate. We're friends, nothing more."

She shook her head. They'd gone over this before. Another argument wouldn't help. Abby figured she'd endured enough emotional turmoil in the past few weeks. She still hadn't spoken to Tate about telling Logan the truth. But she couldn't, not with Tate feeling as sensitive as he did about the whole thing.

"Abby." Logan's voice was deadly quiet. "Don't you see what's happening? You may not think of Tate in a romantic light, but I saw the way he was looking at you in the pizza place."

"You openly challenged him." Abby threw out a few challenges of her own. "How did you expect him to react? You wouldn't have behaved any differently," she said. "And if you've come to ruin my birthday . . . then you can just leave. I've had about all I can take from you, Logan Fletcher." She whirled around, not wanting to face him.

"I didn't come for that." The defeat was back in his voice again.

Abby's pulse thundered in her ears as she waited for the sounds of him leaving—at the same time hoping he wouldn't.

"Aren't you going to open your present?" he said at last.

Abby turned and wiped away a tear that had escaped

from the corner of her eye. "I already know what it is," she said, glancing down at the package. "Honestly, Logan, you're so predictable."

"How could you possibly know?"

"Because you got me the same perfume for my birthday last year." Deftly she removed the wrapping paper and held up the small bottle of expensive French fragrance.

"I like the way it smells on you," Logan murmured, walking across the room. He rested his hands on her shoulders. "And if I'm so predictable, you'll also recall that there's a certain thank-you I expect."

Any resistance drained from her as Logan pulled her into his embrace. Abby slid her arms around his neck and tasted the sweetness of his kiss. A wonderful languor stole through her limbs as his mouth brushed the sweeping curve of her lashes and burned a trail down her cheek to her ear.

"I love you, Logan," Abby whispered with all the intensity in her.

Logan went utterly still. Gradually he raised his head so he could study her. Unflinching, Abby met his gaze, determined that he see for himself what her eyes and heart were saying.

"If you love me, then you'll stop seeing Tate," he said flatly.

"And if you love *me,* you'll trust me."

"Abby." Logan dropped his hands and stepped away. "I—"

"Oh Logan." Glenna Carpenter moved out of the kitchen. "I'm glad to see you're still here. We insist you stay for dinner. Isn't that right, Abby?"

Logan held her gaze with mesmerizing simplicity.

"Of course we do. If you don't have another appointment," Abby said meaningfully.

"You know I don't."

Abby knew nothing of the kind, but didn't want to argue. "Did you see the gift Logan brought me?" Abby asked her mother and held out the perfume.

"Logan is always so thoughtful."

"Yes, he is," Abby agreed, and slipped an arm around his waist, enjoying the feel of him at her side. "Thoughtful, but not very original." Her eyes smiled into his, pleading with him that, for tonight, they could forget their differences.

Logan's arms slid just as easily around her. "But with that kind of thank-you, what incentive do I have for shopping around?"

Abby laughed and led the way to the back patio.

Frank Carpenter, Abby's father, was busy standing in front of the barbecue, basting chicken.

"Logan," he exclaimed, and held out a welcoming hand. "This is a pleasant surprise. Good to see you."

Logan and her father had always gotten along and had several interests in common. For a time that had irked Abby. Defiantly, she'd wanted to make it clear that she wouldn't marry a man solely because her parents thought highly of him. Her childish attitude had changed dramatically in these past weeks.

Abby's mother brought another place setting from the kitchen to add to the three already on the picnic table. Abby made several more trips into the kitchen to carry out the salad, toasted bread, and a glass of wine for Logan.

Absently, Logan accepted the glass from her and smiled, deep in conversation with her father. Happiness washed over Abby as she munched on a potato chip. Looking at the two of them now—Abby busy helping her mother and Logan chatting easily with her father—she figured there was little to distinguish them as unmarried.

Dinner and the time that followed were cheerful. Frank suggested a game of cards while they were eating birthday cake and ice cream. But Abby's mother immediately rejected the idea.

"I think Glenna's trying to tell me to keep my mouth shut because it's obvious you two want some time alone," Abby's father complained.

"I'm saying no such thing," Glenna denied instantly as an embarrassed flush brightened her cheeks. "We were young once, Frank."

"Once!" Frank scolded. "I don't know about you, but I'm not exactly ready for the grave."

"We'll play cards another time," Logan promised, ending a friendly argument between her parents.

"Double-deck pinochle," Frank prompted. "Best card game there is."

Glenna pretended to agree but rolled her eyes dramatically when Frank wasn't looking.

"Shall we?" Logan successfully contained a smile and held out his open palm to Abby. She placed her hand in his, more content than she could ever remember being. After their farewells to her parents, Logan followed her back to her apartment, parking his car beside hers. He took a seat while Abby hurried into the next room.

"Give me a minute to freshen up," Abby called out as

she ran a brush through her hair and studied her reflection in the bathroom mirror. She looked happy. The sparkle was back in her eyes.

She dabbed some of the perfume Logan had given her to the pulse points at her throat and wrists. Maybe this would garner even more of a reaction. He wasn't one to display a lot of emotion, but he seemed to be coming along nicely in that area. His kisses had produced an overwhelming physical response in Abby, and she was aware that his feelings for her ran deep and strong. It had been only a matter of weeks ago that she'd wondered why he bothered to kiss her at all.

"I suppose you're going to suggest we drive to Des Moines and back," Logan teased when she joined him a few minutes later.

"Logan!" she cried, feigning excitement. "That's a wonderful idea."

He rolled his eyes and laid the paper on the sofa. "How about a movie instead?"

Abby gave a fake groan. "So predictable."

"I've been wanting to see this one." He pointed at an ad for the movie she'd seen with Tate.

"I've already been," Abby tossed back, not thinking.

"When?"

Abby could feel the hostility exuding from Logan. He knew. Without a word he'd guessed that Abby had been to the movie with Tate.

"Not long ago." She tried desperately to put the evening back on an even keel. "But I'd see it again. The film's great."

The air between them became heavy and oppressive.

"Forget the movie," Logan said, and neatly folded the

paper. He straightened and stalked to the far side of the room. "In fact, why don't we forget everything."

Hands clenched angrily at her sides, Abby squared her shoulders. "If you ruin my birthday, Logan Fletcher, I don't think I'll ever forgive you."

His expression was cold and unreadable. "Yes, but there's always Tate."

A hysterical sob rose in her throat, but Abby managed to choke it off. "I . . . I told you tonight that I loved you." Her voice wobbled treacherously as her eyes pleaded with his. "Doesn't that mean anything to you? Anything at all?"

Logan's gaze raked her from head to foot. "Only that you don't know the meaning of the word. You want both Tate *and* me, Abby. But you can't decide between us so you'd prefer to keep us both dangling until you make up your mind." His voice gained volume with each word. "But I won't play that game."

Abby breathed in sharply as a fiery anger burned in her cheeks. Once she would have ranted, cried, and hurled her own accusations. Now she stood, stunned and disbelieving. "If you honestly believe that, then there's nothing left to say." Her voice was calmer than she dared hope. Life seemed filled with ironies all of a sudden. Outwardly she presented a clearheaded composure while on the inside she felt a fiery pain. Perhaps for the first time in her life she was acting completely selflessly, and this was her reward—losing Logan.

Without another word, Logan walked across the room and out the front door.

Abby watched him leave with a sense of unreality. This couldn't be happening to her. Not on her birthday.

Last year Logan had taken her to dinner at a restaurant inside the Sheraton Hotel and given her—what else?—perfume. A hysterical bubble of laughter slipped from her. He was predictable, but so loving and caring. She remembered how they'd danced until midnight and gone for a stroll in the moonlight. Only a year ago, Logan had made her birthday the most perfect day of her life. But this year he was ruining it.

Angry, hurt, and agitated, Abby paced the living room carpet until she thought she'd go mad. Dano had wandered into the living room when she and Logan came in, but had disappeared into her bedroom once he sensed tension. Figured. Not even her cat was interested in comforting her. Usually when she was upset she'd ride her bike or do something physical. But bike riding at night could be dangerous, so she'd go running instead. She changed into old jeans and a faded sweatshirt that had a picture of a Disneyland castle on the front. She had trouble locating her second tennis shoe, then threw it aside in disgust when the rainbow-colored lace snapped in two.

She sighed. Nothing had gone right today. Tate had been disappointed that she wasn't able to meet him. Because of that, she'd been fighting off a case of guilt when she went to her parents'. Then Logan had shown up, and everything had steadily and rapidly gone downhill.

Ripping a lace from one of her softball shoes, Abby had to wrap it around the sole of the shoe several times. On her way out the door, she paused and returned to the bathroom. If she was going to go running, then she'd do it smelling better than any other runner in Minneapolis history. She'd dabbed perfume on every exposed part of her body when she stepped out the door.

A light drizzle had begun to fall. *Terrific.* A fitting end to a rotten day.

The first block was a killer. She couldn't be that much out of shape, could she? She rode her bike a lot. And wasn't her running speed the best on the team?

The second block, Abby forced her mind off how out of breath she was becoming. Logan's buying her perfume made her chuckle. *Predictable. Reliable. Confident.* They were all words that adequately described Logan. But so were *unreasonable* and *stubborn*—traits she'd seen only recently.

The drizzle was followed by a cloudburst and Abby's hair and clothes were plastered against her in the swirling wind and rain. She shouldn't be laughing. But she did anyway as she raced back to her apartment. It was either laugh or cry, and laughing seemed to come naturally. Laughing made her feel better than succumbing to tears.

By the time Abby returned to her building, she was drenched and shivering. With her chin tucked under and her arms folded around her middle, she fought off the chill and hurried across the parking lot. She was almost at her building door when she realized she didn't have the keys. She'd locked herself out!

What more could go wrong? she wondered. Maybe the superintendent was home. She stepped out in the rain to see if the lights were on in his apartment, which was situated above hers. His place was dark. *Of course.* That was how everything else was going.

Cupping one hand over her mouth while the other

held her stomach, Abby's laughter was mixed with sobs of anger and frustration.

"Abby?" Logan's urgent voice came from the street. Hurriedly he crossed it, took one look at her, and hauled her into his arms.

"Logan, I'll get you wet," she cried, trying to push herself free.

"What happened? Are you all right?"

"No. Yes. I don't know," she murmured, sniffling miserably. "What are you doing here?"

Logan brought her out of the rain and stood with his back blocking the wind, trying to protect her from the storm. "Let's get you inside and dry and I'll explain."

"Why?" she asked, and wrung the water from the hem of her sweatshirt. "So you can hurl insults at me?"

"No," he said vehemently. "I've been half-crazy wondering where you were."

"I'll just bet," Abby taunted unmercifully. "I'm surprised you didn't assume I was with Tate."

A grimace tightened his jaw, and Abby knew she'd hit her mark. "Are you going to be difficult or are we going inside to talk this out reasonably?"

"We can't go inside," she said.

"Why not?"

"Because I forgot my keys."

"Oh Abby," Logan groaned.

"And the manager's gone. Do you have any more bright ideas?"

"Did you leave the bedroom window open?" he asked with marked patience.

"Yes, just a little, but—" A glimmer of an idea sparked, and she smiled boldly at Logan. "Follow me."

"Why do I have the feeling I'm not going to like this?" he asked under his breath as Abby pulled him by the hand around to the back of the building.

"Here," she said, bending her knee and lacing her fingers together to give him a boost upward to the slightly open window.

"You don't expect to launch me through there, do you?" Logan glared at her. "I won't fit."

Rivulets of rain trickled down the back of Abby's neck. "Well, I can't do it. You know I'm afraid of heights."

"Abby, the window's barely five feet off the ground."

"I'm standing here, drenched and miserable," she said, waving her hands wildly. "On my birthday, no less," she added sarcastically, "and you don't want to rescue me."

"I'm not in the hero business," Logan muttered as he hunched his shoulders to ward off the rain. "Try Tate."

"Fine, I'll do that." She stalked off to the side of the building.

"Abby?" He sounded unsure as she dragged over an aluminum garbage can.

"Go away!" she shouted. "I don't need you."

"What's the difference between going through the window using a garbage can or having me lift you through?"

"Plenty." She wasn't sure what, but she didn't want to take the time to figure it out. All she wanted was a hot bath and ten gallons of hot chocolate.

"You're being totally irrational."

"I've always been irrational. It's never bothered you before." Her voice trembled as she balanced her weight on the lid of the garbage can. She reached the window and had pushed it open enough to crawl through when she felt the garbage can's lid give way. "Logan!" she screamed, terror gripping her as she started to fall.

Instantly he was there. His arms gripped her waist as she tumbled off the aluminum container. Together they went crashing to the ground, Logan twisting so he took the worst of the fall.

"Are you okay?" he asked frantically, straightening and brushing the hair from her face.

Abby was too stunned and breathless to speak, so she just nodded.

"Now listen," he whispered angrily. "I'm going to lift you up to the windowsill and that's final. Do you understand?"

She nodded again.

"I've had enough of this arguing. I'm cold and wet and I want to get inside and talk some reason into you." He stood and wiped the mud from his hands, then helped her up. Taking the position she had earlier, he crouched and let her use his knee as a step as his laced fingers boosted her to the level of the window.

Abby fell into the bedroom with a loud thud, knocking the lamp off her nightstand. Dano howled in terror and dashed under the bed.

"Are you okay?" Logan yelled from outside.

Abby stuck her head out the window. "Fine. Come around to the front and I'll let you in."

"I'll meet you at your door."

"Logan." She leaned forward and smiled at him provocatively. "You *are* my hero."

He didn't look convinced. "Sure. Whatever you say."

Abby buzzed open the front door and unlocked her apartment door for Logan. His wet hair was dripping water down his face, and his shirt was plastered to his chest, revealing a lean, muscular strength. He looked as drenched and miserable as she felt.

"You take a shower while I drive home and change out of these." He looked down ruefully at his mud-spattered beige pants and rain-soaked shirt.

Abby agreed. Logan had turned and was halfway out the door when Abby called him back. "Why are you here?" she asked, wanting to delay his leaving.

He shrugged and gave her that warm, lazy smile she loved. "I don't know. I thought there might be another movie you wanted to see."

Abby laughed and blew him a kiss. "I'm sure there is."

When Logan returned forty minutes later, Abby's hair was washed and blown dry and hung in a long French braid down the middle of her back. She'd changed into a multicolored bulky sweater and jeans.

Abby smiled. "We're not going to fight, are we?"

"I certainly hope not!" he exclaimed. "I don't think I can take much more of this. When I left here the first time I was thinking . . ." He paused and scratched his head. "I was actually entertaining the thought of driving to Des Moines and back."

"That's crazy." Abby tried unsuccessfully to hide her giggles.

"You're telling me?" He sat on the sofa and held out his arm to her, silently inviting her to join him.

Abby settled on the sofa, her head resting on his chest while his hand caressed her shoulder.

"Do you recall how uncomplicated our lives were just a few weeks ago?" Logan asked her.

"Dull. Ordinary."

"What changed all that?"

Abby was hesitant to bring Tate's name into the conversation. "Life, I guess," she answered vaguely. "I know you may misunderstand this," she added in a husky murmur, "but I don't want to go back to the way our relationship was then." He hadn't told her he loved her and she hadn't recognized the depth of her own feelings.

He didn't move. "No, I don't suppose you would."

Abby repositioned her head and placed the palm of her hand on his jaw, turning his face so she could study him. Their eyes met. The hard, uncompromising look in his dark eyes disturbed her. She desperately wanted to assure him of her love. But she'd realized after the first time that words were inadequate. She shifted and slid her hands over his chest to pause at his shoulders.

The brilliance of his eyes searched her face. "Abby." He groaned her name as he fiercely claimed her lips. His hand found its way to the nape of her neck, his fingers gently pulling dark strands free from the braid so he could twine them through his fingers.

His breathing deep, he buried his face in the slope of her neck. "Just let me hold you for a while. Let's not talk."

She agreed and settled into the warm comfort of his embrace. The staccato beat of his heart gradually returned to a normal pace and Abby felt content and loved. The key to a peaceful relationship was to bask in their love for each other, she thought, smiling. That, and not saying a word.

"What's so amusing?" Logan asked, his breath stirring the hair at the side of her face.

"How do you know I'm smiling?"

"I can feel it."

Abby tilted her head so she could look into his eyes. "This turned into a happy birthday, after all," she said.

Now he smiled, too. "Can I see you tomorrow?"

"If you weren't going to ask me, then I would've been forced to make some wild excuse to see *you*." Lovingly, Abby rubbed her hand along the side of his jaw, enjoying the slightly prickly feel of his beard.

"What would you like to do?"

"I don't care, as long as I'm with you."

"My, my," he whispered, taking her hand. Tenderly he kissed her palm. "You're much easier to please than I remember."

"You don't know the half of it," she teased.

Logan stiffened and sat upright. "What's tomorrow?"

"The tenth. Why?"

"I can't, Abby. I've got something scheduled."

She felt a rush of disappointment but knew that if she was frustrated, so was Logan. "Don't worry, I'll survive," she assured him, then smiled. "At least I think I will."

"But don't plan anything for the day after tomorrow."

"Of course I'm planning something."

"Abby." He sounded tired and impatient.

"Well, it's Sunday, right? Our usual day. So I'm planning to spend it with you. I thought that was what you wanted."

"I do."

The grimness about his mouth relaxed.

Almost immediately afterward, Logan appeared restless and uneasy. Later, as she dressed for bed, she convinced herself that it was her imagination.

The lesson with Mai-Ling the following afternoon went well. It was the last reading session they'd have, since Mai-Ling was now ready to move on. She'd scheduled one with Tate right afterward, deciding that what Logan didn't know wouldn't hurt him. Tate was still painfully self-conscious and uncomfortable about telling anyone else, although his progress was remarkable and he advanced more quickly than any student she'd ever tutored, including the talented Mai-Ling. From experience, she could tell he was spending many hours each evening studying.

On her way back to her apartment late Saturday afternoon, Abby decided on the spur of the moment to stop at Patty's and see how she was recuperating. She'd sent her an email wishing her a rapid recovery and had promised to stop over some afternoon. Patty needed friends, and Abby was feeling generous. Her topsy-turvy world had been righted.

She went to a drugstore first and bought half a dozen glossy magazines as a get-well gift, then drove to Patty's home.

Her sister answered the doorbell.

"Hi, you must be from the softball team. Patty's gotten a lot of company. Everyone's been wonderful."

Abby wasn't surprised. Everyone on the team was warm and friendly.

"This must be her day for company. Come on in. Logan's with her now."

Seven

∽

Abby was dismayed as the sound of Patty's laughter drifted into the entryway, but she followed Patty's sister into the living room.

Patty's broken arm was supported by a white linen sling and she sat opposite Logan on a long sofa. Her eyes were sparkling with undisguised happiness. Logan had his back to Abby, and it was all she could do not to turn around and leave. She forced a bright smile and made an entrance any actress would envy. "Hello, everyone!"

"Hi, Abby!" Patty had never looked happier or, for that matter, prettier. Not only was her hair nicely styled, but she was wearing light makeup, which added color to her pale cheeks and accented her large brown eyes. She wore a lovely summer dress, a little fancy for hanging around the house, and shoes that were obviously new.

"How are you feeling?" Abby prayed the phoniness in her voice had gone undetected.

Logan stood up and came around the couch, but his eyes didn't meet Abby's probing gaze.

"Hello, Logan, good to see you again."

"Hello, Abby."

"Sit down, please." Patty pointed to an empty chair. "We've got a few minutes before dinner." Patty seemed oblivious to the tension between her guests.

"No, thanks," Abby murmured, faking another smile. "I can only stay a minute. I just wanted to drop by and see how you were doing. Oh, these are for you," she said, handing over the magazines. "Some reading material . . ."

"Thank you! And I'm doing really well," Patty said enthusiastically. "This is the first night I've been able to go out. Logan's taking me to dinner at the restaurant inside the Sheraton."

Abby breathed in sharply and clenched her fist until her nails cut into her hand. Logan had taken her there only once, but Abby considered it their special restaurant. He could've taken Patty anyplace else in the world and it would've hurt, but not as much as this.

"Everyone's been great," Patty continued. "Dick and his wife were over yesterday, and a few others from the team dropped by. Those flowers"—she indicated several plants and bouquets—"are from them."

"We all feel terrible about the accident." Abby made her first honest statement of the visit.

"But it was my own fault," Patty said as Logan hovered stiffly on the other side of the room.

Abby lowered her eyes, unable to meet the happy glow in Patty's. A crumpled piece of wrapping paper rested on the small table at Patty's side. It was the same paper Logan had used to wrap Abby's birthday gift the day before. He *couldn't* have gotten Patty perfume. He wouldn't dare.

"You look so nice," Abby said. Her pulse quickened. What *had* Logan brought Patty? She thought she recognized that scent . . . "Is that a new perfume you're wearing?"

"Yes, as a matter of fact, Logan—"

"Hadn't we better be going?" Logan said as he made a show of glancing at his watch.

Patty looked flustered. "Is it time already?"

Following her cue, Abby glared at Logan and took a step in retreat. "I should go, too." A contrived smile curved her mouth. "Have a good time."

"I'll walk you to your car," Logan volunteered.

Walking backward, Abby gestured with her hands, swinging them at her sides to give a carefree impression. "No, that isn't necessary. Really. I'm capable of finding my own way out."

"Abby," Logan said under his breath.

"Have a wonderful time, you two," Abby continued, her voice slightly high-pitched. "I've only been to the Sheraton once. The food was fantastic, but I can't say much for my date. I no longer see him. A really ordinary guy, if you know what I mean. And so predictable."

"I'll be right back." Logan directed his comment to Patty and gripped Abby by the elbow.

"Let me go," she seethed.

Logan's grip relaxed once they were outside the house. "Would you let me explain?"

"Explain?" She threw the word in his face. "What could you possibly say? No." She waved her hand in front of his chest. "Don't say a word. I don't want to hear it. Do you understand? Not a word."

"You're being irrational again," Logan accused, apparently having difficulty keeping his rising temper in check.

"You're right," she agreed. "I've completely lost my sense. Please forgive me for being so closed-minded." Her voice was surprisingly even, but it didn't disguise the hurt or the feeling of betrayal she was experiencing.

"Abby."

"Don't," she whispered achingly. "Not now. I can't talk now."

"I'll call you later."

She consented with an abrupt nod, but at that point, Abby realized, she would have agreed to anything for the opportunity to escape.

Her hand was shaking so badly that she had trouble sliding the key into the ignition. This was crazy. She felt secure in his love one night and betrayed the next.

Abby didn't go home. The last thing she wanted to do was sit alone on a Saturday night. To kill time, she visited the Mall of America and did some shopping, buying herself a designer outfit that she knew Logan would hate.

The night was dark and overcast as she let herself into the apartment. Hanging the new dress in her closet, Abby acknowledged that spending this much money on one outfit was ridiculous. Her reasons were just as childish. But it didn't matter; she felt a hundred times better.

The phone rang the first time at ten. Abby ignored it. Logan. Of course. When it started ringing at five-minute intervals, she simply unplugged it. There was nothing she had to say to him. When they spoke again, she wanted to feel composed. Tonight was too soon. She wasn't ready yet.

Calm now, she changed into her pajamas and sat on the sofa, brushing her long hair in smooth, even strokes. Reaction would probably set in tomorrow, but for now she was too angry to think.

Half an hour later, someone pressed her buzzer repeatedly. Annoying though it was, she ignored that, too.

When there was a banging at her door, Abby hesitated, then continued with her brushing.

"Come on, Abby, I know you're in there," Logan shouted.

"Go away. I'm not dressed," she called out sweetly.

"Then get dressed."

"No!" she yelled back.

Logan's laugh was breathless and bitter. "Either open up or I'll tear the stupid door off its hinges."

Just the way he said it convinced Abby this wasn't an idle threat. And to think that only a few weeks ago she'd seen Logan as unemotional. Laying her brush aside, she walked to the door and unlatched the safety chain.

"What do you want? How did you get into the building? And for heaven's sake, keep the noise down. You're disturbing the neighbors."

"Some guy from the second floor recognized me and opened the lobby door. And if you don't let me in to talk to you, I'll do a lot more than wake the neighbors."

Abby had never seen Logan display so much passion. Perhaps she should've been thrilled, but she wasn't.

"Did you and Patty have a nice evening?" she asked with heavy sarcasm.

Logan glanced briefly at his hands. "Reasonably nice."

"I apologize if I put a damper on your *date*," she returned with smooth derision. "Believe me, had I known about it, I would never have visited Patty at such an inopportune time. My timing couldn't have been worse—or better, depending on how you look at it."

"Abby," he said and sighed. "Let me in. Please."

"Not tonight, Logan."

Frustration furrowed his brow. "Tomorrow, then?"

"Tomorrow," she agreed, and started to close the door. "Logan," she called, and he immediately turned back. "Without meaning to sound like I care a whole lot, let me ask you something. Why did you give Patty the same perfume as me?" Some perverse part of herself had to know.

His look was filled with defeat. "It seemed the thing to do. I knew she'd enjoy it, and to be honest, I felt sorry for her. Patty needs someone."

Abby's chin quivered as the hurt coursed through her. Self-respect dictated that she maintain a level gaze. "Thank you for not lying," she said, and closed the door.

Tate was waiting for her when Abby entered the park at eleven-thirty Sunday morning. Since her Saturday sessions with Mai-Ling had come to an end, Abby was now devoting extra time on the weekends to Tate.

"You look like you just stepped out of the dentist's

chair," Tate said, studying her closely. "What's the matter? Didn't you sleep well last night?"

She hadn't.

"You work too hard," he told her. "You're always helping others. Me and Mai-Ling . . ."

Abby sat on the blanket Tate had spread out on the grass and lowered her gaze so that her hair fell forward, hiding her face. "I don't do nearly enough," she disagreed. "Tate," she said, raising her eyes to his. "I've never told anyone the reason we meet. Would you mind if I did? Just one person?"

Unable to sleep, Abby had considered the various reasons Logan might have asked Patty out for dinner. She was sure he hadn't purposely meant to hurt her. The only logical explanation was that he wanted her to experience the same feelings he had, since she was continuing to see Tate. And yet he'd gone to pains to keep her from knowing about the date. Nothing made sense anymore. But if she could tell Logan the reason she was meeting Tate, things would be easier . . .

Tate rubbed a weary hand over his eyes. "This is causing problems with you and—what's-his-name—isn't it?"

Abby didn't want to put any unnecessary pressure on Tate, so she shrugged, hoping to give the impression of indifference. "A little. But I don't think Logan really understands."

"Is it absolutely necessary that he know?"

"No, I guess not." Abby had realized it would be extremely difficult for Tate to let anyone else learn about his inability to read—especially Logan.

"Then would it be too selfish of me to ask that you don't say anything?" Tate asked. "At least not yet?" A look of pain flashed over his face, and Abby understood anew how hard it was for him to talk about his problem. "I suppose it's a matter of dignity."

Abby's smile relaxed her tense mouth. The relationship among the three of them was a mixed-up matter of ego, and she didn't know whose was the most unyielding.

"No, I don't mind," she replied, and opened her backpack to take out some books. "By the way, I want to give you something." She handed him three of her favorite Dick Francis books. "These are classics in the mystery genre. They may be a bit difficult for you in the beginning, but I think you'll enjoy them."

Tate turned the paperback copy of *The Danger* over and read the back-cover blurb. "His business is kidnapping?" He sounded unsure as he raised his eyes to hers.

"Trust me. It's good."

"I'll give it a try. But it looks like it'll take me a while."

"Practice makes perfect."

Tate laughed in the low, lazy manner she enjoyed so much. "I've never known anyone who has an automatic comeback the way you do." He took a cold can of soda and tossed it to her. "Let's drink to your wit."

"And have a celebration of words." She settled her back against the trunk of a massive elm and closed her eyes as Tate haltingly read the first lines of the book she'd given him. It seemed impossible that only a few weeks before he'd been unable to identify the letters of the alphabet. But his difficulty wasn't attributed to any learning disability, such as she'd encountered in the past with others. He was already at a junior level and advancing so quickly she had trouble keeping him in material, which was why she'd started him on a novel. Unfortunately, his writing and spelling skills were advancing at a slower pace. Abby calculated that it wouldn't take more than a month or two before she could set him on his own with the promise to help when he needed it. Already he'd voiced his concerns about an application he'd be filling out for the bank to obtain a business loan. She'd assured him they'd go over it together.

Abby hadn't been home fifteen minutes when Logan showed up at her building. She buzzed him in and opened the door, but for all the emotion he revealed, his face might have been carved in stone.

"Are you going to let me inside today?" he asked, peering into her apartment.

"I suppose I'll have to."

"Not necessarily. You could make a fool of me the way you did last night."

"Me?" she gasped. "You don't need *me* to make you look like a fool. You do a bang-up job of it yourself."

His mouth tightened as he stepped into her apartment and sank down on the sofa.

Abby sat as far away from him as possible. "Well?" She was determined not to make this easy.

"Patty was in a lot of pain when I drove her to the hospital the night of the accident," he began.

"Uh-huh." She sympathized with Patty but didn't know why he was bringing this up.

Logan's voice was indifferent. "I was talking to her, trying to take her mind off how much she was hurting. It seems that in all the garble I rashly said I'd take her to dinner."

"I suppose you also—rashly—suggested the Sheraton?" She felt chilled by his aloofness and she wasn't going to let him off lightly.

An awkward silence followed. "I don't remember that part, but apparently I did."

"Apparently so," she returned with forced calm. "Maybe I could forget the dinner date, but not the perfume. Honestly, Logan, that was a rotten thing to do."

Impatience shadowed his tired features. "It's not what you think. I got her cologne. Not perfume."

"For heaven's sake," she said, exasperated. "Can't you be more original than that?"

"But it's the truth."

"I know that. But you can't go through life giving women perfume and cologne every time the occasion calls for a gift. And even worse, you chose the same scent!"

"It's the only one I know." He shook his head. "All right, the next time I buy a woman a gift, I'll take you along."

"The next time you buy a woman a gift," she interrupted in a stern voice, "it had better be me."

He ignored her statement. "Abby, how could you believe I'm attracted to Patty?"

She opened her mouth and closed it again. "Maybe I can believe that you really do care about me. But I've seen the way Patty looks at you. It wouldn't take more than a word to have her fall in love with you. I don't want to see her hurt." *Or any of us, for that matter,* Abby mused. "I don't believe you're using Patty to make me jealous," she said honestly. "I mean, I wondered about it, but then decided you weren't."

"I'm glad you realize that much." He breathed out in obvious relief.

"But I recognize the looks she's giving you, Logan. She wants you."

"And Tate wants you!"

Abby's shoulders sagged. "Don't go bringing him into this discussion. It's not right. We were talking about you, not me."

"Why not? Isn't turnabout fair play?" The contempt in his expression made her want to cry.

"That's tiddlywinks, not love," she said saucily.

"But if Patty looks at me with adoring eyes, it only mirrors the way Tate looks at you."

"Now you're being ridiculous," she said, annoyed by his false logic.

Slowly Logan rubbed his chin. "It's always amazed me that you can twist a conversation any way you want."

"That's not true," she said, hating the fact that he'd turned the situation around to suit himself.

"All right, let's put it like this—if you mention Patty Martin, then I mention Tate Harding. That sounds fair to me."

"Fine." She flipped a strand of hair over her shoulder. "I won't mention Patty again."

"Are you still seeing him?"

"Who?" Abby widened her eyes innocently.

Logan's jaw tightened grimly. "I want you to promise me that you won't date Harding again."

Abby stared at him.

"A simple yes or no. That's all I want."

The answer wasn't even difficult. She *wasn't* dating him. "And what do I get in return?"

He bent his head to study his hands. "Something that's been yours for more than a year. My heart."

At his words, all of Abby's defensive anger melted. "Oh Logan," she whispered, emotion bringing a misty happiness to her eyes.

"I've loved you so long, Abby, I can't bear to lose you." There could be no doubt of his sincerity.

"I love you, too."

"Then why are you on the other side of the room when all I want to do is hold you and kiss you?"

The well of tenderness inside her overflowed. She rose from her sitting position. "In the interests of fairness, I think we should meet halfway. Okay?"

He chuckled as he stood, coming to her, but his eyes revealed a longing that was deep and intense. A low groan rumbled from his throat as he swept her into his arms and held her as if he never wanted to let her go. He kissed her eyes, her cheeks, the corner of her mouth until she moaned and begged for more.

"Abby." His voice was muffled against her hair. "You're not going to sidestep my question."

"What question?" She smiled against his throat as she gave him nibbling, biting kisses.

His hands gripped her shoulders as he pulled her slightly away from him so he could look into her face. "You won't be seeing Tate again?"

She decided not to make an issue of semantics. He *meant* date, not see. What she said in response was the truth. "I promise never to date anyone else again. Does that satisfy you?"

He linked his hands at the small of her back and smiled deeply into her eyes. "I suppose it'll have to," he said, echoing her remark when she'd let him in.

"Now it's your turn."

"What would you like?"

"No more dating Patty, okay?"

"I agree," he replied without hesitation.

"Inventive gift ideas."

He hesitated. "I'll try."

"You're going to have to do better than that."

"All right, all right, I agree."

"And—"

"There's more?" he interrupted with mock impatience.

"And at some point in our lives I want to drive to Des Moines."

"Fine. Shall we seal this agreement with a kiss?"

"I think it would be only proper," Abby said eagerly as she slid her arms around his waist and fit her body to his.

His large hands framed her face, lifting her lips to meet his. It lacked the urgency of their last kiss, but was filled with promise. His breathing was ragged when he released her, but Abby noted that her own wasn't any calmer.

Not surprisingly, their truce held. Maybe it was because they both wanted it so badly. The next Sunday they met at her place for breakfast, which Abby cooked. Later, they drove over to her parents' house and during their visit Frank Carpenter speculated that the two of them would be married by the end of the year. A few not-so-subtle questions about the "date" popped up here and there in the conversation. But neither of them seemed to mind. Logan was included in Abby's every thought. This was the way love was supposed to be, Abby mused, as they returned to her apartment.

After changing clothes, they rode their bikes to the park and ate a picnic lunch. After that, with Logan's head resting in her lap, Abby leaned against an elm tree and closed her eyes. This was the same tree that had supported her back during more than one reading session with Tate. A guilty sensation attacked the pit of her stomach, but she successfully fended it off.

"Did you hear that Dick Snyder wants to climb Mount Rainier this summer?" Logan asked unexpectedly, as he chewed lazily on a long blade of grass.

In addition to softball, Dick's passion was mountain climbing. She'd heard rumors about his latest venture, but hadn't been all that interested.

"Yeah, I heard that," she murmured. "So?"

"So, what do you think?"

"What do I think about what?" Abby asked.

"They need an extra man. It sounds like the expedition will be canceled otherwise." Logan frowned as he looked up at her.

"Climbing the highest mountain in Washington State should be a thrill—for some people. They won't have any trouble finding someone. Personally, I have trouble making it over speed bumps," she teased, leaning forward to kiss his forehead. "What's wrong?"

He smiled up at her and raised his hands to direct her mouth to his. "What could possibly be wrong?" he whispered as he moved his mouth onto her lips for a kiss that left her breathless.

The next week was the happiest of Abby's life. Logan saw her daily. Monday they went to dinner at the same Mexican restaurant Tate had taken her to weeks before. The food was good, but Abby's appetite wasn't up to par. Again, Abby dismissed the twinge of guilt. Tuesday he picked her up for class, but they decided to skip school. Instead, they sat in the parking lot and talked until late. From there they drove until they found a café where they could enjoy their drinks outside. The communication between them had never been stronger.

Tate phoned Abby at work on Wednesday and asked her to meet him at the park before the softball game. He wanted to be sure his application for the business loan had been filled out correctly. Uneasy about being in public with him for fear Logan would see or hear about it, Abby promised to stop off at his garage.

Later, when Logan picked her up for the game, she was short-tempered and restless.

"What's the matter with you tonight?" he complained as they reached the park. "You're as jumpy as a bank robber."

"Me?" She feigned innocence. "Nervous about the game, I guess."

"You?" He looked at her with disbelief. "Ms. Confidence? You'd better tell me what's really bothering you. 'Fess up, kid."

She felt her face heat with a guilty blush. "Nothing's wrong."

"Abby, I thought we'd come a long way recently. Won't you tell me what's bothering you?"

Logan was so sincere that Abby wanted to kick herself. "Nothing. Honest," she lied, and tried to swallow the lump in her throat. She hated this deception, no matter how minor it really was.

"Obviously you're not telling the truth," he insisted, and a muscle twitched in his jaw.

"What makes you say that?" She gave him a look of pure innocence.

"Well, for one thing, your face is bright red."

"It's just hot, that's all."

He released a low breath. "Okay, if that's the way you want it."

Patty was in the bleachers when they arrived, and waved eagerly when she saw Logan. Abby doubted she'd noticed that Abby was with him.

"Your girlfriend's here," Abby murmured sarcastically.

"My girlfriend is walking beside me," Logan said. "What's gotten into you lately?"

Abby sighed. "Don't tell me we're going over all of that again?" She didn't wait for him to answer. She ran onto the field, shouting for Dick to pitch her the ball.

The game went smoothly. Patty basked in the attention everyone was giving her and had the team sign her cast. Abby readily agreed to add her own comment, eager to see what Logan had written on the plaster. But she couldn't locate it without being obvious. Maybe he'd done that on purpose. Maybe he'd written Patty a sweet message on the underside of her arm, where no one else could read it. The thought was so ridiculous that Abby almost laughed out loud.

They lost the game by a slim margin, and Abby realized she hadn't been much help. During the get-together at the pizza place afterward she listened to the others joke and laugh. She wanted to join in, but tonight she simply didn't feel like partying.

"Are you feeling all right?" Logan sat beside her, holding her hand. He studied her with worried eyes.

"I'm fine," she answered, and managed a half-hearted smile. "But I'm a little tired. Would you mind taking me home?"

"Not at all."

They got up and, with Logan's hand at the small of her back, they made their excuses and left.

The silence in the car was deafening, but Abby did her best to ignore the unspoken questions Logan was sending her way.

"How about if I cook dinner tomorrow?" Abby said brightly. "I've been terrible tonight and I want to make it up to you."

"If you're not feeling well, maybe you should wait."

"I'm fine. Just don't expect anything more complicated than hot dogs on a bun." She was teasing and Logan knew it.

He parked outside her building and kissed her gently. Abby held on to him compulsively, as if she couldn't bear to let him go. She felt caught in a game of cat and mouse between Tate and Logan—a game in which she was quickly becoming the loser.

The following evening, Abby was putting the finishing touches on a salad when Logan came over.

"Surprise," he said as he held out a small bouquet of flowers. "Is this more original than perfume?" he asked with laughing eyes.

"Hardly." She gave him a soft brushing kiss across his freshly shaven cheek as she took the carnations from his hand. "Mmm, you smell good."

Logan picked a tomato slice out of the salad and popped it into his mouth. "So do you."

"Well, if you don't like the fragrance, you have only yourself to blame."

"Me? You smell like pork chops." He slipped his arms around her waist from behind and nuzzled her neck. "You know I could get used to having dinner with you every single night." The teasing quality left his eyes.

Abby dropped her gaze as her heart went skyrocketing into space. She knew what he was saying. The question had entered her mind several times during the past few days. These feelings they were experiencing were the kind to last a lifetime. Abby wanted to share Logan's life. The desire to wake up with him at her side every morning, to marry him and have his children, was stronger than any instinct. She loved this man and wanted to be with him always.

"I think I could get used to that, too," she admitted softly.

Someone knocked at the door, breaking into their conversation. Impatiently, Logan glanced at it. "Are you expecting anyone? One of your neighbors?"

"You," she said. "Here, turn these. I'll see who it is and get rid of them." She handed him the spatula.

Abby's hand was shaking as she grasped the knob, praying it wouldn't be Tate. If she was lucky, she could ask him to leave before Logan knew what was happening.

Her worst fears were realized when she pulled the door open halfway.

"Hi. Someone let me into the lobby."

"Hello, how are you?" she asked in a hushed whisper.

"I'm returning the books you lent me. I really enjoyed them." Tate gave her a funny look. "Is this a bad time or something?"

"You might say that," she breathed. "Could you come back tomorrow?"

"Sure, no problem. Is it Logan?"

Abby nodded, and as she did, the door was opened all the way.

"Hello, Tate," Logan greeted him stiffly. "I've been half expecting you. Why don't you come inside where we can all visit?"

Eight

~

The two men regarded each other with open hostility.

Glancing from one to the other, Abby paused to swallow a lump of apprehension. Her worst fears had become reality. She wanted to blurt out the truth, explain to Logan exactly why she was seeing Tate. But one look at the two of them standing on either side of the door and Abby recognized the impossibility of making any kind of explanation. Like rival warlords, the two blatantly dared each other to make the first move.

Logan loomed at her side, exuding bitterness, surprise, hurt, and anger. He held himself still and rigid.

"I'll see you tomorrow, Abby?" Tate spoke at last, making the statement a question.

"Fine." Abby managed to find her voice, which was low and urgent. She wanted to scream at him to leave. If his ego wasn't dominating his actions, he'd recognize what a horrible position he was putting her in. Apparently, maintaining his pride was more important than the problem he was causing her. Abby's eyes pleaded with Tate, but either he chose to ignore the silent entreaty or he didn't understand what she was asking.

The enigmatic look on Tate's face moved from Logan to Abby. "Will you be all right? Do you want me to stay?"

"Yes. No!" She nearly shouted with frustration. He'd read the look in her eyes as a plea for help. This was crazy. This whole situation was unreal.

"Tomorrow, then," Tate said as he took a step in retreat.

"Tomorrow," Abby confirmed, and gestured with her hand, begging him to leave.

He turned and stalked away.

Immobile, Abby stood where she was, waiting for Logan's backlash.

"How long have you been seeing each other?" he asked with infuriating calm.

If he'd shouted and decried her actions, Abby would have felt better; she could have responded the same way. But his composed manner relayed far more adequately the extent of his anger.

"How long, Abby?" he repeated.

Her chin trembled and she shrugged.

His short laugh was derisive. "Your answer says quite a bit."

"It's not what you think," she said hoarsely, desperately wanting to set everything straight.

His jaw tightened forbiddingly. "I suppose you're going to tell me you and Tate are just good friends. If that's the case, you can save your breath."

"Logan." Fighting back tears of frustration, Abby moved away from the door and turned to face him. "I need you to trust me in this."

"Trust you!" His laugh was mocking. "I asked you to decide which one of us you wanted. You claimed you'd made your decision. You even went so far as to assure me you wouldn't be seeing Tate again." The intense anger darkened the shadows across his face, making the curve of his jaw look sharp and abrupt.

"I said I wouldn't *date* him again," she corrected.

"Don't play word games with me," he threw back at her. "You knew what I meant."

She merely shook her head, incapable of arguing. Why *couldn't* he trust her? Why hadn't Tate just *told* him? Why, why, why.

"I suspected something yesterday at the game," Logan continued wryly. "That guilty look was in your eyes again. But I didn't want to believe what I was seeing."

Abby lowered her gaze at the onrush of pain. This deception hadn't been easy for her. But she was bound by her promise to Tate. She couldn't explain the circumstances of their meetings to Logan; only Tate's permission would allow her to do that. But Tate couldn't risk his dignity to that extent and she wouldn't ask him to.

Logan's short laugh was bitter with irony. "Yet when the doorbell rang, I knew immediately it was Tate. To be honest, I was almost glad, because it clears away the doubts in my mind."

Determinedly, he started for the door, but Abby's hand delayed him. "Don't go," she whispered. "Please." Her fingers tightened around his arm, wanting to bind him to her forever, beginning with this moment. "I love you and . . . and if you love me, then you'll trust me."

"Love?" he repeated in a contemptuous voice. "You don't know the meaning of the word."

Stunned, Abby dropped her hand and with a supreme effort met his gaze without emotion. "If that's what you think, maybe it would be better if you did leave."

Logan paused, his troubled expression revealing the inner storm raging within him.

"I may be wrong, but I was brought up to believe that love between two people requires mutual trust," Abby added.

One corner of his mouth quirked upward. "And I assumed—erroneously, it seems—that love requires honesty."

"I . . . I bent the truth a little."

"Why?" he demanded. "No." He stopped her from explaining. "I don't want to know. Because it's over. I told you before that I wouldn't be kept dangling like a schoolboy while you made up your mind."

"But I *can't* explain now! I may never be able to tell you why."

"It doesn't matter, Abby, it's over," Logan said starkly, his expression impassive.

Abby's stomach lurched with shock and disbelief. Logan didn't mean that. He wouldn't do that to them.

Without another word, he walked from the room. The door slammed as he left the apartment. He didn't hesitate or look back.

Abby held out her hand in a weak gesture that pleaded with him to turn around, to trust her. But he couldn't see her, and she doubted it would've had any effect on him if he had. Unshed tears were dammed in her throat, but Abby held her head up in a defiant gesture of pride. The pretense was important for the moment, as she calmly moved into the kitchen and turned off the stove.

Only fifteen minutes before, she had stared lovingly into Logan's eyes, letting her own eyes tell him how much she wanted to share his life. Now, swiftly and without apparent concern, Logan had rejected her as carelessly and thoughtlessly as he would an old pair of shoes. Yet Abby knew that wasn't true. He *did* love her. He couldn't hold her and kiss her the way he did without loving her. Abby knew him as well as he knew her. But then, Abby mused, she had reason to doubt that Logan knew her at all.

Even worse was the fact that Abby recognized she was wrong. Logan deserved an explanation. But her hands were bound by her promise to Tate. And Tate had no idea what that pledge was doing to her and to her relationship with Logan. She couldn't believe he'd purposely do this, but Tate was caught in his own trap. He viewed her as his friend and trusted teacher. He felt fiercely protective of her, wanting in his own way to repay her for the second chance she was giving him by teaching him to read.

Logan and Tate had disliked each other on sight. The friction between them wasn't completely her fault, Abby realized. The ironic part was that for all their outward differences they were actually quite a bit alike.

When Abby had first met Tate that day in the park she'd found him compelling. She'd been magnetically drawn to the same strength that had unconsciously bound her to Logan. This insight had taken Abby weeks to discover, but it had come too late.

The weekend arrived in a haze of emotional pain. Tate phoned Friday afternoon to tell her he wouldn't be able to meet her on Saturday because he was going to the bank to sign the final papers for his loan. He invited her to dinner in celebration, but she declined. Not meeting him gave Abby a reprieve. She wasn't up to facing anyone right now. But each minute, each hour, the hurt grew less intense and life became more bearable. At least, that was what she tried to tell herself.

She didn't see Logan on Sunday, and forced herself not to search for him in the crowded park as she took a late-afternoon stroll. This was supposed to be their day. Now it looked as if there wouldn't be any more lazy Sunday afternoons for them.

Involved in her melancholy thoughts, Abby wandered the paths and trails of the park, hardly noticing the people around her.

Early that evening, as the sun was lowering in a purple sky, Abby felt the urge to sit on the damp earth and take in the beauty of the world around her. She needed the tranquility of the moment and the assurance that another day had come and gone and she'd made it through the sadness and uncertainty. She reflected on her feelings and actions, admitting she'd often been headstrong and at times insensitive. But she was learning, and although the pain of that growth dominated her mind now, it, too, would fade. Abby stared at the darkening sky and, for the first time in several long days, a sense of peace settled over her.

Sitting on the lush grass, enjoying the richness of the park grounds, Abby gazed up at the sky. These rare, peaceful minutes soothed her soul and quieted her troubled heart. If she were never to see Logan again, she'd always be glad for the good year they'd shared. Too late she'd come to realize all that Logan meant to her. She'd carelessly tossed his love aside—with agonizing consequences.

The following afternoon Abby called Dick Snyder about Wednesday's softball game. Although she was dying for the sight of Logan, it would be an uncomfortable situation for both of them.

"Dick, it's Abby," she said when he answered. She suddenly felt awkward and uneasy.

"Abby," Dick greeted her cheerfully. "It's good to hear from you. What's up?"

An involuntary smile touched the corners of her mouth. No-nonsense Dick. He climbed mountains, coached softball teams, ran a business with the effectiveness of a tycoon, and raised a family; it was all in a day's work, as he often said . . . "Nothing much, but I wanted you to know I won't be able to make the game on Wednesday."

"You, too?"

"Pardon?" Abby didn't know what he meant.

"Logan phoned earlier and said he wouldn't be at the game, either. Are you two up to something we should know about?" he teased. "Like running off and getting married?"

Abby felt the color flow out of her face, and her heart

raced. "No," she breathed, hardly able to find her voice. "That's not it at all."

Her hand was trembling when she replaced the receiver a couple of minutes later. So Logan had decided not to play on Wednesday. If he was quitting softball, she could assume he'd also stop attending classes on Tuesday nights. The possibility of their running into each other at work was still present, since their offices were only half a block apart, but he must be going out of his way to avoid any possible meeting. For that matter, she was doing the same thing.

Soon Abby's apartment began to feel like her prison. She did everything she could to take her mind off Logan, but as the weeks progressed, it became more and more difficult. Much as she didn't want to talk to anyone or provide long explanations about Logan's absence, Abby couldn't tolerate another night alone. She had to get out. So after work the following Wednesday, she got in her car and started to drive.

Before she realized where she was headed, Abby pulled into her parents' driveway.

"Hi, Mom," Abby said as she let herself in the front door.

Her father was reading the paper, and Abby paused at his side. She placed her hand on his shoulder, kissing him lightly on the forehead. "What's that for?" Frank Carpenter grumbled as his arm curved around her waist. "Do you need a loan?"

"Nope," Abby said with forced cheer. "I was just thinking that I don't say *I love you* nearly enough." She glanced up at her mother. "I'm fortunate to have such good parents."

"How sweet," Glenna murmured softly, but her eyes were clouded with obvious worry. "Is everything all right?"

Abby restrained the compulsion to cry out that *nothing* was right anymore. Not without Logan. She left almost as quickly as she'd come, making an excuse about hurrying home to feed Dano. That weak explanation hadn't fooled her perceptive mother. Abby was grateful Glenna didn't pry.

Another week passed and Abby didn't see Logan. Not that she'd expected to. He was avoiding her as determinedly as she did him. Seeing him would mean only pain. She lost weight, and the dark circles under her eyes testified to her inability to sleep.

Sunday morning, Abby headed straight for the park, intent on finding Logan. Even a glimpse would ease the pain she'd suffered without him. She wondered if his face would reveal any of the same torment she had endured. Surely he regretted his lack of trust. He must miss her—perhaps even enough to set aside their differences and talk to her. And if he did, Abby knew she'd readily respond. She imagined the possible scenes that might play out—from complete acceptance on his part to total rejection.

There was a certain irony in her predicament. Tate had been exceptionally busy and she hadn't tutored him at all that week. He was doing so well now that it wouldn't be more than a month before he'd be reading and writing at an adult level. Once he'd completed the lessons, Abby doubted she'd see him very often, despite the friendship that had developed between them. They had little in common and Tate had placed her on such a high pedestal that Abby didn't think he'd ever truly see her as a woman. He saw her as his rescuer, his salvation—not a position Abby felt she deserved.

She sat near the front entrance of the park so she wouldn't miss Logan if he showed up. She made a pretense of reading, but her eyes followed each person entering the park. By noon, she'd been waiting for three hours and Logan had yet to arrive. Abby felt sick with disappointment. Logan came to the park every Sunday morning. Certainly he wouldn't change that, too—would he?

Defeated, Abby closed her book and meandered down the path. She'd been sitting there since nine, so she was sure she hadn't missed him. As she strolled through the park, Abby saw several people she knew and paused to wave but walked on, not wanting to be drawn into conversation.

Dick Snyder's wife was there with her two school-aged children. She called out Abby's name.

"Hi! Come on over and join me. It'll be nice to have an adult to talk to for a while." Betty Snyder chatted easily, patting an empty space on the park bench. "I keep telling Dick that one of these days *I'm* going mountain climbing and leaving him with the kids." Her smile was bright.

Abby sat on the bench beside Betty, deciding she could do with a little conversation herself. "Is he at it again?" she asked, already knowing the answer. Dick thrived on challenge. Abby couldn't understand how anyone could climb anything. Heights bothered her too much. She remembered once—

"Dick and Logan."

"Logan?" His name cut into her thoughts and a tightness twisted her stomach. "He's not climbing, is he?" She didn't even try to hide the alarm in her voice. Logan was no mountaineer! Oh, he enjoyed a hike in the woods, but he'd never shown any interest in conquering anything higher than a sand dune.

Betty looked at her in surprise. She'd obviously assumed Abby would know who Logan was with and what he was up to.

"Well, yes," Betty hedged. "I thought you knew. The Rainier climb is in two weeks."

"No, I didn't." Abby swallowed. "Logan hasn't said anything."

"He was probably waiting until he'd finished learning the basics from Dick."

"Probably," Abby replied weakly, her voice fading as terror overwhelmed her. Logan climbing mountains? With a dignity she didn't realize she possessed, Abby met Betty's gaze head-on. It would sound ridiculous to tell Betty that this latest adventure had slipped Logan's mind. The fact was, Abby knew it hadn't. She recalled Logan's telling her that Dick was looking for an extra climber. But he hadn't said it as though he was considering it *himself.*

Betty continued, apparently trying to fill the stunned silence. "You don't need to worry. Dick's a good climber. I'd go crazy if he weren't. I have complete and utter confidence in him. You shouldn't worry about Logan. He and Dick have been spending a lot of time together preparing for this. Rainier is an excellent climb for a first ascent."

Abby heard almost nothing of Betty's pep talk, and her heart sank. This had to be some cruel hoax. Logan was an accountant. He didn't have the physical endurance needed to ascend fourteen thousand feet. He wasn't qualified to do any kind of climbing, let alone a whole mountain. Someone else should go. Not Logan.

Not the man she loved.

Betty's two rambunctious boys returned and closed around the women, chatting excitedly about a squirrel they'd seen. The minute she could do so politely, Abby slipped away from the family and hurried out of the park. She had to get to Logan—talk some sense into him.

Abby returned to her apartment and got in her car. She drove around, dredging up the nerve to confront Logan. If he was out practicing with Dick, he wouldn't be back until dark. Twice she drove by his place, but his parking space was empty.

After a frustrating hour in a shopping mall, Abby sat through a boring movie and immediately drove back to Logan's. For the third time she saw that he hadn't returned. She drove around again—for how long, she was unsure.

Abby couldn't comprehend what had made him decide to do this. A hasty decision wasn't like him. She wondered if this crazy mountain-climbing expedition was his way of punishing her; if so, he'd succeeded beyond his expectations. The only thing left to do was confront him.

Abby drove back to Logan's building, telling herself that the sooner they got this settled, the better. Relief washed over her at the familiar sight of his car.

She pressed his apartment buzzer, but Logan didn't respond. She tried again, keeping her finger on it for at least a minute. And still Logan didn't answer.

Abby decided she could sit this out if he could. Logan wasn't fooling her. He was there.

When he finally answered and let her into the building lobby, Abby ran in, rushing up to his third-floor apartment. He'd opened the door and she stumbled ungracefully across the threshold. Regaining her balance—and her breath—she turned to glare angrily at him.

"Abby." Logan was holding a pair of headphones. "Were you waiting long?" He closed the door, placing the headset on a shelf. "I'm sorry I didn't hear you, I was listening to a CD."

Regaining her composure, Abby straightened. "Now, listen here, Logan Fletcher." She punctuated her speech with a finger pointed at him. "I know why you're doing this, and I won't let you."

"Abby, listen." He murmured her name in the soft way she loved.

"No," she cried. "I *won't* listen!"

He held her away from him, one hand on each shoulder. Abby didn't know if this was meant to comfort her or to keep her out of his arms. Desperately she wanted his arms around her, craved the comfort she knew was waiting for her there.

"You don't need to prove anything to me," she continued, her voice gaining in volume and intensity. "I love you just the way you are. Logan, you're more of a hero than any man I know, and I can't—no," she corrected emotionally, "I *won't*—let you do this."

"Do what?"

She looked at him in stunned disbelief. "Climb that stupid mountain."

"So you did hear." He sighed. "I was hoping none of this would get back to you."

"Logan," she said and gasped. "You weren't planning

to let me know? You're doing this to prove some egotistical point to me and you weren't even going to let me know until it was too late? I can't believe you'd do that. I simply can't believe it. You've always been so logical and all of a sudden you're falling off the deep end."

Now it was his turn to look flabbergasted. "Abby, sit down. You're becoming irrational."

"I am not," she denied hotly, but she did as he suggested. "Logan, please listen to me. You can't go traipsing off to Washington on this wild scheme. The whole idea is ludicrous. Crazy!"

He knelt beside her and she framed his face with both hands, her eyes pleading with his.

"Don't you understand?" she said. "You've never climbed before. You need experience, endurance, and sheer nerve to take on a mountain. You don't have to prove anything to me. I love you just the way you are. Please don't do this."

"Abby," Logan said sternly, and pulled her hand free, holding her fingers against his chest. "This decision is mine. You have nothing to do with it. I'm sorry this upsets you, but I'm doing something I've wanted to do for years."

"Haven't you listened to a word I've said?" She yanked her hands away and took in several deep breaths. "You could be killed!"

"You seem to be confusing the issues. My desire to make this climb with Dick and his friends has nothing to do with you."

"Nothing to do with me?" she repeated frantically. Had Logan gone mad? "If you think for one instant that I'm going to let you do this, then you don't know me, Logan Fletcher."

He stood up and smoothed the side of his hair with one hand as he regarded her quizzically. "You seem to be under the mistaken impression that I'm doing this to prove something to you."

"You may not have admitted it to yourself, but that's exactly the reason you are." She shook her head frantically. "You're climbing this crazy mountain because you want to impress me."

Logan's short laugh was filled with amusement. "I'm doing this, Abby, because I want to. My reasons are as simple as that. You're making it sound like I'm going in front of a firing squad. Dick's an experienced climber. I expect to be perfectly safe," he said matter-of-factly.

"I don't believe you could be so naïve," she told him flatly, "about the danger of mountain-climbing or about your own motivations."

"Then that's your problem."

"But . . . you could end up dead!"

"I could walk across the street and be hit by a car tomorrow," Logan replied with infuriating calm.

Abby couldn't stand his quiet confidence another second. She leaped to her feet and stalked across the floor, gesturing wildly with her hands, unable to clarify her thoughts enough to reason with him. Pausing, she took a moment to compose herself. "If this is something you always wanted to do, how come I've never heard about it before?"

"Because I knew what your reaction would be—and I was right. I—"

"You're so caught up in the excitement of this adventure, you can't see how crazy it is," Abby interrupted, not wanting him to argue with her. He *had* to listen.

Logan took her gently by the shoulders and turned her around. "I think you should realize that nothing you say is going to change my mind."

"I drove you to this—" Her voice throbbed painfully.

"No," he cut in abruptly, and brushed a hand across his face. "As I keep telling you, this is something I've always wanted to do, whether you like it or not."

"I don't like it and I don't believe it."

"That's too bad." Logan breathed in harshly. "But unlike certain people I know, I don't bend the truth. It's true, Abby."

Abby's mouth twisted in a smile. "And you weren't even going to tell me."

His look was grudging. "I think you can understand why."

Abby shut her eyes and groaned inwardly.

"Now if you'll excuse me, I really do need to get back to the audiobook I'm listening to. It's on climbing. Dick recommended it."

"I thought you were smarter than this. I've never heard of anything so stupid in my life," she said waspishly, lashing out at him in her pain.

His smile was mirthless, as if he'd expected that kind of statement from her.

"I'm sorry," she mumbled as she studied the scuffed-up toe of her shoe. The entire day had been crazy. "I didn't mean that."

A finger under her chin lifted her eyes to his. "I know you didn't." For that instant all time came to a halt. His eyes burned into hers with an intensity that stole her breath.

Seemingly of their own volition, her hands slid over

his chest. She wound her arms around his neck and stood on the tips of her toes as she fitted her mouth over his. The slow-burning fire of his kiss melted her heart. Every part of her seemed to be vibrantly alive. Her nerves tingled and flared to life.

Angrily, Logan broke the kiss. "What's this?" he said harshly. "My last kiss before I face the firing squad?"

"Hardly. I expect you to come back alive." She paused, frowning at him. "If you don't, I swear I'll never forgive you."

He rammed his hands into his pants pockets. Then, as if he couldn't bear to look at her, he stalked to the other side of the room. "If I don't come back, why would it matter? We're not on speaking terms as it is."

From somewhere deep inside her, Abby found the strength to swallow her ego and smile. "That's something I'd like to change."

"No," he said, without meeting her gaze.

"You're not leaving for two weeks. During that time you won't be able to avoid seeing me," she went on. "I don't mind telling you that I plan to use every one of those days to change your mind."

"It won't work, Abby," he murmured.

"I can try. I—"

"What I mean is that I have two weeks before the climb, but we're flying in early to explore several other mountains in the Cascade Range."

"The Cascades?" From school, Abby remembered that parts of the Cascade mountain range in Washington State had never been explored. This made the whole foolish expedition even more frightening.

"My flight leaves tomorrow night."

"No," she mumbled miserably, the taste of defeat filling her.

"There's a whole troop who'll be seeing us off. If you're free, you might want to come, too."

Abby noted that he didn't ask her to come, but merely informed her of what was happening. She shook her head sadly. "I don't think so, Logan. I refuse to be a part of it. Besides, I'm not keen on tearful farewells and good wishes."

"I won't ask anything from you anymore, Abby."

"That's fine," she returned, more flippantly than she intended. Involuntary tears gathered in her eyes. "But you'd better come back to me, Logan Fletcher. That's all I can say."

"I'll be back," he told her confidently.

Not until Abby was halfway home did she realize that Logan hadn't said he was coming back *to her*.

Later that night Abby lay in bed while a kaleidoscope of memories went through her mind. She recalled the most memorable scenes of her yearlong relationship with Logan. One thing was clear: She'd been blind and stupid not to have appreciated him, or recognized how much she loved him.

Staring at the blank ceiling, she felt a tear roll from the corner of her eye and fall onto the pillow. Abby was intensely afraid for Logan.

The following afternoon, when Abby let herself into her apartment, the phone was ringing.

Abby's heart hammered in her throat. Maybe Logan

was calling to say good-bye. Maybe he'd changed his mind and would ask her to come to the airport after all.

But it was her mother.

"Abby." Glenna's raised voice came over the line. "I just heard that Logan's joining Dick Snyder on his latest climb."

"Yes," Abby confirmed in a shaky voice, wondering how her mother had found out about it. "His plane's leaving in"—she paused to check her watch—"three hours and fifteen minutes. Not that I care."

"Oh dear, I was afraid of that. You're taking this hard."

"Me? Why would I?" Abby attempted to sound cool and confident. She didn't want her mother to worry about her. But her voice cracked and she inhaled a quivering breath before she was able to continue. "He's in Dick's capable hands, Mother. All you or I or anyone can do is wait."

The hesitation was only slight. "Sometimes you amaze me, Ab."

"Is that good or bad?" Some of her sense of humor was returning.

"Good," her mother whispered. "It's very good."

The more Abby told herself she wouldn't break down and go to the airport, the more she realized there was nothing that could stop her.

A cold feeling of apprehension crept up her back and extended all the way to the tips of her fingers as Abby drove. Her hands felt clammy, but that was nothing compared to her stomach. The churning pain was almost more than she could endure. Because she hadn't been able to eat all day, she felt light-headed now.

Abby arrived at the airport and the appropriate concourse in plenty of time to see the small crowd of well-wishers surrounding Dick, Logan, and company. They obviously hadn't checked in for their flight. Standing off to one side, Abby chose not to involve herself. She didn't want Logan to know she'd come. Almost everyone from the softball team was there, including Patty. She seemed more quiet and subdued than normal, Abby noted, and was undoubtedly just as worried about Logan's sudden penchant for danger as she herself was.

Once Abby thought Logan was looking into the crowd as if seeking someone. Desperately she wanted to run to him, hold him, and kiss him before he left. But she was afraid she'd burst into tears and embarrass them both. Logan wouldn't want that. And her dignity wouldn't allow her to show her feelings.

When it came time for Logan and the others to check in and go through security, there was a flurry of embraces, farewells, and best wishes. Then almost everyone departed en masse.

Abby waited, studying the departures board until she knew his plane had left.

Nine

Abby rolled out of bed, stumbled into the kitchen, and turned on the radio, eager to hear the weather report. They were in the midst of a late July heatwave.

Cradling a cup of coffee in her hands, Abby eyed the calendar. In a few days Logan would be home. Each miserable, apprehensive day brought him closer to her.

Betty Snyder continued to hear regularly from Dick about the group's progress as they trekked over some of the most difficult of the Cascade mountains. Trying not to be obvious, Abby phoned Betty every other day or so, to hear whatever information she could impart. Abby still didn't know the true reasons Logan had joined this venture, but she believed they were the wrong ones.

The first week after his departure, Abby received a postcard. She'd laughed and cried and hugged it to her breast. An email would've been nice. Or a phone call. But she'd settle—happily—for a postcard. Crazy, wonderful Logan. Anyone else would have sent her a scene of picturesque Seattle or at least the famous mountain he was about to climb. Not Logan. Instead, he sent her a picture of a salmon.

His message was simple:

How are you? Wish you were here. I saw you at the airport. Thank you for coming. See you soon.

   Love, Logan

Abby treasured the card more than the bottles of expensive French perfume he'd given her. Even when several other people on the team received similar messages, it didn't negate her pleasure. The postcard was tucked in her purse as a constant reminder of Logan. Not that Abby needed anything to jog her memory; Logan was continually in her thoughts. And although the message on the postcard was impersonal, Abby noted that he'd signed it with his love. It was a minor thing, but she held on to it with all her might. Logan did love her, and somehow, some way, they were going to overcome their differences because what they shared was too precious to relinquish.

"Disturbing news out of Washington State for climbers on Mount Rainier . . ." the radio announced.

Abby felt her knees go weak as she pulled out a kitchen chair and sat down. She immediately turned up the volume.

"An avalanche has buried eleven climbers. The risk of another avalanche is hampering the chances of rescue. Six men from the Minneapolis area were making a southern ascent at the time of the avalanche. Details at the hour."

A slow, sinking sensation attacked Abby as she placed a trembling hand over her mouth.

During the news, the announcer related the sketchy details available about the avalanche and fatalities and concluded the report with the promise of updates as they became available. Abby ran for the TV and turned it to an all-news channel. She heard the same report over and over. Each word struck Abby like a body blow, robbing her lungs of oxygen. Pain constricted her chest. Fear, anger, and a hundred emotions she couldn't identify were all swelling violently within her. When the telephone rang, she nearly tumbled off the chair in her rush to answer it.

Please, oh, please don't let this be a call telling me Logan's dead, her mind screamed. *He promised he'd come back.*

It was Betty Snyder.

"Abby, do you have your radio or TV on?" she asked urgently. Her usual calm manner had evaporated.

"Yes . . . I know," Abby managed shakily. "Have you heard from Dick?"

"No." Her soft voice trembled. "Abby, the team was making a southern ascent. If they survived the avalanche, there's a possibility they'll be trapped on the mountain for days before a rescue team can reach them." Betty sounded as shocked as Abby was.

"We'll know soon if it's them."

"It's not them," Betty continued on a desperate note, striving for humor. "And if it isn't, I'll personally kill Dick for putting me through this. We should hear something soon."

"I hope so."

"Abby," Betty asked with concern, "are you going to be all right?"

"I'll be fine." But hearing the worry in her friend's voice did little to reassure her. "Do you want me to come over? I can take the day off . . ."

"Dick's mother is coming and she's a handful. You go on to work and I'll call you if I hear from Dick—or anyone."

"Okay." Her friends at the clinic and on the team would need reassurance themselves, and Abby could quickly relay whatever messages came through. She'd check her computer regularly for any breaking news.

"Everything's going to work out fine." Betty's tone was low and wavering, and Abby realized her friend expected the worst.

The day was a living nightmare; her every nerve was stretched taut. With each ring of the office phone her pulse thundered before she could bring it under control and react normally.

Keeping busy was essential for her sanity those first few hours. But by quarter to five she'd managed to settle her emotions. The worst that could've happened was that Logan was dead. The worst. But according to the news, no one from the Minneapolis area was listed among those missing and presumed dead. Abby decided to believe they were fine; there was no need to face any other possibility until necessary.

After work Abby drove directly to Betty's. She hadn't realized how emotionally and physically drained she was until she got there. But she forced herself to relax before entering her friend's home, more for Betty's sake than for her own.

"Have you heard anything?" she asked calmly as Betty let her in the front door. She could hear the TV in the background.

"Not a word." Betty studied Abby closely. "Just what's on the news. The hardest part is not knowing."

Abby nodded and bit her bottom lip. "And the waiting. I won't give up my belief that Logan's alive and well. He must be, because I'm alive and breathing. If anything happened to Logan, I'd know. My heart would know if he was dead." Abby recognized that her logic was questionable, but she expected her friend to understand better than anyone else exactly what she was saying.

"I feel the same thing," Betty confirmed.

Dick's mother had gone home and Abby stayed for a while to keep Betty and the kids company. Then she went to her apartment to change clothes and watch the latest update on TV. The television reporter wasn't able to relate much more than what had been available that morning.

Tate was waiting for her at the little Mexican restaurant where they met occasionally, and he raised his hand when she entered. They'd arranged this on the weekend, and Abby had decided not to change their plans. She needed the distraction.

Her relationship with Tate had changed in the past weeks. He'd changed. Confident and secure now, he often came to her with minor problems related to the business material he was reading. She was his friend as well as his teacher.

"I didn't know if you'd cancel," Tate said as he pulled out a chair for her. "I heard about the accident on Mount Rainier."

"To be honest, I wasn't sure I should come. But I would've gone crazy sitting at home brooding about it," Abby admitted.

"Any news about Logan?"

Abby released a slow, agonizing breath. "Nothing."

"He'll be fine," Tate said. "If anyone could take care of himself, I'd say it was Logan. He wouldn't have gone if he didn't know what to expect and couldn't protect himself."

Abby was surprised by Tate's insights. She wouldn't have thought that Tate would be so generous in his comments.

"I thought you didn't like Logan." She broached the subject boldly. "It seemed that every time you two were around each other, fireworks went off."

Tate lifted one shoulder in a dismissive shrug. "That's because I didn't like his attitude toward you."

"How's that?"

"You know. He acted like he owned you."

The problem was that he held claim to her heart and it had taken Tate to show Abby how much she loved Logan. Her fingers circled the rim of the glass and she smiled into her water. "In a way he does," she whispered. "Because I love him, and I know he loves me."

Tate picked up the menu and studied it. "I'm beginning to realize that . . ." he murmured. "Look, I'll try to talk to him, if that'll help."

Abby reached across the table and squeezed his hand "Thanks, Tate."

The waitress approached them. "Are you ready to order?"

Abby glanced at the menu and nodded. "I'll have the cheese enchiladas."

"Make that two," Tate said absently. "No." He paused. "I've changed my mind. I'll have the pork burrito."

Abby tried unsuccessfully to disguise her amusement.

"What's so funny?" Tate asked.

"You. Do you remember the first few times we went out to eat? You always ordered the same thing I did. I'm pleased to see you're not still doing it."

"It became a habit." He paused. "I owe you a great deal, Abby, more than I'll ever be able to repay."

"Nonsense." They were friends, and their friendship had evolved from what it had been in those early days, but his gratitude sometimes made her uncomfortable.

"Maybe this will help show a little of my appreciation." Tate pulled a small package from inside his pocket and handed it to her.

Abby was stunned, her fingers numb as she accepted the beautifully wrapped box. She raised her eyes to his. "Tate, please. This isn't necessary."

"Hush and open your gift," he instructed, obviously enjoying her surprise.

When she pulled the paper away, Abby was even more astonished to see the name of a well-known and expensive jeweler embossed across the top of the case. Her heart was in her throat as she shook her head disbelievingly. "Tate," she began. "I—"

"Open it." An impish light glinted in his eyes.

Slowly she raised the lid to discover a lovely intricately woven gold chain on a bed of blue velvet. Even with her untrained eye, Abby recognized that the chain was of the highest quality. A small cry of undisguised pleasure escaped before she could hold it back.

"Tate!" She could hardly take in its beauty. For the first time in months she found herself utterly speechless.

"Abby?"

"I . . . I can't believe it. It's beautiful."

"I knew you'd like it."

"Like it! It's the most beautiful necklace I've ever seen. Thank you." Abby smiled at him. "But you shouldn't have. You know that, don't you?"

"If you say so."

"*Now* he's agreeable." Abby smiled as she spoke to the empty chair beside her. "Here, help me put it on."

Tate stood and came around to her side of the table. He took the chain from its plush bed and laid it against the hollow of her throat. Abby bowed her head and lifted the hair from the back of her neck to make it easier for Tate to fasten the necklace.

When he returned to his chair, Abby felt a warm glow. "I still think you shouldn't have done this, but to be honest, I'm glad you did."

"I knew the minute I saw it in the jeweler's window that it was exactly what I was looking for. If you want the truth, I'd been searching for weeks for something special to give you. I want to thank you for everything you've done for me."

Abby didn't think Tate realized what a small part she'd played in his tutoring. He'd done all the real work himself. He was the one who'd sought her out with a need and admitted that need—something he'd never been able to do before, having always hidden his inability. Abby doubted Tate recognized how far he'd come from the day he'd followed her home from the park.

Later, when Abby undressed for bed, she fingered the elegant chain, remembering Tate's promise. Maybe now he'd be willing to explain to Logan why Abby had met with him. The chain represented his willingness to help repair her relationship with Logan. That would be the most significant gift he could possibly give her.

Before leaving for work the next morning, Abby checked the news. Nothing. Then she phoned Betty in case there'd been any calls during the night. There hadn't been, and discouragement sounded in Betty's voice as she promised to phone Abby's office if she heard anything.

At about ten that morning, Abby had just finished updating the chart on a young teen who'd visited the clinic when she glanced up and saw Betty in the doorway.

Abby straightened and stood immobile, her heart pumping at a furious rate. Suddenly, she went cold with fear. She couldn't move or think. Even breathing became impossible. Betty would've come to the office for only one reason, she thought. Logan was dead.

"Betty," she pleaded in a tortured whisper, "tell me. What is it?"

"He's fine! Everyone is. They were stuck on the slopes an extra night, but made it safely to camp early this morning. I just heard—Dick called me."

Abby closed her eyes and exhaled a breath of pure release. Her heart skipped a beat as she moved across the room. The two women hugged each other fiercely as tears of happiness streaked their faces.

"They're on their way home. The flight will land sometime tomorrow evening. Everyone's planning to meet them at the airport. You'll come, won't you?"

In her anger and pain Abby had refused to see him off with the others . . . until the last minute. She wouldn't be so stubborn about welcoming him home. Abby doubted she'd be able to resist hurling herself into his arms the instant she saw him. And once she was in his arms, Abby defied anyone to tear her away.

"Abby? You'll come, won't you?" Betty's soft voice broke into her musings.

"I'll be there," Abby replied, as the image of their reunion played in her mind.

"I thought you'd want to be." Her friend gave her a knowing look.

Logan was safe and coming home. Abby's heart leaped with excitement and she waited until it resumed its normal pace before returning to her desk.

"Tonight," Abby explained to Tate at lunch on Thursday. She swallowed a bite of her pastrami sandwich. "Their flight's arriving around nine-thirty. The team's planning a get-together with him and Dick on Friday night. You're invited to attend if you'd like."

"I just might come."

Tate surprised her with his easy acceptance. Abby had issued the invitation thoughtlessly, not expecting Tate to take her up on it. For that matter, it might even have been the wrong thing to do, since Logan would almost certainly be offended.

"I was beginning to wonder if you were ever going to invite me to any of those social functions your team's always having."

"Tate." Abby glanced up in surprise. "I had no idea you wanted to come. I wish you'd said something earlier." Now she felt guilty for having excluded him in the past.

"Sure," Tate chimed in defensively. "They'll take one look at a mechanic and decide they've got something better to do."

"Tate, that's simply not true." And it wasn't. He'd be accepted, as would anyone who wished to join them. Plenty of friends and coworkers attended the team's social events.

"It might turn a few heads." Tate expelled his breath as if he found the thought amusing.

"Oh, hardly."

"You don't think so?" he asked hopefully.

Tate's lack of self-confidence was a by-product of his inability to read. Now that reading was no longer a problem, he would gain that new maturity. She was already seeing it evolve in him.

Moonlight flooded the ground. The evening was glorious. Not a cloud could be seen in the crystal-blue sky as it darkened into night. Slowly, Abby released a long, drawn-out sigh. Logan would land in a couple of hours and the world had never been more beautiful. She paused to hum a love ballad playing on the radio, thrilled by the romantic words.

She must have changed her clothes three times, but everything had to be perfect. When Logan saw her at the airport, she wanted to look as close to an angel as anything he would find this side of heaven.

She spent half an hour on her hair and makeup. Nothing satisfied her. Tight-lipped, Abby realized she couldn't suddenly make herself into an extraordinarily beautiful woman. Sad but true. She could only be herself. She dressed in a soft, plum-colored linen suit and a pink silk blouse. Dissatisfied with her hair, Abby pulled it free of the confining pins and brushed it until it shimmered and fell in deep natural waves down the middle of her back. Logan had always loved her hair loose . . .

A quick glance at her watch showed her that she was ten minutes behind schedule. Grabbing her purse, Abby hurried out to her car—and she noticed that it was running on empty. Everything seemed to be going wrong . . .

Abby pulled into a gas station, splurging on full service for once rather than pumping her own. *Hurry,* she muttered to herself as the teenager took his time.

"Do you want me to check your oil?"

"No, thanks." Abby handed him the correct change, plus a tip. "And don't bother washing the window."

Inhaling deep breaths helped take the edge off her impatience as she merged onto the freeway. A mile later an accident caused a minor slowdown.

By the time she arrived at the airport, her heart was pounding. Checking the arrivals board revealed that Logan's flight was on schedule.

Abby ran down the concourse. Within minutes the

team, as well as Karen, Logan's assistant, came into sight.

Warmth stole over Abby as she saw Logan, a large backpack slung over one shoulder. His face was badly sunburned, the skin around his eyes white from his protective eye gear. He looked tanned and more muscular than she could remember. His eyes searched the crowd and paused on her, his look thoughtful and intense.

Abby beamed, wearing her brightest smile. He was so close. Close enough to reach out and touch, if it weren't for the people crowding around. Abby's heart swelled with the depth of her love. His own eyes mirrored the longing she was sure he could see in hers. These past weeks were all either of them would need to recognize that they should never be apart again.

Abby edged her way toward him and Dick. The others who'd come to greet Logan were chatting excitedly, but Abby heard none of their conversation. Logan was back! Here. Now. And she loved him. After today he'd never doubt the strength of her feelings again.

In her desire to get to Logan quickly, Abby nearly stumbled over an elderly man. She stopped and apologized profusely, making sure the white-haired gentleman wasn't hurt. As she straightened, she heard someone call out Logan's name.

In shocked disbelief, Abby watched as Patty Martin ran across the room and threw herself dramatically into Logan's arms. He dropped his pack. Sobbing, she clung to him as if he'd returned from the dead. Soon the others gathered around, and Dick and Logan were completely blocked from Abby's view.

The bitter taste of disappointment filled her mouth.

Logan should have pushed the others aside and come to her. *Her* arms should be the ones around him. *Her* lips should be the ones kissing his.

Proudly Abby decided she wouldn't fight her way through the throng of well-wishers. If Logan wanted her, then she was here. And he knew it.

But apparently he didn't care. Five minutes later, the small party moved out of the airport and progressed to the parking lot. As far as Abby could tell, Logan hadn't so much as looked around to see where she was.

After all the lonely days of waiting for Logan, Abby had a difficult time deciding if she should attend the party being held at a local buffet restaurant in his and Dick's honor the following evening. If he hadn't come to her at the airport, then what guarantee did she have that he wouldn't shun her a second time? The pain lingered from his first rejection. Abby didn't know if she could bear another one.

To protect her ego on Friday night, Abby dressed casually in jeans and a cotton top. She timed her arrival so she wouldn't cause a stir when she entered the restaurant. As she'd expected, and as was fitting, Logan and Dick were the focus of attention while they relived their tales of danger on the high slopes.

Abby filled her plate and took a seat where she could see Logan. She knew she wouldn't be able to force down any dinner; occasionally she rearranged the food in front of her in a pretense of eating.

Sitting where she was, Abby could observe Logan covertly. Every once in a while he'd glance up and search the room. He seemed to be waiting for someone. Abby would've liked to believe he was looking for her, but she could only speculate. The tension flowed out of her as she witnessed again the strength and vitality he exuded. That experience on the mountain had changed him, just as it had changed her.

Unable to endure being separated any longer, Abby pushed her plate aside and crossed the room to his table. Logan's eyes locked with hers as she approached. Someone was speaking to him, but Abby doubted that Logan heard a word of what was being said.

"Hello, Logan," she said softly. Her arms hung nervously at her sides. "Welcome home."

"It's good to see you, Abby." His gaze roamed her face lovingly. He didn't need to pull her into his arms for Abby to know what he was feeling. It was all there for her to read. Her doubts, confusion, and anxiety were all wiped out in that one moment.

"I'm sorry about what happened at the airport." His hand clasped hers. "There wasn't anything I could do."

Their eyes held as she studied his face. Every line, every groove, was so familiar. "Don't apologize. I understand." Who would've believed a simple touch could cause such a wild array of sensations? Abby felt shaky and weak just being this close to him. A tingling warmth ran up the length of her arm as he gently enclosed her in his embrace.

"Can I see you later?"

"You must be exhausted." She wanted desperately to be with him, but she could wait another day. After all this time, a few more hours wouldn't matter.

"Seeing you again is all the rest I need."

"I'll be here," she promised.

Dick Snyder tapped Logan on the shoulder and led him to the front row of tables. After a few words from Dick about their adventure, Logan stood and thanked everyone for their support. He relayed part of what he'd seen and the group's close brush with death.

The tables of friends and relatives listened enthralled as Logan and Dick spoke. Hearing him talk so casually about their adventures was enough to make Abby's blood run cold. She'd come so close to losing him.

Abby stood apart from Dick and Logan while they shook everyone's hand as they filed out the door and thanked them for coming. When the restaurant began to empty Logan hurried across the room and brought Abby to his side. She wasn't proud of feeling this way, but she was glad Patty hadn't come. Abby was also grateful that Tate had called to say he couldn't make it. In an effort to assure him he'd be welcome another time, Abby invited him to the team picnic scheduled that Sunday in Diamond Lake Park. Tate promised to be there if possible.

Logan led her into the semidarkened parking lot and turned Abby into his arms. There was a tormented look in his eyes as he gazed down on her upturned face.

"Crazy as it sounds, the whole time we were trapped on that mountain, I was thinking that if I didn't come back alive you'd never forgive me." With infinite tenderness he kissed her.

"I wouldn't have forgiven you," she murmured, and smiled up at him in the dim light.

"Abby, I love you," he said. "It took a brush with death to prove how much I wanted to come home to you."

His mouth sought hers, and with a joyful cry, Abby wrapped her arms around him and clung. Tears of happiness clouded her eyes as Logan slipped his hands into the length of her hair. He couldn't seem to take enough or give enough as he kissed her again and again. Finally he buried his face in the slope of her neck.

He held her face as he inhaled a steadying breath. "When I saw you across the restaurant tonight, it was all I could do to be polite and stay with the others."

Abby lowered her eyes. "I wasn't sure you wanted to see me."

"You weren't sure?" Logan said disbelievingly. He slid his hands down to rest on the curve of her shoulders. His finger caught on the delicate gold chain and he pulled it up from beneath her blouse.

Abby went completely still. Logan seemed to sense that something wasn't right as his eyes searched hers.

"What's wrong?"

"Nothing."

His eyes fell on the chain. "This is lovely and it's far more expensive than you could afford. Who gave it to you, Abby? Tate?"

Ten

~

Abby pressed her lips so tightly together that they hurt. "Yes, Tate gave me the necklace."

"You're still seeing him, aren't you?" Logan dropped his hands to his sides and didn't wait for her to respond. "After everything I've said, you still haven't been able to break off this relationship with Tate, have you?"

"Tate has nothing to do with you and me," she insisted, inhaling deeply to hide her frustration. After the long, trying days apart, they *couldn't* argue! Abby wanted to cry out that she loved him and nothing else should matter. She should be able to be friends with a hundred men if she loved only him. Her voice shaking, she attempted to salvage their reunion. "I know this is difficult for you to understand. To be honest, I don't know how I'd feel if you were to continue seeing Patty Martin."

His mouth hardened. "Then maybe I should."

Abby realized Logan was tired and impatient, but an angry retort sprang readily to her lips. "You certainly seem to have a lot in common with Patty—far more than you do with me."

"The last thing I want to do is argue."

"I don't, either. My intention in coming tonight wasn't to defend my actions while you were away. And yes"—she paused to compose herself, knowing her face was flushed—"I did see Tate."

The area became charged with an electricity that seemed to spark and crackle. The atmosphere was heavy and still, pressing down on her like the stagnant air before a thunderstorm.

"I think that says everything I need to know," he said with quiet harshness.

Abby nodded sharply, forcing herself to meet his piercing gaze. "Yes, I suppose it does." She took a step backward.

"It was kind of you to come and welcome me back this evening." A muscle twitched in his jaw. "But as you can imagine, the trip was exhausting. I'd like to go home and sleep for a week."

Abby nodded, trying to appear nonchalant. "Perhaps we can discuss this another time."

Logan shook his head. "There won't be another time, Abby."

"That decision is yours," she said calmly, although her voice trembled with reaction. "Good night, Logan."

"Good-bye, Abby."

Good-bye! She knew what he was saying as plainly as if he'd screamed it at her. Whatever had been between them was now completely over.

———

"I expect you'll be seeing a lot more of Logan now that he's back," Tate commented from her living room the following afternoon.

Abby brought out a sandwich from the kitchen and handed it to him before taking a seat. "We've decided to let things cool between us," she said with as much aplomb as she could manage. *Cool* was an inadequate word. Their relationship was in Antarctica. They'd accidentally run into each other that morning while Abby was doing some grocery shopping and had exchanged a few stilted sentences. After a minute Abby could think of nothing more to say.

"You know what I think, Tate?" Abby paid an inordinate amount of attention to her sandwich. "I've come to the belief that love is a highly overrated emotion."

"Why?"

Abby didn't need to glance up to see the amusement on Tate's face. Instead she took the first bite of her lunch. How could she explain that from the moment she realized how much she loved Logan, all she'd endured was deep emotional pain. "Never mind," she said at last, regretting that she'd brought it up.

"Abby?" Tate's look was thoughtful.

She leaped to her feet. "I forgot the iced tea." She hurried into the kitchen, hoping Tate would let the subject drop.

"Did I tell you the bank approved my loan?"

Returning with their drinks, Abby grinned. "That's great!"

"They phoned yesterday afternoon. Bessler's pleased, but not half as much as I am. I have a lot to thank you for, Abby."

"I'm so happy for you," Abby said with a quick nod. "You've worked hard and deserve this." Abby knew how relieved Tate was that the loan had gone through. He'd called Abby twice out of pure nerves, just to talk through his doubts.

Tomorrow afternoon they were going to attend the picnic together, and although Abby was grateful for Tate's friendship, she didn't want to give her friends the wrong impression. Logan had already jumped to conclusions. There was nothing to say the others wouldn't as well. Tate was a friend—a special friend—but their relationship didn't go beyond that. It couldn't, not when she was in love with Logan.

"Abby," Tate said quietly. "I'm going to talk to him."

Sunday afternoon Abby was preoccupied as she dressed in shorts and a Twins T-shirt for the picnic. She was glad Tate was going with her, glad he'd promised to explain, but she hoped Logan didn't do or say anything to make him uncomfortable.

Logan. The unhappiness weighed down on her heart. Her thoughts were filled with him every waking minute. Even her dreams involved him. This misunderstanding, this lack of trust, had to stop once and for all. From the moment Logan had left for Washington, Abby had longed for Tate to explain the situation and heal her relationship with Logan. She'd assumed that as time went on they'd naturally get back together. Now, just the opposite was proving to be true. With every passing hour, Logan was drifting further and further out of her life. Yet her love was just as strong. Perhaps stronger. Whether

Tate went through with his confession and whether it changed things remained to be seen.

Since Tate was meeting her at the park, Abby got there early and found a picnic table for them. When Logan came, he claimed the table directly across from hers and Abby felt the first bit of encouragement since they'd last spoken. As quickly as the feeling came, it vanished. Logan set out a tablecloth and unpacked his cooler without so much as glancing her way. Only a few feet separated her from him, but it felt as if their distance had never been greater. He gave no indication that he'd seen her. Even her weak smile had gone unacknowledged.

Soon they were joined by the others, chatting and laughing. A few men played horseshoes while the women sat and visited. The day was glorious; birds trilled their songs from the tree branches and soft music came from someone's CD player. Busy putting the finishing touches on a salad, Abby sang along with the music. The last thing in the world she felt like doing was singing, but if she didn't, she'd start crying.

Tate arrived and Abby could see by the way he walked that he was nervous. He'd met some of the people at the softball game. Still, he looked surprised when one of the guys called out a greeting. The two men talked for a minute and Tate joined her soon afterward.

"Hi."

"There's no need to be nervous," she said, smiling at him.

"What? Me nervous?" he joked. "They're nice people, aren't they?"

"The best."

"Even Logan?"

"Especially Logan."

Tate was silent for a moment. "Like I said, I'll see what I can do to patch things up between you two."

Unhurriedly, she raised her gaze to his. "I'd appreciate that."

His returning smile told her how difficult revealing his past would be. Abby hated to ask him to do it, but there didn't seem to be any other way.

As he wandered off, Abby laced her fingers tightly and sat there, searching for Logan. He was standing alone with his back to her, staring out over the still, quiet lake.

Abby spread out a blanket between the two picnic tables and lay down on it, pretending to sunbathe. She must have drifted off, because the low-pitched voices of Tate and Logan were what stirred her into wakefulness.

"Seems to me you've got the wrong table," Logan was saying. "Your girlfriend's over there."

"I was hoping we could talk."

"I can't see that there's much to talk about. Abby's made her decision."

The noises that followed suggested that Logan was arranging drinks on the table and ignoring Tate as much as possible. Abby resisted the urge to roll over and see exactly what was happening.

"Abby's a friend," Tate said next. "No more and no less."

"You two keep saying that." Logan sounded bored.

"It's the truth."

"Sure."

There was a rustling sound, and faintly Abby could hear Tate stumbling over the awkward words in the list of ingredients on the side of a soda can.

"What are you doing?" Logan asked.

"Reading," Tate explained. "And for me that's some kind of miracle. You see, until I met Abby here in the park helping Mai-Ling, I couldn't read."

A shocked silence followed his announcement.

"For a lot of reasons, I never properly learned," Tate continued. "Then I found Abby. Until I met her, I didn't know there were good people like her who'd be willing to teach me."

"Abby taught you to read?" Logan was obviously stunned.

"I asked her not to tell anyone. I suppose that was selfish of me in light of what's happened between you two. I don't have any excuse except pride."

Someone called Logan's name and the conversation was abruptly cut off. Minutes later someone else announced that it was time to eat. Abby joined the others, helping where she could. She and Tate were sitting with Dick and Betty when she felt Logan's eyes on her. The conversation around her faded away. The space between them seemed to evaporate as she turned and boldly met his look. In his eyes she read anger, regret, and a great deal of inner pain.

When it came time to pack up her things and head home, Abby found Tate surrounded by a group of single women. He glanced up and waved. "I'll call you later," he told her cheerfully, clearly enjoying the attention he was receiving.

"Fine," she assured him. She hadn't gotten as far as the parking lot when Logan caught up with her.

He grabbed her shoulder as he turned her around. The anger she'd thought had been directed inward was now focused on her.

"Why didn't you tell me?" he demanded.

"I couldn't," she said simply. "Tate asked me not to."

"That's no excuse," he began, then paused to inhale a shuddering breath. "All the times I questioned you about meeting Tate, you were tutoring him. The least you could've done was tell me!"

"I already told you Tate was uncomfortable with that. Even now, I don't think you appreciate what it took for him to admit it to you," she explained slowly, enunciating each word so there'd be no misunderstanding. "I was the first person he'd ever told about this problem. It was traumatic for him and I couldn't go around telling others. Surely you can understand that."

"What about me? What about *us*?"

"My hands were tied. I asked you to trust me. A hundred times I pleaded with you to look beyond the obvious."

Logan closed his eyes and emitted a low groan. "How could I have been so stupid?"

"We've both been stupid and we've both learned valuable lessons. Isn't it time to put all that behind us?" She wanted to tell him again how much she loved him, but something stopped her.

Hands buried deep in his pockets, Logan turned away from her, but not before Abby saw that his eyes were narrowed. The stubbornness in his expression seemed to block her out.

Abby watched in disbelief. The way he was behaving implied that *she'd* been the unreasonable, untrusting one. The more Abby thought about their short conversation as she drove home, the angrier she got.

Pacing her living room, she folded her arms around her waist to ward off a sudden chill. "Of all the nerve," she snapped at Dano, who paraded in front of her. The cat shot into her bedroom, smart enough to know when to avoid his mistress.

Yanking her car keys out of her purse, Abby hurried outside. She'd be darned if she'd let Logan end things like this.

His car was in its usual space, and he'd just opened the driver's door. She marched over, standing directly in front of him.

Logan frowned. "What's going on?"

She pointed her index finger at his chest until he backed up against the car.

"Now, listen here, Logan Fletcher. I've had about all I can take from you." Every word was punctuated with a jab of her finger.

"Abby? What's the problem?"

"You and that stubborn pride of yours."

"Me?" he shouted in return.

"When we're married, you can bet I won't put up with this kind of behavior."

"Married?" he repeated incredulously. "Who said anything about marriage?"

"I did."

"Doesn't the man usually do the asking?" he said in a sarcastic voice.

"Not necessarily." Some of her anger was dissipating

and she began to realize what a fool she was making of herself. "And . . . and while we're on the subject, you owe me an apology."

"You weren't entirely innocent in any of this."

"All right. I apologize. Does that make it easier on your fragile ego?"

"I also prefer to make my own marriage proposals."

Abby paled and crossed her arms. She wouldn't back down now. "Fine. I'm waiting."

Logan squared his shoulders and cleared his throat. "Abby Carpenter." His voice softened measurably. "I want to express my sincere apology for my behavior these past weeks."

"Months," she inserted with a low breath.

"All right, months," Logan amended. "Although you seem to be rushing the moment, I don't suppose it would do any harm to give you this." He pulled a diamond ring from his pocket.

Abby nearly fell over. Her mouth dropped open and she was speechless as he lifted her hand and slipped the solitaire diamond on her ring finger. "I was on my way to your place," he explained as he pulled her into his embrace. "I've loved you for a long time. You know that. I hadn't worked out a plan to steal your heart away from Tate. But you can be assured I wasn't going to let you go without a struggle."

"But I love—"

His lips interrupted her declaration of love. Abby released a small cry of wonder and wound her arms around his neck, giving herself to the kiss as his mouth closed over hers.

Gradually Logan raised his head, and his eyes were

filled with the same wonder she was experiencing. "I talked to Tate again after you left the park," Logan said in a husky murmur. "I was a complete fool."

"No more than usual." Her small laugh was breathless.

"I'll need at least thirty years to make it up to you."

"Change that to forty and you've got yourself a deal."

His eyes smiled deeply into hers. "Where would you like to honeymoon?"

Abby's eyes sparkled. "Des Moines—where else?"

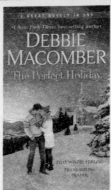